THE PROGRAM

HAYNER PLD/ALTON SQUARE

JUL 0 3 2008

MIAM

THE PROGRAM

a novel

Charlie Lovett

PEARLSONG PRESS
NASHVILLE, TN

Pearlsong Press
P.O. Box 58065
Nashville, TN 37205
www.pearlsong.com
1-866-4-A-PEARL

ISBN-10: 1-59719-013-6
ISBN-13: 978-1-59719-013-8

Original trade paperback

Cover design by Zelda Pudding, photo by Tobago Cays

Also by Charlie Lovett:

Books	Plays
Love, Ruth: A Son's Memoir	*Twinderella*
Sparrow Through the Hall	*Wooing Wed Widing Hood*
Lewis Carroll's Alice	*Snew White*
Alice on Stage	*A Hairy Tale*
Lewis Carroll's England	*Porridgegate*
Lewis Carroll and the Press	*Romeo and Winifred*
Lewis Carroll Among His Books	*Omelette: Chef of Denmark*
Everybody's Guide to Book Collecting	*Unwrapped*
Olympic Marathon	*A Nose for the News*
J.K. Rowling	*Supercomics*
Onward and Upward	

Library of Congress Cataloging-in-Publication Data

Lovett, Charlie, 1962–
  The program : a novel / Charlie Lovett.
     p. cm.
  ISBN-13: 978-1-59719-013-8 (trade pbk. : alk. paper) 1. Overweight persons—
Fiction. 2. Women journalists—Fiction. 3. Body image—Fiction. I. Title.
  PS3612.O86P76 2008
  813'.6—dc22

                                                2007044337

To all those who have ever feared
that because they were different
they were inferior.

K aren Sumner stood naked in front of her bathroom mirror contemplating her breasts. On the countertop lay an open copy of *Perfect Woman* magazine sporting a pouting portrait of Celinda, the sexiest woman in the world. Karen looked back and forth between the glossy image in the magazine and her own reflection in the mirror. There could hardly have been a greater contrast.

Celinda leaned in a doorway, clutching a sheer piece of fabric that barely kept her decent. Her form was all about straight lines. A straight line from her ankle to her armpit—undisturbed by bulging hips or thighs, a straight line across her shoulders, and a straight line down each arm. Her torso, from belly to breasts, was as flat and smooth as the prairies of western Kansas where Karen had grown up, the plane interrupted only by the ridges of her ribs rippling across the surface like summer wheat in the breeze. Celinda was a perfect geometric figure of a woman—even her face was square.

Karen was all curves and roundness. Her thighs sprouted from her knees like giant tree trunks that spread into the mighty width of her hips. Just when this line seemed to be going somewhere it curved tightly back into her waist. But the roller coaster ride of flesh was not over. Crowning her trunk were her breasts. They were—well, they were big. She had been a 36-C since ninth grade, and lately her cup had been running over. She cringed at the thought of reaching to the back of the rack searching for the elusive D-cup. Perched above Karen's curving body, above her sloping shoulders, was her round head with cheeks not like the beautiful pale hollows of Celinda, but full and florid. *God,* she thought, *even my cheeks are fat.*

Of all the places where her body deviated from the model of perfection in the magazine, Karen was most annoyed by her breasts. When she was fourteen they had just grown there—cropped up unbidden and unwanted, these escarpments of roundness, flouting straight line perfection and mortifying her with embarrassment until she learned how to hide them. Hold books in front of you, lean forward with your shoulders, wear loose blouses and armature bras—she had done all this for ten years now, as if through sheer willpower she could banish them. But there they still stood, already starting to sag, but massive as ever.

Her left breast was slightly larger than her right. Its nipple no longer pointed straight forward but a few degrees down, as if indicating some sight far off on the horizon. Her right breast, perhaps because of its smaller size, still rode closer to its original position. Two dark hairs, which she plucked religiously every Monday morning, sprouted where her skin changed color from pasty white to faded pink. Her right nipple had always been the more sensitive. Even now, in the cool air of the bathroom, it stood erect—a rigid button of nearly half an inch that her bras were chosen to conceal.

She didn't need to see a picture of Celinda naked to know what *her* breasts looked like. Nothing interfered with her lines, and the line across her chest was as straight as any. Celinda never wore a bra, had never gone through the humiliation of trying on a size too small in a department store fitting room. True, her nipples were always visible, pressing through the sheer fabric of her high fashion gowns, but those buds were enough to assert her femininity. She had no need for mountains of flesh. Celinda was perfect.

Below her picture, in large gold type set off by the plush blue carpet under her feet, were the words "Get With The Program."

The Program. According to the television ads, over half a million women had attained bodily perfection through The Program, with more signing up every day, anteing up the $5,000 fee and disappearing behind the blue and gold doors that had appeared in every major American city in the past few months. No one knew what went on behind those doors, but the bodies that came out were Celinda-perfect—not a curve in sight.

Five thousand dollars. This morning Karen's bank balance was $428.45, her unpaid bills amounted to about $300, the refrigerator was empty, and *Ear to the Ground*, the alternative paper for which she wrote feature articles, was skating on thin financial ice. Karen couldn't afford the perfect body.

But I can dream, thought Karen, and for a moment she flicked her eyes back and forth between her reflection and Celinda's picture so fast that the two images became one, and for a moment she saw the angular version of herself trapped beneath the curves. It was a daily ritual, this exercise in persistence of vision, a way of tricking herself into believing that another Karen existed, a Karen of lines and angles, a perfect Karen.

She pulled on her control-top panties and her bra—"guaranteed to reduce by one cup size," though all it really did was push flesh over the tops of the cups—and a new forest green sweater set and khaki skirt she had bought from Land's End on credit. She'd bought the sweater set a size too big so it wouldn't stretch so tightly across her chest. As she smoothed the front of the skirt she heard the locks to the outside door clicking open one at a time.

"Jesus, it's cold out there," said a shivering voice. Karen shared a third-floor walk-up studio in TriBeCa with Georgia Phillips, who worked the night desk at the *Daily News*, answering the phone and listening to the police scanner. The hours were brutal and the pay was a pittance, but at least it was a real newspaper.

Karen emerged from the bathroom in time to see Georgia shed the last of her outermost layer. On the floor behind her was a trail of winter clothing.

"God, I hate nights like this," said Georgia, slapping a copy of the *Daily News* onto the coffee table. "Killer Frost Grips City," read the headline.

"Two more homeless deaths last night," she said, collapsing onto the couch. "A Vietnam vet and a forty-year-old woman."

"A Vietnam vet?" asked Karen, her voice edged with fear.

"It wasn't him," said Georgia. "I thought the same thing when I first heard."

Karen relaxed against the doorway. "It's pretty heartless of me to feel

9

relieved just because I didn't know the guy."

"But you do. Feel relieved, I mean. We both do."

"Yeah," said Karen, "we do."

Karen slumped silently for a moment, then did her best to shake off the gloom Georgia had brought into the apartment. "What do you think?" she said, striking a Celinda-leaning-in-the-doorway pose.

"Of the outfit?"

"Yeah, does it make me look fat?"

"No. It makes you look—the way you look."

"Fat."

"No, not fat."

"Well then, chubby."

"No—"

"Chunky, stout, big-boned, portly?"

"Jesus, what are you this morning, a thesaurus? You look fine. You look better than I do. My thighs look like fire hydrants in these pants." Georgia wore a pair of black stretch pants that pulled taut around her. "Add that stupid ski jacket and I look like a damn blue marshmallow. I swear if I have to watch one more of those skeletally thin Programmed bitches get promoted ahead of me I think I'll scream."

"You *are* screaming," said Karen.

"Yeah, well, what did I tell you?"

"Maybe we should just get with The Program ourselves," said Karen, laughing. "I think I left a few thousand dollars around here somewhere."

"Yeah, the day I enroll in The Program is the day my great aunt dies and leaves me five grand."

"Do you even have a great aunt?"

"Actually, I think I might," said Georgia, finally smiling.

"Look, it's just a fad," said Karen, trying to hide her insincerity.

"Well, it's a fad that's lasted all my life," said Georgia, sinking into the cushions. "Do we have any coffee?"

"Couldn't afford it," said Karen. "I just go to work early and drink it there." And with this Karen pulled on a ten-year-old parka with a fake fur hood that completely destroyed any impression she might have hoped to make with her outfit, and left for work. As she pulled the door closed she heard Georgia's voice echoing in the empty refrigerator.

"I think her name is Aunt Ethel."

LOUISE CRAWFORD STOOD in front of the blue and gold door of The Program while the Christmas shopping mob swirled around her on Fifth Avenue. She had taken the train in from Braintree that morning as she did every year at Christmastime. But this year, clutched inside her coat pocket with her usual wad of Christmas shopping money, was a cashier's check for five thousand dollars—all the money she and Phil had been saving for the trip to Hawaii. *To hell with Hawaii,* she thought. Phil would understand. This Christmas she would give every-one she knew the gift of a new Louise.

Phil claimed to love her body—he told her so every night after she weighed herself and came to bed depressed. He said he wanted a wom-an he could hold on to, a woman with curves and hips and breasts. But she knew he was only being kind, or wanted to buck up her self-es-teem so she would make love to him. She knew what the perfect body looked like—she had seen it plastered on every bus in the city, and it wasn't hers. Not yet.

The man on the phone from The Program understood. "You're hid-ing behind a wall of fat, aren't you?" he said. "You can't wear the clothes you want to wear, you're ashamed to go to holiday parties. Just once you'd like to put on a sleeveless dress and not worry about how your arms look."

"Yes," Louise had cried, and he had given her the address.

"No need to make an appointment," he said, "we'll be waiting for you."

Now the doorman smiled at her and asked, "Going in, ma'am?"

Louise stared at the door, rubbing the folded check with her sweaty fingers. "Just give me a minute," she said. All the Hawaii money and then some, she thought. But what better present could she give Phil?

She felt a sharp elbow jab her back. "Jesus, lady," came a woman's voice from behind her, "you're blocking the entire sidewalk."

"OK," she said to the doorman, without turning towards the voice. "I'm ready."

AS FEATURES EDITOR Karen spent much of her time at *Ear to the Ground* rewriting other people's copy and handing out freelance assignments. She even sold advertising—with a fulltime staff of only eight, everyone had to pitch in. But the heart of her young journalistic career had been a series of interviews with the homeless of New York. She had prowled under freeway overpasses, in dark corners of Central Park, and in narrow alleys that most young women slipped uncomfortably past with quickening steps. She had helped put a human face on the city's homeless problem. Her efforts had even been the subject of a feature article in the *Daily News*, thanks to a suggestion from Georgia.

She had no interviews today, but after what Georgia had told her about the Vietnam vet she wanted to check on someone. She was reasonably sure she could find him under a certain bridge in Central Park at midday—that gave her less than three hours to clear her desk of more mundane tasks and change into her street clothes.

The offices of *Ear to the Ground* huddled at one end of a block of warehouses gradually being converted into office space. When Karen arrived at 8:30, the sound of jackhammers and power saws echoed in the street.

"Good morning!" said a voice as Karen extricated herself from her parka. "I thought you had an interview today."

"Morning, Steve. Actually, I don't," said Karen, handing her coat to the eager young man camped out in her cubicle.

"So you're not going to the park?"

"Well, yes, I am."

"But you're not going to change?"

"I am going to change, but we have some work to do first. Cup of coffee?"

"Coming right up." It seemed silly to send Steve for coffee when the urn was only ten feet away, but he liked to pretend he was an executive assistant, so why not enjoy the service.

Steve Collingwood worked as an intern between journalism classes at Columbia. Karen's old advisor, Susan McCorkle, had phoned a few months ago recommending him as a student who was passionate about social issues and disenchanted with the mainstream press. But the important thing was he put in long hours and worked for free. He brought Karen a tall coffee, two creams and three sugars, and slid into the folding chair across from her. "So," he scoffed, eying her new sweater set, "what's with the outfit?"

Steve himself looked like an intellectual, homeless lumberjack. He wore dark-rimmed glasses, which disappeared under a shock of unkempt curly black hair, and his plaid flannel shirt, blue jeans and work boots were carefully distressed to look as if they came from the Salvation Army thrift store.

"Tell me, Steve, did you have a dress code when you went to Exeter?" Karen loved to tease Steve about his establishment roots whenever he took his rebel act too far. His father was a corporate attorney with an apartment on Park Avenue and a house in the Hamptons. Steve was the product of Exeter, Princeton, and now graduate school at Columbia. He had probably paid five hundred dollars at a Fifth Avenue outfitter for his costume.

"Don't get me started on those stuck up country club, golf playing—"

"So, are we going to do some work this morning, Steve?"

"Yeah, sure. You name it."

"Ever seen these?" she said, dropping the Manhattan Yellow Pages on the desktop in front of him with a mighty thud.

"I've heard of them."

"Well, you can spend your day cold-calling businesses, talking to those country club golfers and convincing them to buy advertising in our pathetic little rag. And it wouldn't hurt to call some folks you know, remind them of the good old days at Exeter, and sign them to a twelve-issue contract."

"I can do that," said Steve. "I can tell them our circulation is up, right?"

"Right, Steve. Every homeless person in New York sleeps under our paper."

"Don't worry, I know how to work rich people. I've been doing it since I could crawl."

With Steve occupied, Karen took a moment to freshen up in the phone-booth-sized bathroom. She squinted into the tiny mirror as she tried to tame her parka hair. She would keep on her new outfit for the rest of the morning. Clifton probably wouldn't notice, but she couldn't break the habit of trying to impress him. She glanced at her watch, saw it was five till nine and tugged the comb one more time through her uncooperative hair before scurrying back to her desk.

THE PROGRAM

Clifton Garrett, founder and editor of *Ear to the Ground*, always arrived at the office at precisely nine o'clock. Karen watched surreptitiously as he strode through the door in his double-breasted blazer, wool slacks, and William Morris tie. Clifton seemed to think that if he dressed like a successful businessman, his business would be successful. He was not only an immaculate dresser, he was also drop dead gorgeous, and Karen had been in love with him since approximately ten seconds after she walked into his office for a job interview.

Not that he knew—nobody knew, except maybe Marjorie Jenkins, the production manager. Karen and Marjorie usually ate lunch together—lately it had been peanut butter on a park bench—and last week Marjorie had suggested a new hairstyle for Karen. "Maybe Clifton will notice," she had said, but Karen had let the comment pass and made a joke about what kind of hairstylist she could get for a dollar fifty.

Even if Marjorie did know, Clifton remained clueless. Karen was fat and in love, he was gorgeous and oblivious, and that's the way it would always be.

"Morning, Karen," said Clifton, settling into the chair in the corner of her cubicle.

"Good morning, Clifton," she said.

"Tell me, Karen," he said as he pulled a pipe out of his breast pocket, "have we ever run a review of The Toxic Dump?"

"I beg your pardon?"

"The Toxic Dump. It's a sort of grunge jazz club. I saw a great band there last night. They had this energy you just don't see in the old jazz clubs. And they make this drink with peppermint schnapps and a clove of pickled garlic—"

"No, Clifton, we haven't reviewed them."

"I think we ought to send somebody over there. It's new—I think we could get them before the *Voice*."

"You know, Clifton, I've been meaning to talk to you about our reviewers." Karen ran her fingers through her hair, hoping she didn't look too idiotic.

"Is there a problem?" He propped his feet up on the front of Karen's desk and began an elaborate cleaning of his pipe.

Oblivious, Karen thought, but she only said, "The problem is they can't write."

"But Karen, that's what I have you for. They're good at hanging around in loud, smelly bars; you're good at writing. Besides, we don't even give them drink money—you can't expect too much."

"I at least expect coherence. Lately I've been making up half the reviews myself—not just the clubs, but books, movies, galleries."

"And what you make up is beautiful, Karen. Who cares if it's your writing or theirs as long as it fills the space."

Karen had a hard time arguing when he called her writing beautiful, but at least he wouldn't see her blushing—he was still preoccupied with his pipe. "You don't think that's a little dishonest?"

"Karen, one of the things I pay you for is to be an editor, and as an editor it's your job to make other people look better—and you're damn good at it. If I hired people who could actually write, they'd never go to the kind of places we want to review—and I have to throw these guys the occasional books and movies to make them think we're not just paying them to be barflies. So you keep on making beauty out of garbage. Now, if you'll excuse me, I have a meeting with our accountant, who's going to tell me how much longer we can keep having conversations like this before we all head to the unemployment office."

Karen gazed at his slim hips as he sauntered off to his office.

"Watching something?" asked Marjorie, her head appearing over the top of Karen's cubicle.

"Em—just thinking how to edit this story," Karen stammered. She looked at the paragraph in front of her. *If this is editing,* she thought, *then Michelangelo was a housepainter.*

"Kim Jacobs movies are so unique that no two are alike. Her new movie is based on a book by Jonathan Thompson starring two unknown actors. There performance gives a new meaning to the word performance. Their totally intense from the moment I sat down with my popcorn which I ordered with no butter but which…"

The digression about popcorn continued for several sentences and was the best-written part of the review. Karen "edited" another four pieces before eleven. Then, handing the edits to Marjorie, she took a bag of clothes out from under her desk and squeezed into the bathroom to change. Ten minutes later she pulled on her parka, pushed out the door into the cold, and headed uptown. Across the street she saw Clifton hail a cab, but she turned the corner quickly so he wouldn't offer her a ride. She didn't like him to see her dressed like this, and besides, she preferred to take the subway. It put her in the proper frame of mind.

Karen emerged from the depths at Rockefeller Center and headed north, shuffling through midtown. She liked to walk Fifth Avenue on these forays, to watch the shoppers and tourists lean away from her. If you want to walk up Fifth Avenue during the Christmas season and not get jostled, Karen had learned, dress like a homeless person. If the crowd starts to press in on you, mumble out loud.

She wore an outfit which, unlike Steve's, *had* been bought at the Salvation Army thrift store—running shoes with twine for laces, a pair of corduroy pants two sizes too big, a denim shirt under a green wool sweater and another, looser sweater that had once been white. Her clothes were thick with dirt and frayed at the edges, the sweaters were riddled with moth holes, and a long tear in the left pant leg revealed a strip of flesh that Karen had smeared with grime. She looked the part, but her smell wasn't quite right—too much citrus-scented shower gel and not enough urine. She kept a grimy red ski cap pulled down over her forehead, hiding her clean hair and giving her hazel eyes a menacing look.

The first time she had worn this costume, her invisibility had shocked her. People looked at the space she occupied as if it were empty. To the population of Fifth Avenue she did not exist. She didn't know whether this reaction was due to guilt, fear, or genuine indifference, but she had come to take it for granted. So when someone spoke to her as she crossed Grand Army Plaza, she was tempted to hurry on, to ignore as she had been ignored, but her journalist's instinct made her stop and turn towards the voice.

The man sat on a concrete bench next to a clear plastic garbage bag full of aluminum cans. His eyes squinted at her from under a tangled mass of gray eyebrows. His cheeks were sunken and the bones of his face clearly discernible beneath taut skin. A dirty growth of beard could not disguise his skeletal appearance.

"You're that newspaper lady," he said matter-of-factly.

"Yes," said Karen, trying to sound cheerful, "I am." This had happened once before. A homeless man had recognized her from the picture that ran next to her byline. He had thanked her, told her that what she was doing meant so much to all of them. Karen had stood bewildered—in spite of what she thought of as her own enlightenment, she still imagined the average street person as more likely to sleep under newspapers than to read them. There had stood a man who loyally read her column and whom she had touched with her writing. In the winter sun in front of the Plaza Hotel, she had found another fan.

"You should learn to mind your own business," the man growled, and before Karen could think what to say he went on, spraying her with plosives as he spoke. "Suppose we come after you some day. Suppose we share your dirty laundry with the world, tell everybody how you like to play dress-up and pretend to be one of us and then you go back to your heated apartment and your clean clothes and all you can think of is your cheeks are too fat and maybe you should go on a diet while we're just as hungry as ever."

Karen's face burned hot in spite of the cold wind that blew down from the park. How had he seen through her so easily? How did she know she stared at her roundness in the mirror every morning wishing for a body like Celinda's—like his?

The man did not move, and his face wore a static scowl of hatred. Wasn't she one of the good guys? Was she trying to help or was she just playing games? With a shiver she turned away from the bench and dashed out of the square and across the street towards the park.

She stopped at Seventy-Ninth Street, breathless and clammy from the sweat that trickled down her back. She had covered twenty blocks at a near run. As she stood on the sidewalk staring at the yellow blur of cabs rushing by and trying to banish the stranger's venom from her mind, his accusations of hypocrisy were replaced by the memory of her first interview with Professor McCorkle at Columbia.

"Tell me honestly, Karen, why do you want to go into journalism?"

And instantly Karen had known the answer—"to make people like me." But she had feigned thoughtfulness and said, "I suppose so I can try to do some good in the world," and with those words she had looked her professor in the eye and discovered that, though she might one day make a good journalist, she would never make much of a liar. Professor McCorkle had merely nodded. Now, just when Karen had convinced herself that writing could be used to win the affection she yearned for, it had had the opposite effect.

"You crossing the street or what?" said a teenage boy's voice. Karen had no idea how long she had stood there, mesmerized by the passing traffic, but the sweat on her back had dried and her breathing had returned to normal. She crossed the street and headed west, looking for a coffee vendor.

"Let me have four large with cream and sugar," Karen said, rubbing her arms to stay warm as the wind picked up again.

"You got anything to pay with?" came the skeptical reply. Karen had forgotten about her outfit, and though tempted to storm down the street to the next vendor, she didn't have the energy for righteous indignation. She dug a ten-dollar bill out of her pocket and handed it to the man.

Fifteen minutes later she walked under a bridge where the smell of urine and unwashed humanity accosted her. Two men lay sleeping under newspaper against the stone walls. Three others huddled around a smoldering fire in a metal can. No one looked up.

"Got some hot coffee if anybody needs some," she said, holding up two brown paper bags. With a loud rustling, the men under the papers rose and shuffled towards the fire. The others turned towards Karen— not smiling, or moving from their tiny circle of warmth, but with looks of anticipation on their faces. They all remained silent.

Karen stepped towards the fire, took the cups out of the bag, and passed them around the circle. For several minutes the six of them passed the cups around, sharing equally in their bounty. To Karen a cup of coffee never tasted so rich as when she shared it like this.

When the last cup had been drained she turned to a man with a long grey ponytail. "Hi, Gus," she said.

"Miss Sumner," he nodded. "Appreciate the coffee."

"I saw the paper this morning. Thought I'd check up on you."

"You know I can take care of myself," said Gus. "It's these fools who won't go to the shelter on a cold night you gotta worry about—like David over here." Gus slung his arm around the shoulders of the youngest man there. He didn't look more than twenty, and a boyish smile shone through the filth on his face. "This here's the lady I was telling you about."

"Karen Sumner," said Karen. "I did a story on your friend here for a newspaper…" Karen extended her hand, and the young man hesitantly shook it in his gloved right hand. Karen didn't think it odd that he didn't also wear a glove on his left. Such were the vagaries of homeless life.

"*Ear to the Ground*, I know," said the man. "I'm David. And I go when it's cold enough."

"You should write about this young fella," said Gus. "He can tell you a story or two."

"I'd like that," said Karen, "I mean, if you'd be willing to talk to me." All eyes in the circle turned to David, who blushed deeply.

"She won't bite, I promise you," said Gus.

"Not here," said David quietly. "I'll talk, but not here. Out in the light. Let's walk." Without waiting for an answer, he turned and walked towards the semi-circle of daylight at the edge of the bridge.

Karen didn't have a tape recorder, but she always carried a steno pad, and she never turned down an opportunity for a story. She gave Gus a quick hug, said goodbye to the others under the bridge, and stepped back into the sunlight. She saw David disappearing around a curve in the path, and rushed to follow him.

The young man she caught up to was tall and lanky, and though his clothes hung on him as loosely as on a coat hanger, something about his blue eyes and the glow of his smile struck Karen. Her first thought, on seeing him in the sunshine, was that unlike so many of the homeless she had met, he did not feel rejected by the world. Here, she thought, was a man who still had hope.

"So, David," she said as she caught up to him, "can we talk about how you ended up here?"

"No place else to go."

"I'm sure there's got to be more to the story than that."

"Tell me, where would you go? I mean, suppose you lost your job and you couldn't pay your rent. Who would take you in?"

Karen tried not to think about how precarious her position was, how her job could evaporate tomorrow. "I don't know," she said. "I'm not sure anybody would."

"No place to go?"

"Not really."

"Tell me about it."

"Wait a minute," said Karen, "*I'm* supposed to be interviewing *you*."

"You show me yours and I'll show you mine," David smiled.

"Why?"

"Because talking to you is the most interesting thing I'm going to do all day." David sat down expectantly on a bench.

Karen had been here before; she had traded her secrets for someone else's—and she had found it a highly effective means of getting what she wanted. Besides, it wasn't like this guy was going to write about *her* in a paper.

"What the hell," she smiled, sitting down. "What do you want to know?"

"How an attractive professional woman could believe she has the potential to become homeless."

"Did you just call me—"

"Well—journalism. That's a profession, isn't it?"

Karen blushed. No one ever called her attractive.

"Sure it is," she said, and she told him. It was a story she had learned to tell with emotional detachment—how she had only known her father as an inmate in a state prison in Kansas, and how she had gone to visit him on her ninth birthday only to discover he had been paroled and had disappeared.

"Did he ever turn up?" he asked.

"No," said Karen, distantly, focusing her mind not on the pain of her past, but on the clouds of her breath dissolving in the air.

"Would you like to know?" asked David. "I mean, know what happened to him?"

"Sure," said Karen, "I'd like to know. But I never will."

"Is that why you do this? I mean, interview homeless people. Do you think someday you'll find him?"

Karen saw the disruption in the pattern of her breath in the air before she felt the catch in her chest. It had never occurred to her that her father might be sleeping under a bridge in New York. In a few seconds of silence, broken only by the labored breathing of a passing jogger, a scene passed before her eyes. An old man in an alley recognizes her. "I've read your articles," he says. "I was afraid to contact you," he says. "I love you," he says. Then, as quickly as they had reared up, the images melted away like her breath before her.

"No," she said. "He's dead. I can feel it."

"And your mother?"

Karen could see that he still wasn't ready to talk, so she went on with the story—how she had been an outsider all through school, shunned even by her fellow journalism geeks because her writing was so much better than theirs; how her mother had been diagnosed with cancer at the beginning of Karen's senior year in high school; how she had died just days before Karen was offered a full scholarship at Columbia; how a flash flood that tore through the trailer park that summer meant Karen spent her last few weeks in Kansas at a shelter in the high school gymnasium.

"What was the shelter like?" asked David.

"It sucked. I was surrounded by people I had done my best to avoid for years, and they each thought it was their personal duty to comfort me. I couldn't very well tell them that, after everything that had happened, I was glad to see my old life washed away and couldn't wait to get out of Kansas. So I gave everyone the silent treatment, and of course they thought that meant I was sinking into depression, so they tried to comfort me even more."

"No privacy," said David. "It destroys your sense of self after a while. I think that's why a lot of the older guys just stay on the street. They might freeze to death, but they don't get stripped of their identity."

"I was only there for a month, David. And I had a job during the day and clean clothes that the Red Cross handed out. I can't even pretend to know what it's like to live on the streets of New York with Christmas coming."

"But still, you've been there. You've had a taste."

"A highly sanitized taste, but yes."

David looked straight ahead without speaking.

She decided she'd have to bring her story up to date if she was going to get him to tell his.

"So I worked my ass off all the way through college, enrolled in every summer program, got a scholarship for grad school, and now I'm working for slave wages for a newspaper that could go out of business any day. So the streets are never far from my mind."

"So that's why you do this?"

"I do it because I care, because I think it's important, and believe it or not, because I'm good at it. There's not much in this world that boosts my self image, but seeing my byline and knowing I've written a solid piece does." Karen looked for her breath again, but the day had turned warm enough that only a trace remained visible. "And yes," she said, "on some level I probably do it because I can see myself here if everything doesn't go just right. And," Karen hesitated, "I do it because it makes people...it makes some people respect me, even like me. For a fat ugly girl from the trailer park, that's an accomplishment."

"So tell me," said David, sliding his gaze across Karen's body, "what happened to the fat ugly girl?"

"Trust me, if you could see me out of these clothes—"

"If only," David said with a wistful leer.

"No, seriously. I am overweight. I am not this society's ideal of beauty. Not even close."

"Well, I'm not so sure that—"

"Look, I told you my story. Now let's hear yours."

"OK, OK, fair enough. But we're going to revisit this issue. You are *not* fat and ugly."

"Your story, David," said Karen, pulling out a pad and pencil from within the folds of her sweaters.

"Can we walk?" asked David. "I think I can do this better if I'm walking. Besides it's a great city for walking."

Hours later, Karen and David stood outside the offices of *Ear to the Ground*. They had wandered through the park, past statues of Alice in Wonderland and Hans Christian Andersen. They had rested by the fountain at Lincoln Center, and crisscrossed midtown, passing Carnegie Hall, and lingering outside the Museum of Modern Art. They had strolled on Park Avenue and through Grand Central Station, and taken 42nd Street past the Public Library to Times Square. They had headed south through the garment district, stopped to admire the Flat-iron Building and crossed Washington Square Park among chess players and NYU students. As her feet began to ache he had dragged her through Little Italy and Chinatown, down Delancey Street and then to the financial district. They sat in a pew in the back of Trinity Church, sheltered from the rush hour noise outside. Then he led her past the canyon of Wall Street to Ground Zero, where they stood staring at the empty space in the sky. They eventually made it to Battery Park, where they sat and watched the Staten Island Ferry and the Statue of Liberty while David finished his story. Finally, they walked in silence back up Broadway.

The only less-than-perfect moment in all their wanderings came on Fifth Avenue just past the blue and gold doors that marked the Manhattan headquarters of The Program. Just as they passed, a woman as slim and linear as Celinda burst out of the door and barreled right into Karen, knocking her towards the gutter. Without apology the woman shot down Fifth Avenue and disappeared into the crowd. But the rest of the day had been an exultation of everything that was New York.

"Thank you, David," Karen said, her cold hands shoved deep in her pockets. "Thank you for everything."

"It's a pretty great city, isn't it?"

"Yeah. It's been a long time since I've stopped to think about that."

"I just want you to know that I'm not unhappy. I'm not saying I like being homeless, but I'm not unhappy. I get to wander these streets every day. That's a gift, really, when you think about it. So don't paint me as pathetic and miserable, OK?"

"Of course not."

They stood in silence outside Karen's office for a moment. Karen knew she should get to work, that she had a lot of writing to do, but another minute or two of standing here with him couldn't hurt.

"Do you know what really sucks?" David leaned against the brick wall of the building, blowing warm breath into his cupped hands.

"What?"

"No social life. I mean, look at me. I'm twenty-two and living in the greatest city in the world. I should be going to clubs and parties, having dates every night. Do you know what the dating scene is like at the shelters?"

"I can imagine."

"I'll bet you can't. You know, if I wasn't homeless, I'd ask you out. But where could I take you? 'Gee, would you like to sit in a gutter outside a movie theatre with me?'"

"You'd ask me out?"

"Sure I would." David's voice suddenly lost its sardonic edge as he turned to face her. "I like you, Karen. I know it's just your job, but you're the first woman who's really listened to me in a long time."

"Well, then, ask me out, David." Karen fought to keep the excitement out of her voice. This could make a great story. Besides, she had never been the girl guys were afraid to ask out; she had been the girl they ignored. To be asked out, even by a homeless man, was a minor milestone. And it wasn't like she was dating Clifton; she was just secretly in love with him. Anyhow, this wasn't dating, it was research.

"Like I said, where would I take you?" asked David.

"I'll treat."

"No. Not like that. I don't want a sympathy date. I either do it right or I don't do it at all." Karen could see the fire of pride in his eyes and knew not to press the point.

"Well, then, take me to a shelter."

"You're going to dress up like that," he indicated her costume, "and spend the night on a crappy bed in a room with twenty other smelly women, just so you can have dinner with me?"

Karen looked David in the eyes. "Yes."

He returned her stare for several seconds, challenging her, but when she did not laugh or speak or indicate by the slightest twitch of her face a willingness to budge from her resolve, he shrugged and broke into a smile. "OK. Pick you up Saturday at six?"

"Fine." Karen felt a twinge of guilt that she was pursuing her story into the realm of dating. But, she reasoned, if she was using him, she was also doing him a kindness. She scrawled her address on the last blank page in her steno pad, and pressed the paper into his hand.

"I'd better go," he said. "I need to scout out some romantic shelters before Saturday." He winked at her and Karen felt the color rising in her cheeks, as it had earlier in the park.

"And I've got work waiting for me," she said, turning quickly towards the office door in an effort to deflect the moment. "See you Saturday?"

"Right," said David. "See you then." He turned and headed north.

Karen stayed in the office typing until dawn.

Three hours after she entered the doors of The Program, Louise Crawford emerged onto Madison Avenue through a heavy metal door. She carried a bag of old clothes and, beneath her overcoat, she wore a new little black dress, "Compliments of The Program." Had she unzipped her coat, anyone who knew her could have seen that since morning she had lost at least sixty pounds.

She had meant to walk to Toys–R–Us to shop for the children once she finished at The Program, but when she stepped into the winter sun, she couldn't resist the temptation to turn left and head to Bloomingdale's. *Just for a few minutes,* she told herself. But limiting herself to a few minutes was not so easy when, for the first time in her life, the high fashion outfits on the mannequins not only fit but looked—well, honestly, they looked fabulous on her.

Louise knew she couldn't afford any of the dresses that she took two at a time into the fitting room, but the sheer joy of seeing herself in the mirror sporting dresses by designers whose names had been like salt in the wounds of her self-esteem was worth far more than the four-digit prices of the outfits she slipped on. And the saleswomen, who had always ignored her before, fawned over her as if she were a movie star. "Yes, Mrs. Crawford." "You look divine, Mrs. Crawford." "Can I get you some espresso, Mrs. Crawford?"

Louise luxuriated in their attention for an hour, then, with a sigh, worked her way through the sales rack until she found the perfect dress for her new figure—a bright red sheath that clung to her straight lines and left nothing to the imagination. The hem was high enough to display her new thighs, and her bare nipples pressed through the fabric just like a supermodel's. She almost cried in the fitting room as she gazed, mesmerized, at her image in the mirror. *My God,* she thought, *I look just like Celinda.* Louise had never been so happy—and the dress was only four hundred dollars.

She had a little more than an hour to catch her train when she sprung through the doors of Bloomingdale's. She hurried down to Toys-R-Us, amazed at how speedily her new body moved. The old Louise would have reached the toy store sweaty and panting if she had walked this fast. Andrew was easy to take care of—he had perseverated on the same video game for the past two months. Louise ignored the parental warning as she pulled it off the shelf. Gretchen had been less sure what she wanted, so Louise grabbed a Barbie doll and playset and headed for the checkout line. Fifteen minutes later she was on her way to Grand Central Station, spending her last ten dollars on a cab ride. She opened the box from Bloomingdale's just far enough to glimpse her new dress nestled in the tissue paper, then smiled to think that Phil's Christmas present would be wrapped in red.

STEVE COLLINGWOOD SCRUTINIZED the transformed figure scowling at him from the mirror. If Karen could only see him now, he thought, he'd never hear the end of the Exeter jokes. He'd spent the day cold-calling businesses to sell advertising, and sold a one-time eighth-of-a-page to a dry cleaner in the East Village and a four-week package to a vintage clothing store. Hardly enough to end the financial woes of *Ear to the Ground.* But Steve's day was far from over. He had left the office early, and by five o'clock sat in the study at the Park Avenue apartment flipping through a book he hoped would be much more effective than the yellow pages—his father's black leather address book.

Steve had known most of his father's friends since his grade school days, and while he found the majority of them typical rich snobs who wouldn't know a socially important idea if it hit them in the surgically enhanced face, he knew how to play their game. Nearly everyone in the black book was a partner in a law firm or owned a business—and not dry cleaners and vintage clothing stores. As he thumbed the pages he recognized the names behind two publishing houses, a chain of radio stations, an insurance company, and a retail clothing chain—and he hadn't even gotten to the G's. "F" had been far enough.

Linda Foretti. She had taken over her husband's chain of trendy boutiques in a messy and highly publicized divorce. Now rumor had it she was expanding. Sixteen weeks of full-page ads in *Ear to the Ground* would be just the thing to help generate a surge in growth. Linda was definitely a solid prospect. How would he reel her in? Linda was thirty-five and notorious for her taste for younger men. Steve knew what he'd need to do.

He reached her at her office and made a dinner date for eight o'clock at Twenty-One. "You'll hardly recognize me," Linda cooed.

A face lift already? Steve wondered. Certainly not. In fact, he couldn't remember anything that needed changing on Linda. At the Collingwood Thanksgiving party she had been as curvaceous as ever—wide hips that begged you to wrap your arms around them and breasts that overflowed the low-cut gown she cradled them in. He wondered what Karen would look like in a gown like that. Probably even more bounteous and tempting than Linda.

Two hours later, Karen would hardly have recognized Steve. His hair was perfectly in place, except for a curly lock that hung down across his forehead, just left of center, giving him a carefully designed unkempt charm. He had shaved with a blade and anointed himself with his father's cologne. He wore a steel gray Brooks Brothers suit with a dark blue shirt and a yellow-and-blue-striped tie. From a drawer filled with dozens of choices he picked a pair of solid gold square cufflinks. The tie and cufflinks he borrowed from his father; the suit was one of a closet full his mother had bought for him in hopes he would one day require a gentleman's wardrobe.

He stood almost straight up, but not quite. He wanted to have the lanky slouch of a young man who has grown up very fast very recently. Linda would like that. He decided to keep her waiting a few minutes—just long enough to pique her anticipation without making her impatient. Then he would lope over to her table, tossing that curly lock off his forehead and looking hurried but in complete control. "I'm young and handsome and my time is in incredible demand, but I've made room in my busy day for a quiet dinner with you," he would say.

And he'd say it all without opening his mouth.

She would arrive at ten past eight, he figured, so at twenty past he slipped a ten to the *maître'd,* who pointed to the back of Linda's head. She was sipping a martini. His entrance was just as he'd planned—slightly breathless. He came up to her from the side, and leaned to kiss her cheek.

"Sorry I'm late," he said. "Glad to see you've gotten started."

"Well," said Linda softly, letting her eyes travel slowly the length of his frame, "just as long as you're worth waiting for. Sit down and let's get you a drink."

Steve slid into the chair opposite her, and only then did he see the transformation. His shock must have registered on his face, because Linda smiled, spread her arms, and said, "So, what do you think?"

As always Linda wore a plunging neckline, but the breasts which had so gloriously filled it in the past had disappeared, leaving nothing but her collarbone jutting through taut skin. Her outstretched arms had lost their feminine roundness and were little more than skin stretched across bones. He could only imagine what must have happened to her tantalizing hips. She reminded Steve of the stick figures he used to draw when playing Hangman with his little brother—nothing but lines and angles, not a curve in sight.

He had seen Linda's full curvaceous body two—at the most, three weeks ago. What could have happened? His first thought was that she had contracted some horrible disease—anorexia or cancer—but he could tell by the smile of pride on her drawn face that words of commiseration would not be appropriate. What could he say?

"You were right, Linda. I hardly recognize you."

"I tell you, it's the best five thousand dollars I ever spent. I hear they're raising it to ten, and that's still a bargain."

"I guess I don't understand," said Steve. "Five thousand dollars for—?"

"Darling, The Program! Goodness, you have been a busy little thing up at that school. Don't tell me that none of the little rich girls at Columbia have done it?"

"Right, right," said Steve, vaguely aware that he had heard some classmates talking about a new weight loss craze. "The Program—that's some sort of diet, right?"

"Darling, are you kidding? Believe me, I'd tried every diet known to man and then some. That's the beauty of The Program—I can eat whatever I want, do whatever I want, and still I look like this."

"How does it work?" said Steve, fighting to keep the false excitement in his voice.

"We're not really supposed to talk about it, but it's all in the mind. Now," she said, laying a bony hand on his forearm and giving him a gentle squeeze. "You *are* going to let me pay for dinner, aren't you?"

As the evening wore on, Steve rediscovered his charm. He tilted his head down and looked up at Linda with his perfectly stray lock of hair hanging across his forehead; he tossed his whole body back in his chair and laughed towards the ceiling when she tried to be funny, flipping the lock of hair out of his face for an instant; he even reached out and put his hand over hers, feeling the sharpness of her exposed knuckles, while they waited for the dessert menu. And whenever he had the chance, he looked her straight in the eye.

"You'll come back to my place for a nightcap, won't you?" Linda asked as she wrapped her tongue around a spoonful of crème caramel. "You know you're my first—night out since The Program."

"Of course. A nightcap would be—delicious," he said, smiling and raising an eyebrow ever so slightly. "I did want to talk to for just a minute about business—"

"Oh, please, darling, not business. I hate business. Business should officially end at five o'clock. Why is it that men never understand that?"

"It's just a tiny favor, really," Steve purred, "hardly worth mentioning. Give me five minutes?"

"Two minutes," she said, leaning back and crossing her arms over her narrow chest.

"It's just that I came across this great advertising opportunity for you today. It's this wonderful little offbeat paper called *Ear to the Ground* that's picking up quite a following—"

"You wouldn't happen to work for this little paper, would you, darling?"

"They don't pay me, if that's what you mean."

"How much?"

"Well, of course that depends on the size of the ad, the number of weeks—"

"Look, sweetie, the two minutes are up. Just tell me how much so we can get out of here."

"Twenty thousand would really help. And it's a good investment, honestly. I wouldn't come to you for a hand out."

"Be a dear, Steve, and tell Walter to get us a cab. I'm going to powder my nose." She slid back her chair and reached for her evening bag.

"And what about—"

"I'll write you a check after breakfast," she whispered to him as she passed.

STEVE STOOD ON THE PATIO of Linda's Fifth Avenue penthouse overlooking Central Park. Out there somewhere were the people Karen wrote about. He felt obscene standing here surrounded by fifty thousand dollars worth of plants and trees, sipping a glass of hundred-dollar-a-bottle champagne, while people in the park slept under nothing warmer than yesterday's newspaper. But he knew he was helping them in a way. If he could keep the paper going, then Karen could keep writing and maybe, if enough people read her column, things would start to change.

"Come in from the cold," said Linda behind him. "There's a fire in the den and this fabulously soft bearskin rug. I think it must be a fake. There's just no way a bear could feel so good against naked skin." She wore a full-length silk robe and leaned in the frame of the French doors. Steve did not know Celinda had made this pose famous.

He followed her inside through three lavishly decorated and dimly lit rooms. From behind she looked like a boy—a straight line from her shoulders to her ankles. He longed for even the suggestion of hips to assist in his arousal. Her tiny buttocks were not rounded enough to assert their presence through the shiny fabric of her robe. He wasn't even sure exactly where they were.

Linda stood on the bearskin rug in the flickering light of the fire, eyes closed, running fingers through the blonde hair that cascaded to her shoulders and swaying to the quiet jazz that suffused the room. Normally such a sight would have driven Steve crazy. But dammit, a woman should look like a woman. A woman should have breasts and hips and curves. A woman should look like Karen.

Linda locked her eyes on his, stopped her dance, and slowly untied the sash of her robe. It fell open slightly, then she shrugged it to the floor and stood before him completely naked. Where her breasts should have been were two erect nipples, not much more impressive than his own. The lines of her ribs were visible in the dim firelight. Her wispy patch of pubic hair was the only feature that Steve found remotely feminine, but even that oasis of womanhood seemed lost in a desert of boyish limbs and boniness. The perfect angles of the pubic delta were supposed to form a scintillating contrast with the curves that surrounded them. Linda was nothing but angles.

He followed the line of her left leg down to her high arched foot, which seemed too narrow to support an adult human body. There, splayed out against the darkness of the rug, was the only thing in his whole tour of her body that aroused his interest. Linda Foretti had six toes on her left foot. He didn't want to offend her by staring at this anomaly, so he returned his eyes to her gaunt figure.

"I see you like to watch," said Linda, misinterpreting his inaction and twirling slowly for the benefit of what she supposed were his hungry eyes. Steve wanted to walk away, but he thought of the twenty thousand dollars; he thought of the paper. He thought of Karen.

Karen. Now Karen had the flesh of a woman. She wore her clothes too loose, but he could tell. As Linda swayed in front of him, he mentally clothed her in Karen's flesh. Fleshy woman's thighs that spread up towards that pubic triangle and gave it a soft place to nestle; curvy hips that would magnify every undulation and invite his hands to grab hold; gloriously full breasts that would overflow his hands when he cupped them from behind. With the vision of Karen's imagined shape superimposed onto Linda, Steve coaxed himself into arousal.

He threw his empty champagne glass into the fire, grabbed Linda, thrust himself against her and kissed her deeply. But even as her tongue darted between his lips the feel of her ribs against his hands shattered the illusion of shapeliness and withered his erection. She must have felt his deflation, for she broke the embrace and stepped back towards the fire, wrapping her arms around herself.

"What's the matter?" she purred.

"I'm sorry, Linda, I just can't. It just—it wouldn't be right." Steve backed away, almost tripping over the head of the bear.

"Oh my God," she said in a stunned voice. "You don't find me attractive, do you?"

"No, that's not it," Steve lied. He knew perfectly well if she were shaped like Karen he would have gone through with it.

"Do you realize," said Linda, her voice rising, "that this is the body of the most beautiful woman in the world?" She elbowed past him and rifled through a pile of magazines on the coffee table. Pulling one from the middle of the stack, she furiously flipped the pages. "There," she said, holding up a picture of Celinda in a minuscule black bra and panty set. "Look what it says!" She held the magazine out so Steve could see the caption—"The most beautiful woman in the world." Then she held the magazine next to her own body.

"Admit it. It's the same body. I have the body of the most beautiful woman in the world."

"It's certainly the same body," said Steve quietly. "I'm lucky to have seen it—" He had been about to say "in the flesh," but it didn't seem the right phrase. "But I really have to go."

Linda picked up her gown off the floor and clutched it to her chest. *As if she had something to hide,* thought Steve. "I'll let myself out," he said, and he left her standing alone with her new body and her twenty thousand dollars.

Steve needed a walk, so he crossed Fifth Avenue and turned south. The cold seemed to ooze out of the darkness of the park. He buried his hands in his pockets, hunched his shoulders and walked a little faster. He passed through Grand Army Plaza, where horses stamped in the cold, waiting to take after-theatre tourists for rides through the park. He saw a man covered with newspapers sleeping on a bench, his left hand clasping a plastic garbage bag that bulged with cans. Steve dug in his pocket and found nothing but a credit card and a fifty-dollar bill. He wondered what Karen would do. Wake the man up and give him the fifty, probably.

Steve crossed the square and found a newsstand on Central Park South. He picked up a copy of the *Wall Street Journal*. He was just about to hand it to the man in the booth when his eye caught a stack of *Perfect Woman* magazines. Staring at him from the cover was the same sunken face Linda had displayed in her apartment, with the same caption—"The most beautiful woman in the world," and below, "Find out her secret." Steve whisked up a copy of the magazine and added it to his purchase. Then he crossed the square again, shook the man awake, and pressed a ten dollar bill into his hand. To his shame, Steve felt both afraid and embarrassed when the man looked up at him with puzzled eyes, so he turned and walked as quickly as he dared back towards Fifth Avenue. Twenty minutes later he was home.

He undressed quickly, pulled on an old sweat suit and settled onto his bed with *Perfect Woman*. Page after page showed women with Linda's new figure—women with fast rising film careers, women anchoring network news programs, women on fashion runways or in rock bands or chairing major corporations or running for Congress—all of them billed as having "perfect" figures, and all of them, apparently, products of The Program. Though it was never explicitly stated, the magazine implied these women had achieved success because of their "perfect" bodies. Steve wondered if America had become subject to some sort of mass hypnosis and had forgotten what women were supposed to look like.

Steve had not forgotten. Carefully hidden away in his closet was a *Playboy* magazine from his middle school years. He dug it out and sat on the edge of the bed looking first at Celinda in her "Get With The Program" advertisement and then at the Playmate of the Month, unfolded in all her glory. Now there, thought Steve, was a woman. Her hips were wide and round, her breasts full and heavy enough to haunt the dreams of any red-blooded American male. Her arms and legs had flesh on them—not rolls of fat, but plentiful, soft, female flesh. Celinda, by comparison—well, Steve thought he could detect the possibility of attractive features in "the most beautiful woman in the world," but they all seemed deflated. Put fifty pounds on her and who knows, she might be gorgeous.

For a moment he flicked his eyes rapidly back and forth between the two women, trying to clothe Celinda in the womanly flesh of the Playmate, but it didn't quite work. He tossed the perfect woman into the trash can, shoved the *Wall Street Journal* into his backpack, and retired down memory lane with a ten-year-old *Playboy*.

On Friday Karen's article, headlined "David," started on the front page of *Ear to the Ground* and extended over most of pages four and five. There were not many advertisements to interfere with its flow.

DAVID IS HAPPY. Some people might think he has no right to be—after all, he lives under a bridge in Central Park, sleeps in crowded shelters on the coldest nights, and never knows where his next meal will come from. But spend a day with David walking the streets of what he calls "the most glorious city in the world," and you can see that, in spite of all life has thrown at him, David is happy.

"Sure, I'd like to have a job," says David as we sit on a bench in Battery Park watching the lights of the Staten Island Ferry in the December dusk. "I'd like to have a warm bed every night and a hot shower every morning. I'd like to be able to walk down the street and not see fear and disgust on people's faces. On the other hand," he says, motioning towards Liberty and Ellis Islands, "look at that view. How can you feel impoverished when you can see that every day?"

David doesn't see his homelessness as a permanent state. "It's a phase of my life," he says. "Things will turn around eventually." He's been living on the streets for eight months now. Most days he sets out not wondering how he will eat or keep warm, but what part of the city he should explore. He already knows New York better than most lifelong New Yorkers, yet he's never taken a tour, read a guide book, or even looked at a map. "All you need is time and a strong pair of legs," says David. "I've got both."

David came here from a small town upstate he prefers not to name. "It's not their fault," he says, "except maybe the D.A., and he was just doing his job." On his way to the City he spent four years as a guest of the Empire State at what we delicately term a "correctional facility." "That's one I never understood," he says. "There was nothing correct about that place."

At seventeen, David became an emancipated minor when his single mother entered an alcohol treatment facility. He has not seen or heard from her since. For two years he lived alone in the house he and his mother had shared. He paid his food and utility bills with a welfare check and the income from odd jobs he did in a suburban development three miles away. He walked to school every day, walked to the suburbs when he had a job, and walked home. "I guess I averaged about seven or eight miles a day," he says. Two weeks before his high school graduation he came home on a Friday afternoon to find the doors of his house padlocked and a foreclosure notice pasted across the front window. David didn't know what foreclosure meant, had never heard of a mortgage, and had no idea where he would spend the night.

"Do you ever just sit here and watch the kids playing on the Alice in Wonderland statue?" David asks me in the middle of this story. "It doesn't matter how cold it gets, that statue is always swarming with kids. They climb on the mushroom and into her lap, they crawl underneath and discover the crocodile, they pose on the Mad Hatter's hat. Look, her finger is all shiny from millions of little kids hoisting themselves up. I just love that."

Even though I've walked past that statue in Central Park scores of times I've never looked at it closely enough to know there *was* a crocodile, much less seen the endless enjoyment it gives the children of New York. When we leave the park and begin our long trek through the city that will end that evening at the Battery, I learn more of David's history.

Kicked out of his house and with nowhere to go, David set out for the suburbs, hoping one of the families he sometimes worked for might take him in until the bank reopened on Monday and he could talk to someone. When he passed three classmates on the sidewalk and explained his situation, they invited him out for pizza.

David thought nothing of it when the boys suggested they drive to a park by the river outside of town and drink a few beers. That was a typical activity for his classmates, and the law generally looked the other way as long as there was a sober driver. "You mind driving?" one of the boys asked David, and what could he

THE PROGRAM

say after all their kindness? "Of course not."

"It's hard to believe I was ever such an innocent," David says—with more humor in his voice than malice. "Did you know that Winnie-the-Pooh lives in there?" We are standing almost across the street from the Museum of Modern Art, looking up at the unimpressive façade of the Donnell Branch of the Public Library.

"I did know that," I say. "England wanted him back, didn't they?"

"Yes," says David. "I think the mayor said he'd send Pooh back when they send the Elgin Marbles back to Greece. Or if he didn't, he should have. Have you ever seen him?"

"The mayor? Yes, I saw him in a parade last fall."

"No, Winnie-the-Pooh."

I haven't, so David leads me to the second floor, where we gaze through a plate glass window at a row of tatty stuffed animals, formerly the property of Christopher Milne, a.k.a. Christopher Robin. "They're one of the great free attractions of the city," David says. "No one is ever up here. I can't understand it. If you put those toys in the Met they'd be the most popular exhibit." We stand in the hushed corner of the library for a few moments gazing at Pooh, Piglet, Eeyore, Rabbit, and Kanga. "Roo was lost," David says at last, shaking his head as we head back to the street.

The other boys never told David the car was stolen. When the sheriff pulled them over for a routine Friday night breathalyzer, David blew a 0.0. He hadn't had a sip. But when the license check showed the car had been stolen earlier that day, the sheriff arrested all four boys. Within an hour family lawyers had retrieved three of them. David never made bail.

The other three turned state's evidence against him, claiming he had lured them into the stolen car. The prosecution painted David as a desperate youth who had lost his home and decided to take revenge on the innocent citizens of the community. The D.A. was running for re-election. "There was one person who spoke out for me," whispers David, as we stand in the back of St. Bartholomew's Church on Park Avenue. "An Episcopal priest. He liked stirring up the establishment. He threw dinner parties where he would invite all these old stick-in-the-muds and get them talking about gay rights or gun control—anything to get them riled up. First I thought I was just another issue for him to inspire debate with, but he came to see me in jail before the trial, and I could tell he really cared. He was the only person who talked to me like I was a human being and not some sort of animal."

The trial lasted less than a day. The rich boys walked and David was sentenced to four to eight years for grand theft auto. "I

38

think if the trial had taken a month or even a week, Father Martin might have been able to draw some attention to the injustice of the whole thing," David says. "But the sword of injustice can be mighty swift."

David served his four years without applying for parole. "I didn't have anything waiting for me," he says as we swim through crowds of Christmas shoppers in Grand Central Station, "no family, no friends, no money. As bad as it was in there, at least I had a bed to sleep in and three square meals a day." When he did get out, David headed for the highway and hitchhiked to New York City.

"You know, most New Yorkers hate this place," David says as we stand at the nadir of Times Square waiting for traffic to clear on 42nd Street. The sign opposite flashes "Walk" and I start to cross with the assembled crowd, but David doesn't move, so, like a salmon swimming upstream, I fight my way through harried pedestrians back to the corner. "Not me, though," he says, finishing his thought. "I love to watch the tourists fresh off their planes. They take a bus or a cab into town and check into their hotels and then they pour into Times Square with awe on their faces. I think New Yorkers need to be reminded of that—of the fact that they live in a city that inspires awe, that should inspire *their* awe."

We stand on the corner for several cycles of the light and look into the upturned, awestruck faces of those experiencing New York for the first time. David is right—every cynical New Yorker who makes wisecracks about tourists should stand here and rediscover the awe.

David spent his first three nights in New York on a bench in Central Park. The spring air was warm, and with a few dollars in his pocket he knew he could eat for several days while he looked for a job. But like so many of New York's homeless, he discovered that having no address was a serious impediment to employment. "I first learned about the city looking for work," David says. "Every day I'd pick a neighborhood and walk up one street and down the next, stopping at every business and asking for a job."

He asked at restaurants, grocery stores, shops and offices of every description. Occasionally someone would let him sweep out a back room or help unload a truck for a few dollars, but no one wanted to offer steady employment to an ex-convict who lived on a park bench. "I could have made up an address and lied about my past," says David, "but it didn't seem right." Gradually he got to know the city, earning enough money for food. But as his clothes got more worn, even those jobs became scarce. David began to learn about the vortex that is homelessness.

THE PROGRAM

"I had friends," says David as we amble across Washington Square. "After those first three nights on the bench I met Gus and Jimmy, and they took me to their place under a bridge and I met Bob and Andy." These men had nothing to gain by befriending David—just another body to have to share their space with, another producer of the sour smell of sweat, another person clamoring for warmth when the cold weather came. The four of them had been living on the street for a combined total of twenty-three years. "They showed me where the shelters and the soup kitchens were, and taught me when to linger behind which bakeries waiting for the old bread to get thrown out." David was twenty years younger than the youngest of his friends. "But I'd never had that feeling of being treated like an equal before—not in school, certainly not in prison," he says.

David lets me buy him some take-out in Chinatown, and we eat with chopsticks from cardboard containers as we walk towards the financial district and the heart of rush hour. "Gus taught me how to eat with chopsticks," David tells me. "We found a pair in the garbage one day and we spent the whole day practicing picking things up. What else did we have to do?"

David has learned more than how to survive on the streets and how to eat with chopsticks in the past seven months.

Andy, who found a deck of cards one day, taught David how to play bridge. "We were missing the ace of clubs," David says, "so Gus made one out of a magazine cover." Jimmy taught him Tai Chi. "Some mornings we all go up to one of the big fields and do Tai Chi while the sun rises," David says.

We fight our way through the rush of five o'clock in the financial district. "Another great New York experience," he says as we are swept across the street by two hundred dark-suited brokers who do their best to ignore us. "I really scare them," says David. "You can see it in their eyes. These guys live on a mountain of paper and they know if the thing collapses they'll be right where I am."

David has not had a job in over a month. He's been eating at shelters lately, and with winter coming on has even spent a few nights there. When the forecast calls for temperatures below freezing, his friends agree to go to a shelter. More and more often, David joins them. They rarely find a place that can accommodate all five of them. "I'm always scared to go back to the bridge the next day, because I know any one of them might not have made it through the night," David says. He has read articles about the recent spate of deaths among the city's homeless. And he knows it will only get colder.

We are sitting in Battery Park, with the weight of the city looming behind us and the hope of Liberty's torch shining in the evening gloom, when I ask David about the future. "I'll turn something up," he says, and I note the proactive phrasing—not "something will turn up," but "I'll turn something up."

David will turn twenty-three next month; he's been on his own nearly seven years, four of those spent in prison on an unjust conviction. Now he faces a cold winter without any of the comforts most of us take for granted. Yet he has hope. He is less cynical than most of the people who ignore him in the street.

If we could all see the city through his eyes, what a glorious place it would be—perhaps even glorious enough to make room for a young man like David.

"I HOPE I didn't get too preachy there at the end," Karen said.

"No, I like it," said Clifton, "It's a nice balance of hope and guilt. Give them something to gnaw on."

He sat with his freshly polished wingtips propped on Karen's desk, where she knew they would leave scuff marks. She didn't care, though. Watching Clifton read her work was the most intimate experience she shared with him. For those few minutes every week when he was lost in her words she felt almost one with him, like she was inside his head and he was inside hers. It was like great sex—or so she'd heard.

Clifton read the paper cover to cover every Friday morning, then called everyone together and told them what they had done wrong. He called them his nit-picking sessions, and while Karen dreaded them, she always learned from them. Clifton's stern manner could hurt when he was talking about your writing, but in addition to secretly loving him, Karen thought he was a damn fine editor. The paper got better every issue.

This morning the critique never came. After reading Karen's lead article, Clifton slapped the paper on her desk and trudged into his office without a word, leaving a worried staff behind.

"Something's wrong," said Marjorie, stepping into Karen's cubicle with Steve. "I've been with Clifton for two years and he's never skipped a nit-picking session."

"He has been sort of distant lately," said Steve. "I think he's just distracted—you know, year end number-crunching and all that."

"Maybe it's another woman," said Marjorie, smiling at Karen, who scowled back at her and turned so Steve wouldn't see her blush. With her back to the others, she pretended to examine the paper on her desk. Something about the masthead looked odd, and it took her a moment to realize what.

"Hey, what's this?" she said, pointing to a small line of type under the date.

"'Double Issue?'" said Steve. "What the hell does that mean, 'Double Issue?' It's not any bigger than usual."

"Maybe it means we get a break for Christmas," said Karen.

"It means," said Marjorie, "that this financial crunch is a lot worse than we thought, and Clifton wants to wait until after the holidays to drop the bombshell."

The three of them stood silent for a moment, listening to the gurgling of the coffee urn.

"Well, Karen," said Marjorie at last, "I hope your friend David has some extra room under that bridge."

It's not just a question of denigrating the self-esteem of normal people," said Martin, pouring another glass of Pinot Noir, "it's an affront to God's design. No offense, Darcey."

"Well," said Darcey, "we're talking in theoreticals here, right? So I won't be offended—for now, at least. Besides, you know my stance on God."

"But you should be, my dear," said Jackie. "You absolutely should be offended. Just because he's the host, you don't have to let him insult you. Besides, Martin, doesn't everything we do change God's design—exercise, your annual grapefruit diet, cutting your hair, wearing clothes, for goodness sake?"

"Yes," said Martin, "but this takes something innately female—that God has created—and it removes a part of that femaleness. It ignores His own wisdom in creating it the way he did."

There they sat, the five of them, surrounding the detritus of Friday night dinner, sipping their various beverages—wine for Martin and Gareth, beer for Nick, gin for Jackie, club soda for Darcey—smiling their way through this month's debate, the pros and cons of The Program.

Father Martin Stewart, rector of the Episcopal Parish of St. Alban's in Braintree, New York, had replaced the long dining table in the rectory with a round one so no one would hold a position of superiority in these discussions he hosted. The guest list for his dinner parties, which had gained a certain notoriety among local gossips, varied from month to month, but lately these five always seemed to be last at the table—Nick Leonard, district attorney for Braintree County, a tall, well-padded man packed into a khaki suit; Darcey Thayer, who had moved to Braintree two years ago after graduating from law school at NYU and who worked for a small local firm; Jackie Leblanc, a wealthy middle-aged widow with a country estate on the fringes of the parish who treated Martin like an adopted son; Gareth Lloyd, a seminary student who had taken a year out of school to work with Martin; and Father Martin himself, a charismatic priest who, despite his love of controversy, was as gentle a man as any of the others had ever known.

Martin was surprised how long this discussion had dragged on, from cocktails three hours ago through dessert, and still it raged. He had hoped for an early night, but found himself, at nine o'clock, staunchly defending a position and simultaneously worrying that he might be offending Darcey.

Jackie had met Darcey a year ago and had introduced her to Martin. Darcey had declined an invitation to attend church, and was open with Martin about her atheism. When he said he respected her beliefs, she agreed to come to one of his dinner parties, and she fit right in. "We need as much variety in our viewpoints as we can get," said Martin to Nick one night when the D.A. asked him why a non-believer had become a regular at the rectory. "Besides, Darcey may not believe in God, but it's surprising how often she seems to speak for Him."

"You should see Darcey," Jackie had murmured to Martin after Communion one Sunday a few months ago, "she's a good fifty pounds lighter than last week." So Darcey had become the star guest at to-night's dinner—someone who had participated in The Program and could offer a perspective from the inside.

But she had stayed fairly quiet most of the evening. As for Martin, he generally sat back and let the others do the arguing. But tonight he led the vanguard of opposition to The Program. He didn't attack Darcey personally, but for some reason he could not exercise his usual restraint on this topic.

"Listen," he said. "You know as well as I do that if you clear your mind of all the images you see on television and the movies and forget all the expectations of your parents or your children or your teachers or your boss or your spouse—if you let all that slide away and just look at who you really are, you can see the person that God created, thin or—not so thin."

"So these kids who look inside themselves and see an innate urge to steal a car," said Nick, "they're just living up to God's design, and I should let them off with a slap on the wrist, even though *society* says that stealing is wrong?"

"Yes, but God says it, too," said Martin.

"But you *can't* leave society out of it," said Jackie. "Like it or not, Martin, we were created by society as much as by God. Without this society that you look down your nose at we'd have no language, we'd wear no clothes, we'd live to be maybe twenty-five, and we certainly wouldn't indulge ourselves in organized religion."

"Yes," said Martin, "but in the shaping of our image by the Almighty, all is good; in the shaping of that image by society there is good and evil—we have to learn to separate the two."

"But we *live* in society," said Darcey in a strong level tone that instantly silenced the others. Like a good lawyer, she had been waiting for the right moment to present her argument. "You say this God of yours loves us whatever we look like—tall or short, fat or thin. Well, that's fine, but I don't live with God, I live with society, and with society it's not quite the same. Let me tell you about society."

Darcey fixed her eyes on Martin. "I was a thin kid. God made me thin, if you want to look at it that way. And then He put me into a society that fed me on fried food and ice cream and sat me in front of a television all day long. My parents never told me to exercise or cut back on candy bars. All the other kids ate crap and sat around watching TV, why should I be any different? Only God made me with a metabolism that couldn't handle that lifestyle, and by seventh grade I was the fat kid. Do any of you have any idea what it's like being the fat kid in seventh grade?" She moved her gaze around the table.

"The girls made fun of me, the boys wouldn't talk to me. The counselor and my parents said to ignore them, said they would mature in a year or two, said it was just adolescence. But it never changed—not in high school, not in college, not in law school, and certainly not out in the real world. Sure, the way they did it was different. But do you know how many dates I'd been on before The Program? Not drinks with friends, but actual 'I'll pick you up at eight o'clock' dates? Four. I'm twenty-seven years old! I'm smart and I'm funny, and everybody knows the fat chick is an easy lay, right? Four dates. Isn't that pathetic—I kept count." Darcey paused to let this bit of information seep in.

"But that's not the worst of it. Even the way people look at you, with that expression that says, 'Thank God that's not me,' is not the worst of it. The worst is being ignored, treated like I don't even exist. I could stand at a makeup counter in a department store for twenty minutes, and as long as there was a thin girl there, too, no one would wait on me. When I was interning for a law firm in New York, I walked to work every morning, and every morning someone in front of me held the door open for some thin woman, then let it close in my face. Cabs would drive right past me and pick up some skinny lady a block further on. Guys at the deli counter would look past me and take someone else's order. Believe me, unless you've been there, you can't imagine. The same society that made me fat discriminated against me in a way that—well, if I'd been black or Asian or Hispanic, or even gay, people would have been outraged. As it was, if I told anyone, they'd say it was my imagination, that I was suffering from low self-esteem.

"So I started making money, and I went to The Program. I went back to being that thin person I remembered, that you say God created. It took me two weeks to go on my next four dates; my law firm took me out from behind a desk and let me appear in court; the repairman who would never show up at my house is there every day; and you," she looked at Martin, "the person who voices the strongest disapproval of my right to choose my body shape, are the very person who defends people's right to choose everything else—from their sexual expression to their religious beliefs. So don't you," she looked around the table again, "don't *any* of you tell me that I don't have those same rights, and don't you dare tell me to ignore the opinions of society."

The table sat in stunned silence for several seconds. They had come to think of Darcey as the meek, quiet type. She provided a counterpoint for religiously based arguments, but she did it calmly and in few words. Tonight, when the debate turned on her own choices, she had argued with a passion that earned her new respect.

"Anyhow," said Darcey, finally breaking the uneasy silence, "the guys have been duds so far, but at least I'm finding that out."

"I hate to be indelicate here," said Gareth, leaning forward, "but how much did you actually lose?"

"Sixty-four pounds," said Darcey.

Gareth let out a low whistle. "How does it work?" he asked.

"We're not really supposed to talk about it," said Darcey, "but it's all in the mind."

"Now if she was thin to start out with, how is it a betrayal of God's design for her to get thin again?" asked Nick.

"I think I was wrong," said Martin, "to assume that one set of rules is appropriate for everyone. But I still don't understand why society has created an ideal for women which is so unfeminine. Whatever happened to Rubenesque? You say you lost sixty-four pounds, Darcey. Don't you think if you'd only lost twenty, you'd feel a little more like a woman?"

"It's sort of an all or nothing proposition," said Darcey. "The Program is tailored to produce women who fit this societal ideal, which is there whether we like it or not. So even if I'd wanted to stay more—I don't know, more voluptuous—that's not an option with The Program. And besides, the same society that ignored me when I was fat is the society that created this ideal. So yes, I'm succumbing to societal pressures, but like I said, I live in society, and anything is better than being treated the way I was."

"So you see, Martin," said Jackie with an air of finality, "like it or not, society is here to stay. You can claim that it's wrong for us to wear clothes, but you're going to have to effect some pretty big changes in society before we stop doing it. And you can claim that God made people every shape and no matter how big we are, as long as we're healthy, we should rejoice in the shape God gave us—but you're going to have to effect some pretty big changes in society for that to work, too.

"Now," she said, turning to Darcey, "what nice man can we find for you?"

As the party broke up a few minutes later, Jackie reached into her purse and pulled out a pair of tabloid newspapers. "I thought you two might find this interesting," she said, handing one copy of *Ear to the Ground* to Martin and one to Nick. "I picked it up in New York this morning. Start reading here," she said, pointing to a headline that said simply, "David."

L ouise Crawford and her new body arrived home at four o'clock. On the train from New York, three thin women invited her to occupy the remaining seat in their section. Thin women! In the past she had spent this trip propped up in the aisle desperately moving her packages from one side to another as people passed on the way to and from the restroom. This time she sat and actually spoke to people who before had only given her annoyed looks. And they spoke back!

Two of the women were graduates of The Program; one was simply, as she put it, "thin by the grace of God." But how you became thin was irrelevant. Once you were a member of the club, all past shapes, sizes, and programs were forgotten. And she, Louise Crawford, who had hidden her arms from sight for decades, was now a member.

She took off her coat, stretched her thin bare arms out over her head for all the travelers to see, and fell into a long conversation with her new friends about how, before The Program, their men had always looked at other women.

"Yes," said the naturally thin one, "they were looking at me."

And they all laughed without malice or jealousy—after all, they were sisters.

KAREN WASN'T USED TO dressing for dates. Sure, she had fantasized plenty of times about what she would wear if Clifton asked her out, but that fantasy fell short of helping her tonight on two counts: she was going out with a homeless man, not Clifton; and she didn't actually own any of the clothes she fantasized about. No, her problem tonight was whether to wear her homeless garb—which seemed a bit deceitful—or to dress as she usually did, like a refugee from a 1990s college dorm.

She opted for a denim skirt and pink T-shirt, both of which fit more snugly that she liked, or remembered. No one would see the shirt anyway, she thought, pulling on a grey wool sweater. David was nice enough, but she didn't want him to get the wrong idea. She was standing in front of the mirror, applying a modicum of makeup and lost in a daydream about how nice it would be if Clifton got the wrong idea, when she heard the buzzer.

"David, is that you?"

"Hi, Karen," came his voice.

She thought for a moment about asking him in, but Georgia, sprawled on the couch with the *Times* crossword, saw Karen's finger on the buzzer and shook her head.

"Be right down," said Karen.

"This is not going to end well," said Georgia. "You know the rule about getting emotionally involved with a story."

"Oh, please," said Karen, "I am not emotionally involved. It's just a good opportunity. I'll either write a follow-up on David, I'll meet another prospect, or maybe I'll do a feature on homeless dating."

"Is there such a thing as homeless dating?"

"How do I look?"

"Like you don't want him to get the wrong idea."

"Perfect," said Karen.

"You look fantastic," said David as Karen descended the steps to the sidewalk. "I had no idea you had such beautiful hair." She wore her hair down, the auburn ends just grazing her shoulders.

"Thanks." She wasn't sure what compliment to offer in return. David looked tired, dirty, hungry and cold, but she had to say something.

"You look great, too," she said.

"Aw, I look awful," he grumbled. "I wanted to go to a shelter last night so I could take a shower this morning, but Gus was being stubborn. Somebody robbed him at a shelter Thursday night, and now he won't go no matter how cold it gets. I'm not going to let him sleep under that bridge alone, so I've been staying with him. Sorry."

"Don't be," said Karen. "Gus is lucky to have a friend like you. You know he was my first interview."

"I know," said David. "He's very proud of that."

Karen smiled to think she could make Gus proud.

"I've made reservations at the Lower Manhattan Samaritan Shelter," said David, "I hope you'll find the cuisine suitable."

"Sounds divine," said Karen. "I read an excellent review in the *Times*."

Karen had done her homeless research on the streets, so the Lower Manhattan Samaritan Shelter was a new experience. The outside door was unmarked, but by six forty-five a line of men and women stretched down the block.

"Lots of business when it's cold," David said. "They can feed three hundred, but they only sleep fifty men and fifty women, so a lot of us will be back out at ten. Still, that's a square meal and three hours of warmth. You can't complain."

At seven o'clock the line began to move, and ten minutes later David and Karen entered a large room that looked like an old warehouse. Piles of cots lined three walls; on the fourth was a cafeteria line. Folding tables and chairs filled the room. The line shuffled quietly forward, and Karen felt a pang of guilt when she held out her plate for a serving of roast chicken, green beans, and mashed potatoes. She should be on the other side, serving, she thought.

David led her to the end of a table and sat quietly gazing at his plate.

"Aren't you going to eat?" she asked him.

"Waiting for grace," he said, nodding his head towards a man at the end of the food line. "Some do and some don't," he said.

Karen saw that about half the diners sat waiting for the food to be blessed while the rest gobbled it down before it got cold. When the man at the end of the line had been served he stood at the head of the table closest to the food line. What little conversation had fluttered through the room evaporated.

"Let us pray," said the man in a baritone voice. "Dear Lord, who taught that whenever we render kindness to the least of your children we do so to you, bless this food to the nourishment of our bodies and this fellowship to the nourishment of our souls, in the name of your Son Jesus Christ, Amen."

A mumbled "Amen" from the tables quickly dissolved into the clattering of metal forks on plastic plates. Karen and David ate, like the rest of the room, without talking. He did not remove the worn glove from his right hand, but gripped his fork tightly through the cloth. "One custom you have to understand here," he told Karen when he had finished, "people eat first, and socialize after."

As plates were emptied, conversations broke out around the room. David smiled at Karen as she finished her last bite of chicken. "I'd like you to meet Blake," he said, putting a hand on the man next to him. "He's an admirer of your work. Blake, this is Karen."

"I thought you must be," said the man, looking up and putting out a hand for Karen to shake. "Who else would come here all dressed up beautiful?"

Karen blushed and shook his callused hand. "It's nice to meet you, Blake. Are you from New York originally?"

"Grew up in Philly," he said. "Worked on the docks here for years. Still get a job once in a while. You wrote the piece about David."

"That's right."

"I thought it was your best one yet. I'm not surprised to see you two together."

Before Karen could respond, she felt a hand on her shoulder and turned to see the smudgy face of a woman not much older than herself. The woman leaned over her shoulder and whispered, "Very nice work. You write just beautifully." Though Karen had encountered individual fans of her work among the homeless, nothing had prepared her for the next few minutes of handshaking and compliments. Everyone who had accepted the hospitality of the Lower Manhattan Samarian Shelter seemed to be familiar with Karen's writing.

Just when this mass adoration seemed at its zenith, she heard a gratingly familiar voice raised at the next table. "She's got no business in here. Look at her—taking the place of somebody who really needs dinner, just like she takes advantage of us in that paper of hers." Without turning to look, she knew it was the man from Grand Army Plaza.

"He's right," she whispered to David, "I kept somebody from eating tonight."

"Don't listen to him," said David, loud enough to be heard at the next table. "Everyone who was on line got in. No one got turned away."

But the man had gathered a posse of like-minded people at his table, and the crescendo of their grumbling gave him the backing to raise his own voice louder.

"We're people, not stories!" he said. "What gives them the right to sell our lives and all we get in return is a sheet of paper to sleep under!" He stood up and looked directly at Karen.

"What gives you the right? Well? Are you going to answer us or are you just going to set there and pretend to be girlfriend with somebody because his story sells your paper? What gives you the right?"

Karen felt a fire leap up inside her; sweat trickled down her back and from under her arms. She longed to be transported outside by magic, to feel the cold night air on her burning forehead. Every eye in the room, the kind and the unkind, focused on her. She could not move or speak, or even turn to David with a pleading look. She heard his chair slide back, and felt him move from her side towards the next table, and then his shadow stopped and she felt a hand on her shoulder.

"I think maybe you two should go," said the man who had delivered the blessing. "We don't want any trouble."

Moments later, in the cold street, she could think of a thousand things to say to the man. "We don't make any money; I'm only trying to help you; I can hardly afford to keep myself off the street but I still buy coffee for homeless men; instead of looking for a job that actually pays something, I try to bring some attention to your problems. I try." As the words cascaded through her mind in a growing torrent, her anger and frustration grew; but no matter how many retorts she thought of, she couldn't escape the nagging feeling that the man was right.

"I try!" she cried out to the empty street. "Goddam it, I try. What else can I do?"

"Don't listen to him," said David, "He doesn't speak for anyone but himself."

Karen whirled around. Of course David was with her; she had been so immersed in her own thoughts she hadn't noticed him.

"What if he's right?" she said. "I mean, honestly, is there one less person on the streets because of me?"

"I think there will be eventually. But I also think that's not the most important thing. You've given people something that a shelter can't give them—you've given us self-respect and self-worth, made us feel like real human beings again, instead of cast-off garbage. You saw those people tonight, you know that's true."

"So if they die cold and alone on the street tonight they'll still have self-worth, is that it?"

"Yes, that *is* it. You don't understand what it's like out there. There are things you fear more than death. We all die, but there's a big difference between facing death with some honor and self-esteem and facing it as the inevitable end of someone forgotten by society. You make society remember us. You give us dignity."

Karen hoped David was right, but she still felt guilty—not so much for taking advantage of other people's stories for her own advancement, but because they were homeless and she wasn't. Through sheer luck she had ended up writing about the streets instead of living on them. It had been haunting her all evening, even before the angry man's tirade—this guilt of being the only person at dinner with clean clothes, with a bed waiting at home and the certainty of *something* for lunch tomorrow. Most of all, she felt guilty for using David, accepting this date just to get a story. In her selfishness what she had wanted most out of this evening was something to impress Clifton.

She walked beside David without speaking, slowly wandering back towards her neighborhood. In the last block, he reached out and took her hand, and she let her fingers rest in his warm glove.

"I'm sorry I ruined the evening," she said, when they reached her building.

"I had a lovely evening," said David, "I'm only sorry I couldn't have taken you some place nicer." He kissed her lightly on the cheek and they stood together for a moment in the lamplight, her hand still in his.

What could it hurt? thought Karen. It would just be a kiss, not a promise of everlasting love. And if it gave him a little dignity, where was the harm in that?

In the yellow of the streetlight his sunken face looked almost ghost-like. His cheeks, with their stubbly growth of beard, felt coarse and harsh in her hands, his pale lips were cracked and chapped, but his eyes, as blue in the streetlight as in the sunshine of Central Park, were not afraid to meet hers. As she pressed her lips to his, it occurred to her that she hadn't kissed a man since she met Clifton over a year ago.

"I need to get up to the park and check on Gus," said David when she broke away.

Karen had climbed halfway up the steps when he called to her.

"Do you know what I want?" he asked.

"What?"

"I want to be able to kiss a woman with lips that haven't spent every night outdoors for seven months. I want a woman to hold my face in her hands and feel the soft cheeks of a twenty-three-year-old. I want to hold someone close and not be ashamed of how I smell. I want to hold a woman's hand and not worry that she'll wonder what's under this glove. I want to not be afraid, when I'm standing outside her apartment, that she might ask me to come up."

"You don't have to be afraid," said Karen.

"I know. But I am."

"Any woman worth having doesn't care about all the other stuff, you know. She cares about the person inside."

"Easy for you to say," said David, but Karen had spent most of her life ashamed of how she looked. Telling someone to ignore external appearances was not easy at all. David shoved his hands deep in his pockets. "It's not just the way I look," he said, "There are other things." He stood staring at the sidewalk for a moment. "Listen, I really am worried about Gus."

"Will I see you again?" asked Karen.

"Soon. Tomorrow. Or Monday. Maybe we could take a walk."

"I'd like that."

"OK. Well, goodnight, then."

"Goodnight, David." She watched as he disappeared into the shadows at the end of the block, then climbed the stairs to her apartment wondering what was underneath his glove.

"You'd better be careful," said Georgia. "Sounds to me like he's falling in love with you."

"He just hasn't ever been on a date, that's all," said Karen. "Besides, he's a story, not a romance."

"To you he's a story; he might not see it that way."

"Any good mail?" asked Karen, eager to change the subject.

"Yeah, actually, there is," said Georgia in a puzzled tone. She slid a piece of paper across the table.

"Jesus! This is a check for five thousand dollars!"

"Yeah, it is."

"We could buy furniture."

"We could," said Georgia slowly.

"Who is this from?"

"My aunt."

"Oh, God," said Karen, "you mean she really did **die** and leave you five thousand dollars? That's so weird after you just said that."

"She didn't die."

"She didn't die?"

"No," said Georgia, "She just sent me five thousand dollars and this." Georgia slid another piece of paper across the table, and Karen recognized the familiar shape of Celinda and the ubiquitous caption, "Get with the Program."

"So, are you going to do it?" asked Karen.

"I don't know. It's tempting, isn't it?"

"Yeah."

"What would you do?"

Karen did not have to think long. She imagined giving up her morning ritual in front of the mirror because she already looked like Celinda. "You're going to look great," she said, handing the ad for The Program back to Georgia.

"Yeah," said Georgia, smiling. "I am."

Steve swiveled the tall black leather chair away from the window and tossed the little black book back onto his father's desk. He had tried nearly every number with no luck. Nobody wanted to sign a new advertising contract this close to the end of the year, and besides, his father had taken the unpopular side in a recent divorce case, and most of the names in the book were not currently interested in doing his son any favors. Steve's visions of saving *Ear to the Ground,* and by extension impressing Karen, were fading rapidly.

He swiveled back towards the floor-to-ceiling plate glass window that looked out over Park Avenue. He sat in a three-thousand-dollar chair that rolled across a twenty-five-thousand-dollar oriental rug on which sat a ten-thousand-dollar antique desk, all of which resided in an apartment that must be worth close to six million. Yet he couldn't raise twenty thousand dollars.

If his parents ever gave him any money, he would have given Clifton whatever he needed, become a silent partner. But all Steve's money was tucked away in trust funds of which Mother or Father held the purse strings. And while they were quite liberal about loosening those strings to pay for college or European travel or double-breasted suits from Brooks Brothers, they were rather more tightfisted when it came to things like financing alternative newspapers.

Steve watched the lights of Park Avenue brighten as dusk deepened into evening. In the limousines and town cars below him were hundreds of people for whom twenty thousand dollars was pocket change. The only advantage of being a part of this illusory world of receptions at art museums and black tie dances was the apparent accessibility of money. But now that Steve needed it, he realized even *that* had been an illusion. For all the trappings of wealth that surrounded him, he felt no more able to raise twenty thousand dollars than the man Karen had written about in her last article.

He reached for the paper in his backpack—to reread Karen's article. He loved her prose, always felt like he was in her presence when reading her work. Unfolding the paper, he discovered he had pulled out not *Ear to the Ground*, but the *Wall Street Journal* he had bought earlier in the week. With a sigh, he began to read the domestic business news.

The Program, a privately held weight loss company, has just announced a major expansion—the opening of 250 new outlets nationwide accompanied by projected expenditures in advertising over the next eight months of nearly $1 billion.

A company press release states that over one million women have now participated in The Program, in only sixteen months of the company's existence. Total revenues for the current fiscal year are estimated at nearly $5 billion. The release also states that The Program will double its client fee from $5,000 to $10,000 effective January 1, explaining that 'the $5,000 fee was part of a strategy to introduce our product to the market.'

The company was spun off last August from a privately held media conglomerate, PW Enterprises, the owners of *Perfect Woman* magazine and producers of several feature films.

Shares of Coca-Cola were up sharply, today, on news that...

Wait a minute, thought Steve. One billion dollars in advertising? One *billion* dollars? Certainly they would go for the Superbowl and the Summer Olympics, a building-sized billboard in Times Square, and multi-page color inserts in *Time* and *Newsweek* and *Cosmo* and *Vogue*. But surely there would be a little left to explore new markets. And after all, twenty thousand dollars out of a billion-dollar-budget—why, they would hardly even notice it was gone.

KAREN SLEPT LATE on Sunday morning. Usually Georgia woke her up at nine with a bag of bagels and a stack of newspapers, and the two roommates spent the day critiquing articles and complaining about their jobs. But when Karen awoke at eleven, Georgia wasn't home. So Karen didn't read the *Daily Mail* that day, and didn't see the *Weekend Magazine* cover article about the Peter Paul Rubens retrospective about to open at the Met. Nor did she read, buried among passages about the artist's staunch Catholicism and his diplomatic efforts on behalf of European leaders, the following sentences: "Yet despite his prolific and generally acknowledged brilliant output, some modern critics believe that Rubens glorified a deformed female shape and gave to unhealthy obesity an inappropriate and dangerous sanction. It has even been suggested that his obsession with the overweight female nude bordered on sexual perversion."

Karen also didn't see the full-page advertisement that appeared in the middle of the article's text—a lush and florid Rubens nude with rippling hips and bulging thighs and buttocks. The caption below read, "Don't be Rubenesque. Get With The Program."

When Georgia came home at noon, Karen was eating Georgia's leftover Chinese takeout off of Georgia's plate at Georgia's table and watching the Jets game on Georgia's television. But Karen didn't recognize Georgia herself; she picked up Georgia's phone to dial 9-1-1 when the slim young woman burst through the door. Not until Georgia spoke did Karen realize her mistake.

"What do you think?" said Georgia, twirling in front of the open door. "Sixty pounds lighter in ninety minutes."

Georgia's transformation was amazing. Her bosom had flattened, her cheeks no longer looked like chipmunk pouches, her arms were lithe and delicate, and her legs, protruding from a new black minidress, hardly looked substantial enough to hold her up.

"You did it?" asked Karen.

"Hey, the price is going up in a couple of weeks. I didn't think they'd be open on a Sunday morning, but apparently The Program is available twenty-four/seven."

"Jesus, you look incredible."

"Don't I?" said Georgia. "I'm a new person, I swear to God, an absolutely new person."

"You're not wearing a bra, are you?" asked Karen.

Georgia pressed her slender hands to her chest and laughed. "Baby, I never have to wear a bra again. I'm a free woman. I'm free from my fat, free from my bra, free from this grungy neighborhood, and next week I'm interviewing for a promotion and with this bod, I'll be free of my piece-of-crap job."

"What do you mean, 'free from this neighborhood?'" said Karen.

"Yeah, I kind of met these other two girls at The Program who are looking for someone to share a walk-up on the Upper West Side."

"The Upper West Side?"

"I know, can you believe it? I mean, I knew my body was holding me back, but I had no idea how fast things would change." She took Karen's fleshy hands in hers. "Karen, you have got to get your hands on five thousand dollars."

"But if you move to the Upper West Side, how am I going to pay my rent?"

"We're paid through the end of the month," said Georgia, shrugging. "And the city is crawling with roommates. You'll find somebody. Besides, you'll get some money, you'll get Programmed, and then you can join us uptown. I have to pack."

Georgia threw open the closet and started pulling clothes off hangars. "Most of this is going to the Salvation Army, of course. Unless you want anything."

Karen felt a panic growing in her gut. Find a roommate the week of Christmas? There was no way. Find five thousand dollars to "get with The Program?" Some fantasy. "Listen," said Karen, "can't you just stay until I find another roommate?"

"Say, maybe you can get the money from Steve Collingwood. He's got Park Avenue parents and he's always had a little crush on you."

"He doesn't have a crush on me," said Karen, desperation in her voice.

Georgia shut the suitcase and headed towards the door. "Sure he does. Five grand is nothing on Park Avenue. It's the maid's tip at Christmas. I'll get the rest tomorrow."

Georgia was halfway out the door when Karen grabbed her arm. "Georgia, what's happened to you? How can you abandon me like this? We said we were in this together." Karen made an expansive gesture to indicate that "this" meant not just the apartment, but all they had shared.

"Call me when you get with The Program," said Georgia, pecking

Karen on the cheek. "You're going to look great." Georgia pulled her arm from Karen's grip and closed the door with the corner of her suitcase.

Karen was left in shock. How could this happen? Yes, Georgia looked great, but the ads for The Program said nothing about personality changes. The old Georgia would never have left her like this, no matter how many uptown skinnies invited her to share an apartment. Karen collapsed on the sofa—the sofa that would soon be gone, along with the dishes, most of the rest of the furniture, and possibly the shower curtain.

When the phone rang she did not stir. On Georgia's answering machine she heard Steve's voice.

"Hey, Karen. I guess you're out at dinner or something. Anyway, I just called to bounce an idea off of you, so if you get in before too late, give me a call on my cell, OK? Right, so, talk to you later, I guess."

He did not sound like a man with a crush.

MONDAY THE TWENTY-THIRD dawned gray and dim, with the first heavy snow of the season forecast to begin falling by midday. New York would have a white Christmas, but Karen felt no delight. She was well into her second cup of coffee and still near the top of a pile of editing when Clifton came through the door followed by a burst of cold air and, a few seconds later, by Steve.

"Meeting!" called Clifton, barging into Karen's cubicle and sitting on top of her desk without removing his overcoat.

Even in her gloomy mood, Karen sighed inwardly at his chiseled profile. He had chosen to sit on *her* desk; did that mean something?

The room rattled with the sound of chairs scraping across the floor and then fell silent. In a crude circle sat Karen, Marjorie, Steve, Clifton, and the rest of the staff. With the exception of Clifton, who wore an inscrutable expression, they all had the look of condemned killers about to receive the death sentence. Marjorie drummed her fingers on her thigh; Steve twirled his pencil between two fingers; Karen sat still, her hands resting on the desk in front of her.

"I'm not going to beat around the bush, folks. We're in a bind here. The accountant and the bank both think we should call it quits right now, but I managed to sweet-talk the bankers into giving us another thirty days. But here's what has to happen. First of all, we're skipping this week's issue—that's why I called Friday's a double issue. So I want everybody to stop working on copy and start figuring out how to save money."

He reached into his leather portfolio and pulled out a neatly arranged pile of papers. "These are the figures for the last three months. Now I know you guys are not accountants, but you all oversee different parts of the paper, so it's up to each of you to go over these numbers and find places to save. Steve has volunteered to work full time during his holidays selling advertising, so if you have any leads in that area, contact him. Christmas is day after tomorrow. This office will be closed starting in ten minutes. We'll all meet back here on Friday to see where we are."

Karen stared at the numbers on the page. *Thirty days,* she thought. *A week to find a roommate and thirty days to find a job.* She could hear Steve's watch ticking beside her, ticking away the seconds until she was out on the street, but the numbers in front of her would not coalesce. They only floated, just out of reach, teasing her with their unreality. *And what about Clifton?* she thought. If the paper went under, she'd probably never see him again. He'd never know how she felt.

Somehow the idea of losing Clifton eclipsed any thought she had of unemployment or homelessness. There just had to be a way.

"We can do this, people," said Clifton. "This is just a growing pain. Now go home and have a happy Christmas."

Chairs scraped once again as Clifton bounced from his perch on Karen's desk and bounded out the door before anyone could respond to his speech. With the others watching, Karen was too embarrassed to give chase, to stop him in the street and say "I love you."

"Hell of a time to be looking for a job," mumbled Marjorie, pulling her coat off the hook by the door. "Karen, will you lock up?"

"Yeah," said Karen flatly. "You guys go on." In morose silence the staff shuffled out into the first flakes of snow. Karen piled up her editing and the contents of her "In" box along with the mysterious sheet of numbers and shoved the whole stack into her canvas bag.

She checked the lights in Clifton's office and stood for a moment looking at his meticulously organized desk. Like everything else about him, it was perfect. Slowly she put on her coat, hat, and gloves, turned the thermostat down as far as it would go, flicked off the lights, and pushed her way through the door. As she was locking the bolt, she heard a voice beside her.

"You never returned my message." Steve stood to one side of the door, leaning against the building, a few flakes of snow dusted in his dark hair.

"Sorry about that," said Karen, "I think I must have been asleep when you called."

"You want to get a cup of coffee?"

Karen shoved the keys into her pocket. "I'm afraid I wouldn't be very good company," she said. She began walking and Steve shuffled into step beside her.

"We'll keep it strictly business, I promise. I just wanted to run an idea by you—see if we can't improve these numbers a little bit." He waved the sheaf of papers in his hand.

"Believe me, when it comes to numbers there's no way I could help you."

"Well, maybe I could help you," said Steve, smiling at her as they waited for a light.

Karen thought of her empty apartment and of no Georgia to commiserate with. "OK," she said. "As long as I don't have to be cheerful or anything."

"Be as grumpy as you like," said Steve. "It won't bother me a bit. If you feel like walking, I know a good place about seventy blocks from here."

The snow was beginning to fall more steadily. Karen tilted her head back, gazed straight into the swirling flakes, and felt a crack opening in her depression. The vision of the snow plucked from her melancholy a sense of the miracle of life's simplest delights. *Don't think about thirty days from now,* she told herself, *don't think about unemployment and homelessness; think about walking seventy blocks in the snow with a friend towards a warm cup of coffee.*

She felt the flakes melting on her cheeks and allowed herself the hint of a smile. "What the hell," she said. "It's not like I have anything better to do."

The snow intensified rapidly, and by the time they had walked a few blocks a layer of white covered the sidewalk. When they reached

Washington Square, children had already begun to scoop together snowballs.

At the corner of Broadway and Eleventh Karen felt her foot slip and waited for the inevitable pain and humiliation of landing on the cold sidewalk. But Steve swept his arm around her waist and checked her fall.

"Steady, now," he said. "You'd better hang on to me if you're going to go ice skating." She clasped her gloved hand around his arm, feeling a little awkward clinging to her intern, but glad he was there. She pulled his arm closer and realized he was wearing not his usual puffy green ski jacket but a gentleman's navy blue wool overcoat. Beneath it he wore a dark green V-neck cashmere sweater, a white button-down shirt, and a burgundy striped tie.

"So," she said at the end of the next block as they waited for a light, "why the fancy outfit—you got a date or something?"

"Not exactly," said Steve. "Just taking a friend out for coffee."

"Oh? Who is she?"

"What do you mean?"

"I mean who's the girl you're taking out for—Oh, God, you mean me?" Was it possible? Was Georgia right? Did Steve really have a crush on her? It seemed absurd. "You didn't dress up for me, did you?"

"Well, you always give me such a hard time about the Exeter boy, I thought you might like to see what he looked like."

"But this is not a date, right?"

"This is absolutely not a date. This is a business meeting in which it will benefit me to show you that I'm capable of masquerading as a member of the establishment."

"OK," said Karen. "Because if it were a date, I'd have to let go of your arm and walk home, and I'd probably slip and fall on my ass at least a dozen times." Steve laughed as they plunged across the street into the driving snow.

By the time Steve pushed open the glass door of Nick's Coffee Shop at Fifty-fifth and Ninth, their feet shuffled through snow two inches deep and the drifts at the edges of the streets had obscured the curbs. Karen sat at a Formica-topped table bolted to the floor while Steve ordered coffee and Danishes at the counter.

"I hope this is untrendy enough for you," said Steve, setting the blue

Styrofoam cups on the table and indicating with a nod the general lack of decor. "I discovered this place when I was in junior high. We thought it was so cool to drink coffee, but all the places in my neighborhood sell five-dollar espressos and lattes and close at ten o'clock. Nick will give you an eighty-cent cup of coffee all night long."

Karen took a long drink from her coffee. As she felt the warmth spread through her body she looked at Steve. A few unmelted flakes of snow still adorned his hair and gave him an almost Hollywood handsomeness. Karen could not resist the urge to reach up and brush them away.

"Snow in your hair," she said.

"You too," said Steve, sipping his coffee but not unlocking his eyes from her gaze. "It looks good, I think." They sat that way for a moment, each sipping coffee, looking straight into the other's eyes. Each, Karen supposed, afraid to break off contact.

Finally Karen shivered from the intimacy and ran her hands rapidly through her wet hair. "So," she said, picking up her Danish, "what was it you wanted to talk about?"

"Have you ever heard of something called The Program?"

Karen froze with her pastry halfway to her mouth, then set it back down on the table. "Look, Steve, I know I need to lose weight. I mean, I look at this body in the mirror every morning, for God's sake. Believe me, I know. But first of all I couldn't afford The Program in a million years, and—"

"Hold on, hold on," said Steve. "Who said anything about your losing weight?"

"Well, you said 'The Program.'"

"God, Karen, you don't really think you need to lose weight, do you?"

"Oh, please, Steve," she said, "at least don't make fun of me."

"I'm not making fun of you, I'm serious. I mean, I don't have the pleasure of seeing you naked in my mirror every morning, but I can imagine—I mean, that is, from what I have seen I think you have a very womanly, very voluptuous, very sexy shape."

"Voluptuous?"

"Yes, voluptuous. I don't know if you remember this, or if you're another victim of this mass-induced hypnosis brought on by Hollywood and the fashion magazines, but women are supposed to be curvy. They're supposed to have thighs and hips and—well—breasts."

"God knows," said Karen, hunching over the table, "I've got those."

"Believe me," said Steve, "I'd be the last person on Earth who would want you to get rid of them. I just wanted to know if you were familiar with The Program as a business enterprise."

"You can hardly miss it these days."

"Well, it's going to get even harder to miss." He pulled the *Wall Street Journal* out of his coat pocket and *thwapped* it down on the table. "The Program is getting ready to spend a billion dollars in advertising."

"A billion dollars?"

"That's right. A billion. Do you know how much Clifton told me we need to make our budget balance over the next three months?"

"How much?"

"Twenty thousand. Do you know what percentage of one billion twenty thousand is?"

"No."

"Two one-thousandths of a percent."

"And you think you can convince The Program to spend two one-thousandths of a percent of their advertising budget on *Ear to the Ground*?"

"Well, actually I was going to shoot for a hundred thousand to play it safe." Steve drained his coffee cup and gave Karen a smile like a little boy who has brought his mother breakfast in bed.

"Have you called them?"

"That's where I need your help. I've been on the phone all morning, but as soon as they hear a man's voice they hang up. I even started dialing random extensions, but it's the same thing. The second I get a human being on the phone and they hear my voice, they all say the same thing. 'I'm sorry, sir, The Program is for women only. Thank you for calling.' And the line goes dead."

"And you want me to be your woman?"

"Well," said Steve, grinning, "I'd at least like you to help me out with these phone calls."

"Oh, ha, ha, ha," said Karen. "Have you talked to Clifton about this?"

"I didn't want to say anything yet, in case it turns out to be a dead end."

"And you've got a strategy for how to sell the biggest new advertiser in the world a hundred thousand dollars of space in a neighborhood newspaper that publishes features on homelessness."

"Actually, yes, I do. I even wrote out a sales script. I put it in your box this morning in case you wouldn't have coffee with me. You want another cup?"

"Yes, thanks," said Karen, shaking her head with a smile of resignation. She reached into her bag and pulled out the bundle of mail and editing she had shoved in two hours before. While Steve stood in line for coffee, she absent-mindedly unfastened the clasp of a large manila envelope that she assumed contained his sales pitch. A handwritten letter and two train tickets slid onto the table.

"Dear Ms. Sumner," the letter began.

I have just read your article "David" in *Ear to the Ground*. I can't tell you how pleased I was to finally discover where David has been these last few months. I wrote to him often in prison, and I hope that my letters helped him keep sight of those things most important in life. I did not learn of his release until several weeks after the fact; by then, he was long gone.

While I am glad David's disappearance is no longer a mystery, I am, of course, troubled by his current situation. I doubt David would accept my invitation to live here, but perhaps you and I together can help him find a more stable and safe arrangement.

I do hope you will be careful with him. David is not quite so impervious as he would like us all to believe. He has been through a great deal, things most of us cannot even imagine, and someday he will have to turn and face that darkness. I fear he will not be able to fully rejoin society until he tames his demons.

I should very much like to see David again and speak with him. Since it is not possible for me to leave the parish at Christmastime, I wonder if you and David would be willing to come stay in the rectory for the holiday? I understand, of course, that you probably have family plans, but if you could get away I imagine David would be more likely to come if you came with him. I have enclosed two tickets good on any train coming here from Grand Central Station in hopes that you will be able to accept this invitation. Just call us from the station to let us know which train you will be on, and we'll have someone collect you at this end.

Wishing you Peace and Joy in this season of His birth,
Father Martin Stewart.
P.S. It occurs to me that you may not know my name. I am the
Episcopal priest who appears as a minor character in your lovely
article.

Steve, coffee, and The Program all disappeared from Karen's mind,
which now swirled like the air outside with the two statements that
could not have stood out more boldly from the letter had they been
written in blood. "Someday he will have to turn and face that darkness;
he will not be able to fully rejoin society until he tames his demons."

What darkness? What demons? What critical chapter of his life story
had David left untold? Would he be under the bridge in the park during this snow storm? And would he agree to go with her back to his
hometown? It was far too good a story not to pursue.

"So what did you think?" said Steve, setting another cup of coffee
next to the pile of papers Karen had left on the table.

"Listen, Steve," said Karen, standing up, "I'll help you, I promise I
will, but it turns out I do have something else to do today." She waved
the letter in front of him. "I just got a hot lead and an invitation to
spend Christmas in the country."

Karen pulled on her coat and, without thinking, kissed Steve lightly
on the cheek. "I'll call you on Thursday." In another moment she had
vanished into the snow, leaving Steve holding a cup of coffee and wondering what, exactly, that kiss had meant.

"Jesus!" said Phil Crawford when he saw his wife Louise reclined seductively across the living room couch. "What happened to you? Did you call a doctor? Is it—is it—" Phil searched for a word besides "cancer," but seeing his wife in such an emaciated state erased every other word from his mind. What else could it be?

"Do you love it?" said Louise, bouncing up off the couch and twirling before him in her red dress. "It's the new me, the thin me, the me I always wanted!"

"But—but—" Phil stammered, unable to reconcile the image of his wife's stricken body with her effervescent behavior.

"It's The Program!" she finally cried, wrapping her arms around his neck and kissing him firmly on the mouth. "God, I feel wonderful. Do you know what I did when I got home today? I took off all my clothes and stood in front of the mirror—just stood there and looked at my body. This body that I've hated for so long, that I've tried so hard to avoid even glimpsing. I stared at it for an hour. An hour! It is so perfect. You know that magazine *Perfect Woman*? Well, I am now the perfect woman.

"How do you like that, Phil Crawford," she said, licking her narrow lips lasciviously. "Your wife is a perfect woman." She snaked her tongue into his left ear and whispered, "Want to test drive the new merchandise?"

Phil could not speak. He had left the children at his mother's house, ostensibly because he didn't want them to see the presents before Louise wrapped them, but actually because he and his wife had planned their annual pre-Christmas tryst. He had come home expecting to see his beautifully rounded and amply endowed wife, tired from her day in New York, ready for a soak in the tub and some slow, languid lovemaking. Now he found himself embraced by this shadow of Louise, this wraith lacking all that was most female about his wife—those curves and bulges he had been fantasizing about all day.

"Come on," whispered Louise as she slid a bony hand down to cup his crotch, "let's go to the bedroom."

Phil shed his coat and followed Louise's narrow shape down the back hall. In a daze he removed his clothes and reached to turn off the lamp by the bedside, knowing she preferred to make love in, if not darkness, at least dimness.

"No," said Louise. "Leave it on. I want you to see your perfect wife." She walked over to his side of the bed and stood before him, smiling. "Take a look at this," she said, and unzipped her dress, letting it fall in a puddle of red on the floor. Beneath she wore nothing, and Phil sensed he'd better react enthusiastically to her withered remains, despite his disappointment.

"Wow!" he said, trying to sound eager, "You certainly have changed."

"You bet I have," said Louise, and she slid her insubstantial body across his as she rolled into bed.

Phil felt the awkwardness of his first time with Louise all over again. All the cozy familiarity of his wife's body had disappeared. When he reached for the soft fullness of her breast he found himself grasping at air; when he lowered his hand to stroke her thigh he had to search through several inches of sheet and blanket before he uncovered it.

She moved on top of him, something she had always been hesitant to do. "I feel so exposed up there," she'd say, and he heard behind those words, "I must look so fat." But he loved to see her nakedness above him as he slipped inside her and reached out to grab his favorite part of her, her glorious hips. Whenever he felt close to a climax, he always grabbed for those hips and held on tightly. Now there was no pliant flesh for his hands to dig into. He looked up at the boyish body that rode his own so fiercely, and saw her looking not at him, but at her reflection in the mirror on the bathroom door.

Phil closed his eyes and imagined the sight of her late beautiful breasts bouncing up and down on her chest as she moved, he imagined the gentle ripples in the flesh of her thighs and stomach, he imagined in his hands those fondly remembered hips and, through the power of imagining, he managed to climax. Later, when she nestled in his arms, he turned his face to the wall, so she would not see he was crying.

BY THE TIME Karen reached the park snow had drifted a foot deep in places, and she began to regret not wearing her boots as powder cascaded over her sneaker tops. She pressed on though, her mind racing with questions. Would David tell her about his demons? Would he come with her to visit Father Stewart? Would he be in the park or would the snow have forced him to seek shelter? And what about Gus? Would he have gone with David someplace warm and safe? By the time she reached the bridge, she feared she'd never be able to track down David before Christmas.

The sound of the wind rushing in her ears died away as she crept into the gloom under the bridge. "David," she said timidly. "David, are you there?" Only the echo of her own voice came back to her, and then a scuffling sound from the far side of the bridge. Rats, she thought, with a shiver. But then she heard another noise: a dull thud that repeated several times, each thud followed by a faint wheeze.

Karen walked slowly towards the noise until the figures of three boys emerged from the darkness. Two stood motionless while one kicked at something on the ground. "Excuse me," said Karen, "but have you seen—"

"Shit," said one of the boys as three heads jerked towards Karen.

"Let's get out of here," said the boy who had been kicking. Before she took another step, they had bolted into the snow.

For a moment Karen heard nothing but the sound of her own breath; then a low moan rose from the shadows. Stooping towards the source, she saw David's face as he pulled himself up against the stone wall. Instinctively she stepped back from him.

David was bent slightly forward, and he clutched his side. His left eye and cheek were red and swollen and blood trickled from his hairline down his face and neck. He stared at his shoes as he gasped for breath.

"Oh my God," said Karen, reaching for him. "Are you all right?"

David recoiled and looked up. "What the hell are you doing here?" he said.

"David, you're hurt," she said. "Let me help you."

"I can handle it," said David, spitting blood onto the ground. "I've handled it plenty of times before." He stumbled into the open, scooped up a handful of snow and held it to his eye. He turned to look at her and Karen stepped towards him, but in another second he had disappeared into the falling snow as if he had been an apparition.

Karen was stunned. She had heard of such attacks before—teenage boys who beat up homeless people for sport. But David wasn't a helpless old man. He could defend himself—or at least run. And these had been schoolboys. Were these the demons that Father Stewart had written about?

Karen didn't even realize she was crying until she felt the hot tears on her cold cheeks. She desperately wanted to help David. This had turned into more than a story. But she knew, with his knowledge of the city, if David didn't want to be found, she would never find him.

As a wave of helplessness washed over her, Karen clambered up the embankment and headed across the park. Around her, children laughed as they slid down hills on toboggans. She crested one rise and nearly collided with a couple about her own age, decorating a snowman. *So innocent,* she thought, and in that moment Karen was suddenly struck by the thought that most people *were* innocent; most people went glibly about their lives with no idea of the darkness that dwelt among them. Perhaps even she was an innocent. David was not.

STEVE HAD BEEN leaning over the *Ear to the Ground* budget for an hour, finding a few hundred dollars here, a thousand there, which could, in an emergency, be trimmed away without causing the entire structure to come tumbling down. He looked at the figure he had circled in red ink on his legal pad. $3,287. Not enough. And there was no pretending even that amount wouldn't hurt. There was one item on his list he was especially proud of, though. He thought there might be a way to give Karen credit for the idea—or at least let her be the one to come up with the piece of the plan that would seem most brilliant. But that would have to wait until she had returned from her mysterious trip to "the country."

In a pile on the floor lay a collection of twenty or so major newspapers and magazines, all of which carried at least one full-page advertisement for The Program. Steve had wanted to see if he could detect anything in these publications that might give him a hint about how to talk to a human being at The Program.

Only after another hour did he finally realize what they had in common. Although The Program was probably the fastest growing enterprise in the history of American business, although it had virtually put an end to the dilemma of weight control, although it had just publicly announced it would be doubling its prices and spending $1 billion on advertising, not one of these publications printed a single story about The Program. Why? Was there some tacit, or even not so tacit, understanding that the advertising dollars would flow only if the journalists kept quiet?

Steve picked up the phone and, for the thirtieth time that day, dialed the number for the Manhattan offices of The Program.

"Good afternoon, The Program," said a crisp male voice.

"Hello, my name is Steve Collingwood, and I'm writing a newspaper exposé about The Program. I wonder if I could speak to—"

"Just a moment, Mr. Collingwood," said the voice cheerfully, "I'll connect you."

K aren stood pressed against the door of a packed A-train, rattling home under midtown, more depressed than ever. She had lost the story, lost her roommate, and was well on her way to losing her job and her apartment. Worse, she had lost all sense that she was doing anything real to help anyone. She could not shake the vision of David dissolving into the snow with blood on his face, nor shake the feeling that, for all her efforts, she was still an impotent outsider when it came to problems like his.

Tomorrow was Christmas Eve, and Karen faced a long, lonely holiday in her empty apartment. She closed her eyes and thought of the one thing that could cheer her up—Clifton. She imagined cuddling with him on a couch in front of a Christmas tree while a fire crackled nearby. She had wrapped her arms around him and was just pressing her lips to his when she felt something poking into her ribs.

She opened her eyes and was back on the subway, rolling into Forty-Second Street station. She reached inside her coat pocket and pulled out the culprit that had yanked her from her reverie—the manila envelope from Father Stewart. The doors opened and the crowd shoved her out of the train and onto the platform. Maybe she hadn't lost the story, she thought, staring at the envelope. After all, there was one person who seemed to know all about David's darkness and demons.

As the train pulled away behind her, she looked down the platform at the sign for the Grand Central Station connector. *Why not,* she thought. After all, Christmas with a complete stranger would be better than Christmas alone.

She reached into the envelope and extracted one of the train tickets. "Braintree, New York," she read in the destination box. Would Father Stewart welcome her if she came alone? There was one way to find out.

CLIFTON GARRETT HAD invested nearly everything he had in *Ear to the Ground*, and he had no desire to go crawling home to Pennsylvania and live in his mother's basement. "Marry a rich New York divorcée," his mother had told him on the phone, "then you won't have to worry about money." It sounded like a reasonable plan—but he had no idea how to put it into action. After all, he did not know many rich New York divorcées, and the way things were going he would need to become a kept man in less than a month.

So when Linda Foretti phoned and asked if he would like to see an early movie and maybe have dinner, Clifton eagerly accepted. He had met Linda only once, at a black-tie museum fundraiser he had been invited to because *Ear to the Ground* had run a feature praising the current exhibit. Clifton had met scores of socialites that night, mostly stick-thin women who all looked alike: malnourished. But Linda had made an impression, not only with her robust looks but with her playful smile and what must have been fifty thousand dollars worth of diamonds hanging around her neck. An evening with Linda, he thought, might prove a worthwhile investment.

Linda chose the film, and since the weather had wreaked havoc on the traffic, she suggested they walk from her place on Fifth Avenue to the theatre. When Clifton arrived at her building she was already waiting in the lobby, so completely bundled up he could tell she was female only by the voice that emanated from the pile of wool beside him.

"I used to wear my furs in weather like this, darling," she said, taking Clifton's arm as they picked their way across the tangle of traffic on Fifth Avenue, "but it's positively dangerous to wear them on the street these days."

They walked south along the park in silence, snow blowing at their backs, but Clifton felt comfortable with Linda on his arm. *I could get used to this,* he thought, and he looked at her with a smile, recalling the

CHARLIE LOVETT

shape hidden beneath all that winter garb.

She had been packed into a sheath of shiny silver fabric from ankles to shoulders when he saw her before. The dress hugged every curve, and he had noticed her full and rounded bottom at the bar even before they had been introduced. From the front the view was even more tantalizing as the fabric plunged in a great V to reveal a wide and fleshy expanse of bosom where her diamond necklace dripped towards a deep crevice of cleavage. The memory of her sweeping curves stirred his blood. He slipped an arm around her waist and she leaned into him, but he could not yet detect, underneath her layers of clothing, the shape so keenly etched in his memory.

The film was one of those mid-December releases timed to generate Oscar buzz in New York and Los Angeles before it went nationwide in February. And it had certainly generated buzz. The lines in New York had been blocks long, and only the weather kept the house from being full tonight. The critics were divided between those who saw a tender and honest story of finding one's place in the world and those who saw an homage to the worst in contemporary culture, but everyone agreed that the acting, by two relative unknowns, was superb.

My Sister, Myself is the story of twin sisters born at a Chicago hospital during a blackout. In the seconds before the emergency lights come on, one of the sisters is inadvertently switched for another baby. All this happens before the opening credits. We then follow the mismatched sisters, Mary and Mandy, through their early years, when the family suspects nothing. The first complication comes on their third birthday when we see Mary daintily take a small nibble of birthday cake while Mandy hoovers up three huge slices. Still the parents do not notice.

As the years pass it becomes obvious that Mary is growing into a woman who, like the woman Louise Crawford met on the train, is "thin by the grace of God." Mandy, on the other hand, is the roundest child in the seventh grade. The film dwells at length on the strain the situation puts on Mary and her sense of identity. Mary's first school dance is ruined because her parents make her "look after" Mandy, and no one will talk to the sister of the chubby girl. Mary suffers humiliation when, to help her raise her mediocre grades, her parents force her to submit to tutoring by Mandy. At a particularly painful moment Mary stares sobbing into the mirror and cries, "But I'm not supposed to be the smart one. I'm supposed to be the pretty one. Let me be myself!"

And that cry becomes the movie's catch-phrase—Mary wants nothing more than to be herself, yet she is constantly thwarted by her association with Mandy. After a disastrous high school prom the film moves quickly to Mary's wedding. She has gone to college in California while her sister remained in Chicago, and she has carefully contrived to keep her fiancé from meeting Mandy ("my ugly stepsister," Mary now calls her). Mary is as thin as ever, and has even done some modeling work during her senior year. Mandy, on the other hand, has grown from a chubby teenager into what Clifton would call a voluptuous young woman. Wide hips and full breasts give her the same sort of enticing roundness that Clifton had seen in Linda. Mary, however, complains that the bridesmaid dress she has selected "only looks good on people without flabby arms." In the fitting room, Mary dissolves into tears in the arms of her thin California friends. "Does she have to be a bridesmaid?" she wails. "She's just my ugly stepsister."

At the rehearsal, Mary's fiancé, Thomas, meets the twin sister about whom he has heard almost nothing. He has never been with a woman who wasn't as thin as Mary, and nodding towards Mandy he whispers to his best man, "that might make an interesting change of pace—for my last night, you know."

The groom and the best man contrive to seduce the inexperienced Mandy. The best man invites her to his room and plies her with romance and champagne. When she is naked beneath the covers and waiting for him, the groom takes his place. In the middle of their lovemaking the best man throws on the lights, and all of the groomsmen are treated to the sight of her moving wildly on top of Thomas. She sees the betrayal she has been lured into, and rushes horrified from the room to the hoots and jeers of the groomsmen.

All night Mandy lies awake wondering what to tell Mary. She knows she can't allow her sister to marry an unfaithful man, yet how can she find the courage to confess her own complicity in his disloyalty? Early the next morning she goes to her sister's room and spills out her story, but Mary only laughs. "He already told me," she says. "Thomas and his buddies just thought it would be funny to see the fat chick naked." The wedding goes on, Mandy's quiet tears taken by the assembled friends as a sign of her joy for her sister's happiness.

Two years later, Mary is enjoying a successful modeling career in New York. Her phone rings one morning and a friend tells her that she must go up to a shoot in Central Park and see a new model. When Mary arrives at the shoot the model is surrounded by men arranging her makeup, hair, and dress. They step back and Mary freezes in shock. There, standing before her, is her real twin sister—as thin as she is herself. My sister, myself. The reunion is tearful, the admiration mutual. Mary's identity is at last secure. A month later the sisters send out a joint Christmas card announcing their discovery and their joy.

In the final scene we see Mary's hand writing, "No matter how hard you tried, you could never be my sister, because you never were." The hand turns over the envelope and writes "Mandy," and the camera pulls back to show Mary's real twin leaning over her shoulder, smiling. She hugs her newfound sister from behind as the camera pulls back just far enough to reveal their faces reflected in the mirror where the sisters are gazing.

"Wasn't she wonderful?" said Linda, as the credits rolled over the frozen image of the twins and their reflections. Clifton was about to open his mouth and say that yes, he thought she was wonderful, and brave to take on a role that belittled her body type. He had been planning to say he only wished the movie found her at the end happy to be released from the curse of this self-centered sister and free to determine her own identity. Maybe now, he thought, they could finally give the Academy Award to someone who would actually look sexy in one of those Oscar night dresses.

"And she's so thin," said Linda. "She'll look divine on Oscar night."

Clifton had assumed Linda would sympathize with Mandy, especially since Mandy's maligned but magnificent body matched Linda's so closely, but he knew enough not to argue the point with promise of a pleasant evening ahead. "Yes," he said, as they moved towards the exit, "she will." They were back out in the cold before the credits finished rolling, so Clifton did not see, among the list of producing organizations, the name "PW Enterprises."

Linda kept up a constant chatter about the film as they walked the few short blocks to the restaurant she had chosen. The snow had stopped, and the city glowed with Christmas lights reflected off the blanketing whiteness. "And the way she played her own twin sister at the end, I just thought that was marvelous. Such subtle differences she gave to the two of them. And didn't you love the dress she wore in the last scene?"

Clifton thought of Linda's money and her body and decided that, even with the chatter, he could get used to this. "Loved it," he said.

The maître'd fawned familiarly over Linda. "So nice to see you again, Ms. Foretti—we have your usual table, Ms. Foretti." He emphasized the "Ms." every time. He whisked the coats and scarves and gloves away and Clifton finally got a good look at Linda as he followed her to the table.

After the first shock of seeing the tiny frame before him—the same shock Steve had experienced two nights before—he decided he must have remembered her wrong, must have her confused with someone else. When they sat down he saw her plunging neckline, which revealed the outline of her ribs. And there on her scrawny chest lay the diamonds, just as he remembered them—though now they no longer pointed the way to paradise. All that remained of her once magnificent cleavage was a flat and empty torso. That, thought Clifton, he could never get used to.

"Now, Clifton," she said, either oblivious to his shock or ignoring it, "I wanted to talk to you about a young man who works for you, Steven Collingwood."

"Steve? He doesn't exactly work for me. I mean, he works, but I don't pay him. He's an intern."

"Well, that's awfully good of him. Anyway, Steve and I had a little date on Saturday, and he told me you might like to sell me some advertising." She leaned forward so the candle in the center of the table cast a yellow light on her face. If she still had breasts, she would have been giving Clifton a tantalizing view. "Twenty thousand dollars' worth."

"We certainly are looking for advertisers, yes," said Clifton, trying to remain calm in the face of potentially fabulous news.

"I think you might have to talk to Steve about how to conduct business negotiations, because he acted very strangely the other night. Just when the bargaining was reaching its most—" she trailed a finger up her gaunt neck, "delicate phase, he—well, let's say he pulled out."

"I'm not sure I understand what you mean," said Clifton.

78

"He told me what he wanted, and I told him what I wanted," said Linda, "a reasonable way for negotiations to begin. I provided him with a—shall we say a conducive setting for providing me with what I wanted, and agreed to meet his demands as soon as—well, as soon as my own needs had been taken care of. I think he understood the arrangement. But before he provided the—the services I required, he left the meeting and I haven't heard from him since. I was very—" Linda leaned back out of the candlelight and ran her tongue lightly across the underside of her upper lip. "Very unsatisfied," she said.

Clifton saw everything clearly. Steve had approached Linda soliciting an advertising contract. She had contracted some sort of disease and wanted to go to bed with a strong, handsome young man, so she offered him the contract in exchange for sexual services and Steve had walked out. The whole thing was more sad than sordid—that this woman who so recently had been so attractive should be reduced to paying for sex, and even then, with all her wealth, she couldn't find a lover. He couldn't decide which would be more humiliating for her, to succeed in buying sex or to fail. Steve had made the right choice.

"I think I understand," said Clifton, slowly. "Of course, since Steve doesn't technically work for me, I'm not—not in a position to tell him exactly how he should conduct his negotiations."

"Of course you're not, darling. I'm sure he just had a little anxiety. You know, he's young, and it may have been his first high stakes negotiation. All I'm saying is to talk to the boy. Let him know that the offer is still on the table. I'm sure he could be a very good negotiator," she said, meeting his eyes with her own. "Good for you and for me."

"Well, of course I'll speak with him," said Clifton. That was honest enough. He would thank Steve for not allowing a desperately ill woman to hold *Ear to the Ground* hostage with her demands for sex.

Never during their dinner did Linda mention The Program or intimate that her appearance was not the painful side effect of a ravaging illness but the happy result of a five-thousand-dollar investment. When Clifton left her in the lobby of her building with a peck on the cheek and a reiterated promise to speak with Steve, he assumed within a few weeks she would be dead.

Gareth Lloyd stood under the harsh yellow platform lights of the Braintree railway station. He did not realize it, but he had come to collect a woman he had met before. Karen had been a year ahead of him at Columbia, and had shared the same eight o'clock Art History class the spring of his sophomore year. Most of the class had been spent in the dark looking at slides. But he had not failed to notice the attentive girl on the front row. As spring wore on and the weather warmed, he discovered that she hid a delightful shape under her mound of winter clothes. But it was her face, which he never saw until late in the semester when he mustered the courage to take the seat next to her, that impressed him most. Her eyes followed the professor with an intensity of concentration he rarely saw in a fellow student.

He had vowed to talk to her after class one day—not to ask her out for coffee or anything so bold as that, but merely to say hello, perhaps hold the door open for her. But she had slipped away before he could get out of his seat, and he couldn't bring himself to try again. He never even knew her name. Gareth had the same problem at Columbia that had brought him to Martin. He was incurably shy.

"Not incurably," Martin had told him. "If it was incurable, there would be no point in your coming here."

Gareth had proceeded from Columbia to Union Theological Seminary, blazing a path of academic excellence but making few friends. He wanted more than anything to become a priest, to someday have his own parish. But he knew as well as his teachers did that his personality was incompatible with the priesthood, that he must learn to talk to strangers and speak in front of large groups and provide counsel to those in trouble. At the end of his first year in seminary his advisor offered him a choice—drop out or spend a year with Father Martin. So, Gareth had come to Braintree hoping for a miracle cure, and had been working by Martin's side for six months. By degrees, Martin was having success with Gareth, but the pace of progress had been glacial.

After three months, Martin put Gareth in charge of collecting visitors at the station. "Talk to them," he said. "Introduce yourself. Remember, you're their first experience of our parish, and we want to make a good impression." And so Gareth stood on the platform, as he had a dozen times before, and prayed for the strength to impress this young woman with the friendliness and compassion of the people with whom she sought shelter.

KAREN STEPPED OFF the train clutching her hastily packed overnight bag. In her pocket she had a letter from a complete stranger, an unused train ticket, and six dollars. The cold air cut into her clothes and the high pale moon cast an eerie light on the tracks. She stood shivering on the platform and watched the train pull away into the night. *Now what?* she thought.

"Excuse me, Miss Sumner?"

Karen started to hear a vaguely familiar voice at her side. Even as an undergraduate she had been honing her journalist's skill of observation, and she recognized the timid-sounding young man the moment she turned to face him.

"Art History, eight o'clock, right?" she said, brightening up.

"I beg your pardon?" said the man, sounding confused.

"I never knew your name," she said, "but you sat on the front row near the end of the semester. I think you watched me more than you did the slides."

"Goodness," said Gareth, whose blush was masked by the yellow light. "Of course I remember. I—I should have known your name when Father Martin showed me the article."

"But did you ever know my name at Columbia?"

"No," Gareth admitted. "No, I suppose I didn't. Well, perhaps proper introductions are in order. I'm Gareth Lloyd. I'm assisting Father Martin for a few months." Gareth extended his hand and did what he had never been able to do four years ago—touched the flesh of the strangely beautiful girl in the front row. Karen shook his hand firmly. "Is that all your luggage?" he asked.

"I'm afraid so," said Karen, handing her small bag to Gareth, who led the way to the parish van in the parking lot.

They rode in silence for the first few blocks, Karen remembering the day Gareth had appeared beside her on the front row. It had unnerved her, especially when he stared at her profile for the entire fifty minutes. In all her years in high school, and in her first two years at Columbia, no boy had ever had a crush on Karen. She hadn't recognized the obvious signs. Convinced of her own unattractiveness, she couldn't imagine why this stern young man would stare at her like this. After class she had rushed from the room. Now she felt a pang of guilt. He'd been trying to ask her out and she had run away.

"I remember your beard," she said. Gareth had grown a goatee and mustache as soon as he arrived at Columbia. Later, at seminary, he had let it grow long and bushy all over his face, but Martin had told him he was hiding behind it, so he had shaved it off. "And you always dressed in black. You looked good in black, I think."

"Practicing for the priesthood even then," said Gareth.

"So you're going to be a priest, then?"

"Well, I'm trying," he said, not taking his eyes from the road. "Father Martin is helping me with some—some people issues I have."

"You were awfully shy," she said.

"Yes," said Gareth, "still a problem."

"You were going to ask me out, weren't you?"

Gareth pulled up to a red light and turned to look at Karen. Her profile was as intent and beautiful now as it had been four years ago— her gently rounded chin and robust cheeks offering a soothing contrast to those deep-set and highly focused eyes he only just glimpsed from the side.

"I was going to start by saying 'hello,'" he said, "but you ran off."

"I know," said Karen. "I'm sorry. I didn't know. You had a little crush on me, didn't you?"

"I suppose so," said Gareth quietly.

"I can't imagine why," Karen said, but she enjoyed the first flicker of warmth she had felt in several hours.

Gareth did not have the courage to say to Karen "because you were so beautiful," or "because you were the only person in the class who looked as serious as I felt," or "because I couldn't help myself," so he simply said, "We're almost there. I take it you've never met Father Martin?"

"No," said Karen, "never."

"You'll like him, I think," said Gareth, pulling into the drive. "Everyone does."

The rectory was a sprawling building with a Tudor façade. It had started life as little more than a cottage but had acquired new additions as the needs of the parish grew. One wing was used for receptions, Bible study groups, and vestry meetings, while another contained offices, storage closets, and guestrooms. Gareth parked behind the building and walked Karen through the dimly lit east wing to the back hall of the residence. From a room ahead, they heard voices.

"One of Martin's soirées," said Gareth. "We get together and solve the world's problems." He touched her gently on the arm and guided her into the shadows of an archway that opened into the dining room.

In the candlelight four diners sat around the carcass of a turkey. A burly man in a tan suit spoke. "That's Nick Leonard, our district attorney," said Gareth. "He's the one who prosecuted your friend David. Martin calls him a fascist, but he respects him. Besides, with Nick around, we're guaranteed an opposing viewpoint to everything."

"Couldn't we set up a system where they could work?" said Nick. "I mean, there must be plenty of work the government needs done. You build dormitories for them and provide food, and in return they provide labor. Solve two problems at once."

"Oh, yeah," said a skinny blonde in a voice dripping with sarcasm. "Great idea. Of course, it's been used before by the government of Germany. What were they called again? —Oh yeah, forced labor camps."

"And that's Darcey Thayer," whispered Gareth. "She's an attorney, works at a little firm here in town."

"He is a Nazi, I agree," said a middle-aged woman sporting an impressive pair of diamond earrings, "but Nick is not altogether on the wrong track. There must be a way to provide food and shelter in exchange for work that is a little less—well, a little less reminiscent of Solzhenitsyn."

"Jackie LeBlanc," said Gareth. "She pretends to be a flighty socialite, but she's got a heart of gold and is brilliant to boot. I think if Martin were ten years older he'd be in love with her."

"So that's Martin?" Karen nodded towards a man who sat between the two ladies. He had a thick head of wavy black hair with graying temples and a rugged face that looked like it belonged more to a lumberjack than to a priest. He was clean-shaven, but his jaw line was dark with a heavy growth of whiskers. If it hadn't been for the candlelight sparkling in his deep-set blue eyes and his elfin smile, Karen would have thought he looked like a bear.

"Yes," said Gareth, an edge of awe creeping into his voice, "that's Martin."

"It's a good point that he makes," said Martin. He did not lean forward into the circle of candlelight but sat back in his chair, his chin gripped firmly between his thumb and forefinger. He spoke in a calm tone, in a voice tinged with the lilt of the North Carolina mountains. But Martin immediately drew the focus of the others.

"There is work to be done," he continued, "and there are people without homes who might be glad of an opportunity to do that work. How do we match the one with the other without compromising the principles of our democracy?"

"How about mentoring?" said Karen.

Nick leapt gallantly from his chair while Jackie and Darcey both turned to see the newcomer. Gareth, taken aback for a moment by the boldness of Karen's entry into the conversation, stepped from the shadows to introduce the guest. Only Martin did not move, but his eyes burned brighter as he looked into Karen's, and his smile twitched. In a way subtler and yet more sincere than the fawning that broke out around her, he welcomed her.

Introductions accomplished, Nick pulled up a chair for Karen and Jackie brought a plate of warm food from the kitchen. The table chattered with small talk as Karen ate. Gareth explained that the snow had delayed the train. Jackie wondered how the storm had affected shopping in the City. Nick complimented Karen on her writing. This surprised Karen, knowing that Nick was the man who sent David to prison. She felt that she ought to hate him, but she found him charming and more solicitous of her than anyone else at the table. Only Martin did not speak, but kept his eyes fixed firmly on Karen.

When Karen had finished eating, Martin finally leaned forward into the light. "So, Karen," he said, "tell us what you meant by mentoring." The room fell silent.

"Well," said Karen, "I've been thinking about David. When he ran off today, I started to think about what I could do to help him, if I ever find him again. It would have to be help he would actually accept. I can't do much. I don't have enough money to pay my own rent, much less someone else's. But I could insist that he stay with me. Then he'd at least be able to bathe and shave and he'd have an address to write down on job applications. I could get my friends at work to give him some old clothes. If my paper wasn't about to go under, I might even be able to get him a part-time job until he could find something better. I guess my point is that as one person I can't do much to help out twenty thousand homeless people on the streets of New York. But one person might be able to help one of them."

"And," said Martin, "if everybody helped just one person—"

"The world would be a significantly better place," said Nick. "Even given that a big part of your homeless population has deeper problems like drug addiction and mental illness, I won't argue with your reasoning."

"Fine sentiments for Christmas Eve," said Martin, as the clock on the mantle struck midnight. "But I'm afraid we're asking for guidance from a guest who has had a long, tiring day. Darcey, why don't you take Karen to her room and get her whatever she needs. Sleep as late as you like in the morning, Karen. You want to be well rested before you save the world."

"Well," said Darcey as she led Karen upstairs, "you've certainly impressed Martin."

"I didn't mean to go on so," said Karen. "I honestly don't know where all that came from. It just came spilling out."

"That's what we do here," said Darcey. "We spill things out. And don't think Martin was kidding about saving the world. He doesn't joke about things like that."

THE PROGRAM

Darcey led Karen down a cinderblock hallway past a row of metal doors. "Jackie and I told Martin he needed some guest rooms that didn't look like Sunday School classrooms, so of course he let *us* fix the place up. Not too bad, eh?" She guided Karen through a plain door into a surprisingly cozy bedroom—plush carpet, floral wallpaper, and antique furniture. "Jackie found all the furniture at antique shops in town, and you should have seen the two of us hanging wallpaper—that was a day. Don't you just love this wardrobe? It took six guys to carry it up here, but I think it looks like the gateway to Narnia."

The massive mahogany wardrobe stood against the far wall and reached nearly to the ceiling. Framing the mirror mounted on the door was a series of odd creatures—three-legged fairies, frogs with human faces, centaurs, squirrels with rabbit ears. Karen couldn't help but think they had been carved to make the image in the mirror look normal by comparison. Certainly her own reflection stood up better against these grotesques than it did in her usual comparison with Celinda.

Darcey pulled open the wardrobe door. "And it's filled with my old clothes—they should be a perfect fit on you, if you want to borrow anything."

"You must be kidding," said Karen, who did not know how to react to this comment. Darcey had seemed so kind, how could she make such a snide remark about Karen's weight? It was preposterous to imagine Darcey, who could not be carrying more than a hundred pounds on her five-foot-four-inch frame, owning clothes that would cover Karen's mountainous terrain.

"I'm sorry," said Darcey, seeing the hurt on Karen's face. "I keep forgetting we just met. I went through The Program a few months ago. Believe me, before that we could have passed for twins. Here," she said, pulling a flannel nightgown from the wardrobe. "The bathroom's just through there."

Karen hung her clothes across the shower rod and pulled the nightgown over her head, feeling the soft fabric envelope her. She stood for a moment, her arms wrapped around herself, reveling in the sensation, but when she looked up and caught sight of her wide face in the mirror she couldn't help thinking, *What are you doing here, Karen Sumner? What the hell are you doing here?*

Karen watched as Darcey turned down the bed. She wore a loose flannel shirt and a long denim skirt, but Karen could still tell how thin she was. Her neck was thin and her face and her wrists were thin. Yet she had been shaped like Karen just months ago. Karen suppressed a sudden urge to ask Darcey to undress—just so she could examine the results of The Program in detail. Instead she said, "What's it like?" She nodded at Darcey's body.

"You mean giving in to my temptation?"

"What do you mean by that?"

"Martin says we all suffer temptation. He won't come right out and say that getting a five-thousand-dollar bonus and learning about The Program all in the same day was mine, but I know he thinks so—and that I didn't have the strength to resist."

"I really meant 'what's it like not to be fat anymore?'"

"Not exactly what I thought it would be," said Darcey, sitting on the stool in front of the dressing table. "I guess a part of me wanted to believe it would solve all my problems. You know, people didn't take me seriously because I was fat, guys didn't ask me out because I was fat, I didn't get the good cases at work because I was fat. I had this tendency to blame all my troubles on my shape. And some people do look at me differently now. But it wasn't like I instantly became another person. I still felt like the same shy girl hiding behind her fat—and when I looked in the mirror, she wasn't there. I wouldn't tell Martin this, but it's screwed with my sense of identity. For twenty-five years I've known who I was, even if I didn't like it. I was the fat kid. Now I'm not sure who I am."

"You looked like me before?" asked Karen.

"Pretty much. I was ashamed of my breasts, constantly trying to hide my hips—"

"I know, I know. You look great now."

"Do I? I'm not sure anymore. I used to be so sure I looked bad, and that feeling is gone, but it hasn't been replaced with a feeling of looking good."

"Do you think I look bad?" said Karen.

"No, no—I didn't mean that at all. I mean, honestly—" Darcey stood up to get a better view of Karen sitting on the bed, "I actually think you look very nice—very womanly. You wear it well. I never felt I wore it well. I was always comparing myself to—"

"To Celinda?"

"Yeah, all those super-thin models."

"I do the same thing," said Karen. "It's like there's this Celinda shape inside me waiting to get out if I ever have five thousand dollars."

"I hear they're raising it to ten thousand."

"It might as well be ten million," said Karen.

Darcey took Karen's hands and pulled her up from the bed, surveying her body. "You know," she said, running her hands down Karen's fleshy arms, "in a way I miss this. This is who I was. Martin says I was denying my true self when I signed up for The Program, that I was trying to be someone other than the Darcey God created. Of course Martin doesn't look at me any differently, but then he never sees shapes, only people."

"I guess if everybody were like that—"

"Then I'd still be shaped like you and The Program would be bankrupt."

"I try so hard to see myself as a person and not a shape," said Karen, "but I see myself through the eyes of the people around me. All the condescension from the thin women and the muscular men, how can it not sink in after a while?"

"How does David see you?"

"David?"

"Martin thinks you're in love with him," said Darcey.

"Hardly!" said Karen with a laugh. "I mean, I do think he's become more than just a story to me—a lot of the people I've interviewed have. He's a friend and I'd like to help him. That's part of why I came here."

"And the other part?"

"Some of what Martin wrote, it—well, let's just say it piqued my journalist's curiosity. He said David has demons to face." Karen let her words hang in the air, not sure if she was asking a question or not.

"You need to talk to Martin," said Darcey, clasping Karen's hand. "Get a good night's sleep and then talk to Martin."

The next morning Karen found a note under her door. "Gone to take communion to shut-ins, plan on lunch with me alone, 1:30, my office, Martin."

Phil Crawford loved to wake up and pull his wife into his arms. He considered it the only guaranteed perfect moment of every day— the two of them lying side by side, the soft, comforting width of her rear pressed into his crotch, his right arm slung through the declivity of her waist, his hand gently cupping the pliant flesh of her left breast. He sometimes felt guilty for loving her shape so much and had always told himself he would love Louise no matter how she looked. But he did adore her body, and the fact that it should contain a woman who loved him and who was willing to wake up with his arms wrapped around her bounty each morning never ceased to give him cause for thanks.

Usually he already had a hard-on when he woke up. If not, a moment or two of pressing himself against her would rouse him to attention. Sometimes, if the children were not likely to wake for a few more minutes, she would snake the agile fingers of her right hand around his hardness. On rare occasions she even turned and took him into her mouth. But on most mornings he was content to ease himself into the waking world with a few moments of feeling the throbbing of his penis against her flesh and of teasing her nipple into hardness. Phil thought he could handle anything life threw at him as long as he could have those few perfect moments each day.

On Christmas Eve, Phil awoke and, as always, reached for his wife. His hard-on was ready to nestle against her, and his hand groped for her breast in the place where it had lain waiting for him every morning for nineteen years.

Only as he began to move further into wakefulness did he realize that his hand was grasping at nothing, and that his pelvis was thrust not against the warm softness he expected but against unyielding boniness. Then last night came tumbling back and his erection withered as he tried to find some way of holding this unfamiliar form beside him.

Yes, he thought, he still loved Louise. He would always love his wife. But oh, how he missed that body it had been his pleasure to hold for all these years.

GARETH FOUND THAT from the moment of her speech the night before, Karen had ceased to be a mysterious and unattainable crush. It wasn't that he had fallen out of love with her, rather that he realized he had never been *in* love with her. Without the tension of adoration, he found conversation was not so hard.

"Tell me," said Gareth as Karen ate the eggs and bacon he had cooked her, "how much do you know about Martin?"

"How much do I know? Only what David told me—that Martin was the one person in town who spoke up for him."

"But David didn't tell you anything about Martin personally, about his life?"

"No, should he have?"

"Well," said Gareth, "there's something you probably ought to know."

"What's that?" asked Karen, gripping her coffee mug a little tighter.

"Do you believe in miracles?"

"I don't know. I never gave the matter much thought, to be honest with you. I certainly don't expect them. Put it this way—in the past few days I may have begun the process of losing my home and my job, and I'd been looking forward to a very lonely Christmas. Then last night I met you and Martin and Darcey, I went to sleep in a warm, luxurious bed, and when I woke up you made me breakfast—that's miracle enough for me."

"Maybe that's a miracle, maybe it's just human kindness. Martin is here because of a miracle, though, and when a real one happens it changes you and everyone you come in contact with."

"What was his miracle?"

Gareth took a long pull on his coffee. He hadn't planned on prepping Karen for her meeting with Martin, but it seemed only right to let her know Martin's history. Besides, he was having an extended conversation, speaking in complete sentences, not his usual truncated clauses. Maybe Karen was his miracle.

"Martin was born blind," he said. "His parents spent about five years hauling him around to different clinics, but they got the same answer from everyone—incurable, nothing to be done. So they moved to New York so he could go to this special school.

"One day, Martin's class goes on a field trip to the Cathedral of St. John the Divine to hear the choir. The class is sitting in the pews listening to the choir sing, and Martin's teacher is describing the cathedral to him. Now remember, Martin has never seen anything—he's been blind since birth."

"How old was he?" asked Karen.

"He's ten years old when this happens. The teacher is trying to describe the stained glass in a way that will make sense to a boy who's never seen a color, and suddenly Martin takes over her description. He starts reciting details about the window that not even the teacher can see, and then he starts asking about colors. 'Is that red?' he asks, 'is Jesus's robe red?' And the teacher says, 'Yes, his robe is red.' He goes on through the colors, asking about blue and green and yellow and naming parts of the window that are blue and green and yellow. Well, the teacher is starting to get a little freaked out by now, and she notices this glowing around Martin's eyes. There's a shaft of light coming through one of the stained glass windows and it's falling right on Martin's face."

Karen set her coffee cup down and stared at Gareth, eyes wide with eagerness for the rest of the story. "Could he see?" she whispered.

"No," said Gareth. "A cloud rolled in front of the sun and the light disappeared from his face and the vision ended. But he could remember. All the way back to school he talked to his friends about what red had looked like and how blue had seemed comforting yet cold all at the same time. When he woke up the next morning he could tell light from dark. A week later he could identify the colors of bright lights. Two weeks after that, he asked his mother to take him back to the cathedral so he could thank God for making him see. When they tested his vision a month later, it was twenty-twenty."

Karen exhaled a breath she hadn't realized she had been holding. "And the doctors?" she said.

"The doctors had no explanation. 'It happens sometimes,' they said, 'we don't know why.' But Martin knew why. God cured him."

"Pretty powerful stuff," said Karen.

"Exactly. And it's defined Martin ever since. Martin believes—no, that's not a strong enough word—Martin *knows* you cannot underestimate the power of God. He knows that every day of his life he is a living miracle, a tribute to God's compassion."

"But if God is all that compassionate, why did he make Martin blind in the first place?"

"Well," said Gareth, turning uncomfortably in his chair, "God is not the only force Martin believes in."

STEVE COLLINGWOOD SLIPPED into his parents' living room when their Christmas Eve buffet luncheon was already in full swing. He would have preferred to skip the affair, but he couldn't get to either the kitchen or the front door without passing through the party, and he didn't relish the thought of starving himself to death until the last of the guests had been lured away by the early round of cocktail parties. So, a little after one, he pulled on a pair of charcoal wool slacks and a white button-down with a red-and-green-striped tie and slunk into the living room, hoping to make his way to the buffet table without being noticed by too many people. *I should have worn a tux,* he thought as he saw one of the caterers passing among the crowd with a tray of hors d'oeuvres. *I might have been able to pass for help.*

He was just squeezing past a clutch of women in slinky, sleeveless dresses that proclaimed not only their thinness but also the fact that they had furs in the coat closet and heated limousines waiting around the corner when he backed directly into the last person he wanted to meet.

"Well, really, Steve darling, if I didn't know better I'd say you were throwing yourself into my arms."

"Merry Christmas, Mrs. Foretti," said Steve, leaning on the "Mrs."

She wore a sparkling gold dress that hardly covered more of her than a decent bathing suit would. "Really," she said, putting her hands on

Steve's waist and leaning forward to whisper in his ear just loud enough
to be overheard by the women behind him, "after the other night, I
think it's all right if you call me Linda."

"I beg your pardon," he said. "I was just trying to get to the bar."

"Wonderful," said Linda. "I'm desperate for a refill. You can guide
me through the throng."

Linda linked her arm through his, and he had no choice but to make
his way through the crowd towards the bar. He didn't want a drink, and
he didn't want to talk to Linda, but she clutched his arm tightly and
leaned her head against his shoulder.

"You know," said Linda as he had handed her a fresh Bloody Mary,
"we never did finish discussing that business proposition the other
night. My offer still stands." She stepped in front of him to shield him
from the crowd and quickly cupped her hand against his crotch. "I
hated for you to leave before I had a chance to write you a check." She
leaned into him, ran her nails up the length of his zipper, and whispered, "You scratch my back—or maybe my front—and I'll scratch
yours."

"I appreciate the offer, Mrs. Foretti," he said, pulling away, "I'll be
sure to think about it."

He tried to walk past her, but in a lightning-quick motion her hand
was around his neck and she pulled his head down towards her. "You
do that," she said, planting a wet kiss on his cheek. She turned from
him and started across the room, tossing her head back and laughing
loudly as if he had just whispered some gem of humor to her. "He is
such a doll," she said to no one in particular, and disappeared through
the door.

"I don't really know you, Karen," said Martin, "but I have a strong feeling you're going to do something important."

He and Karen sat in a pair of wing chairs facing the fireplace in his study. Between them, on a small side table, lay an untouched plate of sandwiches. Their faces were illuminated by the flickering fire and a small lamp. Karen almost felt she could sit there forever in the lush luxury of that chair, her feet propped up on a hassock, the comforting smell of a wood fire infusing the air around her. Even the musical sound of Martin's voice—like a cello, she thought, deep and smooth—calmed her. But all this sensory massage could not erase the knowledge that Martin would tell her difficult things in the next hour, that his soothing voice would not impart soothing information.

"Gareth told me about your miracle," Karen said, looking not at Martin but into the flames.

"And did you believe him?"

"I had no reason not to."

"A lot of people are that way about God," said Martin. "They believe because they have no reason not to."

"I used to hate God," said Karen, still not moving her eyes from the fire.

"Me, too," said Martin.

"I was angry that he killed my mother before I could make her proud. All my life I worked to make her proud, and I was so close. She died of

94

cancer five days before I got accepted to college with a full scholarship. She only had to live for five more days and she would have known, but He wouldn't let her. I thought that was pretty unforgivable."

"Like cursing a child with blindness?"

"I suppose so. So you stopped hating God when you got your sight back?"

"I stopped hating God when I decided he wasn't the one who took it away to begin with." Martin's words hung in the air.

Karen remembered Gareth's remark that Martin believed in other powers besides God. She wasn't sure what she believed in. She went to church on Christmas Eve and Easter, but rarely any other time. She liked the music. She knew that belief in God was central to Martin's life, but she also knew he could accept someone like Darcey, who firm-ly believed there was no God. Surely he would understand her own apathy.

"Did God become less real for you when you stopped hating him?" she finally asked.

"At first, yes," said Martin, "but then He healed me. He led me out of darkness into light. I'm one of the lucky ones, Karen. It's easy for me to believe in God after what He did for me. For you, it's not so clear cut."

"Do you think the same force that killed my mother also made you blind?"

"No, Karen," he said. "Cancer killed your mother; a birth defect made me blind."

"Gareth said you believed in a force other than God."

"I believe in many such forces. Nature, man. Nature killed your mother, and nature made me blind."

"But what about—"

"Darker forces?"

"Yes."

"I believe in those, too."

"You mean like the Devil, Satan, the Prince of Darkness."

"That's right."

"I don't know," said Karen, "It all seems a little too balanced to me—God's up in heaven being good, Satan's down in hell being bad. In my experience the world isn't so symmetrical."

"More often he's working here on Earth."

"Who, God?"

"Satan."

"Satan? The Devil is walking around here on Earth doing evil deeds?"

"Tempting."

"He's tempting? He's walking around the streets of New York tempting people?"

"I couldn't say New York for sure, but it's a good guess. There are a lot of souls to be won in a city of eight million people."

"And how do you know, exactly, that Satan is wandering around tempting people?"

"David met him."

"I beg your pardon?"

"Your friend David met him."

"David met Satan? Face to face?"

"Like I said, Karen, I'm the lucky one. I've been touched by God, but I haven't had to face Satan. Not yet, anyway. Let me show you something." Martin reached into his jacket pocket and pulled out a battered but unopened pack of Camel cigarettes. "Do you know what this is?"

"This is just a guess, but is it a pack of cigarettes?"

"This is temptation. For twelve years I was a smoker. When I got my own parish I quit. But I always carry this pack with me. And not a day goes by that I don't want to open it up and have a smoke. But I don't. I resist temptation. It's my own little temptation workout. It may not be much, but I'm hoping that years of resisting the temptation to open this pack of cigarettes will help me prepare for my real temptation, whenever that comes. A lot of people don't even recognize their moment of temptation; they see opportunity and they don't suspect for an instant the true identity of the person offering it to them."

"What about David?"

"He knew. David has a gift—the gift to be able to recognize Satan incarnate. But it's also a curse."

"What was his temptation?"

"You'll have to talk to him about that."

"But he's disappeared."

"He'll be back," said Martin, slipping the pack of cigarettes back into his pocket. "Stay here through the holiday, Karen. Enjoy Christmas with us and you can go back to New York on Thursday. I'm sure things will be a lot clearer by then."

Martin stood and stirred the fire with a poker. He tossed on another log, then walked to the door, pausing just long enough to lay a beefy hand on Karen's shoulder. "Don't think about all this too much," he said. "When the time comes, you'll know what to do."

He left the room and Karen felt suddenly cold, in spite of the fire that leapt anew upon the fresh wood. She wondered if Darcey and Gareth and the others knew that Martin, in addition to being a gentle and compassionate man of God, was also a lunatic.

KAREN SAT IN church that night and heard the familiar story and sang the familiar songs. During the second verse of "O Come, All Ye Faithful," the final hymn, she slipped out the back door to avoid being introduced to strangers. She stepped into a cold, clear night—more stars sparkled overhead than she could ever see through the lights of New York. Under her feet the crust of the snow crunched as she walked the short distance to the rectory.

From Martin's front lawn she could look back at the yellow glow emanating from the church. Voices trickled across the snow, and she could make out the figure of Martin, silhouetted against the light, shaking hands with parishioners, wishing everyone a Merry Christmas.

Enjoy the holiday, she kept telling herself. *It's Christmas—forget about David and Satan and* Ear to the Ground *and Georgia's moving out; forget about your weight and the stupid Program. It's Christmas. Your troubles will still be there Thursday morning. Leave them be for a while.*

And she almost convinced herself. She came close enough that by the time she slid into bed she could think only of David, and she did something she hadn't done since before her mother had died. She clasped her hands together and whispered a prayer—a prayer that wherever he was, David would pass the night in comfort and safety.

LATE ON CHRISTMAS Eve night, a half moon rose over the snow and cast a blue light into Martin's window. He lay awake thinking about Karen. Obviously the girl didn't believe most of what he had to say, but in Martin's experience, unbelief did not always preclude action. Look at Darcey.

Why was it that Darcey's participation in The Program bothered Martin so much? Wasn't weight loss a good thing, a healthy thing? Didn't the women who had been through The Program seem happier with their new shapes? Darcey certainly brimmed with newfound self-confidence—most of the time, anyway. Yet he could not banish the thought that there was something insidious about The Program, and it wasn't just that the women came out too thin or that the entire process was so shrouded in mystery. There was something else, something he couldn't explain but could only sense.

But what to do about Karen? She would go back to the city after Christmas, and he had no doubt she would find David, but what then? Would he tell her? Would she believe him? And if she did, what would she do?

On Christmas morning Karen awoke far from the nearest copy of *Perfect Woman* magazine. She bathed and dressed with only a cursory glance in the mirror to fix her hair, and did not think to compare her body to anyone else's.

She spent the morning helping Darcey and Jackie cook dinner, and when Martin and Gareth returned from the ten o'clock service and the turkey was firmly ensconced in the oven, she sat by the tree in the living room and watched the men open their presents. Nick came for dinner, and a parade of parishioners rang the rectory bell and were ushered in to wish Martin a Merry Christmas and deliver a pie, a frozen casserole, or a necktie. Karen smiled her way through introductions with the visitors. "She's staying with us for Christmas," was all the explanation they seemed to require.

"They all assume since I'm a single man I can't cook," said Martin, laughing.

"Well, they come over here on Christmas and see Darcey and Jackie fixing dinner," said Nick.

"I fix dinner because I want to," said Darcey, "not because Martin can't cook."

"Could you use another necktie?" Martin asked Nick. "They also seem to forget I only ever wear my dog collar when I dress up."

So Christmas Day passed and Karen focused on her new friends and the warm fire. She listened to Martin's mellifluous voice read the Christmas story and stood in the cold yard with Gareth and Darcey gazing up at the stars, trying to imagine what it must have been like to pick out the unusual one and follow it across a desert.

She crept into bed while Martin and Nick still talked by the fire, and slept a sleep of heavenly peace.

THE NEXT MORNING Karen sat at the breakfast table deciphering the train schedule and trying to decide if December 26th constituted "the holiday period." If so, she could take a train at 11:26; if not, 11:47. She hoped Gareth would fix her a plate of eggs before she left.

"Good morning," said Gareth's voice behind her. "Sleep well?"

"I didn't know what sleeping well meant until I came here," said Karen. "Are you cooking breakfast?"

"Sure," he said, but he stood silent and unmoving in the doorway.

"What is it?" asked Karen.

"I thought you ought to see this." He laid a copy of the *Daily Mail* on the table in front of her, opened to the Metro section. At the foot of the front page a small headline read "More Homeless Deaths in City."

The Christmas snowstorm has claimed the lives of at least three homeless men, bringing the number of homeless deaths in the past week to 16.

Two unidentified men were found dead of exposure in Battery Park early Christmas morning. A third man was rushed to St. Luke's Hospital on Tuesday suffering from severe frostbite and advanced heart disease. He died late yesterday afternoon.

The man was identified as "Gus" by another homeless man who had called the ambulance in an attempt to save his friend. Both the deceased and the good Samaritan, who would only identify himself as "David," were recently profiled in articles in an underground tabloid paper.

"David" declined to be interviewed by this newspaper.

Dr. Roy Eastwood, the attending physician, would only remark that journalistic attention, however well-intentioned, had done nothing to save the man's life.

KAREN FELT AS if the breath had been knocked out of her. Even without looking at the byline she could tell Georgia's writing. Georgia, who had been her roommate and her friend and her confidante, and who was now a skinny stranger insulting her in print for all New York to see.

Georgia's betrayal was old news, though; Karen could have let that pass. But Gus was dead. Her first real story, her first friend among the homeless lay in a cold morgue.

"Sorry to be the bearer of bad news," said Gareth.

Karen tried to answer him, but she couldn't make a sound emerge from her constricted throat. She closed her eyes as the tears welled up and tried to picture Gus, smiling in the park, doing Tai Chi with his friends. Already his face was fading from her memory, floating away. She reached out and grabbed Gareth's arm, squeezing harder than she knew she could, and finally the sobs came and she buried her face in his sweater.

She didn't know how long she had been crying when, with a deep breath, she suddenly thought of David. It seemed more important than ever now to find him, but she also saw there might be a way.

She pulled away from Gareth and wiped her eyes dry with her sleeve. "Sorry about your sweater," she said, looking up to see that he was blushing from the intimacy of her embrace.

"It's OK," said Gareth. "I'm—I'm glad to be here for you. I'm sure he was a good man."

"He was," said Karen. "He was a good man. He deserved better from the world than what he got."

"He's in a better place now," said Gareth.

"I want to believe that, I really do," said Karen. She pushed her chair back from the table. "Listen, do you think I could make a phone call to New York?"

STEVE COLLINGWOOD WAS just stepping out of Bloomingdale's, where he had returned four ties for store credit, when his cell phone rang. Karen didn't say where she was or why she couldn't do what she was asking him to do, but it sounded like real investigative journalism. Besides, it was a favor for Karen. He spent much of the next hour on hold wandering the streets of midtown before he finally clicked his cell phone shut and held out his hand in front of an approaching taxi.

MARTIN SAT AT the kitchen table eating a heaping plate of eggs, bacon, and toast. Karen's eggs had gone cold and Gareth offered to make her another plate, but she didn't feel like eating. She had a plan, and what she really wanted to do was get back to the city and get to work.

"He's going to need some clothes," she said to Martin.

"I don't imagine he'd fit mine," Martin said. "He was thin even before he started living on the street. I'm either burly, portly, or rotund, depending on whom you ask. So far no one has called me outright fat. But Gareth is a stick-man, and isn't he about David's height?"

"About that," said Karen. "You got some new clothes for Christmas, didn't you, Gareth?"

Gareth smiled. "You finish cooking the bacon," he said, handing her a fork, "and I'll go see what I can find."

"Train's in forty minutes," she called after him. "Or an hour," she said more quietly.

Fifteen minutes later Gareth appeared with two large gift bags. "I've got three pair of pants and four shirts," he said breathlessly, "and let's see—" He poured the contents of one bag onto the table—a new sweater, several pair of socks and underwear, three T-shirts, and a shoe box tumbled onto the table. "The shoes are brand new, so you should be able to swap them for the right size."

"Gareth, you don't have to do all this," said Karen. "I mean, this is half your Christmas presents."

"You said it yourself, Karen—if each of us would help to save one person—"

"Thank you," she said, taking his arm in her hand and kissing him lightly on the cheek.

"Oh, and Martin helped, too," said Gareth.

"I did?" said Martin.

"Yeah, in the other bag is a packet of razors and some shaving cream, shampoo, a new toothbrush, toothpaste, and some Opium for men. It really doesn't smell that good on Martin."

"I like that stuff," protested Martin.

"Trust me," said Gareth to Karen, "you're doing us all a favor." Karen laughed as Martin rolled his eyes.

"OK, OK," said Martin, "as long as I'm pitching in, let me put one more thing in that bag of yours. He pulled up his sleeve and unbuckled the leather band of an elegant gold watch, which he handed to Karen.

"That's very generous of you, Martin," said Karen, "but I'm not sure he really needs a watch."

"Of course he doesn't need one," said Martin. "And he certainly doesn't need one as nice as this. That's the point. Everyone should have something they don't need, some extravagance to make them feel special."

Karen slipped the watch into her pocket. "Thank you, Martin," she said. "Thank you for everything." She allowed herself to be enveloped in his embrace, and she held as much of his wide back as she could fit her own arms around.

"You take care of yourself, now," Martin said, "and take care of David, too."

"I will."

"Keep in touch. And let us know when you need us."

"I will," said Karen.

"Gareth, you'd better get our friend down to the station," said Martin, breaking off the embrace and giving Karen a final look deep in the eyes. Not once during the trip back to New York did Karen remember she had thought of him as crazy.

The Central Morgue at Bellevue Hospital, with its green linoleum tile and cinderblock walls, did not strike Steve Collingwood as the sort of place likely to lend comfort to those whose loved ones' corpses lay inside. Nor did the brusque attitude of the attending clerk impress him as the sort of sympathetic solicitude due to those whose lives had just been uprooted by death.

After Karen asked him to track down Gus's body and look for clues to David's whereabouts, he had called St. Luke's Hospital. An hour and six conversations later, he learned that Gus had "probably" been sent to the chief medical examiner's office, since his body had not been claimed by any family. Steve had taken a taxi to the office on the corner of Thirtieth and First Avenue and waited another hour to be told that Gus was "probably" at the Central Morgue at Bellevue a block away. When he finally found the right door, he was told that, yes, unclaimed bodies of the homeless and indigent were sent to Bellevue to await interment in the Potter's Field on Hart Island. Now he sat in a plastic chair hoping to enquire after such a body, the body of the homeless man he knew simply as "Gus."

"We got a Gus Doe?" the clerk had shouted into his telephone when Steve had asked about David's friend. "Have to check on that. Take a seat, fill out this form," the man had told him sharply, as if his inquiry had been an affront to the usual routine. Steve filled out the form and had been sitting in this chair ever since, smiling each time the surly clerk walked by. "You're for Gus Doe, right?" he would say, and Steve would say "Yes" as cheerfully as he could, and the clerk would say, "I'll check on that."

He had been waiting an hour when a young woman in scrubs and a lab coat emerged from swinging doors at the end of the hall. She tossed a mane of red hair back from her face and smiled at him, her green eyes magnified by wide ovals of thick glasses. In her left arm she cradled a clipboard.

"Hi, Mr. Collingwood, is it?" she asked, looking down at her clipboard.

"Yes, that's right."

"You're here for Gus."

"For Gus, yes, right."

"And what is your relation to the deceased?"

"Well, I'm not any relation to him," said Steve, standing up so he would feel a little less like he was being quizzed by his third-grade teacher. "As I understand it he has no family, and I represent a concerned group who would like to give him a proper funeral."

"So you do not represent the daughter?"

"I had no idea there was a daughter," said Steve, feeling increasingly awkward.

"According to Mr. James, Gus had a daughter, but he hadn't had any contact with her in several years."

"Mr. James?"

"Yes, a Mr. David James accompanied the body here from the hospital. He says he was a friend of the deceased."

"David said Gus had a daughter?"

"I have to be honest with you Mr. Collingwood. We find in cases like this the family rarely turns up. Still, we're required to hold the body for seventy-two hours."

"So that means—"

"That means you'll have to wait until Monday morning."

"Monday morning."

"Yes, Mr. Collingwood. If you can come back Monday morning, I imagine we will be able to accommodate your wishes."

"Well, then," said Steve, extending his hand, "thank you very much for your help."

She shook his hand firmly. "Thank you, Mr. Collingwood. Most of our homeless cases never do have a proper funeral. It's nice to see someone take an interest for a change."

"You didn't happen to see Mr. James, did you?" asked Steve.

"Actually, I did," said the woman.

"I don't suppose he mentioned where he was going when he left?"

"Well, he asked me how he ought to look for the daughter. I told him he could try searching for a birth certificate through the Vital Records Office, but he doesn't even have a last name—he wouldn't know what he's looking for."

"Yeah," said Steve, "I see what you mean. Well, thanks again."

"You're welcome, Mr. Collingwood." The woman turned and strode briskly back down the hall.

"Excuse me, Miss?" Steve called after her. She stopped and pivoted towards him.

"Yes?"

"I never got your name."

"Sarah," she said. "Sarah Saunders." And she disappeared through the metal doors, leaving them swinging behind her.

LOUISE CRAWFORD STARED at the telephone on the kitchen counter and visualized the pattern of the number she wanted to dial—the toll-free number for The Program.

Phil was back at work. The children had both gone to play at friends' houses. And why wouldn't they? Christmas at the Crawford house had been awkward and silent. Phil had scowled and sulked his way through the day, and Gretchen and Andrew seemed to be equally scared by Mommy's appearance and Daddy's behavior.

Last Christmas she and Phil had snuck off to their bedroom in the afternoon while the children rode new bikes around the neighborhood. He had murmured to her, "You're so beautiful, Louise. I love to feel your breasts, I love to grab your hips," while she giggled to hurry up before the children came back. How sweet he was, she had thought, to lie to her about her body, to pretend that he really did find her plumpness more attractive than the trim models that graced the covers of her fashion magazines. But now she wondered, was it possible he had been telling the truth?

THE PROGRAM

This Christmas Phil had claimed a headache. A headache! Never in nineteen years of marriage had Phil had a headache when she wanted to make love. Then there was the bathroom. He was always sneaking peaks at her while she dressed, or peeping around the shower curtain to see her standing under the spray. But since Monday, if she came into the bathroom, he suddenly found a reason to leave. If she started to undress, he had some pressing need to look in the opposite direction.

The receptionist for The Program had explained their guarantee to her. The Program was guaranteed to make you more attractive to men. Yet the one man Louise wanted to attract was coming down with headaches and going out of his way to avoid glimpsing her naked body, which before he had stalked like a jungle cat. The guarantee had been written on the contract she had signed, but they had insisted on keeping her copy in their files. "It's always available if you need it," the woman had said. Should she call them? Should she ask about the guarantee? Should she admit she had made a mistake—that however thrilled she was with her new body, her husband preferred the old Louise?

She imagined the thin woman who would answer phone. All her life Louise had wanted to be like that woman, to be part of that elite club of those who got the best seats in the restaurant or on the train and who looked down their noses at those sad, chubby ladies standing in the aisle. What would the woman on the phone think if Louise called up and said she didn't want to be in the club anymore? How much more would the perfect women condescend to her if they knew that she had been one of them and had rejected them because one man didn't understand what made women attractive?

As she poured herself a third cup of coffee, Phil called.

"Both the kids are sleeping over tonight," she said in as sultry a voice as she could muster. But Phil sounded cold and distant.

"We've got a lot of—a lot of year-end things that need taking care of here," he said. "I'm going to work late. Don't wait up."

"But Phil—"

"Look, I gotta go, we're really swamped," he said, and the line went dead.

Louise set the phone on its cradle, then picked it back up and dialed The Program.

STEVE WALKED DOWN Twenty-Ninth Street across Park Avenue, still pondering his next move. David was looking for Gus's daughter. Sarah Saunders had said that looking for birth certificates would be no good, so where would he look? Without thinking, he turned north on Fifth Avenue as he tried to imagine how he would find the daughter of a dead man whose last name he didn't know. What did he know about Gus? He tied to remember Karen's article, but most of that had been about Gus's life on the street. The only thing she had mentioned about the rest of his life was that he served in Vietnam.

Service records, thought Steve. If Gus served in Vietnam, the government would have some record of him. But how to find those records? Steve swerved to miss an oncoming pedestrian and found himself almost face to face with one of the great stone lions that flanked the entrance to the Public Library. Of course, he thought. David would be in the library.

In the main reading room, where scores of fingers tapped busily away at computer terminals, Steve perused the library patrons. Several looked as though they could be homeless, but only one of those was young enough to fit the general description Karen had given him.

"Are you David?" asked Steve, pulling up a chair to the computer terminal where the young man sat.

"How did you know?" said the young man, pulling his hands away from the keyboard and jamming his right hand into a pants pocket. "Who are you?"

"Karen Sumner sent me. I thought we might be able to help you find Gus's daughter. I'm Steve. Steve Collingwood. I work with Karen."

David pulled his chair away from the terminal and looked at Steve in confusion. For the first time Steve saw the bruises on his face and a small bandage near his left temple. Karen had described David as bright and full of life, but the man in front of him now looked tired and beaten, not just physically but emotionally.

"How do you know about Gus's daughter?" asked David.

"I've been to the morgue," said Steve. For a moment, the two men said nothing as the muffled sounds of the library continued around them. "Looking for service records?" Steve finally asked, nodding towards the computer screen.

"Yeah, but without a last name, it's pretty hopeless."

After another moment of silence, Steve asked, "How are you doing? I mean, not with the search, but, you know, with—"

David dropped his eyes to the floor. "I knew he was old, and I knew he wasn't well, but it's hard. He was my friend. I don't have a lot of those. And now," he nodded at the computer, "now I can't even do the one thing he ever asked me. It was his last wish, a dying friend's last wish, and there's no way I can find her."

"Listen," said Steve, "Karen knows all about investigative journalism. If anyone can find Gus's daughter, she can."

"I wasn't exactly polite to her the last time she tried to help me."

"You can talk to her about that when you see her," said Steve. "She wants me to make an appointment."

For the first time in their conversation, David smiled. "Well," he said, "my calendar's pretty open."

KAREN PUSHED OPEN the door to her apartment. Her footsteps echoed as she walked in and surveyed the nearly barren surroundings. Her single bed still stood in one corner, and she could glimpse a single towel hanging in the bathroom, but little else betrayed that the apartment was occupied.

All the way back on the train she had felt energized by her plan. She would take her destiny by the horns, she would become a woman of action and she would save David in the process. But the sight of her empty apartment brought reality and depression crashing back. How could she control her own destiny when she didn't own a plate or a fork? How could she save David when she didn't know where he was?

She felt a lump in her throat and tried to concentrate on what Gareth had told her as the train had pulled into Braintree station. "Just do one thing at a time," he said. One thing at a time—and the first thing was to find David.

She picked up the phone and called Steve.

"IF YOU WOULD like to leave a testimonial about The Program, please press one; to have information on The Program forwarded to a friend, press two; for all other inquiries, please press three."

Louise was on her third level of button pressing and still had not come across any options involving complaints or problems. Was she an idiot for complaining? Should she hang up and keep her glorious new body? Wouldn't Phil get used to it?

"Good afternoon, The Program, how may I help you?" An actual human voice. She even *sounded* thin.

"Yes, my name is Louise Crawford—"

"Are you a client?"

"Yes, I went through The Program last—"

"Mrs. Louise Crawford, 117 Bent Tree Road, Braintree, New York?"

"Yes, that's correct."

"You lost fifty-six pounds with The Program, is that correct, Mrs. Crawford?"

"Yes, yes I did, but—"

"And how are you enjoying your new body, Mrs. Crawford?"

"Well, I like it just fine, but—"

"Excellent. If you'll hold one moment, I'll let you record a testimonial for our potential clients."

"No, no," said Louise, raising her voice. "I don't want to leave a testimonial, I want to register a complaint."

"I beg your pardon?"

"A complaint."

"You wish to register a complaint against The Program?" said the woman in a shocked voice. "Why, I'm not sure I've ever heard of such a thing."

"Yes," said Louise shakily, "a complaint. You see, the guarantee for The Program said that men would find me more attractive. That was a guarantee. But my husband doesn't. He finds me less attractive. He doesn't want to sleep with me. He doesn't even want to look at me." Louise's voice rose towards hysteria.

"Mrs. Crawford, please calm yourself. We're here to help."

"Thank you," said Louise, meekly sniffling, "I just want whatever I'm guaranteed if my new body doesn't—doesn't work."

"Of course, Mrs. Crawford, we'd be happy to refund your investment in The Program and return your fifty-six pounds, if there were any violation of the guarantee. But I'm afraid you've misquoted that document slightly. Clause seven of The Program contract guarantees that you will be more sexually attractive to the average male. I'm afraid it's not our responsibility if your husband is—well, not average. Thank you for calling, though, and have a nice day."

XIV

The spots on the Alice in Wonderland statue where the surface had been rubbed shiny by the hands of millions of children sparkled in the midday sun. Karen stood at the top of the steps leading to the statue for a moment before she noticed a pair of adult legs protruding from behind the rabbit's watch.

David's eyes, which had sparkled with excitement the day they had explored the city together, now looked tired and bloodshot. His shoulders slumped and he hung his head. His voice, when it came, was weak and subdued.

"I'm sorry," he said.

"I know," said Karen, reaching her hand out to his shoulder and pulling him towards her. He shuffled into her embrace, his arms hanging loosely at his side.

"You're coming home with me," she said firmly when she finally let her arms drop. There was no fight left in him, she knew.

"Is this because it will make a good story?" asked David.

Karen considered the question carefully. It would make a good story, but now she was too much a part of it to be an unbiased journalist. "No," she answered. "It's because you're a human being and so am I." Martin would like that answer.

"What about Andy and Bob?" he mumbled, "and Sam?"

"You can't help them until you let me help you, David. Now come home." She took his elbow and guided him slowly down the steps.

III

"I couldn't find her," he said when they had passed the boat pond. "Find who?" asked Karen.

"His daughter. I didn't know where to look, I didn't know how to find her. Steve thought you could help."

"Gus had a daughter?" Steve had neglected to tell Karen this piece of news.

"We were in a hallway at the hospital and Gus was on a rolling bed. He said he was glad he got to die inside where it was warm. 'Feel these sheets,' he said to me, 'Ain't they soft.' And he kept saying, 'Feel these sheets.'" David found Karen's hand and gripped it tightly.

"And then just before he died he took my hand and said, 'You find her for me, David. You find my daughter and you tell her I died on soft sheets.'" Karen pulled him to her once again and this time he responded, hugging her hard and crying into her shoulder. "I didn't even know his last name," he said. "I don't know how to find her."

"Don't worry," said Karen, "I'll help you find her. But first I've got a surprise for you."

LOUISE BEGAN TO eat. By the time Phil came home she had consumed a bag of potato chips, almost a half-gallon of Rocky Road ice cream, and eight homemade chocolate chip cookies. She had cooked mashed potatoes and gravy, corn bread, and pot roast for dinner. She'd baked a chocolate pecan pie for dessert.

If The Program wouldn't give her body back, she'd enjoy rebuilding it herself.

WITH DAVID THERE, Karen's apartment didn't seem so barren. When she saw it through his eyes she saw not an empty space but four solid walls protecting them from the cold. She saw not a single thin towel hanging on the rack, but the promise of a long, hot shower. She saw not the threat of her own eviction, but the reality of David's salvation from the streets. And of course, there were the goody bags from Martin and Gareth.

Karen held up Gareth's shirts to David's back to assess the fit, and when David saw the new sweater the seminarian had sent him, his mouth finally curled into a smile. She gave him Martin's razors and an armful of soap and shampoo and sent him into the bathroom. Then she raced out to the Salvation Army thrift store and picked out another towel, a pillow, two blankets, and a set of sheets. When she explained to the cashier she was living in an apartment with no furniture except a single bed, and she needed to make herself a sleeping nest on the floor so the homeless man she had rescued could rest in comfort, the woman smiled and waved her through without asking for payment. "This one's on me, honey," she said. "Lord knows you're doing enough as it is." Around the corner Karen found a store willing to swap Gareth's new shoes for a pair in David's size.

The water was still running when she got home, and she had comfortably ensconced herself in her nest across the room from the bed when David finally emerged from the bathroom through a cloud of steam. His transformation was hardly less dramatic than that of the clients of The Program.

His hair, which had hung almost to his eyes in greasy clumps, was clean and combed straight back, revealing his broad forehead. His face was clean-shaven, and though his cheeks were still sunken, the narrowness of his features in their new context now gave him a quirky sophistication. Karen was surprised to see that he actually looked a little sexy. He wore a blue Oxford cloth shirt, Gareth's new sweater, and a pair of khakis. The clothes hung on him a little loosely, but that would change after a few weeks of eating well. David had not used Martin's cologne, but he smelled clean. Gone was the stale sweat, the urine, the lingering odor of rotting something. David smelled like a man reborn.

But more impressive than his groomed hair and his clean-shaven face, more than the new clothes and the fresh smell, was the way David carried himself. Karen had not realized he was so tall—over six feet—and with his shoulders thrown back and his scrawny chest doing its best to fill Gareth's shirt he no longer looked like the defeated man she had brought home from the park. He looked ready to take on the world.

Her eyes traveled down his right arm to his hand, and she realized it was the first time she had seen him without his glove on. His palm and fingers were nearly purple, and the skin looked gnarled and shiny. *A burn,* she thought. Best not to mention it. He would tell her when he was ready.

"You look great," Karen said.

"Don't sound too surprised," said David, in a voice just short of a laugh. "You can't imagine what it feels like to take a long, hot shower alone when the best you've had in seven months is a quick duck under tepid water at a homeless shelter. And for four years before that it was speed showers in the state prison. I can honestly say that the past hour has been the most pleasurable experience of my short life." He grinned widely and even his pale cheeks seemed to muster a slight glow. "Thank you, Karen. Thank you so much."

"You're welcome," she said. "Now, I thought maybe we could grab a bite to eat and then tuck you into bed. We've got a lot to do tomorrow—find you a job, find Gus's daughter."

"There's one thing I'd like to do first," said David.

"What's that?"

"Do you think we could find a dumpster somewhere?" He pointed to his discarded clothes lying on the bathroom floor.

Karen laughed. "Absolutely!"

THE OFFICES OF *Ear to the Ground* were cold and dark when Karen arrived the next morning. She had crept out of the apartment before seven, leaving David sleeping. She thought she would have at least an hour to work before anyone else showed up, so she started when Clifton came bursting through the door a few minutes later.

"Oh, it's just you," he said. "I saw the light on and thought we might have a burglar. Coffee on yet?" He hung up his coat and started for the coffeemaker without waiting for Karen's reply.

Karen felt the dismissal of the phrase "it's just you" like a knife in the chest. Why did she waste her time loving a man who barely noticed her? But she knew the answer—she couldn't help herself.

"Good morning to you, too, Clifton," she said. "And thank you for asking—as a matter of fact, I had a lovely Christmas."

"Oh, yeah, Christmas. Have a nice Christmas?"

"Stressful," said Karen, "but nice. And enlightening."

"I see, I see," he said. "And Steve, how was his Christmas?"

"How should I know how Steve's Christmas was?"

"Well I just assumed—"

"Assumed what?" said Karen, trying to keep the defensive edge out of her voice.

"Well, I just thought since he finally got up the nerve to ask you out, maybe you saw something of each other over the holiday."

"Ask me out?" *He really does need coffee,* she thought.

"Well, didn't he? I mean he said he was going to—after we closed up the other day. He's been so cute about it, don't you think? A positive puppy dog."

"Clifton, snap into the real world for a moment here. Steve and I had a cup of coffee after work the other day to discuss business. Since then I talked to him twice on the phone—also regarding business—mostly. And what do you mean by puppy dog?" Karen felt her face burning. Maybe Steve did have a little thing for her, but did he have to tell Clifton, of all people?

"My God," said Clifton. "You are so convinced of your own unattractiveness that you can't even conceive of it."

"Conceive of what?" Karen cried, in a voice edged with exasperation.

"Steve has had the most incredible crush on you ever since he started here."

Damn, thought Karen. *Damn, damn, damn.* This was not the direction she wanted a conversation with Clifton to take. "Steve—has a crush on me?" she said, trying to play dumb.

"Oh, come on, Karen, he'd walk through fire if you asked him, and you know it."

"I don't think he's really the man for me," said Karen, hoping Clifton might take the hint.

"There's nothing wrong with it," said Clifton. "Enjoy the attention. Maybe he'll be the one to convince you what a lovely young woman you are."

Lovely woman? Clifton had called her a lovely woman. "I like Steve, I really do," she said, as casually as her fluttering stomach would allow, "but I don't want to hurt him and—"

"There's someone else?"

"Yes," said Karen quietly.

"Well, good for you. Who is he?"

Karen felt the heat rising in her cheeks again. "Nobody you know," she stammered, wondering immediately why she had said something so idiotic.

"Karen," said Clifton, sitting on the edge of her desk. "It's just a crush. If you don't let it go any further it won't, and soon enough he'll have one on somebody else. That's the way crushes work. What you need to do is look in the mirror and say, 'I'm the kind of woman that a handsome and talented young man can have a crush on.' See yourself that way. And then whoever this other man is, well, he'll thank Steve for helping you to see how beautiful and special you are."

Karen was speechless. Clifton thought she was beautiful and special. If she could only find the way to tell him that he was the man who should be thanking Steve. Her brain played out the perfect confession of love, but her mouth couldn't seem to form the words. Before she could make a sound, the door opened and Steve tumbled in followed by Marjorie.

"Get you some coffee?" said Steve, smiling at Karen.

"Um, no—no, I'll get it," she said, and when Steve looked puzzled, she added, "thanks, though."

THE MEETING TO determine whether *Ear to the Ground* could continue operating ground along slowly as Clifton approved one budget cut after another. After an hour, the total on the board was only a little over six thousand dollars, not nearly enough to keep them afloat. Steve had stayed quiet for most of the morning, but he looked relaxed and confident. Karen could tell he had more up his sleeve than their mutual plot to save a thousand dollars a month. At five till ten, he nodded at Karen.

"Why don't you tell Clifton about your delivery scheme?" he said.

"Well, it was really Steve's idea," said Karen, "but I think I can fill in the final piece. We have approximately one thousand subscribers who live in lower Manhattan. We spend about six hundred dollars per issue in mailing costs on them. Now, imagine if we delivered these papers by hand. First of all, we'd have higher visibility if we had a delivery boy in the streets, carrying an *Ear to the Ground* bag, maybe wearing an *Ear to the Ground* hat. It would give us a certain retro charm. Suppose you could find someone with an intimate knowledge of Manhattan, willing to work extremely long hours a day and a half a week? He comes in when the new issue arrives on Thursday night—if he has strong legs and we plan his route out carefully, he can finish up in less than twenty-four hours. We give him $250 a week, hire an assistant to help fold and pack new batches in the bag and so on, that's another hundred. We still come out ahead by $250 a week—that's a thousand dollars a month." Karen took a deep breath and looked at Steve. She hoped she had explained it all right.

"How are we going to find somebody willing to work hours like that?" asked Clifton.

"That's the beauty of it," said Karen. "I know the perfect person for the job. He knows Manhattan like the back of his hand, he's got a strong pair of legs, he doesn't mind working long hours, and his schedule is very—well, flexible. And on top of all that, if we hire him it will be great P.R. for the paper." Karen glanced at her watch—ten seconds till ten.

"OK," said Clifton, "you got my curiosity up. Who's the guy?"

And right on cue David walked through the door. When the hubbub died down, the *oohs* and *ahs* over an actual piece of social improvement walking into the office, all eyes turned to Clifton.

"It's a great idea," he said, "and I have no doubt that David would be just the person to carry it out. The problem is, that still doesn't get us anywhere near the twenty thousand we need to keep this place going. I'd love to hire David. I'd love to hire all of you," he said slowly, perusing their expectant eyes, "but I just don't see how we can do it."

A hollow silence fell over the room. No one wanted to proclaim the time of death for *Ear to the Ground.*

Only Steve still showed a hint of a smile. "I do have one other item for your list," he said.

"Well," said Clifton, "unless it's going to bring in fourteen thousand dollars in cash in the next week—"

"Not exactly fourteen thousand," said Steve, "but I think you'll want to hear me out."

Clifton had clearly admitted defeat, but he shrugged as he slid further into his chair. "Fine," he said, "let's hear it."

"Well, Karen got me started, actually," said Steve. "She told me to work on selling advertising, and I sold a little bit, but I decided we needed a big client, you know—full page ads for six months running, that sort of thing. I tried negotiating a contract with a woman who runs a clothing store, but I couldn't—I couldn't close the deal." No one noticed that Clifton smiled and shook his head.

"But," continued Steve, "a few days later I saw a story in the *Wall Street Journal* that The Program is going to spend a billion dollars in advertising. You know, this weight loss place? A billion dollars." He let the size of the number settle into the minds of his listeners.

"So I call The Program—but guess what? No matter what department I get connected to, as soon as they hear a male voice they hang up. I mean, they're polite about it and everything, but I can't seem to have an actual conversation with anyone. So, I was going to get Karen to call for me, but she suddenly disappears—"

"Yeah, sorry about that," said Karen sheepishly.

"With my voice," continued Steve, "there's no way am I going to fool anyone into thinking I'm a woman, but I get to thinking—none of the publications that have advertising contracts with The Program are running any stories on this amazingly successful business. I mean, they've gone from nothing to being able to spend a billion dollars on advertising in months. How is that not front page news? So I figure I'll call up their press office and tell them I want to do a story. As soon as I say that, I'm mysteriously connected to someone who wants to buy advertising. 'We can't make any comments to the press,' she says, 'but we would consider advertising in your newspaper— under certain circumstances.'"

"What are the circumstances?" asked Clifton, now leaning forward in his chair, the energy back in his voice.

"That's another funny thing," said Steve. "They never exactly said. It was pretty clear that the deal was 'you lay off your story and we'll buy the advertising,' but they never explicitly stated that. And the contract is all pretty normal." Steve grinned as he pulled an envelope from his inside jacket pocket.

"Contract?" said Clifton, barely able to contain himself.

"Yeah," said Steve nonchalantly, "I guess you need to sign this before they can cut the check." He handed the envelope to Clifton, who opened it and began reading.

"Well," said Karen, "will one of you please tell us if it's enough? Are we in business?"

"It's a hundred thousand dollars," said Clifton, dropping the contract in his lap. "A hundred thousand—"

"So we're in business?" asked Marjorie meekly.

"Damn straight," Steve cried. "We are in business!"

JANUARY
XV

David stood in front of the bathroom mirror studying himself. Though he had repeated this morning ritual for three weeks, the man in the glass was still a stranger. He looked more confident than David had yet learned how to feel; his eyes twinkled with an excitement that David could not yet believe was his own; and his clothes were more fashionable than he had any right to expect. Well, perhaps fashionable wasn't the word for this morning. Today was delivery day. He wore blue jeans and a plain white T-shirt, both fresh out of the wash and smelling of fabric softener, along with a white sweatshirt with the *Ear to the Ground* masthead emblazoned on the front and back. His feet nestled snugly in a pair of cross-trainers Clifton had bought him.

Karen still slept in her bed. David had convinced her to take turns sleeping on the floor, though he had had no luck in forcing her to take over sole possession of the bed. She had complained last night that even though it was her turn, he should take the bed since he had to be delivering all day today, but he won the argument by falling asleep on the floor. He stepped out of the bathroom and watched her for a few moments.

She lay on her side with the sheet pulled back from her shoulders and the tops of her breasts spilling out of her red cotton nightshirt. Under the sheet he could detect the sumptuous curve of her left hip.

One foot hung off the edge of the bed, her tiny toes peeking out from under the covers. He could not pick a favorite part of her. The gentle roundness of her shoulders? The soft femininity of her breasts? That tantalizing curve of hip? Those precious toes? And of course there was her face. How he loved to look upon those full cheeks and imagine those slightly parted lips pressed against his own. But since he had moved in, Karen had kept her distance. Considering all she had done for him, he couldn't complain, but how he longed for her.

Karen's great weakness, he had discovered, was chocolate chip cookies. She would talk all day about a new diet she had started, but if she passed a bakery and smelled the wafting aroma of chocolate chip cookies, her resolve melted away. Waking in the room with Karen each morning, he decided, was like waking up next to a freshly baked chocolate chip cookie, still warm from the oven, the chocolate just cool enough to eat, but still runny. But David was forbidden to taste this cookie. He could look at it, inhale its heavenly aroma, but that was all. Some days, when Karen left early, he would masturbate to the mental image of her. But it was like eating stale saltine crackers while imagining that cookie—it would assuage your hunger for a while, but it did nothing to quell a deeper longing.

He leaned over and inhaled the sweet aroma of her hair where it cascaded across her neck, gave her a quick kiss on the shoulder, and was out the door, dizzily climbing down the stairs, before she stirred.

LOUISE CRAWFORD STOOD in front of her bathroom mirror examining her breasts, or what was left of them. How was it that Celinda could look so sexy in the advertisement that lay on the counter before her, yet the image in the mirror was so— so—well, it did not stir the loins of her husband. Louise had spent three weeks gorging herself on every fattening food she could think of, but she still had the same scrawny reflection she had brought home from The Program.

Propped against the mirror was a photograph of her that Phil kept on his bedside table. She wore a black one-piece bathing suit, and she hated the way her thighs and breasts bulged out of either end of it. Or she *had* hated that. Now she wasn't so sure. On the one occasion they had made love since Christmas, Phil locked his eyes not on her trim body, but on this picture of her former fleshy self.

She tried Celinda's pose, clutching not a piece of gauzy fabric but a white bath towel across her breasts and letting it fall over her crotch, leaving the left side of her body bare from shoulder to ankle. A slight improvement, she thought. As she looked at both her own reflection and Celinda's picture with a critical eye, she realized it was not the model's body that was sexy. The flimsiness of the gauze, the relaxed pose in the doorway, the slightly parted lips that begged to be pressed against something (or, she thought with embarrassment, around something)—all this was sexy and suggestive, but the actual body beneath the gauze was not only unsexy, it was unfeminine. Louise had always known she needed to lose weight, especially after Gretchen was born, but did she really want to look like Celinda?

KAREN AWOKE TO a hint of spice hanging in the air. With her eyes still closed, she smiled as she recognized the smell of Clifton's aftershave. His presence seemed to linger about her, almost as if he had been in the bed with her. If only she had ten thousand dollars to purchase the slim and sexy body of Celinda. With a properly seductive body, she thought, she could properly seduce him. And how she would love to be able to give him the gift of the perfect woman. Then he would have to notice her.

Karen inhaled deeply and let the scent of Clifton wash over her. Then, reluctantly, she opened her eyes and faced reality. She was not the perfect woman, just her usual lumpy self. Clifton had not been in her apartment, leaning over her sleeping body to kiss her cheek; he had merely given a bottle of aftershave to David. Life with Clifton was a fantasy, but life with David was reality, and though Karen ached for her boss, she was not unhappy to be sharing her home with a friend.

With their two incomes they had just been able to pay the rent and utilities. Clifton had given David an advance, now that *Ear to the Ground* was solvent, and Karen had bought plates and forks and a twenty-dollar armchair she found at a thrift store. David had become a regular patron of the Public Library, and in the evenings one of them would sit on the bed and one would sit in the armchair and they would read, sometimes sharing choice passages with one another. It seemed strange to share such domestic moments with a man she wasn't interested in romantically, but it was comfortable.

Well, perhaps "comfortable" was not exactly the right word. There had been awkward moments. She had awoken one day last week and seen his erection pushing up the sheet. Her knees had gone weak and she had been horrified to feel herself moistening more quickly than she thought possible. She had reached out her hand to within an inch of his hidden hardness, so close she could feel his heat. If she stared at it closely enough, she could imagine this was Clifton lying aroused before her. When David stirred, she scurried to the bathroom where she drew a warm bath and contented herself with continuing her fantasy. But again, "contented" was not quite right. Though relieved of her immediate ache by her own dexterous fingers, she was far from contented. When she emerged from the bathroom to see David dressed and eating breakfast, she blushed deeply and apologized for taking so long. Yes, Karen was happy to be sharing her life with David, but she was not content.

STEVE COLLINGWOOD, BACK at Columbia after Christmas break, was busy searching for Gus's daughter. He didn't know her name or her age or even what part of the country she lived in. It seemed a hopeless task. But he called Karen almost daily and she had guided him on his search. Even if he came up empty, at least he got to talk to Karen.

He had run classified ads in all the New York papers, and he had written a short article for *Ear to the Ground*, but what if she didn't live in New York or read the classifieds? He and David had interviewed Gus's friends under the bridge in Central Park, but none of them had known Gus had a daughter. Gus had told the doctors and nurses who treated him at the hospital that he had no family, and to David he had muttered only one cryptic sentence.

With a sigh of exasperation he pulled out his phone and dialed the Central Morgue. He had no reason to believe it would lead him anywhere, but Karen told him when you hit a dead end in investigative work, you return to the beginning, and he had learned about Gus's daughter from Sarah Saunders. He hadn't seen her when he returned several days later and made the arrangements for Gus's cremation, but it was her name he repeated when the surly attendant answered, "Morgue, what do you want."

He did not know what he would say to her, so he occupied his mind during the long wait on the line with imagining what lay beneath her white lab coat and pale green scrubs. By the time he heard her cheerful voice on the other end, he had begun to wonder if she might help him forget his unrequited feeling for Karen. When he hung up five minutes later he hadn't even mentioned Gus, but he did have a date.

"SITTING THROUGH OSWALD Petty's latest three-hour film about the politics of Central Africa is like horseback riding with a scorching case of hemorrhoids—one giant pain in the ass."

Karen considered the sentence before her. She had no doubt that Petty's film was a tremendous bore, but she had to decide if *Ear to the Ground* wanted to publish a sentence that was not only disgustingly scatological but also potentially racially inflammatory. At least the grammar was correct.

Karen had come into the office to edit reviews on Saturday morning so David could sleep in peace after a long day of delivering. She liked working alone. She would see all the reviewers at Clifton's Golden Globes party tomorrow night, and she wanted to return their edited copy to them. Dan Weston, who had written the review of Oswald Petty's film, would not be happy, she thought, as she drew a red slash through the entire first sentence.

When the phone rang she almost didn't answer it. The office wasn't supposed to be open on Saturday, so there was nothing wrong with letting the machine get it. But after three rings she decided it might be Clifton.

"Good morning, *Ear to the Ground*."

"Is this the newspaper?" said a sniffling woman's voice.

"It's *a* newspaper," said Karen.

"You publish those articles about homeless people?"

"Yes, that's right," said Karen, wondering if this was someone who had been moved to tears by her articles or someone who was mad at her.

"Then you'll listen to me," the voice said, slightly louder. "I know you will. I've tried all the papers and they won't listen, they won't even think about doing an article. You're different, aren't you?" Karen was tempted to hang up and file this one under "lunatic call," but something about the desperation in the woman's voice told her to stick with it.

She pulled out a blank steno pad and, making her voice as soothing as she could, said, "Yes, ma'am, we are different. Now, what can we do to help you?"

And so Louise Crawford told Karen her story—how she had spent her vacation money on The Program, how her husband was no longer sexually attracted to her, how The Program refused to either refund her money or restore her figure, how she had binged on ice cream and potato chips and fried chicken and hadn't gained an ounce, and finally how she had decided to go to the press.

"I thought," said Louise, sniffing, "I thought that if there were an article in the newspaper then they would have to compensate me or something. You know, like those consumer alerts on television. It's not even the money. It's the principle."

Karen tried to remember if she had heard any other complaints about The Program—from clients, that is. Darcey had felt some loss of identity, but she hadn't been dissatisfied with her body or found it unattractive. Hadn't she said that men started asking her out after she lost the weight? She was tempted to say, "Put your husband on the phone and let me talk some sense to him." But instead she pressed Louise to go on with her story.

"So you started calling newspapers," Karen prompted after a particularly long pause.

"Yes—yes, I started calling newspapers. I started with the *Daily News*—"

And worked your way all the way down to us, thought Karen.

"But they all said the same thing." Again the line went quiet.

"What did they say, Mrs. Crawford?"

"They said, 'It is not our policy to write defamatory articles about a company that provides such a valuable service to so many women in our community.'"

"They all said that?" asked Karen.

"Yes," said Louise. "They all said *exactly* that. After the third time I wrote it down because I couldn't believe they were all using exactly the same words."

"Mrs. Crawford," said Karen, "do you think it might be possible for us to meet? Just to have a chat."

"You mean you're going to do an article?" she said, her sniffling suddenly disappearing.

"I need to talk to my editor," said Karen, "but I'd like to meet you just in case."

"All right," said Louise. "I'm coming into the city on Monday to do some shopping. I hardly have any clothes that fit anymore. Could we meet then?"

"Sure," said Karen. "Where would you like to meet?"

"Well, I thought I'd try this new store, Program Wear. They're supposed to have clothes for—well, you know, for people who've been through— through *it*."

"Been through The Program?"

"Yes, that's right. I have the ad right here. It's on Fifty-Seventh Street."

"Shall I meet you there about noon?" asked Karen. "We could get some lunch together."

"That would be fine," said Louise, "but how will I know you?"

"Believe me, Mrs. Crawford, if we're in a store full of clothing for people who've gone through The Program, you won't have any trouble picking me out."

KAREN HAD JUST finished her editing when the phone rang and the door opened simultaneously. She smiled at David, who strolled through the door looking well-rested and even like he might be putting on a pound or two. At the same time, she picked up the phone. After her conversation with Mrs. Crawford she was not content to let it ring.

"Karen, I'm glad I found you," said Clifton. "Are you busy? I need you to check out a story for me."

Karen swiveled her chair away from David and shuddered slightly at the unexpected sound of Clifton's voice. "I was just finishing up some editing. What can I do for you?"

"This won't take long. I just think we might want to conduct an interview or two." She knew she shouldn't let him push her into working more hours, but this was Clifton.

"Oh, all right," said Karen in a tone of voice that would let Clifton know she was being inconvenienced. She could think of a thousand ways she'd like him to pay her back. "What's the story?"

"Apparently there's a group of people outside the Met protesting the Rubens exhibit."

"Protesting the Rubens exhibit? What in the world for?"

"Look, Karen, just run up and check it out for me, OK? It'll take you an hour at the most. Have a late lunch. Hell, have a hot dog on the steps of the Met."

"All right, all right, I'm going." The line went dead. "I love you, too," she said to the phone, then turned in her chair and realized David was still standing there. "He hung up," she said, blushing. "Say, would you care to join me for an elegant hot dog luncheon?"

"I'd love to," he said.

Steve spent most of the morning buried in the Columbia library studying. By midday he felt he deserved a break and plopped into one of the vinyl armchairs in the periodical room with a stack of back issues of the *Wall Street Journal*. After his success with The Program, he thought he might look for new possible advertisers. He nearly dropped the paper in surprise when he saw Linda Foretti's name staring out at him from one of the briefs:

> New York Woman, a chain of high-end fashion boutiques, has announced a new affiliation with the weight loss centers known as The Program.
> Linda Foretti, owner of New York Woman, announced that the boutiques have changed their names to Program Wear.
> "Program Wear will cater exclusively to clients of The Program," Ms. Foretti said, "providing them the perfect clothes to complement their perfect figures. We are pleased to have reached an arrangement with the management of The Program that is beneficial to both companies."

A match made in heaven, thought Steve. *Or maybe in hell.* He could just imagine Linda with her scrawny body draping Celinda-style mini-dresses onto the scrawny bodies of her Program cohorts. And she'd probably make a fortune doing it.

AT THE FOOT of the wide steps leading up to the main entrance of the

Metropolitan Museum of Art, three dozen women walked in a loosely arranged circle, holding up a variety of signs that, both implicitly and explicitly, objected to the Peter Paul Rubens retrospective exhibit that was drawing large crowds. A television news crew was just packing up their equipment when Karen and David arrived, and she assumed the demonstrators, now guaranteed a spot on the evening news, would soon disperse.

Karen had brought two steno pads and two pens with her, figuring she could get David to help out. As long as he's working for a newspaper, she thought, he might as well start learning the trade. "Here," she said, handing him a pad and a pen, "copy down as many of the signs as you can."

For the next several minutes David sat on the steps and wrote. "Fat is *not* Beautiful," "Thin is In," "Don't Glorify Obesity," "Rubens should Get with The Program," and "Parisian Pervert." "I don't understand that last one," he would say to Karen later. "Rubens was Flemish."

"Was he?" said Karen. "I had no idea."

"*History of Art* in the prison library," said David.

While David transcribed slogans, Karen picked out the woman whose stride was most strident and fell into step next to her. "I wondered if I could talk with you a minute," said Karen. "I'm from the press."

"We had Channel Six here a minute ago," said the woman, as if this proved the importance of her cause.

"Yes, I saw that," said Karen. "Can you tell me why you're marching today?"

"Isn't it obvious?" said the woman. "Have you seen the paintings in that—that evil exhibition?"

"No, I haven't been in yet," said Karen.

"It's an abomination," said the woman. "The absolute glorification of—" she turned and glared at Karen condescendingly, "of fatness. It's not healthy, and it's certainly not beautiful. You talk about voluptuous—'voluptuous' is a word that fat people invented so they wouldn't feel so bad. Let's face it, fat is fat. I know, I've been there, and when you're walking down the street wearing a size twenty-two, nobody whistles and says, 'Wow, you look voluptuous, lady.'"

"You were a size twenty-two?"

"That's right, sweetheart," said the woman, slapping her narrow thigh with the palm of her hand. "And look at me now. Size two, and that's in cheap clothes."

"How did you do it?"

"All I can say is thank God for The Program. You know, if people would spend their money on that instead of buying oversized paintings of florid fatsos, we'd live in a much healthier society."

"So you see excess weight as a health problem."

"Health and aesthetics. No offense, I mean, but wouldn't it be nice to walk down a city street and see nothing but perfect women?"

Karen imagined herself, for a moment, as one of those women—one of a hundred thousand perfect Celinda bodies walking down Fifth Avenue. For the first time she began to wonder if she really wanted that body. There seemed something almost obscene about the notion of every woman having the same body, no matter how "perfect" it was supposed to be.

"Tell me," said Karen, "how was this protest organized? Do you represent some group?"

"We represent the perfect women of the world, sweetheart, and we're inviting everybody to join us. You, too."

"But you're not affiliated with The Program," said Karen, smelling the possibility of a real story.

"Well, we're mostly former clients, if that's what you mean. But they didn't send us out here or anything."

Karen took down the woman's name and then returned to David. After walking next to the size-two women she felt like a lumbering elephant. She could feel a slight jiggle in the flesh around her middle as she bounded up the steps, and she almost thought she could feel the concrete shaking beneath her feet. Thank God Clifton couldn't see her.

"This is all pretty ridiculous," said David. "I hope you're not seriously considering wasting ink on these people."

"That's up to Clifton," said Karen, "but I certainly won't recommend the story. There's not much to it."

"You know, it's funny," said David. "I've been watching people come down the sidewalk. Most of them ignore the marchers, and the ones that stop to watch end up going into the museum. I think they're actually drumming up business."

"I guess protesters will never learn," said Karen. "Controversy sells."

"What do you say we go in and see what all the fuss is about?" said David.

"Have you ever been in here?" asked Karen.

"Oh, sure, I come here all the time. It's free on Tuesdays. But I've never been to any of the special exhibits. You have to pay for those."

"Well, we can't cover the story properly if we don't look at the exhibit," said Karen, smiling. "I'm sure Clifton will reimburse us."

In the first few rooms of the exhibition hung some of Rubens' religious pictures, as well as a number of paintings from his series of the life of Marie de Medici. Though occasional robust female figures graced these canvases, it was the final room, titled on the entry placard 'The Voluptuous Form,' that had so enraged the graduates of The Program on the sidewalk.

On a single long wall hung four paintings, *The Toilet of Venus*, *The Three Graces*, *Rape of the Daughter of Leucippus*, and *The Little Fur*. David sat on a bench facing that wall for thirty minutes drinking in the baroque opulence of those images, the rich colors, the careful composition, and above all the acres of pale, soft, bulging, and glorious female flesh.

Karen wandered the exhibit, copying captions into her steno pad and trying to overhear the comments of viewers. She spotted a perfect-body woman with red hair that hung down her back and asked her what she thought of the exhibit.

"I love it," the woman said. "It's like this wonderfully rich and textured warning sign. It reminds me of everything I used to hate about myself. You see that one over there?" She pointed to *The Toilet of Venus*, where a woman with pale red hair looked into a mirror, her head turned slightly to one side so her face was beautifully reflected; the wide expanse of her back and one thigh and buttock were exposed to the viewer. "I have a copy of that one taped to my bathroom mirror at home. Every morning I look at that picture, and I look at my body in the mirror and I harden my resolve to stay thin. Rubens is a great motivator."

"So did you used to be—heavier?" asked Karen.

"I used to look like her," the woman said. "The day I decided to lose weight was the day I overheard my husband's boss calling me 'Rubenesque.' I think he meant it as a compliment, but I went out and bought a book about Rubens and there I was. He could have used me as the model for this one."

"She has your hair," said Karen.

"Actually, I have *her* hair. It was the only thing I liked about her. So I lost eighty-two pounds and dyed my hair."

"Did you go to The Program?" ventured Karen.

"Lord, no," said the woman. "I lost my weight the old fashioned way. I work out every day and I eat crappy-tasting food. But I'm never going to look like this lady again."

When she had finished talking to the woman Karen settled next to David on the bench. "So what do you think?" she said.

"I think this is what you should be writing about," said David, his eyes riveted to the body of one of the daughters of Leucippus, held in the arms of her rapist. "Don't waste your time on those scrawny spoil-sports outside. This guy understood." He nodded towards the painting. "There is no perfect woman. But there are womanly women. Look at them." He swept his arm to indicate the seven nude figures on the four canvases that hung before them. "I don't know what those—those people we saw outside were, but up there in those paintings—those are women."

"Why don't you write a review of the exhibition?" suggested Karen.

"I couldn't do that," said David, "I don't know anything about art or painting—"

"Oh, come on," she said, suddenly enthused by the idea. "You read the *History of Art* in the prison library. That makes you better qualified than a lot of our reviewers. Just write a reaction to what you see. An average American male responds to the Rubens form. You can contrast them with the ladies in the street if you like."

David sat quietly for a long minute, staring at the paintings. Karen felt an unexpected longing building up inside her—a longing for David to write a defense of Rubenesque women that Clifton would read. Maybe then he'd give her a second glance.

"OK," David said at last, "I'll do it. But can we stop by the shop on the way out and get some postcards?"

"I DON'T GET it," said Steve as he and Sarah Saunders walked down Sixty-Ninth Street, their shoulders hunched into a cold wind. "Are we supposed to be satisfied by that ending?"

Steve had suggested they go to see *My Sister, Myself* because everyone seemed to be talking about the film, though no one would give away the ending. Now he was hoping she wouldn't misinterpret his choice. "I mean, either it was a shallow and moronic ending that's supposed to make us think it's OK to be cruel to people because of their body type, or it was an incredibly subtle demonstration that the bigger sister, Mandy, is morally superior."

"Hollywood doesn't really go in for subtle," said Sarah.

"Yeah, that's what I was afraid of," said Steve. "Ah, here it is." He steered them into the narrow door of a German restaurant he had been wanting to try.

Their conversation had been brief so far, standing in line at the movie theatre and walking to the restaurant, but Steve felt comfortable with Sarah. He took her overcoat and hung it by the door. She wore a black skirt that hugged her hips and a tight fitting red sweater that presented her substantial bosom in all its glory. The top three buttons were undone, revealing a wedge of cleavage that Steve did his best not to stare at. Not only was Sarah Saunders a substantial woman—her curves manifested themselves from shoulder to ankle—but she seemed proud of her substance. *Here,* thought Steve, *is a woman who would never be taken in by The Program.*

"I'm still trying to find Gus's daughter," he said after they had ordered their drinks. "I'm afraid it's like looking for a needle in a haystack when you don't know what a needle looks like or where the haystack is."

"He didn't have any pictures or anything?" asked Sarah.

"Nothing. No pictures, no name. I don't even know Gus's last name."

"Did you try fingerprints?" she asked.

"Fingerprints?"

"Yeah, whenever we get a John Doe in the morgue we take his fingerprints. They go on a sheet that describes the body—unusual features, scars, that sort of thing."

"The guy at the front window never told me that."

"The guy at the front window wouldn't tell you if the building was on fire," said Sarah, laughing. And in that moment, as she tossed back her hair and laughed with a pure musical tone, a laugh that expressed complete sympathy with his plight and complete ease in his presence, Steve felt something soften within him.

He did not want to stop helping Karen; he did not want to end his crush on her; but looking at Sarah sitting before him, looking at her eyes, not her breasts, and hearing her lovely laugh, Steve could sense the possibility of falling in love with her. He watched her for a long moment, even after she had stopped laughing and returned his gaze, even after she blushed and looked relieved that the waitress had arrived with their wine.

"Well," said Sarah, holding her glass up, "here's to a lovely evening."

"Yes," Steve said, tapping her glass with his own. "So," he said when they had drunk, "is there any way you could get me a copy of that bodily description?"

"You could come by Monday and have lunch with me," she said, smiling, "I could get it for you then."

"I don't suppose you'd like to come to a little party for the newspaper tomorrow night," said Steve, hoping he was not pushing her too hard too soon. "Apparently they get together every year for the Golden Globes—it's an alternative paper, so it would be too mainstream to get together for the Oscars."

"Are you trying to get that report more quickly," said Sarah, "or do you really want to see me?"

"I promise I'll still take you to lunch on Monday," he said.

"Well, then," said Sarah, "Sunday sounds fun, then." She took another sip of wine, and Steve felt her stockinged foot running up the inside of his calf.

THE STREETLIGHTS HAD taken over where daylight had left off by the time David emerged from the Public Library and headed home, a steno pad full of notes shoved deep into his coat pocket. He had spent several hours in the main reading room, learning first about Rubens, and then Titian, and then flitting from artist to artist, finding that each question led to at least two others. By the time he was shooed out by librarians eager to get home on a Saturday night his head was a swirl of information, but what he wanted to write about the exhibit at the Met had started to gel.

After he and Karen shared a dinner of instant macaroni and cheese and Spam ("Not bad for a buck and a quarter apiece," Karen said), he began to write. He sat in the armchair by the window, and when Karen fell asleep he turned out the overhead light and worked in the soft glow of the streetlight. He wrote, and revised, and discarded, and started over. He had never written anything more challenging than a five-paragraph theme for high school English class. Now he saw the stern faces of people who might, if Clifton agreed to publish it, read his article. He felt a powerful compulsion to explain himself to those faces, to get each word just right.

He wrote into the night, and when Karen awoke the next morning, she found him asleep in the chair, with a pencil in one hand and a sheaf of pages in his lap. Careful not to disturb his sleep, she lifted the pages and began to read.

For several millennia the ideal of feminine beauty has been based on a single biological urge: the need to propagate the species. As men we are programmed to be attracted to women with wide hips and large breasts, features either necessary for or symbolic of the bearing and nurturing of children. Since the development of art, this idealized form has attracted the attention of (mostly male) artists, from primitive fertility sculptors to Renaissance painters and beyond.

The female nude occupies a unique place in the world of art— the ultimate example of the beauty of God's creation—and while artists have expressed variations in the feminine ideal that naturally come with the passing of time, the underlying truth has always been with us: that what we find most beautiful in the female form is that which differentiates it from the male; not just curvaceous hips and breasts, but also a softness in the flesh which has always comforted and aroused the harder, more sinewy male.

To enter the Metropolitan Museum of Art this past Saturday afternoon I had to pass through a picket line of women who disapproved of some of the art within, not because it objectified the female form or because it might arouse the male sexual urge, but because they felt the ideals of femininity expressed by a thousand generations of mankind were wrong. Many of these women, one of whom called the current exhibit of works by the Flemish master Peter Paul Rubens a "glorification of fatness," are graduates of an extreme weight loss plan called The Program, and they would look as much at home in Rubens' glorious canvases as his voluptuous models would look on today's high fashion runways.

How is it that, sometime in the twentieth century, a quiet revo-

136

lution took place? How is it that thousands of years of wisdom and artistic endeavor, inspired by our most primitive biological instincts, were cast aside almost overnight, and a new ideal of the female form emerged? For the women who protested my entrance into those centuries of artistic history were the antithesis of the time-honored ideal—narrow hips, flat chests, legs and arms as skinny as a prepubescent boy's. There was nothing soft or feminine about these women. Yet, as the artists of this new century tell us—the fashion designers, the moviemakers, the magazine photographers—this is our new ideal of the feminine form. These are the perfect women. Or are they?

Who am I to judge the feminine ideal? Biologically speaking, I am the person for whom it was designed. I am an average male of the species, of an age to reproduce. Having had my fill of one extreme version of womanhood parading in front of the Met, I made my way through the fracas and into the quieter confines of the museum to see what history had to offer.

Though I could have found well-rounded female forms in many galleries in the museum, I followed the signs to the Rubens retrospective and the paintings that sparked the protest outside. In a single gallery hangs an astonishing series of canvases depicting women of such delightful fleshiness I felt almost as if I could reach out and sink my fingers into the broad hips of Venus in *The Toilet of Venus* or into the tightly curved buttocks of the central of *The Three Graces*, or into the small and gently rounded breast of Castor's victim in *The Rape of the Daughter of Leucippus*. These pictures, executed between 1612 and 1639, leave no doubt about Rubens's own ideal of feminine beauty. Painted with caressing strokes, women who, in our society, would spend their lives feeling inferior because of a "weight problem," here appear erotic and alluring.

I was enchanted, entranced, and, I'm not ashamed to admit, even a little aroused by these stunning canvases. I cannot recommend strongly enough that you go to this exhibit and experience true female forms truly painted. I feel I must pick one on which to focus, one masterful image I can somehow use to demonstrate to the women marching in front of the museum, and to so many others who share their unhappiness, that the traditional ideal of female beauty still has relevance.

Despite what I see as lustfulness in her rolled-back eyes, I reject the daughter of Leucippus. Who would listen to my arguments based on a victim of male sexual violence? Venus at her toilet, her eyes staring out at me from the mirror in which she examines her rounded and astounding face, seduces me more each time I turn towards her. But of her body I can see only the generous backside, each hollow delicately painted, each bulge awaiting my touch. Her breasts, her stomach, the fronts of her thighs, are all left to my active imagination. But in *The Three Graces* we have a classical subject that allows Rubens the opportunity to show us his ideal woman from a variety of angles. From their delicate toes treading on the grass of a forest clearing to their flushed and fabulous faces, these handmaidens seem both ripe and right for my exploration of feminine beauty.

My first impression of these women is that for all their erotic appeal, there is nothing idealized about them—they are real women, and that is why they are so attractive. I am a real man; my ideal woman is a real woman. The faces of the two women on the right are even rather plain; the grace on the left has a face of stunning, realistic beauty. Her face is proof that beauty lies not in perfection, but in perfect imperfections. I am helped to this insight by the fact that she bears no small resemblance to a woman I know and love, but any observer would agree (as I heard many museum-goers say) that her beauty is astonishing.

AND HERE KAREN let her eye move from the text to where David sat sleeping in the chair. On the floor next to him lay the pile of postcards they had bought at the Met. She stooped to pick up the card of *The Three Graces*, curious to study the face that David loved. Was it his mother, perhaps, or a long ago girlfriend?

There was nothing so very remarkable about the face, she thought, and she was just about to put the card on the counter and keep reading when something about the slope of the nose caught her attention. She tiptoed into the bathroom, pulled her hair back with one hand and held the postcard with the other. Turning sideways, she compared the profile in the mirror with the face on the card. She dropped her chin slightly, flashed a smile, and nearly fell against the wall in shock. The face on the left-hand Grace was hers.

This couldn't be right. David was a friend, not a lover. He had never even tried to kiss her in the weeks they had lived together. Besides, she was Clifton's.

But she wasn't Clifton's. That had never been anything more than fantasy. This was real. A real living, breathing man who was sleeping in her apartment loved her.

But of course he loved her. She had rescued him from the streets. It was only natural that he should develop feelings of affection. That's all it was, surely.

Even so, she felt herself blushing when she stepped back into the room and saw him. Quietly she slipped back into the bathroom, pulled the door shut, sat on the edge of the tub, and kept reading.

FOR ALL THE loveliness of this face, for all the delightful playfulness in her eyes, this painting is clearly about the whole female form. Rubens has even lifted the heel of the central figure to give us a glimpse of the bottom of her foot; and, let's face it, today we're more likely to see a woman's breasts, in a movie or magazine, than the bottom of her feet. How can you not want to slip your own toes under her heel and feel the coarseness of that hidden skin? How can a man see the ample buttocks of this central Grace and not want to dig his hands into that flesh, or slide them up that S-curve that defines the left side of her body from her knee to her armpit? How can any heterosexual male see those shoulders and not want to knead them with a firm and masculine grip, and then slide one hand below her right arm and cup that healthy breast of which we see only a tantalizing glimpse? Do we really prefer the emaciated forms of hipless, breastless, bulgeless supermodels to the luscious forms Rubens so lovingly depicted?

I tried a little experiment in the main reading room of the New York Public Library after my encounter with Rubens and his detractors. I took a postcard of *The Three Graces* and an advertisement for The Program featuring the super-slim Celinda and presented them to a dozen male library patrons. "Which one," I asked, "would you want to have sex with?"

Their initial reactions were nearly identical—"Celinda is hot," "Who would turn down a chance to sleep with Celinda," "Celinda is my dream woman," and so on. But then I asked them to take a closer look.

"Imagine," I told them, "the feel of each woman's body in your hands." And they examined, with a lover's eye this time, the generous flesh of the Graces and the paucity of Celinda. "Imagine," I said, "how it would feel to be enveloped in each woman's arms." And I could see their eyes straying away from Celinda, as they felt the sharpness of her elbows and the hardness of her chest, and towards the picture of the Graces, whose soft flesh could enclose a lover in so many comfortable ways. "Imagine," I asked, "not just the act of intercourse, but the myriad variety of touches you might share with a lover."

Twelve men I asked. Not scientifically chosen, I grant you, but twelve red-blooded American men who clearly enjoyed imagining sexual encounters. Not one chose Celinda.

One of the men responded to my initial inquiry by remarking that Celinda had rock-hard abs.

"What exactly is the advantage of that?" I asked.

"Well," he responded, "aren't women supposed to have rock-hard abs?"

Before I could answer him he saw the foolishness of his response, saw that he, too, had been programmed to find certain things desirable, even if he knew he would rather lay his head on softness than on something rock-hard.

Who can we blame for the degradation of the feminine ideal? As tempting as it may be to place responsibility on the narrow shoulders of those women who marched in opposition to the Rubenesque form, they are victims, not instigators. Just as we can credit artists such as Rubens for presenting the realistic female form in a way that shows all its beauty and eroticism, we can blame the popular artistic leaders of our society, those who control motion pictures, television, the fashion industry, and the print media, for creating and then promoting an unrealistic ideal against which contemporary women cannot help but judge themselves. They do it to sell clothes and make-up, to sell movies and magazines, to sell diet drinks and weight-loss cream and cookbooks and aerobics videos and exercise equipment. They do it, most recently, to sell, at $10,000 per customer, the mysteries of The Program. In short, they denigrate the self-esteem of every normal woman in society to make money.

There doesn't seem to be much I can do about it. Except to say shame on them—and to tell you to go to the Met and see Rubens. It may be the sexiest show in town.

KAREN'S HANDS TREMBLED as she set the pages down on the sink. On the floor lay the postcard of *The Three Graces*. She remembered her initial reaction to the painting—*please tell me I don't look like that*, she had thought. She had examined the Graces closely for any resemblance to her own figure, and had been disturbed to find certain similarities. To be sure, she did not have quite their texture of cellulite, but in the way their thighs spread from knee to hip, the way the central figure had a droop in her right buttock, the way the stomachs bulged out from the pubis and a moderate roll of fat traversed the central back—in all these details Karen had seen frightening echoes of herself.

She had been ashamed to see herself in a Rubens painting. But David clearly would have her proud. And not just David, but twelve men at the New York Public Library. The thought that thirteen men actually preferred a figure like Karen's to one like Celinda's—even if they were the only thirteen men in the world who felt that way—turned her whole notion of herself upside down.

She picked up the postcard of the Graces and looked at them again. Some of their features were not so bad, and Karen shared some of those, too. Like the slim calves, with just enough flesh on them to create a smooth, feminine curve. And the flushed, round cheeks. Karen had thought of her own cheeks as plump, but they, more than anything, created her resemblance to the left-hand Grace. And their breasts—well, honestly, Karen's were better; bigger, at least, with more pronounced aureoles, and probably softer. *If those thirteen men liked the Graces, they would love me,* she thought, warmth spreading not just to her face, but also between her legs. And one of those men was sleeping right here in her apartment on a Sunday morning with no place to be until tonight. And apparently he loved her.

Karen crept out of the bathroom. The clock on the stove read quarter past ten, but the pile of papers next to David's feet, the experiments and false starts and corrections and rewrites that had lead to his revolutionary article, indicated he had been up most of the night. She should let him sleep. She took the phone, with its twenty-foot cord, into the bathroom, quietly shut the door, and called Clifton.

"I've got your story," she said when he sleepily answered the phone.

"What story?" he asked.

"The story from the Met. You know—Rubens, the demonstrators?"

"Was there anything to it?"

"Well, I didn't think so," said Karen. "They seemed to me like a bunch of self-centered grouches who didn't deserve to have ink wasted on their stupidity."

"So what's the story?"

"I'm getting to that. Since we were at the Met already, we decided to go in and see this exhibit."

"We?"

"David was with me."

"So."

"You're going to be glad he was, believe me. David loved the exhibit, so I told him to write a review of it. I figured if it wasn't too bad we could use a paragraph or two in the arts section—you know, Rubens as seen by an average guy."

"That's why you're calling me at this hour on a Sunday morning? To tell me we have two paragraphs on Rubens written by a homeless guy and they're not too bad?"

"It's almost ten thirty, Clifton, and David is not homeless."

"OK, OK," said Clifton in an impatient voice.

"I just called to tell you that you have a new writer on your staff, that he's brilliant, that he's written the lead article for this week's paper, and that it's going to be the hottest, most controversial thing we've ever published."

Clifton gave a low whistle. "The guy's good, huh?"

"Believe me, you're going to love this. We're going to need permission to run a picture of a Rubens painting called *The Three Graces.*"

"'Three Graces'—right. So when can I see this groundbreaking piece of journalism?"

"You'll have to wait until the party tonight."

"This is seriously hot?" he asked.

"Clifton," said Karen, "this is hotter than Celinda." And with that cryptic comment, she hung up. She was amazed to realize that not once during their conversation had she thought of Clifton as anything other than her boss.

She replaced the phone, crawled into bed with David's article, and began to reread it. Her editorial red pen, which rarely rested when she was preparing copy, now, for the most part, stayed nestled behind her ear. When she had finished her second reading she closed her eyes and imagined the two of them lying on this narrow bed enfolded in each other's arms. When he lay satisfied beside her, breathing deeply and letting the air cool his skin, she would have to ask him how he had learned to write.

XVIII

In front of a full-length mirror in a suite at the Beverly Hills Hilton stood Anna Camello, the unknown actress who had landed the role of Mandy, the larger sister in the film *My Sister, Myself.* A dresser from the studio was putting the finishing touches on the outfit she would wear to the Golden Globe Awards. Anna was about the only person involved with the film who had not been nominated. There had been some small murmurings in the press about this slight, and some of the entertainment papers had suggested that, now that Anna had shown her talent, she might consider going through The Program so she could play leading roles.

But Anna had ignored the press. It had been her childhood dream to make movies, and while she was happy to watch her friends from *My Sister* collect trophies, her own thrill had come when she stepped in front of a camera her first day on the set. She had already signed a contract for her next film. So what if she wasn't making millions of dollars. So what if she was once again playing the unfortunate fat sister. She didn't mind being typecast, she didn't mind playing supporting roles, and she didn't mind earning comparatively low salaries. She was acting in movies, and that was all that mattered.

In the mirror she saw herself packed into a dress she never would have chosen. A high-necked, tightly fitted bodice pressed the impressive swell of her breasts back and almost under her armpits. The skirt was wide and full length, hiding her shapely legs. The sleeves billowed out from her shoulders and could have covered arms of almost any size. There was no doubt, she thought, looking at herself in the mirror, that she was a large woman. The width of her shoulders, the bulges in the tight bodice, and the neck that emerged from this sea green monstrosity left no question about that. But whether she was sexy, well rounded, generously endowed, voluptuous—or whether she was just plain fat—this dress would never tell.

She had brought with her a silver sequined low-cut dress that came to just above her knee. It showed off her lower legs and would have given her the chance to attract the attention of a few photographers with the expanse of breasts it revealed. But the studio dresser had breezed in two hours ago with a hair stylist and makeup artist and they had set to work. Her long hair, which she wore down, was now piled in a meticulously disheveled arrangement on top of her head. Her face looked frightening—her cheeks caked in rouge and her lipstick a brilliant red that clashed with her strawberry blonde hair. "Trust me," the makeup man had said, "It will look great on TV."

Anna shrugged. What did she care if she looked like a brightly painted sausage? Next week she would be back to making movies.

CLIFTON HAD BEEN intrigued by Karen's phone call. Her instincts were solid, and now was just the time *Ear to the Ground* could use another infusion of her editorial wisdom. After all, Karen had suggested the series of homeless profiles. Everyone had thought she was crazy, including Clifton. How would a series of long, depressing, unillustrated articles help sell newspapers? But Karen's work on the homeless pieces had brought *Ear to the Ground* more attention and more readers than ever. Even if she wouldn't give him details of this new article over the phone, her voice told him this could be another step up for the paper. If so, he thought, he would love to be able to give Karen a raise. But David had written the story, he reminded himself. Would she want him paid a writer's salary now instead of a delivery boy's? Sadly, there was not much difference.

He was just stepping out of the shower when the phone rang again, and he was puzzled for the second time that morning.

"Clifton? Hello, it's Linda Foretti."

"Linda, good morning," said Clifton, trying to sound nonchalant, although he nearly dropped the phone as he grabbed at the towel that was sliding off his waist.

"Listen, Clifton, I'd like to talk to you about advertising in that little rag of yours."

"Certainly, Linda," said Clifton.

"You know I'm opening a new store down near Union Square to sell Program Wear, and I thought those—oh, what do you call them—those types that take your paper?"

"Readers?"

"Bohemians! I thought maybe those bohemians down there ought to know we're coming. I guess a lot of them are anorexic or whatever, because it seems like a lot of them are skinny already."

"A lot of them can hardly afford to eat," said Clifton calmly.

"Right, whatever, but they love clothes, am I right? So listen, I want you to set me up with a six-month contract, half a page per issue. You do ads for The Program, right?"

"That's right."

"Well, we're tied in with them, so I'll need to be opposite their ad. I'm sure it's no problem. You just reserve the spot and we'll e-mail you the paste-up."

"Well, sure, Linda, I can do that."

"You're a darling, Clifton!" With a click her whirlwind voice disappeared and Clifton was left staring at the receiver.

Was it possible that Steve had fulfilled his end of the bargain Linda had proposed? In the flush of Steve's triumph in landing the contract with The Program, Clifton had forgotten to talk to him about Linda. Now he began to wish he had said something. It was nice to have another big advertiser, but Clifton would hate to have acquired the account by compromising the morals of his intern. *Ear to the Ground* was supposed to fight for social justice and strike blows against corruption, not send innocent interns into sexual entanglements.

He would talk to Steve at the party that night, tell him to keep away from Linda. If she canceled the contract, so what. They still had The Program.

KAREN HAD HAD sex three times in her twenty-four years: a fiasco in a back seat with a one-time date in high school; a slightly less brief encounter with a college friend who, it turned out, was only trying to be sure he was really gay; and a drunken night she could not even remember, but which haunted her until her next period. Sex and Karen had not been good friends.

Did she really want David? What if he didn't want her? What if his article had been mere fabrication? What if he only spoke of love for the woman who looked like the left-hand Grace because he thought it would look good in the paper? What if all his praise for the voluptuous form was meant as sarcasm? What if his entire article was a spoof of fat women who think they are attractive?

David stirred in his chair and Karen, who had been standing at the window, retreated to the bathroom. In one hand she clutched his article, in the other a package of condoms Georgia had left in the bathroom cabinet after her sudden departure.

NICK LEONARD SAT in his office reviewing the case file for *New York vs. David James.* Ever since he had read Karen's article the case had gnawed at him. Had he convicted an innocent boy?

All the evidence seemed to point to David—motive, eyewitnesses. But David's story was not without credence. Take away the testimony of the rich kids, and there really wasn't much. Nick had been running for re-election on a "get tough on crime" platform. He needed convictions. But what if he had destroyed a boy's life?

He couldn't give David back those years in prison, but if the boy was innocent, he could at least try to clear his name. He'd need some help, though, and he didn't feel like crawling to the police investigators with this one.

He picked up the phone and called Darcey. She'd be in the office on a Sunday afternoon.

"ARE YOU IN there?" David knocked again on the bathroom door. Karen had suddenly found herself tongue-tied, afraid to answer.

"Yes," she said at last, barely loud enough to be heard through the door.

"Have you got my article?" he asked. "I guess I fell asleep with it in my lap, and I can't find it." His voice was edged with panic, a feeling Karen could well remember from the first time she lost a long night's work to a computer crash.

"Yes," she said, staring at her side of the door. "Yes, I have it with me. I was just—I was just reading it."

"I'd love to know what you think of it, when you get done," he said. "I was up most of the night. This writing thing is not as easy as it looks."

Karen wanted to shout "It's wonderful," she wanted to fling the door open and embrace him and congratulate him and have him say that he meant every word of it and that he loved her and wanted her and needed her. Her hand trembled on the doorknob and a cold sweat trickled down her back. She had been staring at her reflection for almost a half an hour before David knocked, trying to see herself through his eyes, through eyes that preferred Rubens to Celinda.

"I kind of need to use the facilities in there," said David, "if—you know—if you're done."

Karen bit her lip in embarrassment and swung open the door. Seeing a groggy David standing there wanting nothing more than the bathroom somehow relieved the tension that had been building in her.

"Sorry," she said with a sheepish grin as David shuffled past her and pulled the door shut.

She sat down in the chair, still warm from David's body, and stared down at the few pedestrians that passed below while she listened to the sounds of water in the bathroom—first the toilet, then the sink, then the shower. Across the street a heavyset man in a dark blue ski jacket sat on the steps in front of his building. After a few minutes a man in a green ski jacket whistled at him from the end of the block and blue trotted off to meet green. Karen's right hand trembled in her lap. She had just begun to wonder if anyone would buzz in a teenage boy who had been ringing the bell on a building a few doors down when she heard David's voice behind her.

"So, did you read it?"

Karen did not turn to see him, but kept her eyes fixed on the boy. "Yes," she said, "I read it."

"So what did you think? Do you think Clifton will run it? I know it's a little long but—"

"Clifton will run it. I already called him and told him to hold the space."

"But it's too long, right?"

"It's not too long, David. It's well written, it's insightful, it's contro-versial. It's going to sell papers."

"What's the matter, then?" he asked. "Why won't you look at me? And why do you sound so distant? Are you mad at me for something?"

Karen finally swiveled her body away from the window to see David standing in bare feet, his wet hair dripping onto his white shirt leaving a dark circle around the base of the collar. He wore a pair of blue jeans and an expression like a scolded puppy dog. She almost laughed—he was that beautiful. Suddenly all her uncertainties slipped away and she saw standing before her not an intimidating sexual creature, but a friend—a friend who loved her.

"No," she said, softening her tone, "of course I'm not mad at you, David. I'm just a little—well, a little overwhelmed, that's all. I had no idea you were such a good writer."

David's face brightened. "I guess I got a lot of practice writing all those letters to Martin. You really like it?"

"I love it, David. I love it." She stood up and crossed the few feet that separated them, then stood on her tiptoes and kissed him lightly on the lips.

"What was that for?" he asked, blushing.

"That was for saying you love me in a newspaper article."

"You noticed that, huh?"

"Yeah, I noticed that."

They stood in silence, toe to toe, for a long moment.

"So," David finally said, "What do we do now?"

"You really like this body?" asked Karen, taking a step back from him.

"I've been dreaming of it ever since I met you," said David.

"Well, in that case," said Karen, unbuttoning her blouse, "I'm afraid all that hard work you did getting dressed was just wasted effort."

Karen had never imagined a lover like David. Where for others a perfunctory pawing of her chest had served as the sole preamble to the brief main event, David spent so long exploring her every inch—with gentle tracings of his fingertips, firm strokes of his hands, teasing touches from his darting tongue, even the occasional tickle from his toes—that she felt an exquisite agony of anticipation before he ever touched her breasts or ventured between her legs. He paid homage to every curve. How could Karen ever have doubted his sincerity?

She felt a pang of guilt that she should be the recipient of so much pleasure, but when he finally probed between her thighs, first with an artfully wielded finger and then with his flickering tongue, her pleasure overcame her guilt and she slipped into another world where there was only David and each supremely talented piece of his being with which he brought her rapture. When he entered her she laughed and whimpered and did not even try to stifle her cries of ecstasy.

Later, lying in his arms, her breathing slowly returning to normal, she marveled it had been such fun. Fun was the last thing she had expected. She lay for a long time, staring at the ceiling, trying to adjust her mind to the idea that her body could be attractive. She became so lost in this radical shift in her self image that David had to ask her three times if she wanted some lunch. When she finally turned to answer him, he was still smiling.

David and Karen arrived early for Clifton's party. After making love they had spent the afternoon editing David's article, and that had seemed to Karen almost as intimate. They went over every sentence, tweaking and tightening. Karen began to teach David about journalism, trying not to say anything that would interfere with his natural style. He eloquently defended word choices and sentence structures he had clearly agonized over, but he wasn't stubborn or arrogant. When her suggestion was better, he made the change and moved on. Karen felt the buzz of his creative energy in her head all day, like a glass of good champagne.

At three o'clock they went to the office to type. She typed the first half and he typed the second, and they printed out three copies to take to the party. They felt like a team, and Karen had rarely shared that feeling with a man. At work she was either Steve's boss or Clifton's employee. In her few previous experiences with dating she had always felt inferior—the lucky girl some man had condescended to take out. But she and David had worked together as equals.

The word "partnership" kept running through her head as they walked towards Clifton's apartment. When she thought of what they had done in bed as partners, she felt a flash of embarrassment knowing she was about to face Steve, who still seemed to have an inexplicable crush on her, and Clifton, whom she felt she was betraying. She wondered if they would sense the change that had come over her.

Looking down at her wide hips and mountainous breasts, she wrapped her arms around herself and, for a brief moment, actually loved her body.

THE STUDIO HAD timed the arrival of Anna Camello at the Golden Globes red carpet so she would pass through the tunnel of flashes and cheers about fifteen yards ahead of her slender co-star, Lucinda Wilson. Lucinda would arrive with the handsome young actor who played her husband and with the film's director. Accompanied by two tuxedoed gentlemen, she would catch the attention of every photographer with the plunging neckline of her scarlet gown. *Why shouldn't it plunge?* thought Anna when the studio dresser told her about it. *There's nothing for it to reveal.*

Anna would arrive unaccompanied. She would serve as herald for Lucinda's entourage. In the world of Hollywood, Anna had discovered, everything was scripted. Well, almost everything.

With her limo waiting in line a few blocks from the expectant crowd, Anna noticed a clutch of people on the sidewalk who did not look like typical movie fans. They carried signs and their shouts, though distant-sounding through the thick glass, were not cheers of adulation, but jeers and insults. As her car turned the corner, she saw that this was no mere clique of radical malcontents—there must be hundreds of them. And then Anna saw her own name on a homemade cardboard placard.

For a moment she thought the anger of this crowd was directed at her, and she could not imagine what she had done. Then she realized that these demonstrators supported her; this was an outpouring of outrage over the fact that Anna had not been nominated, and this crowd attributed that slight to size discrimination.

Signs read "We love you Anna," and "Big Women Can Act Too." A row of policemen struggled to keep the crowd on the sidewalk.

Anna didn't know whether to be proud or horrified. She didn't mind being slighted. Six months ago she had been an unknown actress and now she was starring in a hit movie. But these women on the sidewalk, normal woman in a normal variety of sizes and shapes, seemed to have appointed her the figurehead in their battle against the cult of thinness. Could she decline the post? She decided the least she could do was acknowledge them. She rolled down her window, leaned out far enough to be recognized, and waved vigorously, flashing the killer smile she had worked on in the mirror for years.

The crowd went berserk. Again they surged against the policemen, and this time a group of women broke through the line and came running towards Anna. In the few seconds before they were dragged back to the sidewalk, Anna managed to shake the hands of several women who wept to be so close to her. She had never imagined such worship. The car turned another corner and the sounds of the cheers faded. Anna rolled up her window and sat back, breathless in her seat

She pressed the button that allowed her to talk to the driver. "What did you think of that," she asked, almost giggling.

"You know movie fans," he said flatly. "Crazy people."

KAREN, DAVID, CLIFTON, and the clutch of reviewers, staff and their dates who stood around the television in Clifton's apartment did not notice Anna's subdued entrance. They did not notice the TV reporters rushing past her for a glimpse of Lucinda and her escorts. Their attention had been distracted by the arrival of Steve Collingwood who, unlike Anna, sported a date on his arm. Clifton, who had been sure Steve was totally smitten with Karen, had stumbled and stuttered his way through introductions in his surprise to see the young man grinning broadly and escorting Sarah Saunders through the door.

Steve and Sarah had overdressed for the party, where a pair of blue jeans without holes was considered elegant, but neither seemed to mind. Sarah wore a flouncy blue dress that showed off her well-formed calves and was nicely filled on the top by her bosom, which drew the attention of a number of the reviewers to the displeasure of their slim and pouty dates. Steve wore a blue blazer and his school tie with a pair of gray flannels.

Karen was surprised to find she felt a sense of loss watching Steve and Sarah. Now that Steve's crush on her was apparently over, and in spite of David, she felt the tiniest hint of regret for what might have been. But she didn't let it show. She smiled warmly at Steve and gave him a welcoming kiss on the cheek. "You're looking very Exeter tonight," she whispered teasingly.

On the coffee table lay a copy of David's article, now titled "The

Case for the Rubenesque." Clifton had read it while David and Karen watched him. When he had started *Ear to the Ground*, he found it nerve-wracking to read an article while an eager young writer stared over his shoulder. He had worried if he didn't laugh on cue, or say "Mmmmm" in a deep ponderous voice, he would crush the poor writer's hopes. He had learned a lot since then—that crushed hopes sometimes led to better writing, that the feelings of reporters were subordinate to the quality of the newspaper, and how to ignore people who stared at you as you read. So he ignored Karen and David.

"Lose another hundred words and run it with the picture on the front page. Two—no, three columns and then the rest on page four and five."

"That's good, isn't it?" said David, looking to Karen, but she was already talking to Clifton.

"Did I tell you? I told you, didn't I?"

"You know this is going to make waves," said Clifton. Our biggest advertiser is a weight loss center and we're going to run a front page story on how it's OK to be fat."

"I know," said Karen.

"Well," said Clifton, standing up, "luckily they've already signed a contract, so we're in business for at least another six months. And I just landed another big account today." Clifton could imagine Linda's reaction when she saw the article, but maybe he could get her to sign the contract before the paper came out. She probably wouldn't read it anyway. "David," he said, "I guess you're going to have to find someone to take your place as delivery boy. It looks like you're a staff writer now."

AT THE *My Sister, Myself* table Anna sat between Oscar Duncan, who had been nominated for best screenplay, and Andy Donnelly, who had done the sound effects editing for the film and was also the nephew of the director. When conversation was permitted—before the ceremonies began and during the commercial breaks—Oscar pitched various screenplay ideas to the director, who sat on his other side. Anna was left to make small talk with Andy, whom she had never met before.

Andy's primary interest was in knowing "what Lucinda is like," a question he repeated in various forms throughout the evening. Anna smiled and told brief anecdotes about working with Lucinda, all of which seemed to delight Andy almost to the point of orgasm. He never looked at Anna, but kept his eyes riveted on the bare, flat chest of Lucinda where she sat across the table. Anna wondered how many glasses of champagne she would have to drink before this rodent faded into the haze of oblivion he so richly deserved.

While Andy was asking the cinematographer on his other side what Lucinda was like, the waiter poured Anna's third glass, and leaning over her shoulder whispered, "You're much sexier than her, and more talented, too."

Before his comment had registered on her brain he was gone. When she turned to look for him, she saw him at the next table, still pouring champagne, but he surreptitiously lifted his eyes to her and—was it possible that he winked?

She lowered her gaze, feeling slightly flushed and more flattered than if she'd received one of the awards. She didn't even hear Andy ask, "So, did you ever share a dressing room with Lucinda?"

FATHER MARTIN HAD turned in early that night and had no idea that the award for Best Picture in the Drama category had just been announced when he felt wrenched from his sleep and sat bolt upright in bed, sweat pouring off his body.

He kept his room completely dark at night, an oddly comforting throwback to his blind childhood, but tonight the darkness only exacerbated the unexplained sense of panic and dread that overcame him. He thought about waking Gareth, but what would he tell him? Then some instinct (later Martin would call it the voice of God) told him to call Karen.

He reached for the phone by the bed, grateful he had committed her number to memory. Her phone rang and rang. Karen was not home, and Georgia had taken the answering machine. He did not try her again that night, but he also did not sleep.

He threw his curtains open and stared into the darkness until the pale light of dawn began to outline the shape of St. Alban's.

MY SISTER, MYSELF had not swept all the awards for which it had been nominated, but many people at Anna's table had made the trek to the podium that evening. Oscar Duncan had given Anna a quick hug when he stood to collect his Best Screenplay award, and Lucinda, who had surprised no one by winning Best Actress, had graciously mentioned Anna in her speech. Lucinda was, Anna knew, a kind and decent person; she couldn't help it if it took The Program to give her a body that producers would cast in a leading role.

The tension at the table before the announcement of Best Dramatic Picture was palpable. Only the producer, whom Anna had never met, seemed calm.

He sat nearly opposite her and had remained quiet through most of the evening, exchanging pleasantries when addressed, but generally abstaining from the conversation. He had never produced a motion picture before—he was a New York businessman with lots of money and a love of the movies. Anything anyone in the cast knew about him came only as rumor. He had remained far behind the scenes during the making of the film. The concept had been his and he had provided the screenwriter with the barest of outlines, but most of the people on the shoot didn't even know his name.

WHEN THE AWARD for Best Dramatic Picture was announced, Steve groaned and beat his head against Sarah's shoulder in exasperation. "I swear that movie is the work of the Devil," he said, and Sarah laughed, nudging him in the ribs with her elbow.

"What's the matter," she teased, "you don't like skinny ladies?"

"No," he whispered, grabbing her around the middle and tickling her warm, soft flesh, "I absolutely do not like skinny ladies."

As a result of their flirtations on the couch, Steve and Sarah did not hear the name of the producer of *My Sister, Myself* who would be accepting the award, nor did they see the somber-looking man mount the rostrum.

He wore a black shirt and black tie with his tux, and his black hair was combed straight back and shined under the lights. This gleaming hair was his only distinguishing characteristic. When they spoke of it afterwards, none of them could agree on exactly what he looked like.

"He looked average," Karen would say, "a little on the short side, is all."

"He looked like someone you would pass in the street and never see," Clifton would add.

THE PROGRAM

"If he'd been at this party," Marjorie would say, "nobody would have noticed him."

Except David.

His name was Arthur Blackburn, and his acceptance speech, as short and bland as his looks, was delivered in a nervous monotone.

"I really had very little to do with the making of this film," the producer said. "I'd like to say thank you to all those who took my little idea and my big bank account and turned out a great picture. The actors and the crew—everybody. I think you did a great job. Thank you very much."

He paused uncomfortably before the words "thank you" both times he used them, as if he had some speech impediment that placed a hesitation before this one expression. As he turned to leave the podium, his right hand shakily moved up to check that his hair was still in place.

When the applause died down and the commercial break had begun, the room was abuzz with comments on what made the speech unique. He hadn't mentioned a single name. No one, least of all a novice producer, was powerful enough in Hollywood to fail to mention names on an awards rostrum.

But the murmurs quickly gave way to discussions of future projects and post-ceremony parties. Only back in New York had the speech made any lasting impact.

At first no one noticed David's reaction to Arthur Blackburn. The party's groans, applause, and a small chorus of "told-you-so's" overshadowed David's more subtle response.

The color drained out of his face, and he began to tremble. He could not take his eyes from the television. Not until one of the reviewers called for quiet so he could hear the acceptance speech did David begin to mumble the word "No," over and over—under his breath at first, but gradually louder and louder.

Karen, who sat on the floor leaning against David's knee, felt the trembling just before the "no" became audible. When she turned to look at David she was afraid he was sick, and she jumped up to help him. But he pushed her away and trembled more violently, still repeating "no" until he commanded the attention of the room with his

156

shouting.

"For God's sake," yelled Steve, "somebody turn the damned thing off!" Clifton reached for the remote control and snapped the picture of Blackburn into darkness. David fell silent, but continued to shake.

When Karen approached him he backed towards the door. "Don't come near me," he said, his eyes flashing what seemed like fury towards her.

"But David," she said, taking another step closer.

"I said don't come near me," he shouted, shoving Karen so that she stumbled backwards onto the couch. "Stay away from me."

Karen sat stunned and breathless on the couch, tears burning in the corners of her eyes. David bolted out the door and she heard his footsteps pounding down the stairs.

"Crap, what was his problem?" said one of the reviewers.

"Is he OK?" asked Steve.

Clifton sat by Karen on the sofa and took her hand. If he had ever done this before she would have been beside herself with delight. Now she felt as if she'd been kicked in the stomach. "Are you all right?" said Clifton.

"I think I'd better go," Karen finally managed to mumble. She desperately wanted to find David, but she couldn't bear to think of him repeating such horrible words to her, so she let Clifton and Steve bundle her into a cab and send her home.

She fell into bed in a trance, wondering how she could have let herself be so happy. How could she have forgotten what Martin had said about David and his demons? How could she have believed everything was fine?

She lay awake in her bed for hours, tears running down her cheeks until the whole pillowcase was damp.

Steve hailed a taxi after the party, and he and Sarah slipped in quietly. He would drop her off at her apartment in the Village first, then sit back for the ride uptown to Columbia. Neither of them spoke about David's bizarre episode. The whole incident had more or less ended the party. No one had known what to say, so no one had said anything.

Steve glanced at his watch and decided that by the time he got back to his dorm it would be too late to call Karen. Besides, he would talk to her in the morning. Hopefully David would be back by then.

He watched Sarah's face appear and disappear as they drove under one streetlight after another. She gazed in silence into the night. When the cab stopped at a light she reached for his hand, still looking out the window. Her hand felt warm and slipped into his easily.

"I had a nice time, really," she said. "I'm just tired, that's all."

"I'm glad you could come," said Steve. "I liked—I liked being with you."

"Me, too," she said, sliding closer to him on the seat. "Oh, I almost forgot," she said, "I got that report for you, the one on Gus Doe."

Sarah reached into her purse and pulled out a folded photocopy just as the cab pulled up to the curb in front of her building. She pressed it into Steve's hand. "I'm not sure it'll do you much good."

"Shall I walk you in?" he asked as she opened her door and stepped out.

"I'm OK," she said.

Steve sighed. *The death knell for a date,* he thought, *the girl who walks herself to the door.* But just as he was about to tell the cabby to head for Columbia, Sarah leaned in at the door. Her breasts swayed tantalizingly close in almost full view. She put a hand around his neck, pulled him to her and kissed him on the lips, holding his head and letting the kiss evolve for several seconds before she broke away.

"I'll see you for lunch tomorrow, right?"

"Right," said Steve, breathlessly, as her head disappeared and the door closed.

On the way uptown, once his pulse had slowed to normal, Steve unfolded the paper she had given him. At the bottom were Gus's fingerprints; Steve would have to ask Karen if she had any contacts in law enforcement who might help with those. The rest of the form seemed fairly useless—height, weight, and so on. The figures flashed in and out of view as the cab made its way under the street lights. Not until he was past Eightieth Street did he notice a small box labeled "anatomical anomalies." The cab slipped into darkness again before he could read what it said, but at the next stoplight he saw the words clearly: "Six toes on left foot."

DEEP IN THE night, long after Karen had given up hope of falling asleep, she heard the street door open. It had opened several times while she lay there, and she no longer dared hope it might be David, but a few moments later she heard a key in the lock and her door swung open, revealing David's slouching profile in a rectangle of pale yellow light.

He closed the door behind him, shuffled across the room and lowered himself into the armchair. For several minutes he was so quiet Karen couldn't hear his breathing. She wondered if she ought to say something. It seemed deceptive to let him think she was asleep.

"I can't stay," he finally said, "but I thought you deserved an explanation."

Karen barely managed to mutter, "OK."

After a long silence, David began to speak in a soft monotone. "I never used to believe in evil," he said. "Even after I got to prison. I figured people made mistakes or grew up in hard circumstances. I believed people could be selfish and sometimes cruel and frequently stupid, but

I didn't believe in pure evil. Martin tried to make me believe in pure good, believe in God and all that. He told me all about his miracle and how God had healed him, but when I asked hadn't God made him blind in the first place, he always changed the subject. He liked talking about good, not so much about evil.

Karen wished she could be closer to David while he poured out this story, wished she could hold him, but after what had happened at Clifton's she didn't dare reach out to him. Instead she lay unmoving on her back, staring into the darkness and letting his voice wash over her.

"When I first got there I shared a cell with this huge black guy named Charlie. He scared the hell out of me, until I'd been in for a few days and I realized he was a pussycat. He liked to tell me jokes—sort of third-grade jokes—and if I laughed even a little bit he would be happy for the rest of the day. He told me the same jokes over and over and I always laughed. Charlie was in for murder, and he told me that he did it, all right. Most people in prison, they claim to be innocent, but not Charlie. He killed his sister's husband when she came crying to him that he was slapping her around and sleeping with another woman. Charlie walked right into the man's bedroom and stabbed him in the back while he slept, sixteen times with a butcher knife. He pled guilty and got fifteen to twenty because of extenuating circumstances, and the fact that the judge thought Charlie had done a service to society.

"He didn't complain about prison except for one thing. He always talked about how much he missed his dog, Scooter. He would tell me stories about Scooter and how he was his best friend in the world. He would sometimes cry himself to sleep after telling Scooter stories. The other way he would fall asleep was by praying, and the way Charlie prayed was to repeat this one phrase from the Lord's Prayer over and over—'Lead us not into temptation,' 'Lead us not into temptation.' Like a mantra. He never did explain that to me.

"So one day Charlie comes back from recreation with this huge smile on his face and tells me he's going to go see Scooter. For a while I can't get him to stop grinning and explain himself, but finally he tells me he met somebody who's going to get him paroled. 'You met somebody at recreation?' 'Yeah,' he says, 'At recreation.' So I figure the next day maybe I better not skip recreation like I'd been doing. But I don't see anything unusual. Charlie wanders around the yard telling jokes. The nice folks laugh. Others don't. After a while I forget all about it and figure somebody was just having a joke on Charlie.

"The next time I stay in from recreation, Charlie comes back and right away I can tell something is different. He still tells his jokes, but when I laugh he just goes on to the next one without smiling. He keeps saying he's going to see Scooter; and that night as I'm falling asleep he's got a new mantra. Instead of praying, he just says, 'I'm going to see Scooter, I'm going to see Scooter,' over and over. Next day, Charlie gets paroled. He's not even supposed to be up for parole for another year and a half. But they come and collect him and he shuffles out of the cell mumbling about Scooter and I never see him again."

The voice stopped for so long that Karen wondered if David had drifted off to sleep. Finally, she began counting passing cars. There were few this time of night, but she had counted to seventeen before the voice emerged again from the darkness.

"I'm in my cell alone that night and for the first time since I got to prison I'm lonely. I go to recreation the next few days and ask around. Does anybody know what happened in the yard that day to make Charlie so different? But nobody's talking. Not like they don't know, just like they won't say.

"Three weeks later I get a new cellmate. This kid is a greenhorn. Barely old enough to qualify for grown-up prison. What's more, he's genuinely innocent. I can tell the second he walks in. He's scared of me. Anybody who's scared of me couldn't possibly have done what they said he did. Supposed to have killed a couple of kids and he's not much more than a kid himself. He won't talk to me about it, or about anything for a long time. So I just talk to him. I read him letters from Father Martin, and I read from whatever book I'm working on. I think it was *Robinson Crusoe* when he first showed up. Eventually he loosens up and starts to talk. His name is Sam. He won't tell me his last name, so I just call him Sam.

"Sam can't read, so I keep reading to him. Every decent book I can get from the prison library. Dickens, Hemingway, *The Three Musketeers*, *Gone with the Wind*. His favorite is poetry. *Songs of Innocence* by William Blake. I read that one over and over until we can both recite it from memory.

The night was dark, no father was there,
The child was wet with dew;
The mire was deep, and the child did weep,
And away the vapour flew."

Blake's words hung in the air as David lapsed once more into silence. Karen had studied the Romantic poets in college. She let her mind drift to the little boy, "lost in the lonely fen." She knew that God found the boy in Blake's next poem, but as she lay there waiting for David to resume his narrative, it seemed the boy might wander forever in the darkness.

"Life moves pretty slow in prison," continued David. "I start teaching Sam to read. A year later he can read to me—when my voice is tired or I need a break. It might take him twenty minutes to get through a page of *A Tale of Two Cities*, but he's making progress. Teaching him how to read, and working our way through the prison library together, gives me something to do, something to relieve the unrelenting tedium of the place. I've almost forgotten about Charlie when a man in a black suit appears at the fence one day, talking to two guys in the yard.

"'That's him,' a prisoner tells, me, nudging me in the back and pointing to the man on the other side of the fence.

"'Who?' I ask, squinting into the sun, trying to get a look at the man's face, but it's shaded by a broad-brimmed hat.

"'That's the guy who cut the deal to spring Charlie.'

"I sit and watch the man for a few minutes. He's silhouetted against the afternoon sun, and his face is obscured not only by his hat and the bright light behind him, but by the silver diamonds of the chain-link fence. The two men speaking to him move on, but the man stays by the fence, completely still, staring into the yard. Staring at me. So I figure what the hell, I'll go talk to him. Maybe he can help Sam.

"I walk over and the guy's face is still sort of gray under the hat. His features just won't coalesce. Still, even though I never got a good look at him, I'd know that face anywhere.

"'Did you help Charlie?' I ask him.

"'I helped him get out,' he says. 'What do you want?'

"I pause before I answer, because my first reaction is to say I want help for Sam, but I realize his question has a broader scope. I am not sure if he means he has the power to give me anything, but I can tell he's asking not just what I want right now, but what I want out of life, what my dreams are, what I hope to accomplish when I've slipped off the shackles of this place.

"'I want a comfortable place to live,' I say. 'And I want not to have to worry about how to pay the bills. And I want someone to love me. That's all, really.'

"'And what does Sam want?' he asks.

"I wonder how he knows about Sam. Did those other two prisoners tell him about the shy kid, the innocent who never speaks outside his cell and spends his evenings listening to Shakespeare and Jane Austen? But something in his face, the way his eyes bore into me, tells me to just answer.

"'Sam doesn't want anything,' I say. 'But I'd like for him to get out of here.'

"'Sam doesn't want anything,' he repeats—a statement, not a question.

"'I don't think so,' I say.

"He stands for a long moment, staring across the yard at the other inmates. After his eyes have scanned from one side of the yard to the other, they return to rest on me. 'I'll talk to you tomorrow,' he says, and before I can answer he walks off across the parking lot. The bell rings and I head back to Sam. I can't decide what to think of this strange man. I keep thinking about how Charlie looked that last night before they let him free, and how he'd stopped praying. Something just doesn't seem right.

"That night after the lights go out I ask Sam, 'What do you want?'

"'What do you mean?' he says.

"'If you could have anything, what would you want? Wouldn't you want to get out of here?'

"'What would I do out there,' says Sam, and I think maybe he's right. Sam's too innocent for prison, that's sure enough, but maybe he's too innocent for the real world, too. Here at least people pretty much leave him alone. It's one of those low security places where they put your less dangerous criminals. Not a lot of shower rapes as long as you're careful. And no one would touch Sam. It would be like child molesting—that's how innocent Sam is. But in the real world? Well, people might not rape him, but I'm sure they'd find a way to strip away his dignity pretty fast.

"'Somebody to read to me,' Sam says from the bottom bunk.

"'I beg your pardon?'

"'That's what I want. Someone to read to me after you're gone.'

"'OK, Sam,' I say, 'I'll see what I can do.'

"Well, I can get somebody to read to Sam. There's a few other life termers here who could probably be coaxed into the job, and I've got at least two years to find somebody and groom them for the position. I figure after I get out I can send books to Sam, because in another two years we'll be through everything in the prison library. That starts me thinking about the man at the fence again. If he can really give me financial security, then I can buy books for Sam. I assume this guy runs some sort of charity that finds jobs for ex-cons, helps them get paroled early, that sort of thing.

"Next day I meet him at the fence again.

"'What does Sam want?' he asks.

"'Nothing I can't give him myself,' I say, and I swear for a second I see this red glow in his eyes. But he speaks very calmly.

"'And you?'

"'I could really use a job when I get out of here.'

"He smiles this wide grin that shows off perfect white teeth. A little too perfect. 'I can offer you an entry-level position in a new corporation guaranteed to make the Fortune 500 in its first year. In less than three years you'll be a millionaire, and that will be just the beginning. If you stick with the company, you'll not only be rich beyond your wildest dreams, but women—well, let's just say whatever you want in that area will be easy to find. A beautiful and faithful wife, perhaps? I sense that would be your choice.'

"'You can take an ex-con with no high school diploma and make him a millionaire?' I ask. And my head is already filling up with visions of my life to be. I can see a beautiful old Victorian house looking out over the Hudson, with a wide lawn and three or four kids cavorting around. A—and here I recreate in my mind his exact words—a beautiful and faithful wife standing on the porch. Rooms full of books to read and plenty of money to buy more for Sam.

"And then I have this other vision, and I'm ashamed to say it pleases me more than the first. The three boys who sent me up to jail with their lies come into my office looking for jobs. Their fathers have cut them off, they tell me. They don't have any skills because they've spent their lives lounging around the country club. Can't I please give them a place in the company? The mailroom, even? And I see my own face as I smile the very smile that smeared itself across their faces when they took the stand at my trial. And I press a button on my desk and I say 'Grace, call security and have these liars thrown out of the building.'

"'Yes,' the man says through the fence, interrupting my reverie, 'I can give you the power you've always longed for. You've spent your whole life being, pardon the expression, being shit on. I can make that stop.'

"'And what exactly do you want in return?'

"'For you I can make an extremely favorable deal. Much better than the deal I offered your friend Charlie.'

"'Is Charlie working for this company?'

"'Charlie didn't want a job. Charlie wanted to see his dog. I get people what they want.'

"'And the price?' I ask.

"'You get me what I want.'

"'Which is?'

"'I think your time's up,' he says, and he walks away.

"I lie awake that night weaving more and more elaborate scenarios of wealth and power and revenge. It never occurs to me to doubt that this man can deliver.

"Gradually I find myself thinking less and less about my beautiful and faithful wife and my lovely house and cavorting children and thinking more and more about power and revenge. It spreads through me like a virus, this lust to punish those who wronged me. Not just the three boys, but their fathers and their lawyers, the D.A., even the judge. I plot a hundred ways to get them back, each punishment more humiliating than the one before. And with each dream I see the smile on my face spread wider. And not once during that long, wonderful night do I give a thought to Charlie's repeated prayer: 'Lead us not into temptation.'

"The next day I go running out to the fence to give the man what he wants. But he isn't there. He isn't there the next day, either. Or the next. And I start to panic. What if he left for good? What if my dreams, which continue unabated, never come true? What if I rot in this prison while those who wronged me flourish on the outside? They set me up once; surely they'll do it again. I might never see the outside.

"I try to read to Sam, but my mind continually wanders into one or another of these fantasies—the glorious or the wretched—and without realizing it I fall silent for ten, twenty, thirty minutes. Sam waits a long time to complain, to ask if there is more.

"By the time I see the man at the fence the next week I am desperate. I would give him my immortal soul if only he'll keep his promise. But he doesn't want my immortal soul. He wants Sam's."

Again David fell silent. Karen closed her eyes and tried to comprehend the significance of his last statement. She heard in her head the echo of her conversation with Martin. "And how do you know, exactly, that Satan is wandering around tempting people," Karen had asked, and Martin had replied, "David met him."

Karen wasn't sure she believed in God, much less the Devil, but David claimed to have met him. And Satan had offered him everything he could ever want in exchange for the soul of an innocent, the sort of soul he could never win on his own. It would be so simple to say David was crazy, that his demons consisted of a mild touch of insanity. The problem was, David was the sanest person Karen knew.

Sometime during her ponderings David had begun again, and Karen suddenly realized she had been hearing his voice without listening.

"—a contract like the one he said Charlie had signed. Only this one has my name under the signature blank, and Sam's name in another blank. His name is beautifully calligraphed in red ink. The paper is hot when he hands it to me. Not that luxurious warmth of paper fresh out of the copy machine, but hot enough to sting your fingertips. And then he said it again.

"'You have three days.'

"Those are the longest three days I've ever known. I don't eat. I don't read to Sam or talk to him or even look at him. I lay on my top bunk with that hot paper under my pillow making my face sweat and I try to fight off the sweet dreams of power and torture and death. On the third day I start to mutter Charlie's prayer. 'Lead me not into temptation, lead me not into temptation.' Over and over, hour after hour. Sometimes it seems the paper is cooling off and the visions start to fade, but then the heat comes again with renewed intensity and new and more glorious apparitions fill my mind—my wife becomes more beautiful, my house bigger, the children more talented, the view from my office more spectacular, and the fate of my persecutors more grisly.

"After three days I stumble out into the yard. As soon as I see him at the fence my strength returns and I walk to him. He holds a pen through the chain link. I grip the contract tightly and reach towards the pen and I can't tell you how glorious the visions are—they've taken on their own life now, far exceeding anything I could conjure from my own imagination. And without taking my eye from those visions, I crumple the contract in my right hand. It grows hotter and hotter, and as I squeeze it I can hear the sound of my flesh burning. I shove the wadded up contract through the fence and it falls on the ground and bursts into flame. In an instant my visions are gone and the pain surges into my hand. I fall to the ground holding my hand to my chest and whimpering.

"'You could have had me,' I gasp through the pain, 'But not him.' I look up at him one last time and now I can clearly see his glowing red eyes and wisps of smoke curling from under his hat.

"I was in the hospital three days to treat the burn. When I got back, Sam read to me all day every day, while I lay in my bunk and tried to forget those visions and recover my strength. When I finally started to feel alive again, I made a vow. The only way to avoid temptation, I told myself, was to desire nothing. I decided when I got out I would make myself happy with nothing. If I could be content living on the street with no possessions, then what could tempt me?

"I had to do one other thing, though, and that was the hardest part. "I had to forgive the people who sent me to jail.

"Not to their faces, necessarily, but in my heart. I wrote a lot of letters to Father Martin about that, and he wrote a lot of letters back, and I did it, eventually. It took most of the rest of my time in prison, but I did it.

"So I came to New York, settled down under a bridge in Central Park, and made myself happy with nothing. Even after I met you and moved here, I still figured I was safe. Because I knew I could be happy with nothing, I could always go back to that if that's what it took to avoid temptation.

"My mistake was starting to care for you. Then I had something to lose, something he could take away from me. So you see why I can't stay, why I can't be near you."

"He was the man on TV," said Karen, speaking for the first time since David had come into the room.

David did not reply, but stood up from the chair and pulled his coat on. "Take care of yourself," he said. And then he was gone.

L ater that morning Clifton opened a stiff manila envelope that had arrived in the mail. Inside he found a note from a prominent politi- cal cartoonist. "Every paper in town refuses to run this, but Georgia Phillips at the *Daily Mail* said you might be interested—I'm afraid she was being sarcastic, but I send it along just in case."

An inner envelope contained a pen-and-ink cartoon of a stick-figure woman standing outside of the front door of The Program. She ad- dresses a couple—a burly, muscular man and a classically curvaceous woman. The stick woman says "The Devil made me do it."

It seemed fairly innocuous to Clifton. Maybe it was rejected, he thought, because it wasn't that funny. On the other hand, coupled with David's article about Rubens and with the caption, "The cartoon the other papers wouldn't let you see," it might stir up a little controversy, sell a few more papers.

"LUNCH TOMORROW? Oh, Steve, dear, I don't think we can cover all the ground we need to cover over lunch. Besides, I'm a busy business- woman—you can't expect me to be available for lunch on just a day's notice. How about cocktails tonight at my place? Seven o'clock."

Steve had called Linda's office before his lunch with Sarah, hoping he might arrange to meet her in a public place. He had not been sur- prised to see those hopes dashed.

"Fine," he said in a flat voice. "Seven o'clock. But just for cocktails.

I have a dinner date at eight-thirty," and before she could respond he hung up.

Who knows, maybe Sarah *would* be available for dinner.

WHEN THE DOORS of Program Wear, Linda Foretti's revamped store on Fifty-Seventh Street, opened at ten o'clock, Louise Crawford joined the throng of recently reduced women who pressed into the shop. She paid little mind to a tall, wide man standing to one side of the door, wearing a dark suit and a heavy coat. Louise did not know that this man was not so much a security officer as a bouncer. Though he did not forbid anyone from coming into the store, he strongly discouraged those who did not possess the "perfect body" from wasting their time and annoying the other customers.

Louise had gotten up early to be one of the first customers at Program Wear, but it was her meeting with a newspaper reporter that had driven her into the city so eagerly. Now she browsed the racks of insubstantial garments, still not quite able to believe they would fit her.

Like Darcey, Louise felt some loss of identity after going through The Program. She had always hated her body, but she had always considered that hatred an essential part of her being. As she walked by a mirror, she couldn't decide whether to hate her new body or not—this far from Phil it was starting to seem perfect again. And she knew she would look fabulous in any one of these outfits. In the past Louise's problem shopping had been finding something to fit. Now she faced a new dilemma—having to develop taste or style or at least a preference for one design over another. This store was full of things that would fit her. Maybe Louise Crawford liked her new body after all. It was her husband who hated it.

After browsing for a few minutes, Louise stopped a saleswoman to ask where the sizes were posted. "Don't worry," explained the woman, If you've been through The Program, everything will fit. Just check for your height on the tag."

Everything will fit. Louise stood quietly for a moment digesting that glorious information. She had spent her entire adult life searching the racks for something that might not look too humiliating in a department store changing room. Now she stood in a sea of chicness and *everything* would fit. It was such a reinvention of her concept of shopping she hardly knew where to begin.

Finally, Louise picked out a short black dress to try on. As she twirled in front of the fitting room mirrors she could hardly believe how good she looked. Since her ninth grade Christmas dance, when Brooke Peterson wore a dress like this, she had wanted to wear one. How she had longed for a body that would look good in a spaghetti-strapped wispy bit of black like what hung from her perfect shoulders now. Louise could not stifle a delighted giggle as she twirled again and felt the silky fabric settling gently on her thighs.

Two hours in Program Wear positively flew by. Louise tried on business suits and eveningwear, bathing suits and lingerie, workout clothes and casual wear. Everything fit and everything looked great. She giggled frequently.

By twelve o'clock Louise was laden with two heavy bags of clothes and was wearing a crisp new suit with matching black pumps. She felt, just as she had when she laughed with the skinny women on the train before Christmas, that she belonged to a club she was happy to be in. After spending years commiserating with her fellow fatties about how hard it was to find an outfit that looked good, she had spent two hours celebrating with her fellow Program girls over how fabulous they looked.

She hated to leave the air of camaraderie in Program Wear, because a part of her knew that the world outside those doors was a very different place.

KAREN AWOKE ALONE. She didn't know when she had finally fallen asleep, but she couldn't have slept more than two or three hours. Last night seemed like a dream; even yesterday morning seemed like a dream. Maybe David hadn't really made love to her; maybe he hadn't written an article extolling the virtues of the voluptuous; maybe he hadn't told a story about meeting the Devil. Maybe David didn't even exist; maybe Karen was the crazy one.

A hot shower washed away the unreality of what had happened. Karen wanted to crawl back in bed and cry and shiver and lock out the rest of the world forever. But she had felt depressed and rejected and abandoned before, so she did what she always did in those situations. She put her emotions on autopilot and she got to work. After all, in two hours she had a meeting that might lead to the biggest story of her career.

BY TEN O'CLOCK the sitting room of Anna Camello's hotel suite had been inundated with flowers, telegrams, phone messages, and hand-delivered letters and cards. Bleary-eyed from champagne, Anna picked up a large manila envelope from a pile of mail on the desk and tore it open. "Dear Miss Camello," read the letter,

> Doubtless by now you have sensed the outpouring of sympathy from the normally shaped community at the way the Hollywood establishment treated you last night. This blatant display of size-ism has angered millions across the country.
>
> I represent a large number of people in the Los Angeles area who have organized themselves as the Army of All Sizes (AAS). AAS is composed of men and women of every natural shape who oppose the super-thin ideal being promoted by Hollywood, the fashion industry and the weight loss scheme known as The Program.
>
> In the past few months we have organized chapters in every major city in the United States. By early spring we hope to organize a "Million Pound March" on Washington. And you, Miss Camello, could be our spokesperson. You could do more to reverse the destructive trend towards ultra-thinness than perhaps any other individual in the country.
>
> Won't you join our crusade, Miss Camello? I would be happy to receive your call at any time. Any "weight" you can lend our cause will be appreciated by millions of normal Americans.
>
> Sincerely Yours,
> Jane Baxter,
> Founder, AAS

Anna only wanted to make movies. She didn't want to be a nationally famous political figure, giving speeches to thousands of cheering women and hope to millions more. But she looked at her reflection in the mirror and remembered the shape of all the women who had mounted the rostrum last night—a shape that stood in stark contrast to her own. And she thought of all the other women who felt inadequate because of the dichotomy between their own reflections and pictures on television or in a magazine.

She picked up the phone and called Jane Baxter.

MARTIN RESISTED THE urge to call Karen again until after he read Morning Prayer at 7:45. After the service Jackie wanted to talk to him about the arrangements for Ash Wednesday, and then he barely had time to grab a cup of coffee before his weekly Bible study group. The discussion ran late, and at ten till twelve he finally found himself alone in his study. When he phoned *Ear to the Ground*, Marjorie told him Karen had not come into the office that morning. She also told him about David's breakdown the night before.

When Martin tried Karen at home again, no one answered. He feared something was wrong. As near as he could tell, David's outburst at the party coincided with his own sudden waking the night before.

By mid-afternoon Martin had arranged for Gareth to take over his duties for the next two days, and he stood on the cold platform awaiting the 3:16 train for New York.

STEVE AND SARAH had an early lunch at a diner a few blocks from Bellevue. As he sat across from her in the booth, he couldn't help thinking about what The Program was doing to thousands of beautiful women like her. He cringed to imagine what Sarah's luscious figure would be reduced to if she were seduced by the false allure of The Program.

But for once, Sarah indulged no such thoughts. She was with a man who smiled at her and laughed with her and held her hand as they walked back towards Bellevue. She longed to pull him into an alley or a doorway and kiss him the way she had on Sunday night, but she settled for a more chaste peck when he said goodbye.

"I'll call you," he said, as so many men had said before; this time, she believed it.

AT THE DOOR of Program Wear Karen found her way blocked by the massive bulk of the security officer. "I'm sorry, Miss," he said, "this is for clients of The Program only."

Karen was just about to deliver a lecture about discrimination based on shape when Louise Crawford slipped past the security officer and intervened.

"Are you Karen Sumner?" she asked.

"You must be Mrs. Crawford," said Karen.

Louise eased Karen a few steps down the sidewalk. "Please, call me Louise," she said. "I'm sorry about all that. I guess they can tell who might be a customer."

"Perfect women?" asked Karen.

"I suppose you could say they are—I mean, we are. Perfect on the outside, anyway."

"I take it you're not pleased with the way you turned out," said Karen.

"Are you kidding? I just spent two hours in a store where everything fits me. Imagine that—everything! I didn't have to suffer the humiliation of finding nothing that would hide my thighs or fit over my hips, or make my bust less—well, less busty. *I'm* extremely pleased. My husband, not so much."

Karen thought about what David had written. "He liked you better before, right?" she asked.

"That's right," said Louise.

"I think your husband and a friend of mine may have something in common."

"What's that?" asked Louise.

"Let's call it a relish for the voluptuous female."

"He likes fat women?" asked Louise.

"Now, Mrs. Crawford," said Karen, "I'm sure you were never a fat woman. Just because you can't fit into clothes designed to look good on nothing bigger than a coat hanger, that doesn't make you fat. It makes you normal." Karen was surprised to find these words coming out of her mouth. She thought Louise's new body looked fabulous, but she seemed to be channeling David.

"If you start writing things like that in your paper, women might think twice before signing up for The Program."

"Do you wish you had thought twice, Mrs. Crawford?" asked Karen.

"I thought about a thousand times. Mostly I worried about the money—what it would do to the family to spend all our savings on something so selfish. But I didn't see it as selfish then. I saw it as this gift I was giving my family. My husband would get a perfectly shaped wife; my kids wouldn't have to be ashamed of their chubby Mom. I actually believed my family would love me more if I looked different. Of course the people at The Program helped me believe that."

"They told you your family would love you more?"

"Not in so many words, but every time I called they would put some woman on the phone who had just been through The Program and she would tell me how wonderful sex with her husband was now, or how the kids wanted her to come have lunch with them at school all of a sudden."

"But it didn't work out that way for you."

"No. And when The Program wouldn't do anything to fix it, I decided I would put the weight back on. You wouldn't believe the way I've been eating, and I haven't gained a pound."

Louise's words sounded positively supernatural. If she was telling the truth, there was something very creepy about The Program, and that could mean one hell of a story.

They stopped at the corner of Fifty-Seventh and Lexington, waiting for an uptown light. Karen, who had been scribbling in her notebook as they walked east, took a long look at Louise Crawford. There it was—that perfect body. Despite all the trouble Louise's new body had caused her, Karen couldn't help being jealous. She couldn't help imagining her own face on that body. Fantasy could be reality for ten thousand dollars.

"I have to ask you," said Karen to Louise, "what exactly do they do to you in The Program?"

"I wanted to tell you," said Louise, "I really did. I mean, there's been all this speculation on late night comedy shows. I thought, if I can tell her what really went on in there, she'll have to print my story. But I just can't remember. It's like the time between when I went in and when I came out didn't even exist. And every time I try to tell somebody what it was like, the same sentence comes out of my mouth."

Karen flipped a few pages in her notebook and said, "We're not really supposed to talk about it, but it's all in the mind."

"Right! How did you know that?"

"You're not the only person who's been through The Program," said Karen, remembering the night she had written what Darcey said about her experience.

"I got an idea, though," said Louise. "I've heard that sometimes people can remember things under hypnosis. So I thought, maybe if we could find someone to hypnotize me—"

"You'd be willing to do that?" Karen asked excitedly.

"Yes," said Louise. "Yes, I would. I told the people at the other papers, but none of them were interested."

"Well, we'd be interested," said Karen, starting across the street as the light changed. For a moment she lost Louise in the crowd, but that was the nature of crossing the street in midtown at lunchtime. She shouldered her way through the oncoming pedestrians when the two groups met in the middle of the wide expanse of Fifty-Seventh Street. When she stepped onto the curb she stopped to find Louise. The other northbound pedestrians surged past her, and in another few seconds, she stood alone by a mailbox.

Karen turned to look for Louise a split second before she heard the bellowing of the bus horn.

Louise stood in the center of one of the westbound lanes, facing an oncoming curtain of traffic that had surged across Lexington. The bus, thought Karen later, must have somehow found an empty lane and a green light—it never could have built up such speed in the width of Lexington Avenue. Karen leapt for the street, instinctively hoping to pull Louise to safety. Instead, she felt a stranger jerk her back to the curb just as a taxi whizzed by in the closest lane. The next two or three seconds seemed to telescope out into minutes of agony—time moved slowly enough for Karen to see that Louise was not completely frozen. She flailed about wildly, her arms spiraling through clouds of exhaust, but her legs and feet never moved.

Afterwards, as she shivered and sobbed on the street corner, replaying that horrifying vision, Karen realized Louise had not been, as most of the casual witnesses reported, frozen on that spot. Louise had not stopped walking in front of an oncoming bus. Her clothes had stopped.

Karen could never explain it satisfactorily to the police, but she knew what she knew. Louise had been halted in the middle of the street by the refusal of her suit and shoes to progress any further.

Karen turned away just before the impact, but she would never forget her final view of Louise's terrified face reflected in the grille of the bus. And there was no escaping the sound. In the midst of the screech-ing of brakes and tires, she heard the unmistakable *thwump* of several tons of bus striking the few remaining pounds of Louise Crawford.

The police report would conclude that the death of Louise Crawford was accidental, and that her progress across the street might have been hindered by her heel catching in a pothole. The reporting officer, however, felt Louise's death was probably the suicidal act of a woman who had spent all her savings to make herself attractive to her husband, only to be rejected. The officer didn't see any point in causing the family further anguish by pursuing this conclusion, so Louise's death was treated not as a suicide that might cast a shadow of controversy on The Program, but as an unfortunate accident.

Karen spent most of the afternoon at the police station, giving her statement. She did not meet Phil Crawford, who arrived at the station just after Karen left, so she was spared the only thing that could have made the day more traumatic—a meeting with Louise's widower. For Karen was convinced she had been the indirect cause of Louise's death—that Louise Crawford had been killed because of what she wanted to tell Karen about The Program. She was equally convinced that the only way to avenge Louise's death was to find out whatever had been covered up by silencing her, and only Karen's journalistic drive to do exactly that kept her from collapsing completely when she emerged into the late afternoon light.

With a trembling lip, but a steely voice, she gave a cab driver the address for *Ear to the Ground*. Only in the cab did she allow herself a long, indulgent sobbing fit. When she arrived outside the offices and saw lights shining from within, she pulled a tissue out of her pocket, blew her nose loudly, wiped her eyes, and hoisted herself onto the sidewalk.

Karen had mastered the ability to push her fragile, emotional self— the Karen with fat arms and low self-esteem—out of the way when hard-nosed journalistic Karen was needed. And it was that second Karen, the Karen who had a story that would put *Ear to the Ground* in the national spotlight, who burst into the offices just as Clifton, Marjorie, and Steve were about to knock off for the day.

"Oh, Karen, good, I'm glad you're here," said Clifton. "I didn't expect you to be gone all afternoon. I want you to write a sidebar for David's article on how he was the subject of one of your homeless profiles and that he's working for us now. You don't have to get too personal or anything. A couple of hundred words should do the trick."

"I'm off," said Steve, pulling on his coat. "I think I might have a lead on Gus's daughter," he said, but Karen seemed unmoved by this piece of intelligence.

"Sit down, everybody," said Karen firmly. "You, too, Steve. Nobody's going anywhere for a while. We need to talk."

"I'm sure it can wait till tomorrow, Karen," said Clifton.

"No," said Karen in a voice so fierce that everyone in the room stopped moving, "it cannot wait until tomorrow. Can murder wait until tomorrow? Can the cold-blooded execution of one of our own informants by a major corporation wait until tomorrow? Can the body of a woman who was only trying to do what was right being splattered all over the front of a cross-town bus wait for tomorrow?" Karen, who had been sharp and composed when she began this speech, trembled as she recalled Louise's death. She slumped into a chair and took several deep breaths, fighting off tears.

"Maybe we can all put off our engagements for a little while," said Clifton.

"I don't see a problem with that," said Steve, who was in no hurry to meet Linda Foretti again, to fend off her advances and question her about her toes.

Slowly, and with many interruptions for questions, Karen told the story of her meeting with Louise Crawford, Louise's decision to undergo hypnosis, her horrible death, and the afternoon with the police.

"If the police ruled the death an accident, we're going to need some pretty solid evidence before we print an article that says otherwise," said Clifton.

"But isn't that what we're all about here?" asked Steve, who could sense the room dividing into two groups—those who believed Karen's story of the supernatural qualities of Louise's clothes and those who did not. Steve, as always, would fight for Karen. "Aren't we supposed to challenge commonly held beliefs? Isn't that the basis of investigative journalism?"

"Sure," said Clifton, "but we don't go to press until we know we're right."

"I'm not saying we need to go to press this week," said Karen, "but we need to investigate. There is something very bizarre going on here."

"I'll grant you that," said Marjorie, "I mean, I'd say Karen was just imagining things if it wasn't for the timing. Louise has just agreed to reveal the best kept secret in American business and—"

"And she's liquidated," said Karen flatly.

"Didn't you leave out part of the story?" asked Steve. "I mean, what was all that last night when David saw Arthur Blackburn on TV?"

"I don't see what that has to do with Louise's death," said Karen defensively. "That was a private matter."

"It has everything to do with Louise's death," said Steve. "I think we've got to assume that Blackburn is involved."

"He's a film producer, Steve," said Karen. "What could he possibly have to do with it?"

Steve waited for someone else to explain the situation to Karen, but when the silent faces of the others only turned back to him he sighed and said, "Don't you people ever read the *Wall Street Journal?* Producing films is a hobby for this guy. Arthur Blackburn is the owner and operator of The Program."

Karen exhaled a short breath that sounded like the whimper of an injured dog.

"So," said Marjorie, "what's the big deal? Who is this guy?"

"The very question I was going to ask," said Clifton, looking at Karen.

"He's the Devil," said Karen softly.

"I beg your pardon," said Clifton.

"He's the Devil," repeated Karen, without altering the quiet, resigned sound of her voice.

"The Devil?" said Marjorie skeptically.

"How many times do I have to repeat it?" shouted Karen, jumping up from her chair and throwing the others back in their seats with the sudden power of her voice. For now she believed it herself. Now Louise's death made sense. "He's the Devil. Satan, the Prince of Darkness, Mephistopheles, the embodiment of all evil. He has a new name now—Arthur Blackburn."

"You have to admit," said Steve, "it makes sense. If you're the Devil and you want to wreak havoc on Earth, you could do a lot worse than to promote a—what did David call it?—an unrealistic ideal of feminine beauty. You destroy the self-esteem of normally shaped women." He tried not to look at Karen as he spoke. "And what's more, you remove from men the pleasure of—well, of the female flesh."

"Those are side effects," murmured Karen, not raising her head. "I'm sure he's pleased about them, but that's just him having fun."

"Well, if that's just fun," said Clifton, "then what's his business?"

"His business," said Karen, who now saw everything clearly, "is the acquisition of souls."

"I think maybe we'd better order in some dinner," said Clifton. "I have a feeling this is going to be a long night."

TWO HOURS LATER Karen had told her co-workers everything David said the night before—everything except his telling her he couldn't be near her.

"Do you realize," said Steve, as he slid another slice of pizza onto his paper plate, "that I was supposed to have a meeting with Linda Foretti tonight?" Clifton glanced at Steve but resisted the impulse to shake his head. He would talk to Steve privately about Linda, not embarrass him in front of the others.

"Who's Linda Foretti?" asked Karen.

"You really *don't* read the *Wall Street Journal*, do you?" said Steve. "Linda Foretti is the owner of Program Wear. She's the first major merchant to reach a marketing deal with The Program, and as a result, she'll probably be a billionaire before too long."

"Do you mean to tell me," said Karen, "that you had an appointment this evening with the woman who sold the clothes that killed

Louise Crawford?"

"Something like that," said Steve.

"What in the world for?"

The room was silent for a moment. Clifton looked away from Steve, pretending to have difficulty opening a can of beer.

"She's an old family friend," said Steve at last, not wanting to reveal the possibility that she might also be the daughter of Gus Doe.

"So," said Karen, "could you use Linda Foretti as a source?"

"It's possible," said Steve.

"Listen," said Clifton, "I don't want you to do anything—anything uncomfortable, Steve. I feel like we've gotten you too deeply involved already. Don't put yourself on the line personally."

"I don't think she's going to tell me much," said Steve. "She certainly won't admit to any involvement in this Crawford woman's death. But maybe I can find out something about her relationship with Blackburn." Steve took a long drink of beer and then added in a soft voice, "The Devil's handmaiden—that would explain a lot."

"Look," said Clifton, "we've got to make a tough decision here. We're talking about pursuing a story that is a direct attack on our biggest advertiser. If we're right, we're firing a shot in the battle against the forces of evil, and we all saw what happened to Louise Crawford when she only threatened to open fire. If we're wrong, we lose our ad contract with The Program, we go out of business, and no self-respecting paper will hire us because we're the people who wrote the story about the Devil running a weight loss clinic."

"Or," said Steve. "If we're right, any price we have to pay is worth unmasking the Prince of Darkness and exposing his work on Earth, and if we're wrong, we're no worse off than we were a month ago. If you ask me, The Program is evil no matter who runs it, and if the job of *Ear to the Ground* is to go where other papers won't, we can do nothing better than attack this guy. The fact that we're doing it with his money is just poetic justice."

"I'm not sure I agree that The Program is evil in and of itself," said Karen. "I mean, I'm sure my self-esteem would be helped if I could lose—" She had been about to say "forty or fifty pounds," but remembered David's article and said, "a few pounds."

"But I believe David," she added, "and if the Devil is running a company on Earth, he can't possibly be up to any good. What difference does it make if he makes women feel better about the way they look, if it costs them their souls to do it? I say it's our responsibility as human beings to go after this guy."

"You know," said Marjorie, "I haven't said a lot this evening, because I'm not sure what to say. I mean, I respect you people, and I love working with you, but what I'm hearing tonight—well, excuse me for being the one to say this, but it just sounds crazy. The Devil is running a weight loss clinic and producing award-winning movies in his spare time. Do you realize how insane that sounds? I'm not saying we should avoid this story because we could all end up as hood ornaments for city buses or because it will run our paper out of business. I think we should avoid it because it will take a serious journalistic endeavor and turn it into a laughing stock. Even if we don't go out of business we'll look like the worst of the tabloids. If I'm anything, I'm loyal, and I love you guys. Whatever you decide, I'll go along, and I'll work my ass off for this story even though I think it's moronic, if that's what you want me to do. But if you ask me," she looked at Clifton, who felt a sheepishness he hadn't known since his last scolding by his mother, "we should drop this story in the trash can where it belongs."

"It's a shame David isn't here to give us his opinion," said Clifton. "He's part of all this."

"I am here," said a voice from the door behind them. Everyone whirled around to see David standing in the open doorway.

Karen wanted to run to him, but his eyes told her to stay away. He pulled the door shut behind him, but did not venture further into the room. "What did you want to ask me?" he said in a low, almost threatening voice.

After quickly explaining their discussion, Clifton said, "So, we're trying to decide whether to pursue this story of Satan incarnate running The Program as a way to acquire women's souls."

David stood silent for a long minute. Finally, he relaxed his stance and stepped far enough into the room to sit on the corner of a desk. "You are a great bunch of people," he said, "and I respect what you do here. And there are a lot of other people out there on the streets who feel the same way. I know it sounds insane to think that a well-respected businessman is the Devil. But unfortunately I've met him face to face. I've been through his temptation, and if you decide to do this story, you may all go through it, too. And it's not an easy thing to resist; it's not a thing I would wish on anyone, least of all my friends."

David looked slowly around the room from one face to another. "This is serious business," he said. "More serious than life or death. We're talking about risking our immortal souls in order to prevent the damnation of innocents. I know that sounds medieval, but if you don't grasp that, if you're not scared to death by the mere thought of doing this story, then you should stay away. Personally, I plan to find a way to go after this guy, but I'm scared shitless. I'm not sure the rest of you are." He looked directly at Karen as he said this. "As far as *Ear to the Ground* getting involved, I'm afraid I have to vote 'no.' If you are crazy enough to do this, I'll help you, but it will have to be in my own way."

"Well," said Clifton after a long pause, "since this seems to be our executive committee, I guess I have the deciding vote. We're all in this together one way or the other, right?"

"Right," answered the room in subdued unison.

"I started this paper with ten thousand dollars I inherited from my grandmother," said Clifton. "She always told me that whatever I did in life, I should try to leave the world a better place than I found it. That was the idea behind *Ear to the Ground*. Karen, you understood that from the start. And even if we haven't been a catalyst for enormous social change, we have helped ordinary people feel better about themselves. And if that's all we ever did, I'd be happy. I'd feel like we'd improved the world a little bit."

Marjorie exhaled a long, slow breath. David stared at a crack in the linoleum tile floor. Steve wrapped a rubber band around his left index finger, then unwrapped it. Karen squelched an urge to run to David.

"But," said Clifton, "Grandma believed in Satan as strongly as she believed the sun would rise every morning, and she'd never forgive me if I missed a chance to strike out at him. I'm not sure whether I believe or not. I am scared, David. I think we all are. But I'm more scared that if we pass this story by, we'll be giving in to something evil without even putting up a fight. So, if you are all with me, I vote 'yes.'"

Again the room fell silent. The traffic had thinned by now, though an occasional passing car or the squealing of tires in the distance reminded them of the outside world. Could it be, thought Karen, that while life went on as usual for the rest of the world, a monumental decision affecting the future of mankind had been made in this room? Could it be that the real history of the world happened like this—in quiet discussions behind closed doors?

"It's happened before," said David, who now appeared serene and composed.

"What has?" asked Steve.

"A few people gathered in a room agreeing to risk their lives to change the world," said David, looking at Karen.

"Is that what we're doing?" asked Steve. "Because if so, I'd like to get started. What do you say we stop waxing philosophical and start doing some investigative journalism."

An hour later they all had their assignments. Karen had fought hard to get hers. None of the men wanted her to do it, but without it, there would be no story. She was the best suited for it in every way, she insisted. Clifton had finally reluctantly agreed.

"We're all going to be called upon to take risks," said Clifton. "Karen has just drawn the first battle assignment."

On the sidewalk outside the office, David approached Karen. "I hope you understand," he said. "It's because I care for you that I have to keep away. But maybe I'll see you at work." Before Karen could respond, he slipped into the shadows.

At least he was alive, she thought, and she would see him again. With a slightly lighter heart, she began the long walk home.

Two hours of sitting on the cold concrete steps outside Karen's apartment had done nothing to alleviate Martin's fears about Karen.

He supposed that he ought to feel foolish, having come all the way to New York just because he had a bad case of insomnia and Karen didn't show up at work on time. But he did not feel foolish as the minutes and hours ticked by, the street darkened, his bones chilled, and still Karen did not arrive.

As other residents of the building came home from work, Martin asked about Karen. No one had seen her. No one even seemed to know her. One young woman asked if Karen was "the chubby girl Georgia used to live with." Martin said he supposed she might be.

"Haven't seen her," the woman said curtly.

KAREN FELT A surge of emotion when she saw Martin standing by her building. She wanted to laugh and sob and hold him and pour out everything that had happened since she had left Braintree. She felt guilty for not keeping in touch with him about David, and she felt desperate for his guidance. When she reached him all she could manage was to throw her arms around him, hold him tight, and whisper, "How did you know?"

"Just had a feeling you might need some company," he said, returning her embrace.

She held him for a long moment, then reluctantly let her arms slide from around him and stepped back to look at his face. "You look freezing," she said. "And I'll bet you could do with some dinner."

STEVE LOOKED ACROSS the table at Linda and wondered how she did it. He had made it through cocktails and had agreed to accompany her to dinner, but she had controlled the conversation, keeping away from the topics he had come to discuss. So how should he begin? He couldn't very well say, "I don't want to have sex with you, but I wondered if you could tell me if your father was a homeless man with six toes, and by the way, are you in business with the Prince of Darkness?"

Between them lay the remains of an appetizer course—a few scraps of smoked salmon and two empty highball glasses. Steve generally stuck to wine at dinner, but when Linda had ordered a Scotch and soda, he decided tonight called for something a little stronger. Now, feeling slightly lightheaded, he tried to prioritize his tasks. Though he had been searching for Gus's daughter for nearly a month and only on the trail of the Devil for a couple of hours, the new assignment seemed more important. In a distant third place was the job of avoiding Linda's sexual advances.

"You know I decided to advertise in your little newspaper after all," she said as she sipped her second glass of wine. "My first ad runs in this week's issue."

"No, actually, I didn't know that," said Steve, wondering why Clifton hadn't mentioned this development, and seeing an opening in the conversation at last. "I suppose you've got a big influx of revenue from your new business partner."

"You mean The Program?"

"It's certainly quite a coup going into business with them," said Steve.

"Steve," said Linda. "Please tell me you didn't call me just to get a story about my silly old clothes shop."

"Of course not," said Steve. "I just felt sort of—well, sort of awkward about—about the end of our last evening together, so I thought we could—put things on a better footing."

"That sounds like a wonderful idea," said Linda, running her toes along Steve's calf.

"You know," said Steve, lightly returning her pressure by pushing his knees closer together, "I couldn't help noticing the other night that—well, I really shouldn't even mention it in the context of a body that's as—as perfect as yours, but I found it intriguing and—well," Steve leaned across the table and whispered, "to be honest, I found it a little sexy—"

"You mean my extra toe?" Linda asked, wiggling all six of her toes against the back of his right knee.

"Yes," he said, twitching involuntarily from ticklishness.

"You think that's sexy, do you?" She ran her tongue around her slightly parted lips.

"Yes, I do," he said. "Is that a family trait or are you—unique?"

"My father has one," she said idly between sips of scotch. "I'm not sure about anyone else."

"So you father's still alive, then?" said Steve. "He must be proud of your success."

"We don't talk much," said Linda.

"I know what you mean," said Steve, feigning exasperation. "I never seem to talk to my father anymore. It's like when he looks at me he still sees this ten-year-old kid. When I was sixteen I started calling him by his first name—Warren this, and Warren that. Boy, did that drive him crazy."

Linda tossed back the last of her second drink and laughed. "I imagine it did," she said. "Your father has always been one to stand on formalities. I'm surprised he didn't make you call him Mr. Collingwood."

"What did you call your dad?" Steve asked nonchalantly.

"Well, one thing's for sure," said Linda, "I certainly never called him Gus."

KAREN FOUND COOKING dinner for Martin and making the sleeping arrangements a welcome distraction from the gravity of recent events. She told Martin most of what had happened in the past day, beginning with David's recognizing Arthur Blackburn on television. Naturally, Martin wanted to help.

"I can offer you friendship and support," he said, "and I can offer you my prayers. But I'd like to do something more concrete."

"Maybe we could use you for deep background," said Karen.

"What do you mean?" asked Martin.

"Well, you're an expert on God and Satan and the Bible."

"I'm not sure I'd call myself an expert."

"You know a lot more than I do," said Karen, "and I'll bet you know a lot more than Steve or Clifton or Marjorie. David has met the Devil, but you know about the Devil's history, Lucifer being thrown out of heaven and all that. If we're going to defeat him, we need to know as much about him as possible."

"So I'm military intelligence?" asked Martin.

"Something like that," said Karen. "Maybe we should call you our special advisor on religious affairs. Just find out everything you can about the Devil."

"I guess that means I go home and read," said Martin gloomily. He had hoped for a more active part in the campaign. He knew, however, that God had called him for a specific part in this battle, and if his role was to learn and to advise, so be it.

Karen and Martin shared a simple dinner, and by ten o'clock she felt her eyes drooping. Martin insisted that Karen take the bed, and she apologized for not staying up longer.

"I didn't get much sleep last night," she yawned. Karen usually lay awake for a half hour or so, digesting the events of her day, but tonight, despite the monumental nature of the past twenty-four hours, she fell almost instantly into a dreamless sleep.

Martin sat in the chair by the window, reading the Bible until deep into the night.

THE GLOW FROM Linda's fireplace flickered off her pale skin. Steve had accompanied her home out of driving curiosity. He had tried to turn the dinner discussion back to The Program, but every time he brought it up they ended up discussing women's bodies, not satanic business partners.

As the scotch flowed and Steve became less circumspect, he gradually described to Linda his ideal female body. Sober, he would never have sung such praises to Linda's rejected former form, but the restaurant had taken on a softness and Linda's body had become blurred around the edges and it seemed right to be frank with her.

Nor did she discourage him. On the contrary, whenever he praised a full bosom or a curving hip, she nodded her hazy head. "I know," she would say in a voice that was the aural equivalent of voluptuous. "Flesh is so sexy, isn't it?"

But it was not Linda's conversation that had piqued Steve's curiosity to the point that he was willing to return to her lair, nor was it only that his own inebriation had weakened any resistance he might have mounted. What caused Steve to slip into the back of Linda's black Lincoln Town Car, and to lay a hand softly on her thigh, was the fact that the more they spoke of curves and bulges and full-figured women, the more Linda seemed to take on that form.

Steve was just drunk enough not to question the transformation that took place in the chair opposite him. He assumed it must all be in his mind—after all, her clothes still fit, and no one could go from post-Program gaunt to Rubenesque while a single dinner progressed from entrée to dessert. Yet the woman who led Steve out of the restaurant sashayed wide hips in front of him, and jiggled bounteous breasts beneath her blouse. But for her face, in fact, she was a perfect replica of Karen, and Steve's forgotten desire for Karen surged within him.

Now he gazed upon the woman who had so repelled him on their previous date and who now sprawled her generous naked body across the bearskin rug that had haunted his dreams of a month ago. Linda the waif had vanished, replaced by a bounteous Linda whose curvaceous flesh had a powerful effect on Steve. Though there was no advertising contract on the line and no business to save, Steve let himself succumb to Linda's tempting pleasures.

He slowly untied his tie and unbuttoned his shirt, never letting his eyes leave Linda, but tracing with his gaze the outlines of her pale flesh—the spread of her rear where her weight pressed it against the rug; her breasts which, though they had slid to her sides as she reclined, were yet firm enough to withstand the full effects of gravity; the padding of her hips that he could already feel his fingers sinking into.

Steve felt himself swell harder, and in another moment he was lying on the rug beside her, letting her enfold him in flesh. To resist the temptation never even crossed his mind; he only thought that here, at last, was a perfect woman.

CLIFTON SLEPT FITFULLY. He wondered if he ought to call the staff together tomorrow and tell them "never mind." Each time he closed his eyes he saw the man who had tempted David by the prison fence. Even though he had seen Philip Blackburn on television, his memory of the face was indistinct, as if it remained hidden in the shadow of that broad-brimmed hat. Clifton asked himself over and over if he really wanted that face made clear.

Any doubt he had about David's story or about Louise Crawford's death or about the true nature of The Program dissolved as the night wore on. He could think only of the shadowy face, and he knew that the horror lurking behind those eyes was real.

IN THE FADING light of the dying fire, Steve made slow, luxurious love to the transfigured Linda. He loved placing a hand on the space between her shoulder blades and feeling soft resilience. He loved grabbing at her arms and having the flesh slip teasingly through his fingers. When she was on top he loved the weight of her pressing down on him, the supple folds above her hips, the heavenly fullness of her breasts, the luscious flesh of her thighs. Undulations rippled through her like waves on a pond, with his vigorous thrusting the pebble dropped at the center of the growing maelstrom.

When he finally exploded inside her he had no idea what piece of godly flesh his hands gripped, only that they were filled to overflowing with the unmistakable feel of womanhood. And in that moment of climax he bit his tongue to keep from crying Karen's name, for even Linda's face now looked like the round and rosy face of Karen Sumner.

Lying on the rug afterwards, feeling the warmth radiate from the fire and from Linda's body, Steve juggled guilt and ecstasy in his mind. He could not be unfaithful to either Karen or Sarah, since he had only a business relationship with one and had been on only three dates with the other. And could he really betray Karen by sleeping with her replica? Or was that the deepest sort of betrayal—to make love to Karen without her even knowing it? Was it tantamount to the rape of an unconscious woman?

But he had not made love to Karen; he had made love to Linda. Sordid as that may have been, it had nothing to do with Karen. However confused he felt about the morality of what he had done, he had no doubt about the physical satisfaction he had drawn from the encounter. It was as if the body to which he made love sensed his every desire and transformed itself by the second to conform to his ideal. Though his mind may have been torn, his body felt no such qualms.

"Goodness," said Linda, as they lay on their backs panting, "I'd say that was a successful test of our new product."

"What do you mean?" said Steve.

"You know The Program uses the power of a woman's mind to change the shape of her body, right?"

"I suppose I knew it worked something like that," said Steve, wishing he had the—the stamina to roll back towards her and continue his exploration of her body.

"Well, soon we're going to introduce The Program for Men. It works basically the same way, except the woman can transform her Programmed body into whatever her man desires. She can look like a movie star, and I mean a specific movie star, or the next-door neighbor, or her eighteen-year-old self—whatever gets him hot." Linda slipped her slim fingers into Steve's hand where it lay on the rug. "And it sure got you hot," she giggled.

"So you—" Steve let his words die in the air, not sure exactly what he wanted to ask.

"I used the power of my mind to transform my body into one you were desperate to make love to. Tell me, was I a specific person, or just your sexual ideal?"

Steve turned and saw the gaunt Linda lying beside him. The breasts and hips, the curves and bulges, the soft folds and tempting creases of flesh had all disappeared. Yet the memory of the other Linda, the Karen-shaped Linda, still lingered.

"I guess you were just my fantasy woman," Steve lied. "Someone I conjured up out of adolescent dreams."

Linda sighed and pulled his hand to her, placing his palm on her hard, flat stomach. "That's funny," she cooed, "because I really had the feeling I was someone you knew."

"A friend of mine knew this woman Louise Crawford," said Steve, eager to change the subject. "It's too bad she didn't know about this—this product."

"I gather complaints like hers were part of the inspiration," said Linda. "The Program really does make an effort to achieve total customer satisfaction. Louise just wasn't patient enough."

How did Linda know about Louise? Steve wondered. Suddenly the scales fell from his eyes. He stared down at Linda's six toes and felt a churning in his stomach. He had just made love to a woman who was in league with the Devil, a woman who had left her own father to die on the streets, who had helped murder an innocent housewife.

And yet, he knew that if she transformed back into Karen an hour from now, he would not be able to resist—he would gladly dive once more into her flesh. It had been a very successful test indeed.

K aren stood on the sidewalk outside the blue and gold door to The Program fingering the check in her pocket. Unlike Louise Crawford, Karen had no doubt she would step forward and allow the hulking uniformed doorman to pull that door open and that she would pass into the semi-darkness she had glimpsed a moment ago. She merely wanted a moment to compose herself, to review her plan of action. The doorman would mistake her immobility for the hesitation he had seen in thousands of women, almost all of whom eventually entered the building.

She had tested her equipment several times that morning, and everything seemed in perfect working order. Marjorie had outfitted her well. She didn't know exactly what to expect behind the door of The Program, but she did know from Louise that she would be asked to sign a contract. A contract that over a million women had signed, and yet no copy of which had apparently left the offices of The Program.

Pulling Clifton's check from her pocket, Karen stepped towards the door. In perfect synchronization with her movements, the doorman pulled the door open in front of her and she stepped in.

She found herself in an elegantly appointed waiting room—overstuffed leather chairs, a plush blue and gold carpet with an interlocking T and P design woven into it, and oversized photographs of fashion models on the walls, lit by narrow spotlights recessed in the ceiling. Karen spotted the image of Celinda she had so often compared to her own body. The other women who graced the walls were of similar form and allure. Beneath each framed photograph was a small gold plaque with the woman's name and the caption "Graduate of The Program."

At one end of the room a woman who might have been Celinda's twin sister sat behind a wide antique table, empty except for a single black telephone. She wore a snug black dress of the type Karen had always admired and never been able to wear.

"Good morning," said the woman in a voice as soft as the surroundings. "Welcome to The Program. If I can have your name, I'll be able to send you right in. And," she added, winking conspiratorially, "by lunch time you'll look just like me."

Karen felt her pulse quicken, and for just a moment, caught up in the wink and the smile from the type of woman who usually huffed at her on the sidewalk or elbowed her on the subway, she forgot the true nature of her excursion into The Program and pictured herself looking stunning in a petite black dress held up by spaghetti straps. She imagined, as she looked at the smiling woman behind the table, that she was looking into a mirror, that she was experiencing her first view of her new, thin body.

Karen could see those narrow shoulders as her own, could envision a closet emptied of bulky sweaters, baggy blouses, and elastic-waist pants. She could feel her chest relieved of the weight of her breasts, feel the muscles that had labored for so many years to support them suddenly relax. She reached up a hand to feel the marvelous smoothness of her front, imagining the straight journey it would take as she ran a flat palm from her neck to her crotch. Only when she encountered first the bulk of her overcoat and then the exaggerated curve of her oversized breasts did she return to the world of the waiting room, where the thin woman still smiled at her and asked for her name.

"Karen Sumner," said Karen, meekly.

"May we call you Karen?" asked the woman, "We like to keep everything informal here at The Program."

"Yes, certainly," said Karen.

The woman picked up the phone, which had no buttons on it. "Karen is here," she said, in a tone of voice that implied the person on the other end had been eagerly awaiting Karen's arrival all morning. After a brief pause the receptionist hung up and smiled again. "They're all ready for you, Karen," she said. A door hidden in the wall behind the woman swung smoothly open revealing a long, dim hallway. "You can go right in."

As Karen walked slowly past her, the woman put a delicate hand on her arm. "We're so glad you're here," she whispered. "It's going to change your life, I promise."

Karen walked down the long, narrow hall. On the walls hung more pictures of Program graduates. The hall was warm, and Karen shed her coat as she walked.

With pictures of Programmed bodies assaulting her from every side, she felt fatter than ever. She was so wide, she could hardly fit through the hallway without brushing a hip against the lower edge of a picture frame. *At least no one can see me,* she thought. *Not yet.*

She cringed at the thought of the impending embarrassment of her next encounter with a human being, doubtless a thin human being who would be repulsed by the bulges and rolls of her fat. When she reached the door at the end of the hallway, her sweaty palm slipped on the knob twice before she finally turned it and pushed open the door. To her shame, she had to turn sideways to fit through.

The room into which she passed was similar to the reception area—high ceilinged and carpeted in the same blue and gold. A pair of large armchairs stood in one corner. One wall was completely filled by a vast video screen, and the opposite wall by a mirror.

A handsome and muscular young man sat in one of the armchairs, holding a clipboard. His blonde hair was combed carelessly to one side. His button-down shirt, which he wore without a tie, seemed incapable of containing the massive muscles of his neck and shoulders. Every inch of skin he showed—his face and neck and hands, even a strip of flesh above his ankle she glimpsed when he crossed his legs—was tanned a deep bronze.

Karen had seen his type on infomercials for weight loss or fitness products. Men just like him had smiled at her while calling out aerobics instructions on videotape or demonstrating tummy-toning machines on late-night television. She had never met such a man in the flesh. He looked up when she came in the door and smiled broadly.

"Hello, Karen," he said. "Welcome to The Program."

Karen could not look at him without seeing her reflection in the wall-sized mirror. What she saw horrified her.

In her bathroom mirror at home, she only saw the upper half of her body, and she usually looked at herself in the mirror naked—the better to compare herself with the nearly nude Celinda. Now she could see her entire body staring back at her, and the way her clothes attempted to restrain her corpulence only served to emphasize the volume of unnecessary and unattractive flesh that padded her every inch.

I must be getting fatter, she thought. *I'm a fat pig.* She tried to remember the last time she had weighed herself, but could not.

"My name is Brad," said the perfect young man, offering a hand to Karen. "Why don't you have a seat?"

Karen felt a pang of dread as she looked at the empty chair. *When I sit down,* she thought, *I won't be able to see that monstrosity in the mirror. But can I fit my—my fat ass into that chair?*

Brad took no notice of her hesitation, and only scribbled on his clipboard while he waited for her to sit. Biting her lip, Karen placed her hands on the wide arms of the chair and began to lower herself. She felt the arms brush against her hips, but managed to wedge herself into the seat.

"I'm here to make sure The Program is right for you," said Brad. "What I'd like to do is show you a computer model of how you look now, and what you'll look like after The Program."

He riveted his dark blue eyes to Karen's as he spoke, which she found unnerving, but she couldn't find any place to turn her gaze. She was afraid if she looked away, she might catch a glimpse of that mirror again.

"Now, I don't want you to be embarrassed as we watch these images, Karen. Remember, I'm a qualified Program technician, and I've seen thousands of these pictures before. While you were walking down our entrance hall, we used a variety of sensors and scanners to create a computer model of your body. Then we ran that model through our special software to show you what The Program will do for your body. So," he said, finally breaking contact with Karen's eyes and turning his attention to the video screen, "are we ready?"

Karen swallowed hard, wishing they could skip the "before" picture and go straight to the "after."

"Yes," she said, "as ready as I'll ever be."

THE PROGRAM

Marjorie spent the morning roaming the Internet looking for accounts of women who had been through The Program and subsequently suffered accidental death. She found six. Considering that a million women had participated in The Program, this did not seem an inordinate number. She wondered, though, how many she did *not* find?

How many obituaries neglected to mention the deceased's enrolling in The Program? It hardly seemed the sort of information likely to crop up in articles about deadly accidents.

What disturbed Marjorie was not the number of deaths, but their nature. None were commonplace accidents like automobile crashes or house fires. Four of the articles actually used the term "freak accident."

One woman was killed skydiving when her parachute failed to open. Afterwards it was found to be in perfect working order. One, whom family and neighbors described as "obsessively careful," got her hand caught in a garbage disposal and bled to death. One was working in her garden when her husband's truck rolled into her. The investigation revealed that the parking brake was engaged and the truck was in park. One drowned in a backyard wading pool while her toddler played beside her.

The two most recent deaths bothered Marjorie the most. Two women had been killed, like Louise Crawford, when they failed to step out of the way of moving traffic.

She stared at the last of these accounts for several minutes, reading the words over and over.

…was killed when she stopped walking in the middle of Maple Avenue and stood in the way of an oncoming truck.
"She seemed to be struggling," said one witness, "like her feet were stuck to the pavement."
Police have ruled the death accidental.

Marjorie had not expected to find any evidence supporting the inane premise of the story she was helping with, but even she could not dismiss as coincidence the similarities between this story and Karen's account of Louise's death.

She made careful notes on each of the articles, and steeled herself for the job of phoning survivors to ask if the wife or mother or sister or daughter had been dissatisfied with The Program.

KAREN SAT MESMERIZED by the larger than life images that filled the wall opposite her.

Slightly more than half the wall was devoted to the current Karen. She wore a flesh colored bikini, but otherwise everything in the picture was painfully familiar. Her body stood with feet together and hands slightly lifted from her sides. The entire image rotated slowly so no bulge, no deposit of cellulite, no unsightly roll of fat or slack bit of flab could hide. Her breasts overflowed the cups of the bikini top, and her thighs spread instantly on emerging from the elastic bands of the bottom. After the image had rotated three or four times, the screen zoomed in and surveyed the lumpy landscape of Karen's flesh in detail—the slackness in her upper arms, the emerging double chin, the fleshy expanse of her back. On and on the tour continued, like some aerial exploration of a hostile environment.

Next to this image was a narrower screen displaying the future Karen, Karen after The Program. As Karen's current body rotated, her new body rotated. As the screen zoomed in on Karen's imperfections, the adjacent image provided an identical tour of her future landscape. This Karen was also dressed in a flesh colored bikini, but no flesh swelled from the top of the cups or from beneath the elastic of the legs. The journey up her potential legs was a glorious exploration of the smooth and the slim. Her torso was so flat that only the thin fabric of the bathing suit varied its plane. Lightly outlined in the skin of her chest was each delicate rib. Karen imagined a breeze must be blowing through the pictures, for while goose-bumps appeared on the saggy arms of the old Karen, the new Karen tossed her head back and let her shining hair flutter behind her, while her stiffening nipples pressed through the fabric of her top.

The point of view changed once again, and now the two images mirrored each other in a series of simple movements. Karen tried to imagine what it would feel like to run her new, streamlined hand down the smooth line of her new side. The Karens in front of her each performed this motion, and she was all too familiar with the circuitous route the hand of the left-hand figure took from her shoulder to her knee. At the same time, she could almost feel in her outstretched palm the smooth sweep of motion made by the right-hand Karen—like skimming the glassy surface of an undisturbed lake.

Each Karen leaned over to touch her toes. One was unable to bend completely at the waist because of the aggregation of flesh at her center. The other folded in half as easily as a pocketknife.

As the bodies moved through one exercise after another, Karen found her eyes drawn more and more to the new Karen, the Karen she could be by mid-afternoon. There was her face, without its puffiness, without the double chin or the round cheeks, but still unmistakably her own face. And there, below it, the body she'd always dreamed of.

How could Phil Crawford have been dissatisfied with this? Didn't men dream of women like this? Super-models, movie stars, all society's sex symbols were shaped like the new Karen. Didn't David dream of women like this? Sure, he wrote with eloquence of the antiquated ideals of womanhood, but hadn't David really written that article for one reason and one reason only—to seduce a fat woman?

If David saw the new Karen, the slim Karen, he would change his tune in a second. He would forget all about his attack on The Program (which, after all, was providing a public service to women and men), and he'd revel in the good fortune of having a perfect woman to love.

Karen felt herself getting wet at the thought of sex with her new body, of how David would worship every smooth, straight, taut, tight inch of her. She had a check in her pocket. In three hours she could have her perfect body in bed with David and they could forget all their idiotic ideas about the Devil.

When the images on the screens faded to blackness, the lights in the room came on and Karen blushed deeply at the thought that Brad now saw the old Karen, for she had already come to think of herself as the perfect woman. In the harsh florescent lights she appeared anything but.

"Well," said Brad, "what do you think? Can we tempt you into joining The Program?"

"You know," Karen said after a short pause, "I'm running a movie in my head, a movie of my life. Only this time I'm the thin girl instead of the fat girl. It's amazing how much changes. My father stays, my mother lives, my classmates like me—"

"It can change your life—forever," said Brad. "Shall we go into the next room and take care of the paperwork?"

"Sure," said Karen, hearing the voice of her father saying, "Of course I could never leave such a perfect little child."

Brad offered Karen a seat in a metal folding chair on one side of a Formica table. The room into which they had passed was tiled with linoleum on the floor, and the barren walls were painted a sickly color of pale green. Eager to return to the plush world of the perfect woman, Karen pulled the check from her pocket and laid it on the table.

"Now," said Brad, "I'd like for you to look over this contract and sign your name at the bottom of the page. Then we'll take you back to the heart of The Program, and by this afternoon you'll look just like that woman on the video screen."

He pushed a single sheet of yellow paper and a ballpoint pen across the table to her. "It's really just a formality," he said, smiling. "Most clients don't even read the thing."

Karen's eagerness to get on with The Program, to inhabit her glorious new body, was not quite sufficient to overcome her habit of always reading before she signed her name. She supposed afterwards that the strength of that habit was what saved her.

The first few paragraphs were worded in an impenetrable legalese that would have discouraged most readers from going further. As she skimmed the words, Karen's mind was distracted, for an instant, from its obsession with her new body, and in that instant she heard two voices. The first was Brad saying, "Can we tempt you into joining The Program?" The other was David reciting his cellmate Charlie's evening incantation, "Lead us not into temptation; Lead us not into temptation."

My God, thought Karen, careful not to alter her expression, *that's what this is. This is temptation.*

She looked at the pen in her hand poised over the paper and realized how close she had come. She didn't dare lift her eyes to Brad, but she lay the pen down and leaned back in her chair, picking the contract up off the table and holding it in front of her.

Marjorie had outfitted Karen with three silent spy cameras. One was disguised as a button on her shirt and could be operated by flexing her right big toe, one was built into a pair of glasses she had almost forgotten she was wearing, and the third was in a pen in her purse. As she held the contract in front of her, she snapped several exposures through her button. She then laid the document back on the table and looked at Brad with a coquettish smile.

"I guess I don't really need to read the whole thing," she said. "I probably wouldn't understand it anyway."

She reached for the pen on the table and knocked it to the floor. "It's OK," she said as Brad bent to retrieve the stray pen, "I have my own." Karen snapped several more photographs of the contract with her pen before Brad stood back up.

"On the bottom line," said Brad. "The other line is for me to sign as witness."

"And what if I decide not to sign?" said Karen, returning the pen to her purse. "What if I decide I don't want to do it? Or I decide I don't want to do it right now?"

"You're perfectly free to back out before signing," said Brad. "If you want to give up that perfect body, no one is going to stop you. I've known a few to get cold feet. Of course they usually come back in a day or two."

"It's just such a big step," said Karen, trying to exude an air of uncertainty.

"It is," said Brad. He smiled at her. "People will never look at you the same way again."

Karen fought back a renewed urge to sign her name as she remembered how people had always looked at her. "I guess—I guess I'm not quite ready yet," she said, sliding the contract back across the table. "I just need a little time to get used to the idea."

She picked up the check and folded it in half, slipping it into her pocket. "I'm sure I'll be back in a few days. Can I ask for you, Brad?" She batted her eyelids at him slightly.

"Of course," said Brad. "I'll be waiting for you. And please don't worry about delaying. It takes time to get used to the idea of not being—well, of being a perfect woman."

"Exactly," said Karen. "I'll see you in a few days. And thank you, Brad. Thank you for everything."

CLIFTON HAD ASKED David to escort Karen back to the office after she photographed the contract. "Don't tell her," Clifton said, "just be there." So David had followed her at a safe distance and watched as she disappeared through the blue and gold door.

After only a few minutes of waiting, he began to suspect that clients never came out the front door. He saw a dozen women in a variety of shapely forms enter through the blue and gold door, but no one emerged. When he walked around to the Madison Avenue side of the building, however, he saw two unmarked gray metal doors. From one issued, at intervals of about two minutes, a stream of Programmed women—dazed-looking ultra-thin waifs. The other door remained shut.

David knew how to disappear in midtown. He slouched in the doorway that never opened, sipping tepid coffee from a blue Styrofoam cup and mumbling. No one paid him the slightest notice.

BRAD SHOWED KAREN into another long hallway with the same carpet and photographs that seemed to be a hallmark of The Program. "The exit is to your right at the end of the hall," he said. "I do hope you'll come back. I don't know about you, but I quite enjoyed what I saw of the new Karen." He winked at her and disappeared as the door swung closed between them.

She made her way down the hall, thinking it must be narrower than the previous one. *I know I'm not any wider than I was an hour ago,* she thought. Again she had to turn herself sideways when she reached the exit.

She pushed against the door, which opened only enough to let a sliver of bright daylight into the pale fluorescence of the hallway. Karen did not want to draw attention to herself now, when she had nearly made her escape. *What if they know already?* she thought. *What if they're keeping the door closed to catch me?*

Her palms turned clammy, and a bead of sweat trickled down her nose. *At least I have some weight to throw against it,* she thought. She backed up slightly, pushed down on the bar that unlatched the door, and hurled her body against the barrier.

"Ow!" she heard a muffled voice cry from the other side, just as the pain in her shoulder caused her to say the same thing. In another second the door flung the rest of the way open and there stood David, rubbing his shoulder.

"You could have knocked," he said. "I would have let you out."

M artin had spent his morning in the cluttered office of the Rev. Donald Hodges, professor emeritus of Union Theological Seminary.

During Martin's years as a seminarian, Father Donald was something of a legend. Rumors about his participation in exorcisms and other bizarre medieval rituals abounded, though none was ever supported by evidence. In those days Father Donald still taught an annual course, outside the required curriculum, called "Archaic Rites of the Christian Church."

With a day in New York to discover ways to defeat the Devil, a visit with Father Donald seemed an efficient use of time.

His office was filled with books and papers from floor to ceiling. Only a small pathway that wound from the door to his desk was free, and even that was being encroached upon by stacks of ancient looking leather-bound volumes. Not until he had rounded two of these obstacles did Martin see a face to go with the voice that had bid him enter when he knocked on the door.

Father Donald's face was as obscured as the floor of his office. A shaggy gray beard covered all but his bulbous nose and thin lips. His forehead and eyes hid behind a mop of hair.

"Forgive me if I don't get up," said Father Donald in a growl. "Rather in the middle of something."

His voice sounded as medieval as the rituals he studied, like the groaning of an ancient doorway opening against its will.

"And you'll forgive me if I don't sit down," said Martin with a laugh. There was no surface on which he could possibly have sat, nor had there ever been on his frequent visits to Father Donald's office as a student. This had become a running joke between them.

"Martin Stewart, bless me, I didn't recognize you. How are you, my son?"

"I'm well, Father," said Martin.

"Well you can't be too well," said Father Donald, lowering his voice, "or you wouldn't be here. People don't come to me for gardening advice."

"You won't believe me."

"I've believed more unlikely prophets than you, Martin."

Martin decided it was best to dive right in. "Some friends of mine believe Satan has become incarnate as a human being, and they want me to help defeat him."

"I had a feeling he was back," said Father Donald flatly. "What's he up to?"

Martin paused to consider how ridiculous it sounded. No more ridiculous, he decided, than the Son of God working as a cabinetmaker. "He's running a weight loss program headquartered here in New York," he said.

"Saint Cuthbert said, 'Do not let the Devil distract you with foolish worries, for he has a thousand crafty ways of harming you.' Looks like your friends have discovered number one thousand and one."

"Do you have any suggestions?" asked Martin.

"Well," said Father Donald, running his fingers through his beard, "Cuthbert believed prayer was the best way to banish the Devil. But a more contemporary tempter may demand more contemporary countermeasures."

"Like what?" asked Martin.

"What is the weakness of the Devil incarnate?"

"I was hoping you could tell me."

"You were my student, weren't you?" said Father Donald, suddenly digging through a stack of papers on his desk as if he were looking for the old grade book that would offer evidence of Martin's previous knowledge. "Surely you haven't forgotten everything we talked about."

"Not everything, I hope," said Martin.

"Lucifer was a former resident of—?"

"Of heaven," said Martin tentatively.

"Correct. He was of heaven and subject to the laws of heaven even after his fall. So you say he is now incarnate as a man. Who else do we know who was the human incarnation of a heavenly spirit?"

"Well, Christ, of course," said Martin.

"Two marks for Rev. Stewart. Now, what was Christ's weakness during his human incarnation?"

"Well," said Martin, feeling as if he were back in school, "he was subject to the weaknesses inherent in humanity. He was subject to temptation."

"Ah, but he resisted the temptation of Satan himself, didn't he? Not an easy task for most humans, though I know a few who have done it."

"Yes," whispered Martin, thinking of David. "So do I."

"So what was Christ subject to that made him susceptible as a human being—not temptation, not even human sin—"

Father Donald used his prompting voice, but Martin could drag no tidbit back from his studies that would answer the question. Christ had been all God, and as thus susceptible to none of the dangers of humanity, yet at the same time he had been all man, and susceptible to all of them. It was the mystery of the incarnation, but he sensed Father Donald was fishing for a simpler answer.

"I'm afraid I don't know," said Martin.

"Quite simply, as a human being, he was subject to the laws of the Roman Empire, an empire whose jurisdiction eventually put him to death."

"But he overcame that death."

"Yes," said Father Martin, "but that doesn't change the fact that he was subject to human laws and human political jurisdiction."

"So if Satan has turned himself into a man," said Martin slowly, "then he's subject to the laws of man."

"He's subject to the laws of the City and State of New York and of the United States of America. You just need to get him convicted of something."

KAREN HAD FELT a surge of relief to see a familiar face outside The Program. Not only would she not have to return to the office alone, but she would get to spend some time with David. Now they sat in the middle of Washington Square Park eating sandwiches. David had let Karen walk in silence, sensing she needed to get well away from the offices of The Program before she talked about what had happened inside. He had made sure her cameras were in working order, though, and that the film had advanced properly. After lunch they would stop by a special lab that could process the miniature film.

"Can you talk about it?" he finally asked her after they had scattered the remains of their sandwiches among the eager pigeons.

"Have you ever had surgery?" she asked

"No," said David. "I thought their ads said there was no surgery involved."

"It's not that," said Karen. "When I was seventeen I had my wisdom teeth out. The doctor said I would be awake for the surgery, that he would just give me a local anesthetic and something to make me a little loopy, but I'd be aware the whole time. I looked at the clock on the wall and it said eight o'clock, and I breathed in this loopy gas and looked right back up and it was nine thirty. It was like that hour and a half just vanished.

"That's what it was like this morning. I remember the feel of the doorman's coat as I brushed past it when I walked in the front door, and then I was out on the sidewalk with you. I just hope the camera can remember what happened."

AT QUARTER TILL two, the offices of *Ear to the Ground* were occupied only by Clifton, who was reviewing Marjorie's layout, and Marjorie herself, who made small changes on each page spread after Clifton returned the proofs. The layout was due at the printer by three o'clock.

Clifton read through David's article one last time. He had rejected Marjorie's suggestion that the end of the piece be placed opposite the advertisement for The Program. "I think we can temper our rebelliousness a little bit," he said. He decided to pull the cartoon, too. He thought it might be overplaying their hand to run that caption, "The Devil made me do it."

The full-page advertisement for The Program that would run on page three featured a picture of Lucinda Wilson, in the daringly cut gown she had worn to the Golden Globes ceremonies. The caption read "Lucinda Wilson: Unknown in January, Graduates from The Program in February, Wins Golden Globe for Best Actress the following January. Congratulations!" Below that, in much larger type, was the usual slogan, "Get With The Program."

As he looked over the proof, Clifton imagined how much fun it would be to run a nearly identical advertisement opposite—a picture of Anna Camello, her ample cleavage revealed by a low cut gown. She would be eating a huge chocolate chip cookie, and the caption would read: "Anna Camello: Voluptuous, Full-Figured Actress in December, Overlooked by the Critics in January. And she's still just as sexy. Congratulations!" And below, in giant type, "Screw The Program." *If only*, he thought.

At five till two Clifton finished going over the proofs and Marjorie e-mailed the final paste-up to the printer. "An hour early this week," she said. "That should surprise them."

She had not told Clifton or anyone else about the other mysterious deaths among Program graduates she had uncovered, nor did she plan to before she had more information. Surely there were reasonable explanations. Surely out of a million people, a few are bound to die under mysterious circumstances every year.

"I'm surprised Karen and David aren't back," said Clifton nervously. "I hope everything went OK." He looked down at his watch and then up at the clock on the wall. It was one fifty-nine.

He stood up, pulled his pipe out of his jacket pocket, and began to tamp it full of tobacco. As he did so, he swayed, shuffled his feet, and stared at the front door.

Marjorie sighed, pulled out her notebook, picked up the phone, and called the husband of the woman whose parachute hadn't opened. As the phone rang on the other end, she followed the second hand of the clock as it swept towards two o'clock. One ring. Two rings. Three rings. One more and the answering machine would probably pick up. As the fourth ring began, she heard a man's voice say, "Hello."

Clifton flicked his lighter just as the second hand reached twelve.

"I DIDN'T EXPECT to see you guys here," said Steve, parting the pigeons as he strode towards the park bench where he had spotted David and Karen. "How did it go this morning?"

"We don't really know," said David.

"You don't know how it went?" asked Steve, plopping down on the end of the bench and pulling a sandwich from a brown paper bag.

"I can't remember anything," said Karen glumly. "I guess they must—brainwash you or something before you leave."

"Not surprised," said Steve through a mouthful of sandwich. "You got the pictures, though?"

"I'm pretty sure," said Karen. "I guess we'll find out when we get them back from the lab."

"What brings you here?" said David.

"Just felt like walking," said Steve. "Got off at Union Square." Steve tried to make this decision seem like the carefree whim of one who simply wanted to enjoy the sun of a warm winter day, but in fact he had felt driven above ground. The subway had seemed altogether too close to hell, and burning with guilt from his seduction the night before, he had fled the underworld. He had almost avoided Karen and David when he spotted them on the bench, still not sure how he could explain what had happened last night, but he was afraid they might see him slinking off, and then what would he say?

And how *would* he explain last night? He had to tell them, had to tell everyone. It was a significant break in the story, and a major scoop. He should have called Clifton last night, he knew. They could have gone to press with the story in this week's edition and scooped the rest of the papers for sure.

But he couldn't muster the courage to pick up the phone. Instead, he had just stood under the shower from midnight until two. That was one nice thing about dormitories—they never ran out of hot water. Now, with only an hour before the paper was due at the printer, there was no question of breaking the story this week. So no hurry in telling anyone. Certainly no hurry in telling Karen.

"You headed to the office?" said Steve.

"Yeah," said David. "I promised Clifton I'd get Karen back in one piece. We've got to drop off this film on the way."

BY TEN TILL two, Martin had been sequestered for three hours in a corner of the reading room of the Public Library with a pile of texts relating to alleged sightings of the Devil in human form over the centuries. After his conversation with Father Donald, he wanted nothing so much as a long session with a good lawyer. He planned to call Darcey as soon as he got back home. Meanwhile, he thought he'd look for precedent of another kind, but his search had yielded little.

Accounts of Satan walking the Earth were unsubstantiated, and details of a single supposed incarnation differed widely from one source to another. In no case did humans use anything as simple as the criminal justice system to defeat the Prince of Darkness. Strange rites and even human sacrifices, but no court cases—unless you counted witch trials, but those women were only accused of serving the Devil, not being him.

When he glanced up and saw the hour hand creeping towards two, Martin decided to give up his work and head over to *Ear to the Ground*. Maybe Karen would be back. He had reserved a seat on the five-fifteen from Grand Central Station, and he wanted to report to Karen and Clifton in person before he left.

He returned his books to the circulation desk, pulled on his overcoat and walked through the ornate marble lobby and into the winter sunshine. As he walked down the wide stone steps and past the great lions that guarded the entrance to that palace of knowledge, a clock inside chimed two o'clock.

DAVID, KAREN AND Steve were close enough to hear the explosion, although in a city of incessant loud noises they paid it no mind. Only afterwards did they realize what they had heard. "I felt it in my chest," David would say, "but in New York you feel things in your chest all the time."

Martin did not hear it, or at least he could not remember hearing it. He later calculated that he must have been leaving the library at two o'clock, but he could not recall any noise beyond the traffic on Fifth Avenue and a jackhammer on Forty-Second Street. He would lay awake for several nights playing those moments over in his head and listening to every sound—the swish of the brush on the bottom of the revolving doors, the clatter of three pairs of high heels on the steps, the honk of a taxicab. Again and again he listened for a distant boom, but he never heard it.

NEITHER MARJORIE NOR Clifton heard more than a millisecond of that sound; their eardrums were burst by the first shock of the explosion.

Clifton, who stood in a line with the outside door, but about fifteen feet away, was blown face first into the street. He passed through the doorway almost without injury since the force blew the door off its hinges in front of him. The sudden and rapid acceleration of his body, however, caused his head to snap back, which broke his neck. The force with which he struck the lamppost outside the door broke most of his ribs and his left arm. It shattered his pelvis and the front part of his skull. The coroner described the cause of death as massive trauma. The immediate cause could have been skull fragments in his brain, a rib ripping through his heart, or the severing of his spinal column. All of these happened at less than one second after two o'clock. The coroner said that Clifton certainly did not live long enough to be aware of any of it.

Marjorie, on the other hand, was cursed with a brief comprehension of the event. Her chair was positioned in front of a large steel support beam, so the force of the explosion took a more circuitous route to her.

She saw Clifton rushing towards the door before the explosion slammed her chair into her desk, breaking six ribs and sending chair, desk, and Marjorie flying across the room. She realized Clifton was being flung through the doorway by some unseen force before the flames hit her and incinerated the outer layers of her flesh.

She lost consciousness within a second of the arrival of the fire, which roared from the back wall and focused its blue hot flame on Marjorie like a blowtorch. She did not live for more than a few seconds after that.

KAREN, DAVID, AND Steve turned the corner at the end of the block and saw six fire engines and a fleet of police and emergency vehicles. A crowd of onlookers filled the street behind hastily erected police barriers. Even from the end of the block they could see that half the building that had housed *Ear to the Ground* was gone.

None of them made any effort to get closer to the scene, to ask the police what had happened. They all knew what had happened—Satan had found them out and had smote their headquarters with the flames of hell.

"Natural gas explosion," one onlooker said to another. "Broke every window in the neighborhood."

Karen held David's hand on one side and Steve's on the other as the three stood motionless, gazing into the fracas. She knew that Clifton and Marjorie would have been going over the page proofs for tomorrow's paper until three o'clock. They were dead; there would be no paper tomorrow.

She glimpsed for an instant, as through a closing shutter, all her worries of a month ago—that she would lose her job, that she would be turned out onto the street, that her figure was not attractive. These seemed like a playful fantasy now. How she wished she had spent the past month living under a bridge in Central Park with David and that she knew nothing of the coming conflagration.

Steve searched his mind for any hint he may have inadvertently given Linda that could have lead to this murderous act. Was that the reason for his seduction? Did he blurt out information in the throes of passion? Unlike Karen, he had an almost photographic memory of his brush with the powers of The Program—a memory too clear for his own comfort, for it made looking at Karen, and holding her hand, painfully awkward.

He thought he had skirted the issue of Linda's business relationship with The Program delicately enough that she would not suspect an investigation. But he couldn't shake the thought that this destruction and death was his fault, that he had been too enraptured by the physical transformation of Linda into Karen to beware of the dangers inherent in sleeping with the enemy.

David could feel a tear trickle down his cheek. If only he had walked away from Karen the moment he had seen her approaching in the park all those weeks ago. If only he had never agreed to be interviewed, never met Karen, never dragged her and her friends into this satanic inferno. Now, because of him, because of his own weaknesses, two of his friends were probably dead, and Karen might be next.

He wished he could turn from her and disappear into the crowd, but she gripped his hand tightly. Besides, it was too late. She was already a part of all this. She was the first woman he had ever loved, and he was probably going to get her killed and put her immortal soul at risk.

All three of the friends who stood stunned by the flames had assumed that the destruction of *Ear to the Ground* was a result of Satan's knowledge that the paper was pursuing a story about Arthur Blackburn and The Program. But had they heard a telephone conversation that took place at the *Daily News* later that afternoon, they might have thought differently.

GEORGIA PHILLIPS WAITED until the cubicles next to hers were unoccupied and then dialed a local Manhattan number.

"Don't you think that was a bit of an overreaction for a cartoon?" she said as soon as the other line was picked up. "It wouldn't be so bad for people to know you can take a joke."

She was silent for a moment as the party on the other end answered.

"I didn't sign up for this," she said. "Not murder and blowing up buildings."

Again the voice answered.

"Fine," she said, "but next time remember that cartoons are jokes. If nobody ever makes fun of you, *that's* when you know you've blown your cover."

BUT KAREN AND David and Steve had no way of knowing the identity of the informant. Steve feared he was guilty of betraying his friends; David thought it was all his fault; Karen assumed Satan's omniscience.

That assumption would later be challenged by two facts: when they returned to the photo lab, Karen's pictures had turned out perfectly, and the final edition of *Ear to the Ground* had not been destroyed in the fire, but was printed that night from the files Marjorie had e-mailed just before the explosion. Had they known this as they watched the bodies of their friends loaded into an ambulance, they might have held out hope for victory.

But in that moment, the Prince of Darkness had destroyed not only their friends and their newspaper, but also their hopes.

"What's all this, then," said a voice behind them. Steve and David each felt a hand on their shoulders, and Karen felt quick breaths against her hair, as if someone had come running down the block to find them.

"I think you'd better take us home with you, Martin," said Karen, moving her eyes from the diminishing fire. "I don't think the City is safe for us any more."

MARCH
XXVI

Karen sat by the window of her bedroom in the rectory and wrote with a ballpoint pen on a yellow legal pad. A stack of pads and a pile of pens lay on a small table by her chair. Several filled pads lay on the floor by her feet. Karen had spent much of her time since arriving at the rectory as a refugee writing. It was her way of contributing to what they called "the war effort," writing a daily account of the battle from the front line. That no one beyond their tiny band was ever likely to read her account did not lessen its importance for her.

Each night they gathered around the fire—Karen in an armchair, Martin in his rocker, Steve behind them all sitting stiffly on a kitchen stool, Darcey and Gareth sprawled on the floor, David lurking in the shadows—and Karen read her account of the previous day's progress. Jackie and Nick sometimes stayed for these readings. Jackie had taken over the role of chef at the rectory, and Nick, as District Attorney, was suddenly in demand from his friends. Darcey begged him to appoint her special prosecutor for the case, but Nick said that as of yet there was no case, so he couldn't appoint her anything. "That means he's not ruling it out," Darcey said to Karen.

Karen had begun her journal the day after they arrived in Braintree, the day of Louise Crawford's funeral at St. Alban's. She had been afraid to approach Phil Crawford and his children, but Martin had introduced her. Karen felt she deserved Phil's wrath for her part in Louise's death, but Phil believed he had lost his wife before the horrible scene on Fifty-Seventh Street, before Louise ever called Karen. Phil had no doubt about whom to blame for taking Louise from him. He blamed The Program.

With Karen's detailed readings each night there were few confidences in the group, and Martin thought that best. "This is not a business in which it pays to keep secrets," he said. "Isn't that right, Steve?" he added, and though the question remained unanswered by Steve and unnoticed by the others who were busy eating Jackie's lamb curry, nothing escaped Karen's notice.

So she had recorded Martin's question and Steve's silence in the chapter she would read before the fire this evening. She did not stop to ponder their significance, because she knew the dangers of allowing personal suspicions or prejudices to creep into one's journalism. Her duty, as she saw it, was to record, and record she did.

Not that there had been much progress to report. The success of Karen's espionage in obtaining a copy of The Program contract had been their first and only strike against the enemy. Steve's meeting with Linda Foretti had, he told them, yielded nothing.

Karen and the others at *Ear to the Ground* had assumed they would wage their battle in the press, but when *Ear to the Ground* and Clifton both went up in flames, their arsenal and their general were taken from them in a single enemy raid. When Martin had suggested they fight the battle in the courtroom, Darcey and Nick moved to the front line, leaving Karen, David, and Steve feeling helpless.

Karen had appointed herself chronicler because she could find no other way to help and she couldn't bear doing nothing. David, for similar reasons, had become Jackie's assistant in the kitchen, but he refused to sleep in the rectory, insisting the only place safe for him to lower his guard was inside St. Alban's. He spent his nights on the marble floor in front of the altar.

Only Steve seemed inert. He stayed in his room most of the time, and spoke little at meals. Karen felt especially shunned. She had once thought Steve had a crush on her, but now he seemed to avoid her, always taking a chair at the dinner table as far from her as possible, rarely speaking directly to her, and casting his eyes to the floor whenever they chanced to pass in one of the long rectory halls.

Not that he held completely aloof from the combat. Martin had obtained a huge cache of books about satanic forces and Steve was working his way through them, looking for anything that might prove helpful. Each night, after Karen's presentation, he offered a synopsis of his reading for the day, delivered in a quiet monotone that belied his previous gregariousness.

They all grieved for Clifton and Marjorie. Karen wept every night, and her dreams were haunted by images of that terrible scene in the street after the explosion. But as Steve withdrew more and more from the group, Karen began to suspect his grief was not progressing along the same path as that of the others. Whether he feared a similar fate or whether it had been Marjorie, not Karen, who was the object of his affections, Karen did not know, but something was troubling Steve. She did not allow such thoughts to cloud her mind when she sat in the chronicler's chair, but in the darkness of her room as she lay waiting for sleep to overtake her, she worried about Steve.

"We don't know where he is, honestly," said the voice of Grace Collingwood over the phone. Sarah Saunders fidgeted with the cord of the yellow wall phone in the hall of the morgue, wondering if Steve had told his mother to give her the brush off. "He just left a message saying he had some important business to attend to and not to worry about him."

"Did you know he hasn't been to his classes in over a month?" asked Sarah.

"I'm sure if he needs to get in touch with you he'll call." The line went dead and Sarah stared at the receiver for a moment before returning it to the hook.

If he needs to get in touch, he'll call. Definitely the brush off.

She had waited two weeks before trying to call and another week before she got up the nerve to phone his parents. Not that she wasn't used to being forgotten after a few dates.

For some men it was finding out where she worked—but Steve had met her in the morgue, so that wasn't a problem. For others she knew, though they never told her, it was her weight. Would Steve have called if she'd been twenty pounds thinner?

She'd tried to find a copy of *Ear to the Ground* on the newsstand when she didn't hear from him for several days, but everyone seemed to be out. She had paid little attention to anyone but Steve on the night of Clifton's Golden Globes party, so the names of Steve's coworkers did not register when their bodies arrived at the morgue. Sarah could not know that Steve blamed himself for their deaths and that he brooded with guilt and mourning over the bodies she processed and placed into dark, silent drawers.

Sarah only knew that she'd had three dates, nice dates, with Steve. Then he disappeared and she found herself still thinking about him a month later. She went back to her lunch, which she ate in the corner of the hallway that passed for a lounge. Leafing absent-mindedly through a magazine, she came across an advertisement for The Program and stared at the sinuous form of Celinda. Sarah wrapped an arm around her midriff, feeling the extra layer of fat she knew didn't belong there. Her thumb grazed the bottom edge of her breast. It had already begun to droop, and she was only twenty-six. Was it possible there was a perfectly reasonable explanation for her obsessing over Steve? Was it possible she was in love with him? And if so, might he return the calls of a Sarah Saunders in the perfect shape of Celinda?

She tore the page from the magazine, neatly folded it, and slipped into the pocket of her lab coat.

WHEN DARCEY CREPT through the side door of the rectory and into the kitchen, David's arms were coated nearly up to the elbow with flour. Jackie had been teaching him to make bread. With his back to the door his shoulders flexed as he leaned into the counter again and again, and Darcey couldn't help giggling at the strength and intensity he put into the job.

"You know, that can be fun if you don't take it quite so seriously."

"I'm having fun," David protested, turning a smiling face towards her and holding up his floured arms. "It's a workout, though." David rolled his dough into two loaf pans and set them in the warming oven to rise before rinsing off his arms in the work sink by the back door. "What brings you to the kitchen?" he asked.

"Well, to start with, I'm hungry," said Darcey.

"Skipped breakfast, I bet."

"And lunch. Make me a sandwich?" Darcey slid into a ladder-back chair by the kitchen table and slipped her feet out of her constricting high heels. "I was in court all morning on a divorce case that never should have gone to trial, then I had lunch with our new intern and he asked so many questions I never ate a bite."

David busied himself at the counter making Darcey a turkey sandwich. He had found in the kitchen a refuge from his nightmares. As long as he could concentrate on the minutiae of baking bread, making sandwiches, and cooking dinner, there was no room in his mind for the horrors of the war they were waging.

"So, this new intern, is he cute?" David had taken to ribbing Darcey about the fact that, although she had the body she'd always wanted, she hadn't been doing much dating.

"Actually, I brought him here to meet you," said Darcey solemnly.

"You know I'm straight, right?" he said, wagging the carving knife at her.

"His name is Tom Watkins."

"Why does that name sound familiar?" said David, setting the sandwich in front of Darcey. She did not answer, but took a bite of the sandwich. "Is this a guessing game?" David asked.

"No," said a voice from the door. David looked up to see a man about his own age, dressed in a blue business suit. Despite his broad muscular shoulders, the man looked timid. He fidgeted nervously and his eyes darted around the room, lighting on everything but David. David had just decided that such a timorous man was not likely to make much of a lawyer when the narrow line of the man's lips brought the name Tom Watkins crashing onto shore from the sea of his memory.

"You're Tommy," said David flatly. "You said it was your car."

"I've come to apologize, for what it's worth," said Tom, still not moving from the doorway. "I was a dumbass, cocky kid." He looked up at David for the first time and saw the man he had unjustly sent to prison smiling at him.

"Nice try, you bastard," David said, looking at the floor and shaking a finger.

"David," said Darcey sharply, "at least give him a chance. It wasn't easy for him to come here and—"

David wrapped an arm around Darcey and laughed a long, loud laugh. "Sorry, Tommy," he said, "I wasn't talking to you. Why don't you come in and have something to drink. Is it too early for a beer?"

Tommy walked slowly to the table, glancing at Darcey as if for reassurance that David was not dangerous. "Do you mind if I ask," said Tommy, "who you were talking to?"

"When I was in prison," said David, pulling three bottles of beer from the fridge, "I was—tempted by someone. He tempted me to take revenge on you—sweet, glorious revenge, it seemed to me at the time."

"I can imagine," said Tom.

"No," said David quietly leaning across the table and handing Tom a beer, "you can't. Anyway, my only weapon against this temptation was forgiveness. I had to forgive you—and not just sit in my cell and say it, but really feel it in my heart. It wasn't easy, believe me. But I did it."

"So why— " said Tom.

"Why did it sound like I called you a bastard? I was talking to him. He was testing me, to see if I'd really forgiven you. You can't be sure about something like that until you come face to face." David smiled again and raised his bottle towards Tom. He felt a rush of euphoria and hope, more hope than he had felt since they left New York. Here was evidence that the tempter could be resisted.

"So," said Tom, finally smiling back at David and taking a swig of his beer, "who is this person, anyway?"

ON THE FIRST Saturday morning in March, Karen decided the events in Washington were closely enough allied to their own efforts to merit monitoring on TV. The early spring had already coaxed a few premature cherry blossoms from the trees that lined the tidal basin, but the cameras soon zoomed beyond those to the steps of the Lincoln Memorial where the speakers' platform had been erected for the Million Pound March.

The march had been billed by the Army of All Sizes as a demand for the civil rights of "men and women who are not unnaturally thin," and had been hailed by many as a blow against one of the last forms of discrimination still generally accepted by American society.

"And why should that be so," cried a voice from the platform, "when we are not even a minority? We are a majority! We are the normal ones! We are the beautiful ones!"

Thus Karen watched the coining of a phrase that would enter American culture with the force of a hurricane—"The Beautiful Majority."

Karen thought the television coverage of the march must be a good sign—the first time the major media, who had seemed to be in cahoots with The Program, aired the views of the anti-Program movement. Not that this rally was specifically aimed at The Program, but many speakers mentioned The Program as one more symptom of what one man called the "national illness of weight obsession."

The rectory residents had not closely followed the goings-on in the world outside during the weeks since the explosion, so Karen was non-plused by the roaring reception given by the crowd to the final speaker of the day, Anna Camello, co-star of *My Sister, Myself.* Karen had watched the Golden Globes and heard the murmurings about Camello's being shut out of the nominations, but she did not know those rumblings had crescendoed into a mighty torrent of protests, nor did she know that Camello had become a national spokesperson for the Army of All Sizes. Karen did not know that Camello had been nominated for an Academy Award and that her Golden Globe winning co-star, Lucinda Wilson, had not, nor did she know that Oscar predictors were calling this the most politically charged race in history and had already made Camello an odds-on favorite.

Discontent with The Program and all it stood for had been brewing not only within the walls of the St. Alban's rectory, but across the country. Had Karen and the others been following the news, they might have felt less alone in their struggle.

Karen had summoned the others to the TV, and they were all stunned by the first words of Anna Camello's speech.

"Where is David James?" she said, and a great cheer rose up from the crowd as her voice echoed across the Mall.

"I'm right here," said David, who had just walked into the room. "Who's asking?" A chorus of shushes greeted David as everyone strained to hear why Anna Camello was looking for him.

Karen jumped up and pulled him towards the TV. "The whole country is watching this," she whispered.

"I have been looking for David for almost a month now. We've all been looking for David. And I think you know why." She held up a copy of the final issue of *Ear to the Ground,* and the crowd erupted once more.

Though they could not possibly see what paper she held, they clearly knew. David's article had circulated like wildfire in the days after the explosion. Though the subscribers never received that final issue, the printers, as they had been paid to, distributed copies to newsstands throughout the city. Within hours readers had posted the article on the Internet, and soon it had become a rallying cry for the Army of All Sizes and similar groups popping up everywhere.

Not only had Anna Camello and the Million Pound Marchers been looking for David, journalists across the country had been looking for him. Papers wanted to reprint his article, talk show hosts wanted to interview him, magazines wanted to hire him to write more.

All this the residents of the rectory would learn in the next few hours as they took turns at the television, combed through a stack of papers and magazines Gareth brought in from the supermarket, and searched online for anything to do with David. For now, they watched and listened as Anna Camello read David's article to the crowd in Washington. The camera occasionally zoomed in on individual women, some of whom were reciting David's words from memory with a look of religious zeal on their faces.

"I didn't think it was that great," said David to Karen later as they sat at the kitchen table over the remnants of dinner. "You've written stuff that was ten times better."

"You don't know about the biggest rule of journalism, do you?" Karen asked with a smile.

"No, I guess not."

"It doesn't matter how good the writing is and it doesn't matter how revolutionary the content is."

"So what does matter?"

"Timing," said Karen. "You have to say what people are thinking a split second before they start thinking it—that's what makes you a leader. If you had written that article a week earlier, before all the mess with the Golden Globes, no one would have noticed it. If you'd written it a week later, you would have been following the herd. You told people what they wanted to hear right when they wanted to hear it, even if they didn't know they wanted to hear it. Most writers go their whole career without pulling that off."

"Guess I was lucky," said David.

"Maybe," said Karen, "but it was well-written." She leaned over and kissed David lightly on the cheek before taking the dishes to the sink. It was the first time she had kissed him since the day of the Golden Globes party, and her stomach fluttered when he did not pull away.

Deep in the night, when the others had retired to their rooms, Martin sat behind his desk and worked on a sermon by the yellow light of an antique lamp. Despite his belief that battling the Prince of Darkness was vitally important work, he could not neglect the more mundane task of running his parish. As he wrote out his sermon for tomorrow he also jotted down notes for what he would say three days later on Ash Wednesday.

By dawn, he hoped, both sermons would be finished and he might grab an hour of sleep before the early service. When he heard Steve's voice at his door, he set down his pen, took off his reading glasses, and resigned himself to a night without rest.

"Can I talk to you for a minute, Father?" Steve asked, hesitating in the doorway.

"It's nice to hear you call me Father," said Martin. "Come in and have a seat."

Steve closed the door behind him and crept towards the chair in front of Martin's desk. He sat down and fixed his eyes on Martin's glasses where they lay on top of a page of sermon.

"I hope you've come to talk about whatever it is that's been troubling you," said Martin. "It goes beyond what the rest are feeling, doesn't it?"

Steve did not answer, but leaned forward in the chair, resting his arms on the desk, still not moving his eyes from the glasses. "Does the

Episcopal Church have a rite of confession?" he asked at last.

"We have a rite called 'the Reconciliation of a Penitent,' which is something like Roman Catholic confession."

"Do we have to be in a church to do that?" Steve asked, now looking at Martin's face for the first time.

"No," said Martin. "I can hear your confession anywhere. Anytime."

"How do we do it?"

"Well, there's an opening prayer and then you confess and then I offer you counsel and then I give you absolution. Pretty simple, really."

"Can we—I mean, can I confess to you—now?"

Martin reached for his well-thumbed copy of the *Book of Common Prayer*. "Of course you can," he said. From the shelf behind him he took another copy of the prayer book and handed it to Steve.

"And is it secret?" asked Steve. "I mean is there some sort of—I don't know— "

"It's absolutely confidential," said Martin, laying a hand on Steve's trembling arm.

"Even if—"

"No exceptions," said Martin. "It starts here on page 407." He waited for Steve to find the proper spot in the book. "Where it says 'Penitent,' that's you."

Steve stared at the book in his lap as the clock on the mantelpiece ticked away the seconds. After a minute, he read, in a quivering voice, "Bless me, for I have sinned."

Martin replied, reading from the book, "The Lord be in your heart and upon your lips that you may truly and humbly confess your sins: In the Name of the Father, and of the Son, and of the Holy Spirit. Amen."

Again a long silence hung in the room as Steve looked at the words on the page, and at the ominous long dash that followed.

"I confess to Almighty God, to His Church, and to you, that I have sinned by my own fault in thought, word and deed, in things done and left undone; especially—" And now Steve had arrived at the place where the prayer book would help him no more. "I—I'm not sure how to start," he mumbled to Martin. "There's so much."

"What troubles you the most?" said Martin.

"I think I might be responsible for Clifton and Marjorie's deaths," said Steve, "but honestly, I'm more troubled by what I did to Karen."

"What was that?"

"It's sort of hard to explain. Lusted after her, I guess."

"That's not so horrible," said Martin. "Karen is an attractive lady. I don't think you've done her any great harm."

"It's more than that," said Steve. "I had sex with her."

Martin knew his job was to remain calm, open minded, and forgiving, but this came as a shock. He had had many private conversations with Karen, some of them about Steve, and she had never mentioned this. "How did that come about?" he asked.

"Well, not actually with her," said Steve. "I mean she wasn't really there, but to me it seemed like she was there—and isn't that even worse?"

"You fantasized about her?" Martin asked, confused.

"More than that," said Steve, and slowly, with frequent questions from Martin, he poured out the story of his encounter with Linda—how his lust for Karen had transformed Linda and he had been unable to resist the temptation; how he felt he had violated Karen, as if he had raped her without her knowing it; how he had betrayed Sarah. And how he had become convinced he must have said something that tipped Linda off to their activities and led to the murder of Clifton and Marjorie.

The rubric at the end of the prayer of confession read: "Here the priest may offer counsel, direction, and comfort." Martin wondered what counsel, direction, and comfort he might possibly offer. He had spoken to parishioners who talked of being "tempted by Satan" before, but never had he imagined such a clever temptation as the one to which Steve had surrendered.

"I don't think you had anything to do with the explosion," he said at last. "Or if you did, it was only a question of timing. If he hadn't found out that day, he would have found out the next morning when David's article came out. And he would have blown the office up then, probably with all of you in it. So if anything, you saved Karen and David and the cause. But something tells me he found out some other way."

"And what about the sex?" asked Steve.

"That's a little more complicated," said Martin. "This rubric says that I 'may assign to the penitent a psalm, prayer, or hymn, or something to be done, as a sign of penitence and act of thanksgiving.' I think maybe I need to do that."

"Something to be done?" asked Steve.

"You know what it is, don't you?"

"You want me to talk to Karen."

"In your heart she's the one you have injured. And until you confess to her and ask her forgiveness, that sin will infect the whole group."

"I know," said Steve. "I'm sorry for the way I've been acting."

"I forgive you," said Martin, "and God forgives you. And Karen will forgive you, too. But not until you ask."

"Yes, Father," said Steve.

"Talk to Karen," Martin repeated firmly, "by sundown tomorrow."

"Yes, Father. I will."

"Now," said Martin, turning back to his prayer book, "are you ready for your absolution?"

AT 3:00 A.M. Gareth sat on the floor of Darcey's living room surrounded by banker's boxes and stacks of spiral notebooks. On top of one box sat the remains of a take-out pizza, now cold and stiff. Darcey had gone to her office to retrieve another fat volume of statutes and left him with the task of uncovering her notes on New York contract law from a class she took in law school. He did not feel particularly useful in his role as legal assistant to Darcey, but it gave him a way to contribute to the effort, so he came to her house every night after dinner and helped in whatever way he could.

He had read The Program contract aloud to her a hundred times as she paced up and down, chewing on one pencil after another. He had cooked meals for her at two in the morning, taken her for long drives in the country while she thought, and pulled a blanket over her when she fell asleep on the couch.

He felt comfortable with Darcey because he was not attracted to her. With her he never found himself imagining a relationship other than what they already had—friends working together. And because he harbored no secret adoration of her, he had, over the past few weeks, managed to emerge from his shyness somewhat.

Even Martin had commented on the difference. "It looks like Darcey is succeeding where I couldn't," he said, and when Gareth protested that he and Darcey were just friends, Martin said, "That's what it takes to overcome your shyness, Gareth—friends."

Gareth dragged one of the banker's boxes across the carpet so he could sit on the sofa and examine its contents. He pulled out a manila file folder and opened it on the coffee table.

He knew as soon as he saw the photographs he should shut the folder and replace it. Not only was it a violation of Darcey's privacy for him to see these pictures, but since he was not sexually attracted to her, why would he want to?

They were glossy eight by tens in color, obviously taken by a professional. But although the face that looked coquettishly out at him was unmistakably Darcey's, the generously endowed body was unfamiliar to Gareth. He had not met Darcey until afterwards, and so he only knew her Programmed body, that trim, boyish figure that held so little attraction for him. But here was Darcey displayed in her pre-Program glory, and Gareth could not look away.

The picture on top showed Darcey leaning in a doorway, in a pose reminiscent of Celinda's famous Program advertisement. But her figure, unlike the linear body of Celinda, traced a beautiful S-curve from shoulders to knees. One luscious hip jutted into the doorway, defying anyone to pass. She wore a pink negligée that hung across the top of her full breasts and stopped just above her crotch, giving a glimpse of pink satin panties beneath. The top of the negligée was cut low enough to show several inches of cleavage, and the round swell of her bosoms. Her soft, fleshy arms and legs were completely uncovered, and Gareth could not help imagining how it might feel to be wrapped in all that wonderful womanly flesh.

Another picture, for he had now given up all attempts at propriety and begun to sift through the pile, showed Darcey in the same negligée, kneeling on a bed. Her rear spread invitingly where she sat on her feet, and she leaned far enough forward that her breasts nearly swung free of the flimsy fabric. Gareth could feel their supple weight in his palms as, in his imagination, he reached out to cup them.

Many of the pictures were posed to show off Darcey's substantial breasts, but others favored her wide buttocks or her scrumptiously shaped legs. Gareth especially liked a series where she wore a man's blue dress shirt. In one she lay on her stomach with her satin-covered rump peeking from beneath the shirttails. In another, she stood in that same doorway, the shirt unbuttoned nearly to her navel and pulled tightly across her breasts.

Gareth swallowed hard as he realized he could take one of these photos and Darcey would probably never know. He mustn't, he knew. He wouldn't.

But still, since he had seen most of them anyway, what harm would it do to play a little game, to look through the stack one more time and choose the image he *would* steal if he were that sort of man?

He felt a tightness in his slacks as he thought over the images he had seen so far, trying to decide which he liked best. He really shouldn't— he should put them back right now before she came home, before he became any more aroused. And yet what a thing to have happen, to be sexually aroused by Darcey. Just admitting it quickened his pulse, made his breaths come shallow, and increased his hardness.

He felt a flush in his face, and he knew he must put the photos back. But he was guided not by reason but by animal urges. *Why not pick out an image,* he thought. One to study just for a minute, to burn into his mind so that later, in the privacy of his own room, he could recall it and—

No. He didn't dare. How could he even think such things about Darcey? He shoved the photos back into the file folder—all but one that fluttered to the floor. He sat frozen for a moment, not wanting to take his eyes off that luscious image. It lay several feet away and had turned itself sideways to his line of sight, but he knew this must be the one, the picture he would not, could not forget.

Darcey wore a red silk teddy held up with spaghetti straps and cut barely above her nipples, which stood out through the thin fabric. She stood blocking the doorway with her feet spread apart and her shoulders thrown back, but the defiance and pride of the posture was tempered by the teddy bear she clutched to her stomach. Her head was tossed back far enough for her blonde hair to dangle behind the slope of her shoulders, and her face was swept up in a delighted laugh.

There, thought Gareth, *is a voluptuous, well-endowed woman, proud of her body.* For all her talk about how The Program had improved her self-esteem, Darcey no longer seemed to have that insouciant joy in her body the photographer had captured here.

Gareth could see himself slipping his arms around the exciting girth of the playful woman in the picture, feeling the folds of flesh return his caress. The image became so real to him he did not notice the change in how the light played across the glossy surface of the photograph as the front door opened.

"So what do you think?" asked Darcey, stooping to pick up the picture. "You can be brutally honest. Pretty sad, isn't it?"

Gareth felt his face go hot with embarrassment, but Darcey sounded more amused than offended. He looked from the photograph she held at arm's length to the body The Program had left her, letting his eyes roam slowly from legs that seemed too thin to support a real human being up the narrow line of her figure to her sparkling, inquisitive eyes waiting patiently for a response. His embarrassment eased as he saw a genuine curiosity in Darcey's eyes. "I should be brutally honest?" he said.

"Please," said Darcey. "These were my last ditch effort to boost my self-esteem before I gave up and got with The Program."

"Well, yes, I think it *is* sad. I think the body in those pictures is about the sexiest thing I've ever seen. I think it's sad you felt you had to get rid of it. I mean, no offense, Darcey, but if you still looked like this—well let's just say that with your brains and this body, you could have had any man you wanted—or at least—well, for what it's worth, you could have had me."

"You are the sweetest, Gareth," she said, plopping down on the sofa beside him and kissing him quickly on the cheek. "If only you'd been around to talk me out of it."

"If only," said Gareth wistfully.

"But I couldn't have had any man, Gareth, believe me." Darcey held the photo up in both hands, tilting it from side to side as if a change of angle might alter her past. "I could feel the way they turned their eyes from me, and they certainly never asked me out."

"I don't suppose it ever occurred to you," said Gareth, who had more than a little experience as a shy man in a world of attractive women, "that maybe they turned their eyes because they didn't want to get caught staring, and they didn't ask you out because they were afraid you were out of their league."

"No, I have to admit, that never occurred to me," said Darcey with a laugh. "You have to understand, Gareth, you're special. Other men are not like you. You're sensitive and honest and kind, and, as I discover much too late, appreciative of the full female figure. But that's not the way most men are. They want us skinny and stupid and submissive. I couldn't make myself stupid, and I sure wasn't going to stop being hard-nosed or hard-headed or whatever you call my personality, but I could at least stop being fat."

"I think you underestimate us, I really do. It's just like the way we let a tiny percentage of women show us what beauty is supposed to be. You let the vocal minority of men define the whole species. Any normal man would find your old body a lot sexier than your new one."

"What did you just say?"

"I'm sorry, Darcey, but you told me to be brutally honest."

"No, no, no—" said Darcey in an excited voice, "I liked it, I just want you to repeat it."

"I said that any normal man would prefer the body in these pictures to the one you got from The Program."

"If you're right, Gareth, then we've got him."

"We do?"

"Look, what was Louise Crawford's complaint?"

"Her husband didn't find her sexually attractive."

"Right, and The Program said 'too bad, because all the contract guarantees is that the average American man will find you more attractive.'"

"Not me," said Gareth.

"Right—not you and not Phil, certainly not David, judging from his article, and not those twelve men he talked to at the New York Public Library. All we have to do is prove in court that the average American man would prefer this," Darcey held up the picture that had so enthralled Gareth, "to this," she indicated her own body with a swipe of her hand. "Then we've got him on breach of contract and maybe even intent to defraud."

"So how do we prove it?" asked Gareth.

"Well, before we figure that out," said Darcey, as a sly smile Gareth had never seen before crept across her face, "you need to tell me what you think of the rest of these pictures—one by one."

D avid and Karen strolled across the lawn towards the rectory after the ten o'clock Eucharist at St. Alban's. Karen had felt comfortable with David on the few occasions they had been alone together since arriving in Braintree, and he seemed to share that easy friendship. She wondered if he still felt any desire for her.

Maybe they had moved too fast. Maybe some day, when this was all over, he would be able to hold her again. For now she contented herself with the fact that he was at least safe and speaking to her. But as she glanced at him out of the corner of her eye, she couldn't banish the exquisite memory of his hands exploring her body.

When they were halfway to the house they heard quick, heavy foot-falls and labored breath behind them. For an instant David thought someone had realized who he was, and that a swarm of press would descend on the rectory by nightfall. He had just begun to manufacture a convincing denial when Steve's voice hailed them.

"Morning," Steve panted.

"Good morning," said Karen and David nearly in unison.

"I must be out of shape. I didn't think I could catch you."

"Steve, I think you're actually smiling," said Karen. "I didn't think you still knew how."

"I assure you, it's only a grin of nervous fear," said Steve. "Listen, Karen, I was wondering if I could talk to you for a few minutes."

"Sure," said Karen.

"Alone. It won't take long, I promise."

"I need to help Jackie get lunch started," said David. "I'll see you two later." He trotted off towards the kitchen.

"So," she said, "what's on your mind?"

Steve had rehearsed what he would say all night, but he still felt tongue-tied. He took a step towards the stream that flowed across the field behind the rectory. Karen fell in beside him and he found himself walking with her. So he spoke a word into the cold morning air and found himself, at last, pouring out all he had wanted to tell her for so long—how he had loved her from afar and how he now realized that what he had taken as love was merely lust; how he thought that perhaps he really did love Sarah, but how he had been distracted from that love by the temptations of the fictitious Karen's flesh; how he had violated Karen so horribly without her even knowing it; how he begged her forgiveness and her friendship.

They stood at the edge of the creek when Steve finished. He felt tears of relief trickling down his face—whatever Karen said, however she responded, the burden he had carried since that night with Linda had finally been lifted.

"You were seduced by my body?" Karen said, wrapping her arms around herself.

"I'm sorry," said Steve, "I'm so, so sorry—" He wiped a sleeve across his eyes.

"I mean, this body, this body that I've hated for so long—this is the body you lusted after?" Karen spoke not in anger but in delight; she seemed on the verge of laughter.

"Yes," said Steve, "It's a—well, no offense, Karen, but it's a very sexy body."

Karen said nothing. Steve drew breath to apologize once again, but was cut short by Karen's laughter. Whatever lingering worries she had that David's kind words about her figure were inspired by something other than his honest opinion of the feminine ideal dissolved into giggles as she saw the memory of his lust in Steve's eyes. Had she strolled into the offices of The Program that day, no amount of temptation could have swayed her to make the slightest change in her body. Her body—her lumpy, curvy, flabby body—had been a greater temptation than Steve could resist.

"You know what, Steve?" said Karen. "I'm not going to forgive you for lusting after me. And do you know why? Because lusting after me is the sweetest thing you could do for me and for every woman who has ever felt like an ugly tub of lard when she compared herself to Celinda." She threw her arms around a shocked Steve and held him tight. "Thank you," she whispered.

"Now," said Karen, when they had almost reached the kitchen door, "this Sarah Saunders—she's got a pretty great body, too, doesn't she?"

"WE'LL NEVER GET this case to court," said Nick, hurling Darcey's file onto his desk and rearing his bulk out of his chair in disgust. "No self-respecting judge is going to think twice before throwing it out."

"Let me just make two points," said Darcey calmly, not rising to meet Nick's scorn, but sitting with her hands resting on the pad in her lap. Gareth, who stood behind her, appeared equally unruffled by Nick's outburst. "First of all, Thompson is the only judge sitting this month, and you know as well as I do that Thompson loves any opportunity to put big business on trial. If there's an iota of evidence, he'll let things proceed. Secondly, The Program has been sued twice already for contract violations in—"

"Orange County, Florida and King William County, Virginia," said Gareth.

"Both judges let the case go to trial, and do you know why?"

"I have a feeling you're going to tell me," said Nick with a sigh.

"Because The Program lawyers wanted to go to trial. You know how most corporate trials drag on for years?"

"Because the corporations can afford the lawyers to drag things out and wear down the opposition," chimed in Gareth.

"Well, The Program is just the opposite," said Darcey. "The lawyers could have used a thousand delay tactics, but they rushed both cases to trial."

"Florida took three weeks, Virginia six days," said Gareth.

"And who won?" asked Nick.

"The Program won, of course," said Darcey, "because neither of those cases was any good, but the point is these guys actually want to go to court. They think they're unbeatable, that their contract is iron-clad, and they figure if they prove that in a few quick cases, no one will bother them anymore."

"And were these criminal cases?" said Nick.

"Civil suits," Darcey said.

"But the law's different in New York," said Gareth.

"There's still a law on the books that allows criminal prosecution for breach of contract if you can prove malicious intent to defraud," said Darcey, "and since The Program is a sole proprietorship, it means we can prosecute him personally."

"These guys shake off civil suits like snowflakes," said Nick, "and now you want to come at them with a criminal case based on—on this?" Nick held up the file between two fingers.

"That's right," said Darcey.

"And what about this other charge?" asked Nick.

"Misdirection, nothing more," said Darcey.

"And you honestly think Thompson will let this go to trial?"

"Let me argue it, Nick. You can appoint me special prosecutor and you can wash your hands of the whole thing."

"It looks to me," said Nick, tapping the file on his desk, "like you're a piece of evidence in this case."

"Nick, I know I can—"

"You want to win this case, right?" said Nick harshly.

"We have to win this case," said Darcey.

"Right. We by God do have to win this case. So we've got to play it as clean as we know how. Without you as evidence your flimsy-ass case falls apart, and I'm not going to have the thing thrown out because the prosecutor is also the main piece of evidence."

"So who argues it?" asked Darcey meekly.

"I fucking argue it," said Nick, banging a fist on his desk. "And you coach me every fucking step of the way. I want you in my office at seven o'clock tomorrow morning and I want a legal assistant with you, a real one. Now get out of here."

In the hall outside Nick's office, Darcey and Gareth stifled their laughter. "How did you know he would take it?" Gareth asked.

"I told you," said Darcey, "He'll take any case to keep it away from a woman. And it's better than I thought."

"How?" asked Gareth.

"When Nick uses the f-word," said Darcey, taking Gareth by the hand and leading him down the hall, "he doesn't lose."

Steve estimated he had spent three hours staring at the phone since his apology to Karen, but every time he picked up the receiver to call Sarah, the image of Linda's writhing, naked body leapt up in his mind. So he rationalized his inability to call her. If he really loved her, he told himself, he would stay as far away from her as possible. After all, since he was involved in battling Satan, calling Sarah would only drag her into the dangerous fray. And he almost believed this argument. Almost.

He picked up the receiver ten more times that afternoon, but never dialed further than the area code.

Nick prepared for trial by buying himself the biggest belt buckle he could find and having a spittoon that had languished in the basement of the courthouse for decades reinstalled by the prosecutor's table. He sloshed his work boots through the mud behind his house and found an old pair of khakis that was not only well-worn at the seams, but also too tight in the waist and a good two inches too short. For two days before the trial he didn't shave.

"You want them to take us lightly, right?" he said to Darcey. "If I look like this, the little Harvard Law prick they send up here will figure he doesn't even need to open his briefcase." Nick motioned for Darcey to sit down. "So," he said, "how do we start?"

"Stipulation," said Darcey, tossing a file folder onto his desk. "These guys will stipulate to all sorts of things to speed up the trial and to keep their corporate documents from being entered into evidence."

"Well," said Nick, "if you tell me what to do, I can promise I'll look stupid doing it."

"Your honor, I'd like to open this hearing with a motion to dismiss the charge of second-degree murder," said the defense attorney. He was a narrow, bespectacled man who looked as if he rarely saw the light of day. "Even if Louise Crawford had committed suicide, there is no precedent for such a charge. But she didn't commit suicide. The death of Louise Crawford was ruled accidental. I have the police report right here."

"Your honor," said Nick, "I'd like to address that point, if I may." He pushed his hands against the prosecutor's table and lifted his bulk to a standing position, making as much of a show of his size as he could. He spoke in a gruff voice that implied he only occasionally came in from the farm to prosecute a few criminals.

"Your honor, you know I wouldn't file a charge without evidence to back it up." Nick hitched up his pants and strode around the end of the table towards the bench. "But hell, I don't want to waste your time or the time of the honorable counsel for the defense." Nick nodded towards the defense table. "So if the defense will agree to proceed directly to trial on the breach of contract issue, I'll be glad to drop these murder charges and save everybody some time."

"That arrangement is suitable to the defense, your honor. We're prepared to go to trial immediately on the contract issue."

"Well, then," said Nick, "there you go. You see, your honor, we're all prepared to be reasonable here." He winked at the defense table and sauntered back to his seat.

"He actually bought it," whispered Tom excitedly to Darcey.

They sat in the back of the courtroom surreptitiously taking notes. They had dressed in shabby clothes, hoping to look like the kind of derelicts who hung around the county courthouse for entertainment. Tom, whom Darcey had chosen as her assistant, pretended to be asleep. Nick had told the others to stay home. "No point arousing suspicion," he said. "We want them to think they're being prosecuted by arrogant nincompoops in some hick town."

Other than Darcey and Tom, there were no spectators. The Program had mastered the art of keeping out of the press, so the proceedings inside the Braintree County Courthouse went on unnoticed by the outside world.

Nick's only request for jurors was that none of them be clients of The Program, a requirement that proved superfluous, as none of the members of the jury pool fell into that category. Within three days the jury had been seated.

A rthur Blackburn, charged with criminally breaching his contract with Louise Crawford, looked more respectable than any defendant who had ever come before Judge Thompson. He smiled at the members of the jury; the jury suppressed their desire to whisper to one another about their first sight of the man behind The Program, and the trial began.

"Good morning, your honor," began Nick, but instead of continuing, he stood silent and motionless for as long as he dared. Finally, he stooped to the prosecution table and fumbled through his papers, which he had wadded up and flattened back out the night before and had been careful to scatter across the entire surface of the table. "Um— the prosecution is wondering if the defense might be willing to—to—" Nick pretended to search desperately for a document. "I beg your pardon, your honor," he said, rising to approach the bench, "What's that called when the defense agrees on the facts of the case?"

"Stipulation," came the exasperated reply from the defense table.

"Thank you, counsel," said Nick, turning to smile at the defense lawyer. "Stipulation. I wonder if the defense might stipulate a few basic facts for us."

"What are the facts?" groaned the defense lawyer.

"First, we'd like the defense to stipulate to the existence of some sort of clause in the contract for The Program that guarantees clients will be more—well, that they'll be sexier following treatment."

THE PROGRAM

"Your honor, the defense is happy to enter into evidence a copy of Clause Seven of our standard client contract, which I will read to the court with your permission."

"Proceed," said the judge.

"The Program and its proprietor guarantee the client that she will be more sexually attractive to the average male following her participation in The Program." The defense lawyer passed two copies of a single-page document to the bench, one of which the judge handed to Nick.

"Thank you, counselor," said Nick, bowing slightly towards the defense table, "thank you very much."

He leaned against the witness booth for a moment, pretending to read the clause. "I see, I see," he mumbled. "I beg the court's pardon for using such crude language before. 'Sexually attractive to the average male.' That sounds much more genteel. I wonder if the defense could help me understand this a little better, though. I assume you aren't encouraging any kind of perversion, so when you say the average male, you mean grown men, is that right?"

"Your honor, the defense stipulates that the words 'average male' in Clause Seven are meant to indicate heterosexual American males over the age of eighteen." Turning to Nick, who had crossed back over to his table and was once again rooting through papers, the lawyer went on. "Is that suitable to the prosecutor?"

"Oh, yes," said Nick, smiling again towards the defense table. "That's a great help. I thought that must be what you meant. Now, I'm a little confused about precisely what 'more sexually attractive' means. Let me see if I understand. If one person is more sexually attractive to the average American heterosexual male over eighteen than another person, it means that, all else being equal, the average male would rather have sexual relations with the first person?"

"I'm not sure," said the defense lawyer with a chuckle, "that we want to enter into the dangerous legal ground of defining 'sexual relations,' but yes, I'd say you are correct. That's the meaning of the contract."

"So the defense would be willing to stipulate," said Nick, running his fingers along the text of the document he still gripped in his left hand, "that the client contract for The Program guarantees the average American heterosexual male over eighteen would rather have sexual relations with a client after she has participated in The Program than before?"

The lawyer for the defense had carefully copied out Nick's words, but still asked the clerk to read them back. After a moment he replied, "Yes, the defense is willing to stipulate that statement concerning Clause Seven."

"Now," said Nick "just so I can be absolutely clear on this, would you say by average that you mean, what—a simple majority of these men?"

"Yes, I'd say that."

"So to determine what the average male thinks about something, it wouldn't do me much good just to talk to one person—say, to Phil Crawford?"

"Absolutely," said the defense lawyer, smiling as if he'd caught Nick in a trap. "The testimony of any single person, including Phil Crawford, concerning the sexual attractiveness of Louise Crawford or any other client of The Program, cannot prove anything about her attractiveness to the average male."

"I understand," said Nick in a troubled voice, dropping one stack of papers onto his table and picking up another. "Just for the record, your honor, I'd like to enter into evidence a photograph and physical description of Louise Crawford before and after her participation in The Program, but I'd like to ask one more question of the defense, if I may."

"What is it?" said the defense lawyer in an exasperated tone

"Well it's just this," said Nick, holding up the two pictures of Louise Crawford. In both she wore a long brown overcoat, and in neither was more than her face visible. "These are the only before and after pictures of Louise Crawford the prosecution has been able to obtain. They were taken about a week apart, but I think the defense will agree that they don't really show the dramatic weight loss that Louise experienced."

"Yes, the defense would agree to that."

"Louise Crawford was five feet two inches tall and she weighed one hundred and sixty pounds before she went to The Program and ninety-seven pounds afterwards. Now, I have to think that Louise Crawford is not the only five foot two, one hundred and sixty pound client The Program has had in the State of New York."

"Certainly not," said the defense lawyer.

THE PROGRAM

"And since we're not able to bring Louise Crawford into this court-room," said Nick, "because of her tragic and untimely *accidental* death—" Nick leaned hard on the word "accidental," "I wonder if the defense would stipulate that what holds true for Louise Crawford in terms of sexual attractiveness before and after The Program would also hold true for other clients of The Program, say, between the heights of five one and five six and between, let's say, a hundred and fifty and one hundred and eighty pounds."

"Absolutely," said the defense counsel eagerly. "Any statements that could be made about Louise Crawford's sexual attractiveness would apply to any members of the group you mentioned. The defense is proud to stipulate that."

"Pride goeth before the fall," whispered Darcey to Tom. "He's almost got him."

Nick leaned over his table, shuffling papers from one side to another, finally pulling a yellow sheet out from under a large pile. "You wouldn't have any idea how many women would be in that group, would you, counselor?"

"Well, we've had over seventy-five thousand satisfied customers in the state of New York," the defense lawyer spouted, "and I'd guess at least a third of those fit into the category you describe."

"So you'd be willing to stipulate that twenty-five thousand women, of a similar shape, size, and sexual attractiveness to Louise Crawford, have undergone The Program in the state of New York?"

"Sure," said the lawyer, "we'll stipulate to that."

"Well, that's mighty impressive." Nick strolled back to his seat and dropped himself down with a thud. He began to pile all his scattered papers into a single stack, while the judge cleaned his glasses and the defense attorney tapped his pen on the table.

Throughout the proceedings the defendant sat impassive but smiling at the defense table. He occasionally glanced at his watch, but generally had an air of being entertained by the entire proceeding and showed no signs that he regretted assigning the case to a junior attorney. There was no point, after all, in wasting good high-priced lawyers on such a simple chore.

"Your honor, I think that's all I have for this morning. The defense has been so kind in stipulating all these facts, I'm finished up ahead of schedule. Do you think we might take an early lunch?"

Judge Thompson knew Nick was up to something strange, but there was no law against making a fool of yourself in court—people had certainly done it in his courtroom before—and Thompson knew Nick well enough to know that the snotty kid from New York would end up being the fool by the time the trial was over. "Fine, counselor," said the judge. "This court is adjourned until 2:00 P.M."

PHIL CRAWFORD STRAIGHTENED his tie in the mirror of the men's room for the fifteenth time. The face looking back at him hung so loosely on the skull beneath it seemed in danger of sliding off. He wondered, looking at his sagging cheeks and the dark circles beneath his eyes, if that face had always existed below the surface, if the round-cheeked, smiling visage he had shown the world before December had merely been a mask, hiding what lay below.

Phil had discovered his own weight loss program—lose your wife one step at a time, first her body, then her life. He'd shed forty pounds since Christmas.

He hadn't believed one word of what Darcey and Martin had told him about the Devil running The Program, but that didn't stop him from jumping at the chance to help bring the company down. Whatever The Program was, it had taken his wife from him, taken their mother from his children. Now he prepared to walk into a courtroom and confront the man responsible.

Why having a straight tie mattered to him, he did not know, but once again he pulled on the silk, trying to perfectly align the knot with his Adam's apple. He did it four more times before Nick stuck his head through the door and whispered, "It's time."

NICK MADE A show of helping Phil down the aisle and sitting him as close to the jury box as he could, so they could see the gap between his stiff, starched collar and his narrow neck.

"Your honor," Nick began, after he had carefully spread his crinkled papers across the prosecution table and selected one as if he were selecting a grapefruit in the produce department, "the facts of this case, so kindly stipulated by the counselor for the defense," Nick made a slight bow to the defense table, "have—well, they've taken the prosecution a bit by surprise, your honor."

The defense lawyer raised a hand to his face, but failed to hide his smirk from the jury.

"I had hoped to call to the stand this afternoon Mr. Phil Crawford," he gestured to where Phil sat slumped in the front row. "But the defense has kindly pointed out to me that given the wording of this—" he looked down at the papers he held for a long moment, "Clause Number Seven, anything this poor widower has to say would be irrelevant."

Phil gave Nick a beseeching look, a look Nick knew the jury would remember—a broken man desperate to say something against those who destroyed his life.

"Your honor," said the defense lawyer, rising quickly from his chair, "given the prosecution's own admission that the testimony of its star witness is irrelevant, I move for the immediate dismissal of the charges." He sat back down, now making no attempt to hide his condescending smile.

"Well, counselor," said Judge Thompson, "is there any reason I shouldn't listen to the rather obvious advice of the defense?" Thompson looked forward to Nick's next move. The prosecutor had turned in some impressive performances in his courtroom over the years, but this one, from the muddy boots and the wadded-up notes to the sacrificing of his one witness, topped them all.

"I'm glad you asked me that, your honor, because I've been thinking about what the esteemed counselor for the defense said this morning." Again Nick rifled through a sheaf of papers, but this time he shook his head, apparently unable to find what he was looking for, and tossed the papers into the air. As they fluttered to the floor, he went on.

"Aw, hell, I ain't got it written down, ladies and gentlemen—" he strode over to the jury box and addressed the jury directly, "but you heard it as well as I did. This man—" he pointed to the defense table, "said that the majority of grown men would find a woman more sexually attractive after she went through The Program. And that's all this case is about. If he's right, he wins. Hell, if he's right I'll drop the charges myself. But if he's wrong, the defendant is guilty of breach of contract in the state of New York, and by the admission of the counselor for the defense he's guilty of not one count, but twenty-five thousand."

Nick had gradually been raising his voice during this speech, so that the words "twenty-five thousand" echoed through the nearly empty courtroom.

"Your honor," he said sharply, "the prosecution calls the adult male population of Braintree County."

The courtroom was silent for a moment, just long enough for the jury to see the stricken look on the defense attorney's face and to observe the sharp elbow of the defendant jab his counsel in the side.

"Your honor, I object," said the defense attorney, leaping to his feet. "The male population of Braintree County was not on the witness list and furthermore the delay—"

"Counselor, I'm going to overrule your objection for the time being, while I give the prosecutor an opportunity to explain himself. But—" he glared down at Nick above his half glasses, "I shall keep your objection very much in mind."

"Thank you, your honor," said the defense lawyer.

"Now," said the judge to Nick, "you've heard the objection, and you can imagine what this courtroom will look like with goodness knows how many—"

"Fourteen thousand seven hundred and six, your honor," said Nick. "I looked it up during lunch."

"With fourteen thousand witnesses parading through here. So what have you got to say for yourself?"

"Your honor, I'll admit that our witness list did not contain fourteen thousand names, but because I did not know the wording of Clause Seven until the defense so kindly informed me this morning. I did not expect to have to prove the opinions of the average male. Surely I have the right to expand my witness list based on the revelation in trial of information previously unknown to me."

"You ought to be ashamed that it wasn't known to you," said the judge, "since your whole case revolves around that clause, but there's no law against incompetence, so I'll grant you the right to expand your witness list. But not by fourteen thousand."

"Thank you, your honor. Now, obviously if we are to exhibit the opinions of the average male, we are going to require more than one or two witnesses. I agree that fourteen thousand is too many, but if the defense would suggest a number they feel would be representative of the general population, I'd be happy to reduce the list." Nick turned to face the defense table and crossed his arms, giving a look of great patience as if he were waiting for a small child to perform a complicated addition problem.

"Your honor," said the defense lawyer with a sigh, "the defense believes that to obtain an accurate sampling of adult males and determine the opinions of the average member of that group, a minimum of—of one thousand witnesses would need to be examined."

"Well, there you are, your honor—we've trimmed the list by thirteen thousand, just like that."

"Counselor," said the judge, "I am not any more prepared to let a thousand witnesses troop through this courtroom than fourteen thousand."

"Of course, your honor, I understand completely." Nick paced back and forth in front of the bench several times, muttering "one thousand," under his breath. Stopping in front of the jury box he looked up and smiled. "That's a lot of witnesses, isn't it, ladies and gentlemen?" Three of the jurors chuckled, and they all smiled.

"You know, your honor," he said, turning back to the bench, "I only have one question to ask these witnesses, and it occurs to me that the Braintree High School auditorium has a capacity of twelve hundred. Now, I know this is a bit unorthodox, but if your honor would agree to convene court there, I believe I could examine all one thousand witnesses at once. A simple show of hands, it seems to me, would be sufficient to determine the answer to my question."

"Your honor, I must object in the most strenuous—"

"You must do nothing of the sort," snapped Judge Thompson at the defense attorney. "You've already objected, and I've already told you that I'm keeping your objection in mind. This is my courtroom, and if I want to take a field trip, it's my business. Bailiff, call the principal of Braintree High and tell him I want to use the auditorium tomorrow morning after assembly."

"But your honor—"

"Counselor, your objection is overruled," said the judge. "Now, Mr. Prosecutor, I will convene court tomorrow morning at eleven o'clock. If you don't have your thousand witnesses in their seats by then, I'm throwing this case out."

"Your honor," the defense lawyer jumped to his feet again. "How is the defense to be assured that these one thousand men are randomly chosen and haven't been screened by the prosecution?"

"Counselor," said the judge, "the prosecution will be lucky to get one thousand bodies by tomorrow morning, much less screen them, but the court hereby orders the prosecution to allow the defense counsel to be present at the recruitment of these witnesses. Court is adjourned."

"Well," whispered Darcey to the apparently sleeping Tom in the back row, "now the question is, will it work?"

Martin, Gareth, David, Steve, Karen, Darcey and Tom all helped out at Nick's office well into the night. There were three phone lines and two more next door in the assistant prosecutor's office. Everyone but Nick and Darcey took turns on the phone—the two lawyers kept a log of those who had agreed to show up in the morning, their ages, addresses, and phone numbers.

After a few hours of listening in on phone conversations, the defense attorney decided the selection process was as blind as it could be, and he spent most of the night dozing in the high-backed chair behind Nick's desk.

By dawn they had disturbed over two thousand homes in Braintree County, and twelve hundred and sixteen self-professed heterosexual men over the age of eighteen had agreed to come to the high school at nine o'clock.

Nick paced nervously backstage as the auditorium filled. He liked being in control, and he could control a single witness. But he couldn't control a thousand men. Even if enough of them showed up, there was no guarantee how they would answer the question. And what a fool Nick would look if they sided with the defense.

This case was no longer a quiet matter. Everyone in Braintree knew something was going on. Half of them had been woken by phone calls in the middle of the night. Nick was hanging his career on a great uncertainty. If he won the case that everyone in town participated in, he could keep the D.A.'s office as long as he liked. If he lost—well, he'd just have to hope that the men of Braintree knew sexy when they saw it.

Outside the school, the parking lot and nearby streets were jammed. Not only the thousand witnesses but also wives, friends, and families had come along to see the action. At the doors to the auditorium, officers of the court checked IDs against the list Nick had provided. Karen, David, Jackie, and Steve circulated through the crowd, herding witnesses towards the door and trying to move everyone else out of the building. They all worried that in the confusion, the auditorium would never be filled by eleven o'clock.

A makeshift jury box had been arranged in front of the curtain with folding chairs, and tables had been provided for the defense and the prosecution. Judge Thompson would stand at the podium. When the judge's watch reached eleven he signaled for the jury, who had been milling about behind the curtain, to take their places. He and the lawyers followed them through the curtain.

The crowd quieted quickly when the figures of authority strode onto the stage. Curiosity seethed though the room, but it seethed silently. When court had been called to order, Judge Thompson asked the officer at the back door to close the entrance and make his report on the witnesses.

"Your honor, there are twelve hundred and sixteen names on the prosecution's list. Of those, eleven hundred and seventy-two have presented themselves with proper identification this morning and are seated in the auditorium."

Nick breathed a sigh of relief.

"And are there any members of this audience who are not registered witnesses in this proceeding?" asked the judge.

"No, your honor, there are not," came the reply.

"Very well, swear the witnesses in."

The swearing-in was accomplished en masse, and Nick stood up to address the witnesses. "Gentlemen," he said. "I'd like to thank all of you for coming here this morning. I know this is an imposition on many of you, and I'll try to take as little of your time as possible. I only have one question for you this morning, and Judge Thompson has agreed that you can answer that question by a simple show of hands.

"I'd like to show you two photographs. Both were taken by the same photographer in the same studio and with the same instructions— please make this subject look sexy. So I'm going to show you two sexy pictures." A murmur rippled through the audience. "You see, now, I told you this wouldn't be so bad," said Nick, smiling.

"Your honor, I'd like to enter these two photographs into evidence," Nick said, passing two eight-by-tens to the Judge. "And here's a set for you, counselor." He passed another set to the defense attorney before adding, with a smile towards the audience, "I know you'll enjoy those." Light chuckling scattered through the auditorium.

"Now, if we could have the slide screen down and the lights dimmed, please. Gentlemen, I'm going to show you the same two pictures that I just entered into evidence. They are of the same woman. On the left—that's your left as you look at the screen—will be a picture with the caption 'before.' The picture on the right will be captioned 'after.' I'm going to give you ninety seconds to look at these photographs, and I ask you to please to look at them carefully and quietly without sharing your thoughts with your neighbor. Then I'm going to ask you to answer this simple hypothetical question. If you had to engage in sexual relations with either the 'before' woman or the 'after' woman, which would you choose? Does everyone understand?"

More murmurs and chuckles, but no raised hands. The lights went down, the slide screen descended, and two photographs of Darcey appeared.

The 'before' picture was the image Gareth had seen on top of the stack of lingerie photographs. The 'after' picture had been taken just a week ago and showed Darcey's post-Program body in the same pose, wearing the same pink negligée and pink satin panties, though in a smaller size, and the same come-hither look on her face.

Nick watched the defense counsel as he compared the images on the screen with the glossies he had just been handed. He knew the defense would be desperate to find a reason to object, but there was none. The only difference in these pictures was the difference created by The Program.

In fact, the attorney for the defense was thrilled when he saw the pictures. Who could fail to notice the resemblance between the 'after' picture of Darcey and the now famous portrait of Celinda? Surely these men would associate Darcey's post-Program photograph with Celinda, and their natural desire to connect sexually with perfection and fame would override any lingering childish desire they might have for big breasts and wide hips.

The Program had done a magnificent job on Darcey—transforming the dumpy looking young lady, whose seductive pose in pale imitation of Celinda made her all the more pathetic, into the perfect woman, her smooth chest revealed by the low-cut nightie, the perfect line of her narrow legs breaking ever so slightly where her almost unnoticeable hip leaned against the door frame. *In ninety seconds,* the defense counsel thought, *this case will be over.*

The eleven hundred and seventy-two witnesses sat in silence for those requisite ninety seconds, every eye fixed on the screen. Nick couldn't watch, couldn't bear to look into those faces and try to ascertain which way the eyes were drifting. Instead he stared at the second hand of his watch as it crept, at a glacial pace, towards the deadline.

In the hall outside the auditorium Jackie had joined Karen, Steve, Darcey, Gareth, and David. They knew from the silence within that the moment of truth had come. They stood in a circle and held hands while Gareth led them in prayer. Martin, they knew, was praying back at St. Alban's.

"Well, gentlemen," said Nick in an amiable tone that belied his fear, "I appreciate your attention. We can bring the lights up now and take out the slide screen."

Nick walked slowly to the front of the stage. "Now," he said, "we're going to pretend we're back in grade school, because I don't want anybody to change their vote when they see their neighbor, or their buddy—or their father—" here Nick glanced at a father and son pair in the front row, "vote the other way. So I'd like everyone to please close your eyes."

Groans rose from the audience.

"I know, I know, it seems silly, but we want to be completely fair about this thing. Now, eyes all closed?"

There was a general noise of assent.

"OK, now I'd like to ask those men who would prefer to have sexual relations with the 'before' picture—that's the picture that was on your left—to please raise your hands. Raise them nice and high and keep them up, please, so the officer of the court can count." Up went the hands.

Nick felt his pulse slow as the count progressed. It looked like more than half, but he couldn't be sure. After nearly fifteen minutes, the officer of the court announced he had made an accurate count.

"You may put your hands down, gentlemen, but please keep those eyes closed." Further groans. "Now, those gentlemen who did not raise their hands yet, are there any of you who do not prefer the figure in the 'after' picture?"

No hands were raised.

"Fine. Your honor, I'd like to suggest in the interest of time that we simply subtract the number of 'before' votes from eleven hundred and seventy-two to determine the number of 'after' votes."

"Any objection?" the judge asked the defense.

"No objection," said the counsel for the defense, who looked pale and was clearly perspiring.

"Would the officer of the court be so kind," said Judge Thompson, "as to read the results of the polling?"

"Your honor," came a voice from the left aisle, "Of eleven hundred and seventy-two witnesses, the number who would prefer to have sexual relations with the woman in the 'before' picture is —seven hundred and ninety-six."

A great cheer went up from the crowd, or from at least seven hundred and ninety-six of the crowd. Nick suppressed an urge to join the celebration.

The defense attorney dropped his head into his hands and flinched as the defendant kicked him under the table, in clear sight of the jury, and hissed, "Object, damn you, object."

The defense attorney did object, once order had been restored by the judge's repeated gaveling. "Your honor, this is highly irregular. I am not aware of any precedent in the state of New York that allows this sort of polling of witnesses."

"Have you searched for such a precedent?" asked the judge, who seemed at last to be enjoying the proceedings.

"No, your honor, I have not, but— "

"Well then, don't tell me there isn't one," said the judge sternly. But then he added, "However, I sustain the objection. I did search for a precedent, and I didn't find one. I allowed this carnival to go forward because it gave me the possibility of throwing this case out if these fine gentlemen voted the other way. But they didn't, and I'm not going to let this type of testimony stand."

Nick's elation crashed into the hard wooden floor of the stage. He almost couldn't muster the energy to respond to the judge, but he knew he must. He pulled himself from his chair, where he had plopped so triumphantly thirty seconds ago.

"But your honor—"

"And I don't want to hear anything else from you," the judge snapped at Nick. "Now here's what we're going to do—and I apologize to you folks in the—well, in the witness box," he said to the audience, "because this is going to take up a lot of your valuable time, but I've got to try to dispense some justice here. We're going to get a signed affidavit from every one of these gentlemen notarized by an officer of the court saying which one of those pictures they'd rather have sex with. We're going to do it today, and if the count of men who vote for 'before' isn't within five votes of —what was the count?" he asked the officer.

"Seven hundred and ninety-six, your honor."

"Isn't within five votes of seven hundred and ninety-six, then I'm going to throw this whole circus out of court!"

Despite his stern words, Judge Thompson was not without sympathy for the prosecution. Anticipating the possibility that the affidavits might be needed, he had instructed his office to photocopy twelve hundred blank forms that could be quickly filled in with the requisite information. He also had six notaries standing by to speed things along.

To avoid any appearance of arm-twisting, Nick and the rest of his team left the building and loitered on the playground for the next three hours while the witnesses trickled out and returned to their lives. Not until the next morning would they know the results of the balloting.

"One thing's for sure now," said Nick to the others. "If that guy is the Devil, he knows we've got him in a tight spot, and it doesn't seem too likely that he won't fight back."

"My thoughts exactly," said a voice behind them.

"Martin," cried Karen, throwing her arms around him in welcome, "have you heard what happened? Nick was great!"

"I heard," said Martin quietly, "but right now I think it would be best if we all got back to the church."

THEY PASSED THE night, nine battle-weary soldiers, in the sanctuary of St. Alban's. Martin and Gareth took it in turns to kneel in prayer at the altar, and others joined them throughout the night. Whether because of the protection afforded them by St. Alban's, or because Blackburn thought an attack might overplay his hand, they never knew, but they passed the night safely.

Nick, who had been distracted by the trial, took the opportunity to approach David and broach the subject of exoneration. Tom joined Nick and David and the three talked most of the night, planning the process that could, in a few months, lead to the overturning of David's guilty verdict.

Karen and Steve sat up most of the night whispering in the back of the church, though afterwards they would not tell anyone what they talked about. Only Jackie seemed to get much sleep—stretched out on a pew.

Darcey sat for a long time by the altar in one of the short pews that normally held acolytes. When he was not taking his turn in prayer Gareth sat with her, sometimes in silence, sometimes in whispered conversation. He read her scriptures and prayers from the *Book of Common Prayer*, and she listened passively. He spoke of his own path towards the priesthood, and he explained as well as he could why he believed in God. He did not ask her to justify her atheism, nor did he ask her to accept his belief; he merely talked and read and, when she felt inclined to respond, he listened.

When the first light of dawn turned the east window above the altar from black to a glimmer of blues and reds, Gareth slept, leaning into the corner of the pew. Darcey walked softly to where Martin knelt before the altar and placed a hand on his shoulder. When he looked up at her face, bathed in the colored light that filtered through the window, she nodded almost imperceptibly to him, and offered him the tiniest of smiles and a squeeze on the shoulder.

Martin understood. He stood up and took her hand for a moment, then let it slip from his as he went to join Gareth. Darcey sunk to her knees before the altar and, for the first time in her life, she prayed.

The next morning a curious crowd milled around outside the court-house, and the courtroom was packed with spectators. The only way Darcey and Tom were able to watch the proceedings was to join Nick at the prosecutor's table, but their presence was unremarkable compared to the radical transformation of the defense table. The cowed figure of the lead attorney still sat at the end of the table, but between him and the defendant now sat four other lawyers, all of them oozing confidence. Nick recognized two from television talk shows.

Judge Thompson brought the court to order, banging the restless crowd into submission with his gavel, and the officer of the court who had been charged with the collection and tallying of the affidavits stepped forward.

"Do we have an affidavit from each witness present at yesterday's proceedings?"

"Yes, your honor, we do."

"Very well. I'd like to thank the officers of the court for their tireless work in collecting these affidavits, and I know the counselors for the prosecution and the defense will want to do the same."

"Absolutely," said Nick enthusiastically.

"Now, if I recall, counselor—" the judge glared over his glasses at Nick, "you were hoping that seven hundred and ninety-six of these affidavits would show a preference for this picture," he held up the "before" picture of Darcey, "over this one." He held up the "after" picture. Darcey smiled at the judge and gave a little wave from behind the prosecutor's table, and Nick had to bite his lip to keep from laughing when he saw Judge Thompson's expression of surprise. Though he had seen Darcey in court a number of times, the judge had not recognized her pictures. Nick could have sworn he saw Thompson blush.

"It is my hope, your honor," said Nick, "that the affidavits will accurately record the testimony of the witnesses given in open court."

A tall lawyer with slicked back dark hair and a closely trimmed beard stood up at the defense table.

"Before you object to the prosecutor's using the term 'testimony' to describe the circus of yesterday, counselor," said the judge, now glaring at the defense table, "let the court hear the contents of these affidavits." He nodded towards the court officer.

"Your honor," said the officer, "I have in this hand three hundred and seventy-six affidavits," he held up a sheaf of papers, "that indicate the witnesses' preference for the 'after' photograph shown in court yesterday. If the counselor for the prosecution is quick with numbers," which Nick, already smiling, was, "he'll know that leaves exactly seven hundred and ninety-six affidavits expressing a preference for the 'before' photograph."

A smattering of applause broke out among the spectators, but was quickly quelled by a few strikes of the gavel. Darcey squeezed Tom's hand under the table.

"Well, your honor," said Nick, standing to face the jury, "not only have we proven that the men of this county are honest folk—" here he nodded to the spectators, "but I think the prosecution has offered overwhelming evidence that Clause Seven of The Program contract has been violated not just in the case of this woman—" Nick pointed to Darcey, and the jurors and spectators realized for the first time that the woman in the photographs now sat before them. Several of the spectators blushed to recall their thoughts of yesterday when looking at lingerie photos of the woman who now sat so nonchalantly in open court.

"Not only in the case of Darcey Thayer," continued Nick, "not only in the case of Louise Crawford, but in twenty-five thousand cases up and down this great state of New York. Your honor, when the current proceedings have ended, I plan to bring before this court a new proceeding in which we will charge the defendant with an additional twenty-four thousand nine hundred and ninety-nine counts of criminal breach of contract, and we will prove those counts with the evidence so thoughtfully provided by the men of this fine county."

More vigorous applause erupted from the gallery, as a broad member of the defense team—rather too broad, Darcey thought, to be representing The Program—extricated himself from behind the table and buttoned his suit jacket around the expanse of his belly.

"Your honor," he said with a chuckle, "the defense appreciates the fact that the prosecuting attorney is running for re-election, but I'm afraid he fails to note the fact that to prove criminal breach of contract he must prove intent to defraud. Now, I assure you my client was led by the society in which we all live, by the movies and the magazines and the supermodels, to believe that skinnier is sexier. There is no intent to defraud here, your honor—or if there is," he said smugly, "I would challenge the prosecutor to prove it."

"That's exactly what I intend to do," said Nick. "The prosecution calls Steve Collingwood."

The door at the rear of the courtroom opened and Steve strode down the aisle.

Nick had no worries about Steve's testimony. His sexual experience with Linda Foretti and Linda's admission that her transformation had been the test of a new product from the man who brought the world The Program would prove beyond any doubt that Blackburn's understanding of human sexuality was far too advanced for him to have believed in Clause Seven. Steve's testimony would be incriminating. The problem was, would anyone believe him?

Steve told his story well and stuck to every detail under a rough cross-examination by the defense team. Only the original defense lawyer was not part of his grilling. But it was the smiles and chuckles of the defense lawyers, more than their words, that endangered Steve's testimony. Every look one of those famous lawyers gave the jury said, "this man is crazy—why would you believe such a story?" And indeed, why would they?

After two hours on the stand Steve stepped down and Judge Thompson adjourned court for lunch. Nick watched the jurors as they left and saw from their smiles and the wags of their heads that they, being normal, intelligent people, had dismissed Steve's story as fantasy.

WHILE STEVE WAS taking the stand, Gareth and David were riding the morning commuter train to New York. Nick and Darcey had kept tight-lipped about their strategy. "The less you know the safer you are," Nick had said. But he had asked Gareth to go into the city and retrieve a woman, any woman, who was ready to undergo The Program. David had volunteered to go along, for the change of scenery, he said, but in truth because he didn't think any of them ought to be alone. "Besides," he said, "I know the city a lot better than you do."

By noon the two men stood on the sidewalk outside the blue and gold door of The Program. "What do we do now?" Gareth asked when they had loitered for ten minutes while six or seven women had been welcomed in by the burly doorman.

"Look at their faces," David said. "They all have the same look—not quite confident, not quite excited, steeled for something frightening, but defying every man who ever overlooked them because of their weight. We memorize that look. Then we stand on the corner a block to the south and wait for somebody with that expression to show up."

"And then we just say, 'Come with us upstate. We don't know exactly why, but what the heck, we're two strange men on the street corner, so we must be safe to travel with'?"

"I'm not sure we should word it exactly like that," said David.

The first two women they accosted ignored them completely. David was gratified to see, however, that both passed through the blue and gold door in the next block. At least he had recognized the look. When he saw the look on another face in the approaching crowd, he smiled to think how impressed Gareth would be at the ease with which they would convince this woman to join them.

"Excuse me," said David as the woman stopped at the crosswalk, "but you're going to The Program, aren't you?"

"How did you know?" the woman asked, without looking at him.

"Just a hunch," he said. "Listen, I really think you ought to consider coming with us instead. I'm a friend of Steve Collingwood, and I know he'd like to see you."

The woman turned towards David. Her hands were thrust deep into the pockets of her lab coat. "You know Steve?" she asked quietly.

"Yes," said David. "I met you at Clifton Garrett's Golden Globes party, remember? I'm the one who sort of ran out screaming."

"I remember," said the woman, dropping the tension from her shoulders and letting the crowd surge past her across the street.

"My friend and I have been living with Steve in a little town upstate for the past few weeks. We've been working on sort of a secret project, which is why Steve hasn't called you, but he'd love to see you if you can get away."

"Steve wants to see me?" said the woman in a quavering voice.

"There's a train in half an hour," said David.

"OK," said the woman, as if in a trance. "I took a few days off because of—you know." She nodded towards the blue and gold door in the next block.

"Great," said David, and turning to his slack-jawed companion he said, "Gareth, I'd like you to meet Sarah Saunders. Sarah, this is my friend Gareth Lloyd."

AFTER THE LUNCH break, the composition of the prosecution table had changed yet again. Now, for the first time, Martin appeared in court, sitting between Nick and Darcey.

Once court had reconvened, Nick stood at his chair and said flatly, "Your honor, the state rests." He glanced at the jury with a look that said, "Oh, well, I tried," and sat back down. A murmur ran through the spectators.

Nick sat still and quiet, doing his best to look defeated, and hoped that the defense would take the bait. Martin, who appeared in court without his collar, simply clutched his Bible under the table and prayed.

"Your honor," said the defense lawyer with the potbelly, "I think we can wrap this case up fairly quickly. The defense will limit itself to a single witness to rebut this farce that has masqueraded as a prosecution. I regret to inform your honor, however, that our witness is a resident of New York City, and as the defense was not aware until this morning, when we heard the fanciful story of Mr. Collingwood, that her testimony would be needed, it may take us until tomorrow morning to have her present in court."

Nick breathed a silent thanksgiving as Martin thumped his knee under the table with his Bible.

"Call your witness," said Judge Thompson, "the court will give her until noon tomorrow to present herself."

"The defense calls Linda Foretti."

A slim woman standing in the back of the courtroom pulled off her hat and veil and marched up the aisle. "I'm here, your honor," she said.

The startled defense lawyer scrambled to meet her at the bar and usher her to the witness box, but his colleagues could not pull their chairs out of his way quite quickly enough for him to accomplish this piece of gallantry. When the attorney was able to present himself in front of the witness box, he turned and smiled to the jury as suavely as he could manage. "Well, ladies and gentlemen, I see Miss Foretti has been able to join us today after all. What a piece of luck."

Linda was sworn in and the defense attorney poured her a glass of water from a pitcher on his table. But Linda did not touch the water. As anyone in the jury box could see, Linda was caught in the crossfire of two intense stares—one from the defendant, whose look might have been a threat but also might have been a silent show of support and encouragement; and one from the new man at the elbow of the prosecutor. A few members of the jury knew this man as Martin Stewart, priest of the Episcopal parish of St. Alban's, but none knew why he stared so intently at Linda.

"Ms. Foretti," said the defense attorney, "this morning the court heard the testimony of a Mr. Steve Collingwood. Mr. Collingwood claims that, through the knowledge and power of the defendant, you were able to seduce him—that is, Mr. Collingwood—into sexual relations by hypnotically transforming your body into the overweight form of a woman to whom he was sexually attracted." He said all this with an edge of sarcasm and amusement. "Could you please tell the court if that is true?"

"Not exactly," said Linda with a little laugh.

"I thought not," said the attorney, returning her chuckle.

"First of all, I wouldn't use the term 'overweight.' And the metamorphosis was not hypnotic," Linda said quickly. "My body was actually physically transformed. He told me—" for the first time she looked towards Martin, "the defendant told me he knew exactly what men

were sexually attracted to. 'Men as a group and individual men' were
his exact words. And he said he could transform me into whatever Mr.
Collingwood would be most attracted to—I mean sexually, that is."

"Your honor, I object," said the dark-haired defense attorney, jumping to his feet.

"You object to your own witness?" asked the judge.

"I'd like permission to treat Ms. Foretti as a hostile witness," said the
attorney.

"She doesn't seem hostile to me," said the judge. "She's merely answering the question."

While this altercation took place, observant jurors might have noticed two changes at the opposing counsels' tables. Behind the prosecutor's table Martin nodded to Linda, his lips pressed tightly together; behind the defense table, the eyes of the defendant, which had remained
impassive throughout the trial, glowed red deep within their irises.

Before dinner, Steve asked Sarah and Linda to join him in the study. He didn't know what to say, but he knew he couldn't face sitting down to dinner without speaking to them. Steve had still been at court, suffering the shock of seeing Linda again, when Sarah arrived at the rectory, and though he was thrilled to be enfolded in Sarah's arms when he returned, the testimony he had given that morning made the timing rather awkward. He had spent much of the afternoon trying to decide how to broach the subject of his dual transgression—that he had slept with Linda and lusted after Karen when he should have been thinking only of Sarah.

"I'm not sure how to say this," Steve began, unable to look at either of the two women who stood before the fire, "but I thought maybe the three of us should—well, should talk about—" He dug his hands deep into his pockets, wishing, praying for some words to come.

"Well," said Linda, nudging Sarah in the ribs, "we could talk about what a great lover you are."

"Or," said Sarah, with a giggle, "we could talk about how you prefer well rounded women to—"

"To Programmed ones," finished Linda. Steve looked up from the stain on the rug where he had fixed his gaze and saw the two women grinning at him.

"It's not funny," said Steve.

"Oh come on," said Sarah, "it's a little funny. We really should have

Karen in here, though, shouldn't we?" Sarah and Linda dissolved into giggles.

"Listen," said Steve, "I think it's pretty serious. The thing is, Sarah, I just want you to know that I'll never cheat on you again."

"Oh, God," said Sarah, suddenly stopping her laughter, "that is so sweet."

"That he won't cheat on you?" asked Linda.

"No," said Sarah, crossing the room to take Steve by the hand and look into his eyes, "that he felt like he was cheating on me to begin with. You wouldn't feel guilty, Steve, if you didn't—"

"I know," he said quietly, "and I do."

"Oh, shit," said Linda, opening up her purse, "now you two are going to make me cry." She pulled out a wadded-up tissue and dabbed at her eyes. "I'd better leave you alone," she said, and, sniffing, she slipped out of the room.

"I guess I can forgive you this one time," said Sarah, smiling. "After all, you did help put the Devil behind bars."

Steve pulled her into his arms and stood for a long moment holding her as tightly as he dared. All his memories of Karen fell away as Sarah's soft body melded into his own, and he could think of nothing but holding her forever. Only Gareth's call to dinner parted them.

Sarah, who had forgiven Steve more completely than she had thought possible, would often tease him about his encounter with Linda. "Please," she whispered into his ear as they walked hand in hand into dinner, "tell me I was at least the third person with you on that bearskin rug."

"When I try to remember it now," said Steve, "it seems like you were the only one."

ALTHOUGH THEIR WORK was not finished, the dinner that night at the rectory was one of celebration and relief. The jury had taken only thirty minutes to return a verdict of guilty; there only remained the proceeding that would determine Arthur Blackburn's sentence.

But while there was joy at the rectory table, nearly everyone had the same question: why did Linda Foretti, handmaiden to the Devil, turn state's evidence, and why did she now sit happily dining with the band of impertinents who had undertaken to bring him down? When Martin had said grace and seated himself behind the leg of lamb, all eyes silently turned to him for an explanation.

"Why is everyone looking at me?" asked Martin.

"Don't you have something to tell us?" said Karen. Linda was grinning, but Martin still feigned puzzlement.

"Something about Linda?" prompted Steve.

"Ah, yes, Ms. Foretti," said Martin, now returning Linda's smile. "Well, the defense had to believe she was on their side, you see, so I couldn't risk telling anyone. I didn't even tell Nick until this morning. The day I spent in New York doing research—the day of the explosion—I went and talked to Linda. I felt her out, and gradually I realized she didn't know anything about Blackburn. She just had a business arrangement with him, that was all. She didn't know the clothes she sold killed Louise Crawford; she honestly thought it had been an accident. She was as amazed by her bodily transformation as Steve was. But when she told me the story of how she had seduced him, well, I think just the process of confessing made her realize the truth."

"It all seems so obvious now," said Linda, "but at the time—well, this guy could make you believe anything. I guess it was like hypnosis, but talking to Martin helped me break out of it."

"When she saw the truth, she agreed to help me out. That was the last time I talked to her until yesterday, when I told her to get to Braintree courthouse by two o'clock this afternoon. I really believed we could count on her, but I knew with him in the room nothing was guaranteed."

"I just drew on your strength, Martin," said Linda, raising her glass to him. They all toasted Martin and toasted Linda and toasted Nick, but even though Steve was awash in the swell of love, he knew he needed to tell Linda something else, something even Martin didn't know.

"I'd like to propose a toast, too," said Steve, standing up with his wine glass. "I'd like to toast a man who is not here tonight, but whom some of us here remember. I never met him, but he was a friend to David in his time of greatest need. We lost some friends in this battle—Clifton and Marjorie, Louise Crawford—but let's remember that first friend we lost, before we even knew we were in a battle, the friend whose ashes Martin buried in an unmarked grave. I think he still deserves a service with mourners," he glanced up at Linda, "and with family. So I'd like to propose a toast to Gus Cooper, and I hope we all remember that it's not too late to mourn him—or to love him." Steve looked again at Linda, and saw tears glistening in her eyes.

Linda spent most of the night in confession with Martin, remembering for him the events that had estranged her from her father. That conversation, which lasted until both Linda and Martin had fallen asleep in the easy chairs by the fire, would remain forever private.

At breakfast, Linda sat with David and asked him to tell her everything he remembered of Gus, a task that took several days. But she never spoke of her relationship with her father to anyone other than Martin.

In the kitchen after breakfast, as he helped Karen and David with the dishes, Steve said quietly, "I told you I'd find Gus's daughter."

"Yes," said Karen, kissing his cheek, "you did."

A FULL MOON hung above the rectory that night, and though the exhaustion of the restless night before, together with the euphoria of the verdict, led everyone to an early bed, sleep was not foremost on every agenda. Steve found that the comforts of Sarah's body easily eclipsed the fading memories of his night with Linda and his crush on Karen. He had never experienced sex as an outgrowth of love, but as he rested in her arms afterwards, sex without love seemed as preposterous as life without Sarah.

Darcey had cried softly as she made love with Gareth—tears of joy to be enfolded in his arms, and tears of regret that she could not offer him the entire Darcey, the original Darcey, the "before Darcey" that most men preferred. But Gareth whispered to her over and over that he had not fallen in love with the pictures. They had only jarred him into realizing that he was already in love with her. "Whatever your shape," he said, and she drifted off to sleep with her head on his chest and a smile on her lips.

Though Arthur Blackburn was in jail awaiting sentencing, David still felt the need to sleep in the church. Karen sighed as she slipped between the cold sheets, wondering if David's need for divine protection was just a ruse to avoid her. Just as she was drifting into a dream of that Sunday morning so long ago—the one and only time she had truly made love—the door to her room creaked open.

THE PROGRAM

"If you're not asleep," said David, "I could use some company."

"Do you want me to come downstairs?" said Karen, sitting up to see his outline in the doorway.

But David closed the door behind him. "I think this might be a better place," he whispered.

As he slid his body next to hers, Karen was too exuberant for anything so silly as tears of joy. She laughed giddily as she wrapped him in her womanly flesh. Later, as she kissed her way down his torso, she stopped to give him a sly smile and whisper, "Why Mr. James, I do believe you have rock-hard abs."

She loved the way her soft and plenteous flesh melted against his hardness when she moved on top of him, and afterwards she pulled him to her and fell asleep clinging to his lean, masculine body. When she awoke the next morning she thought for a moment that the second time had been a dream, so vague was her recollection of David's caresses coaxing her out of sleep in the middle of the night, but when he rolled towards her, pressed his morning erection against her pliant thigh and said, with a twinkle in his eye, "You know, they say the third time's a charm," she knew that with David in her life, she didn't need to dream.

"YOUR HONOR," SAID Nick, now dressed in a perfectly tailored black suit with a red and white silk tie, "I would like to introduce two pieces of evidence for you to take into account when considering your sentence. I believe these go directly to the issues of malice of intent and of the likelihood that the defendant, if not incarcerated, will continue to be a danger to society. I'm especially eager to establish this danger now, as I'm sure that your honor's sentence will serve as a model for sentences in the other counts pending against the defendant." Of course Nick would bring the other counts himself, so he was merely reminding the judge that he hoped the sentence would eventually be multiplied by twenty five thousand.

The courtroom had been emptied of the jury and, at the request of both counsels, of the spectators. Martin, Darcey, Tom, Karen, David, Steve and Sarah crowded around the prosecution table while Nick paced in front of them. The defendant had not even glanced in their direction, and so had given no indication that he recognized David from his prison temptation.

"First of all," said Nick "I'd like to introduce a copy of the entire contract for The Program."

"Objection, your honor," said the tall, dark defense attorney, leaping from his seat. "That document was never subpoenaed from The Program, and could only have been obtained through an illegal search and seizure."

"Your honor, this document was brought to us by a young woman who was considering becoming a client of The Program and felt it important to look over the contract carefully first. There were no law enforcement officials involved in obtaining this document, I assure you."

"Surely, counselor," said the judge to the defense table, "if The Program has over one million clients, this contract must be a fairly common document. Do you have any evidence of an illegal search?'

"No, your honor."

"Well, then. I'll allow it."

"I should particularly like to draw your attention to Clause Sixteen, your honor." Nick handed the judge a copy of the contract, made from Karen's photograph. "If I may, I'll read that out. 'In addition to the initial payment of ten thousand dollars, the client having completed the course of care at The Program and reduced her weight to the figure indicated in schedule C, shall, upon the natural termination of her life, immediately surrender up her immortal soul to the proprietor of The Program for all eternity, at which time said soul shall be transferred to the place of eternal punishment.'"

Nick let the word "punishment" hang in the air while the judge read over his own copy of the document.

"Your honor, I put it to this court that the defendant is none other than the Devil incarnate, that he started The Program as a means to purchase the souls of innocent women and consign them to eternal damnation, and that this court has a unique opportunity, if not to inflict eternal punishment, at least to put Satan behind bars for a very long time."

"Your honor—" now the wide defense lawyer raised himself awkwardly to his feet, "I really must object most strenuously. If the prosecution is claiming that my client believes he is the Devil, then the court must allow us to counter with an insanity plea. I mean clearly, your honor—"

"Tell me, counselor," interrupted the judge, "did you have an opportunity to read this contract before this trial began?"

"Yes, your honor, I did and—"

"And did you attempt to file an insanity plea at that time?"

"No, your honor, but I didn't think this issue would become relevant."

"Your honor," said Nick, "I think I can put this issue to rest with my second piece of evidence." The defense lawyer sighed loudly and wedged himself back into his chair.

"It is not the contention of the prosecution, your honor, that the defendant *believes* he is the Devil, but that the defendant *is* the Devil. How else could he cause women to lose up to one hundred pounds in less than an hour?"

"Your honor, again I must object. The prosecution offers no evidence of the inner working of The Program and no evidence that the process takes less than an hour. How The Program works is, for obvious reasons, an industrial secret, but I fail to see how the prosecution hopes to use the success of our company as proof that it's run by the Devil."

"Very simply, your honor. I'd like to ask the defendant to use the method employed in The Program to help this young woman—" Sarah stood up as he gestured towards her, "to lose fifty-seven pounds. That's the amount of weight she would lose in The Program according to the chart on their contract."

"Objection," said both the wide and the tall defense attorneys. The bespectacled one who had begun the trial still sat with his head in his hands.

"Overruled! I think the prosecution has made an excellent suggestion. If this court finds that the powers used in The Program are supernatural, then I will naturally impose the maximum sentence, which I am tempted to do after reading this contract anyway. Miss—?"

"Saunders," said Sarah. "Sarah Saunders."

"Miss Saunders, are you sure you want to undergo this process?"

Sarah looked at Steve, who so loved the body he had experienced the delights of for the first time last night. He reached forward and caught her hand and gave it a squeeze as he grimly nodded his head. "Yes, your honor," she said. "Although I'd be obliged if the process might be reversed after this demonstration."

"Your honor, this amounts to forcing the defendant to testify against himself," objected the tall attorney.

"The defendant is not under oath," said the judge, "nor is he under any compunction to demonstrate The Program. Surely if you have hundreds of locations around the country, there must be plenty of people who could undertake this demonstration for the court. If no one does, I will base my sentence on the other evidence of this case. However, I am giving the defendant an opportunity to demonstrate his product. Frankly," he said, rolling his chair forward again and leaning across the bench to look right into the glowing eyes of the defendant, "I don't think he can do it."

The defendant turned his red-hot stare towards Sarah and raised his hand at her as if in benediction. Sarah wore a short, low cut dress Darcey had loaned her. "You need to show as much flesh as possible," Darcey had said, "so we can see what happens."

Almost immediately Sarah's ample cleavage began to melt away. Her thighs disappeared in a cloud of white mist that rose to envelope the rest of her body, but did not sufficiently obscure her to keep Steve from seeing, with a sinking heart, the gradual deflation of her chest. Sarah stood completely still, as if in a trance, until not more than a minute after the process had begun the defendant lowered his hand, pursed his lips, and blew a tiny puff of breath in her direction. The mist cleared and there stood Sarah, fifty-seven pounds lighter, with her dress hanging loosely from her narrow shoulders.

The defendant turned his glare back to the judge. "Don't ever tell me I can't do something," he said.

"Can you put the weight back on?" the judge asked.

"Let her do it herself," spat the defendant.

WHEN ARTHUR BLACKBURN had been sentenced to the first of what would ultimately be 26,376 consecutive eighteen-month prison terms in the state of New York alone, he was led past the defense table towards a cell where he would await transportation to a high-security facility. Stopping in front of the table, he smiled at David.

"You'll come around one of these days," he said. And then, directing his glowing glare at Martin, he hissed, "I never should have let Him cure you."

"He doesn't need your permission," said Martin calmly.

"Doesn't He?" said Blackburn with a smile. "Look around you. Who do you honestly think is stronger? Look at the sick children, the people dying for no good reason—hunger and war and senseless crime on the streets. A two-year-old was shot to death last night by his eight-year-old brother. Don't you think He would stop me if He could?"

"He's not going to prison," said Martin, unable to hold the gaze any longer and casting his eyes down to the table.

"No," said the Devil, "you sentenced Him to death." He let out a blood-chilling laugh and was dragged from the courtroom.

IN THE GRAVEYARD of St. Alban's, by the light of the moon, Martin conducted a second burial service for Gus Cooper. Gus's daughter Linda threw the first handful of dirt into the small hole that would be her father's grave, and nine people—Martin, Linda, Darcey, Gareth, Tom, Steve, Sarah, Nick, and Jackie—held hands in a circle and said a prayer for the souls of Clifton Garrett, Marjorie Drake, and Louise Crawford.

Martin added a prayer for the souls and bodies of the more than one million women whose contracts with The Program would be made null and void by a succession of court rulings over the next few months. Sarah had signed no such contract, but before the circle dispersed, Steve muttered a prayer for her health. He wished for the return of her figure, but he already knew he would love her no matter what her shape.

XXIII

Father Donald Hodges
General Theological Seminary
New York, New York

Dear Father Hodges,

A dear friend of mine, Father Martin Stewart, suggested I send you the enclosed journal I kept of events that happened about a year ago. He felt you would know best where such a document should be stored.

Since my journal ends abruptly with the sentencing of Mr. Blackburn, you might like to know what has happened since.

Fittingly, Anna Camello won the Academy Award for best actress just two days after the producer of *My Sister, Myself* was sentenced to a prison term. When the court ordered the closing down of The Program a few weeks later, the Army of All Sizes and the other groups that had been involved in the Million Pound March began to feel they had turned the corner in the battle against the cult of thinness.

The so called "Beautiful Majority" has begun to wield its influence in Hollywood and the fashion industry, and the mass hypnosis that Steve Collingwood thought he saw the first time he looked into the pages of *Perfect Woman* magazine has started to loosen its grip.

Most of the women who were clients of The Program have gained back at least some weight, and the three who are close friends of mine, Linda Cooper (formerly Foretti), Darcey Thayer, and Sarah Saunders, have returned, after a few months of indulgent eating, to their former voluptuous selves.

Sarah, in fact, was featured as the cover girl on the first issue of *Zaftig*, a new men's magazine that "tastefully celebrates the full-figured woman." *Zaftig* was founded by Steve Collingwood after he dropped out of Columbia. You may know that the title is an old Yiddish word literally translated as "luscious" or "ripe," but usually applied to well-rounded women.

The whole first issue was a parody of the now defunct *Perfect Woman* magazine. Sarah wore nothing but her lab coat on that first cover, and she left enough buttons undone to sell out the entire issue in three days.

My old roommate, Georgia Phillips, called me a few days after I got back to New York and told me she felt like she'd been in a trance since December. She asked me if she could move back in, but David and I decided that two was enough. Georgia and I keep in touch, though, and she's contributed a couple of pieces to Steve's magazine.

Many former employees of The Program described their months there as trancelike, and many of them experienced religious conversions after the company went under. As for Celinda, she's gained thirty pounds and can be seen on late night infomercials for the "Tone Not Trim" fitness program, where she promises women they can improve their muscle tone "without losing their feminine figures."

Linda Cooper seems to turn everything she touches into gold. Not only is she a silent backer of *Zaftig*, but her new line of clothing stores, called Real Woman and catering to the curvaceous figure, has been an extraordinary success. Linda is carrying on a long distance romance with Father Martin. She told me the other day that if he keeps refusing to make a dishonest woman of her, she might have to marry him.

David and I were married last month at St. Alban's. We are both in business for ourselves now.

David, whose conviction was officially overturned a few months ago, was in great demand as a freelance writer in the weeks following the trial. He took the money from the first article he sold and bought a huge box of books for Sam, the cellmate he had taught to read. He thought I didn't see, but when he packed up the books, he slipped in the watch Martin had given him with a note. I can only guess what it said.

Since then David has started a company that gives walking tours of New York. His first three employees were his old friends, Jimmy, Bob, and Andy from underneath the bridge in Central Park.

Since he's on the streets all day, he can help me with my endeavor, too. Thanks to some financial help from Linda, I'm now the head of a mentoring program for homeless men and women in New York.

I write freelance pieces every now and then, but my work with the homeless takes up more and more time. Since we started four months ago, we've helped one hundred and forty people make the transition off the street and into a stable home.

We don't talk about it much, but I still keep an eye out for my father, and David watches out for his mother. I know he'd also love to find Charlie, his old cellmate from prison. Every day brings new hope.

Of course you know Gareth is back at seminary. Whether or not you know that he's engaged to Darcey, I don't know, but the two of them plan to marry after his ordination next year.

Martin had a dinner for him before Gareth left St. Alban's, and pronounced his shyness cured. "I wasn't your miracle, though," he said, "and neither was God. Darcey was your miracle." And she was.

Darcey let Steve publish her famous courtroom "before" and "after" pictures in *Zaftig*, and had to decline a number of other marriage proposals when he let slip in the captions that she had returned to her "before" proportions, but other than that she has managed to stay out of the public eye since the trial. She worked on Nick's re-election campaign last fall, and he offered her a job in the D.A.'s office after he won, but she decided to stay in private practice, so it will be easier for her to move when Gareth gets his call.

And The Program? After the courts shut down their operations and invalidated their client contracts the suits started coming, and the money that had poured in from women convinced they were overweight poured back out (in smaller amounts) to thinner versions of those same women. Even Phil Crawford got a check for two thousand dollars—an unexpected and unwanted gift that arrived on what would have been his twentieth wedding anniversary.

Even in its demise, The Program managed to keep the worst of things—that it had been run by the Devil—out of the papers. All the publicity centered on health risks and the breach of contract so aptly demonstrated by Nick and Darcey. Clause Number Seven was the only part of The Program contract ever made public.

As far as I know, Steve Collingwood was the only person ever subjected to The Program's proposed product for men, though what goes on behind the walls of the New York State Penitentiary,

I couldn't really say.

Please do with this journal whatever you feel is right. Personally, I never want to see the thing again.

Yours Sincerely,
Karen Sumner

IN THE LAUNDRY of the New York State Penitentiary a newly arrived inmate leaned against the hot, vibrating dryer and sighed. "I'd sell my soul for a pack of smokes," he said wistfully.

A voice from the darkness behind him replied, "That can be arranged."

ABOUT THE AUTHOR

Charlie Lovett is Writer-in-Residence at Summit School in Winston-Salem, NC. His plays for children have been seen in over 1,000 productions in all 50 states and five foreign countries.

He is the author of 11 previous books, including works on Lewis Carroll and the acclaimed memoir *Love, Ruth*. *The Program* is his first novel.

More information about Charlie and his works is available at www.charlielovett.com.

ABOUT PEARLSONG PRESS

PEARLSONG PRESS is an independent publishing company dedicated to providing books and resources that entertain while expanding perspectives on the self and the world. The company was founded by Peggy Elam, Ph.D., a psychologist and journalist, in 2003.

PEARLS ARE FORMED when a piece of sand or grit or other abrasive, annoying, or even dangerous substance enters an oyster and triggers its protective response. The substance is coated with shimmering opalescent nacre ("mother of pearl"), the coats eventually building up to produce a beautiful gem. The self-healing response of the oyster thus transforms suffering into a thing of beauty.

The pearl-creating process reflects our company's desire to move outside a pathological or "disease" based model into a more integrative and transcendent perspective on life, health, and well-being. A move out of suffering into joy.

And that, we think, is something to sing about.

PEARLSONG PRESS endorses **Health At Every Size**, an approach to health and well-being that celebrates natural diversity in body size and encourages people to stop focusing on weight (or any external measurement) in favor of listening to and respecting natural appetites for food, drink, sleep, rest, movement, and recreation.

While not every book we publish specifically promotes Health At Every Size (by, for instance, featuring fat heroines or educating readers on size acceptance), none of our books or other resources will contradict this holistic and body-positive perspective.

WE ENCOURAGE YOU to **enjoy, enlarge, enlighten and enliven yourself** with other Pearlsong Press books and products, which you can find at www.pearlsong.com, Amazon.com or your favorite bookstore. Sign up for our free e-newsletter or keep up with the latest about our books and authors at our blog at www.pearlsongpress.com.

Off Kilter: A Woman's Journey to Peace with Scoliosis, Her Mother. & Her Polish Heritage
Linda C. Wisniewski

Splendid Seniors: Great Lives, Great Deeds
by Jack Adler

The Singing of Swans
a novel about the Divine Feminine
by Mary Saracino

*Beyond Measure:
A Memoir About Short Stature & Inner Growth*
by Ellen Frankel

*Unconventional Means:
The Dream Down Under*
by Anne Richardson Williams

*Taking Up Space:
How Eating Well & Exercising Regularly Changed My Life*
by Pattie Thomas, Ph.D.
with Carl Wilkerson, M.B.A.
(foreword by Paul Campos, author of
The Obesity Myth)

Romance novels and short stories featuring
Big Beautiful Heroines
by Pat Ballard, the Queen of Rubenesque Romances:
  The Best Man
  Abigail's Revenge
  Dangerous Curves Ahead
  Wanted: One Groom
  Nobody's Perfect
  His Brother's Child
  A Worthy Heir

& Judy Bagshaw:
  At Long Last, Love: A Collection

& Pat Ballard's *Ten Steps to Loving Your Body
    (No Matter What Size You Are)*

Printed in the United States
106148LV00003B/130/P